THE MILK OF ALMONDS

THE MILK OF ALMONDS

Italian American Women Writers on Food and Culture

Edited by Louise DeSalvo and Edvige Giunta

The Feminist Press
at The City University of New York

Published by the Feminist Press at the City University of New York
The Graduate Center, 365 Fifth Avenue, Suite 5406, New York, NY 10016
feministpress.org

First edition, 2002

09 08 07 06 05 04 03 02 5 4 3 2 1

Library of Congress Cataloging-in-Publication Data
The milk of almonds : Italian American women writers on food and culture / edited by Louise DeSalvo and Edvige Giunta.— 1st ed.
    p. cm.
  ISBN 1-55861-392-7 (alk. paper) — ISBN 1-55861-435-4 (pbk. : alk. paper)
  1. American literature—Italian American authors. 2. Italian American women—Literary collections. 3. Italian Americans—Literary collections. 4. American literature—Women authors. 5. Gastronomy—Literary collections. 6. Italian Americans—Civilization. 7. Food —Literary collections. 8. Gastronomy. 9. Food. I. DeSalvo, Louise A., 1942- II. Giunta, Edvige.
PS508.I73 M55 2002
810.8'09287'08951—dc21

                                                                        2002005262

The Feminist Press would like to thank Mary Bisbee-Beek, Florence Howe, and Genevieve Vaughan for their generosity in supporting this book.

Text design and typesetting by Dayna Navaro.
Printed on acid-free paper by Transcontinental Printing.
Printed in Canada.

To our mothers and grandmothers,
children and grandchildren

Annunziata (Mildred) Calabrese
Libera Calabrese
Assunta Calabrese
Cettina Minasola Giunta
Nunziatina Nuncibello Minasola
and
Deborah Jean
Emily Alice
Jason
Judith Lynn
Julia Frances May
Justin
Matteo Stuart
Steven Louis

Contents

Acknowledgments, xi

Editors' Note, xii

LOUISE DeSALVO AND EDVIGE GIUNTA   Introduction, 1

Part One: BEGINNINGS

CAROLE MASO   Rose and Pink and Round, 17

MARY BUCCI BUSH   Aperitivo, 22

DOROTHY BARRESI   Mother Hunger and Her Seatbelt, 24

KIM ADDONIZIO   Beer. Milk. The Dog. My Old Man. 27

CRIS MAZZA   Our Father, 28

RACHEL GUIDO deVRIES   Italian Grocer, 37

MARY SARACINO   Smoke and Fire, 38

KIM ADDONIZIO   Outside, 44

DONNA MASINI   Sacred Hearts and Tar, 45

Part Two: CEREMONIES

CAMILLA TRINCHIERI   Kitchen Communion, 49

DOROTHY BRYANT   Dizzy Spells, 56

JANET ZANDY   My Children's Names, 64

MARY RUSSO DEMETRICK   Jazzman, 65

KIM ADDONIZIO   Bedtime Story, 65

MARY BETH CASCHETTA   The Seven Sacraments, 67

SANDRA M. GILBERT   Kissing the Bread, 76

LUCIA PERILLO   Pomegranate, 78

MARY ANN MANNINO   The Anthology Poems, 81

DOROTHY BARRESI   The Prodigal Daughter, 82

EDVIGE GIUNTA   The *Giara* of Memory, 84

Part Three: AWAKENINGS

NANCY CARONIA   Go to Hell, 95

MARY JO BONA   Motherlove, 101

ROSETTE CAPOTORTO   We Begin with Food , 102

Breakfast in My Seventeenth Year, 104

CHERYL BURKE   Bone, Veins, and Fat, 105

RITA CIRESI   Big Heart, 112

DANIELA GIOSEFFI   The Origins of Milk, 121

LORYN LIPARI   Cracked, 123

ROSETTE CAPOTORTO   Broke, 130

Part Four: ENCOUNTERS

PAMELA E. BARNETT   Other People's Food, 135

DIANE DI PRIMA   What I Ate Where, 143

ROSETTE CAPOTORTO   The Stereotype, 148

REGINA BARRECA   My Grandmother, a Chicken, and Death, 148

SANDRA M. GILBERT   "No Thank You, I Don't Care for Artichokes," 150

RINA FERRARELLI   Hot Peppers, 152

ROSETTE CAPOTORTO   If You Were a Boy, 152

GIOIA TIMPANELLI   Tridicinu and 'Mmaculata, 153

VITTORIA REPETTO   she's doing the dishes, 158

pasta poem, 159

AGNES ROSSI   Breakfast, Lunch, and Dinner, 160

Part Five: TRANSFORMATIONS

ANNE MARIE MACARI   I Can Be Bread, 167

SANDRA M. GILBERT   Finocchio, 168

ADELE REGINA LA BARRE   Pomodori, 170

VITTORIA REPETTO   lovers and other dead animals, 175

LUCIA PERILLO   Tripe, 175

ANNE CALCAGNO   Let Them Eat Cake, 176

ANNE MARIE MACARI   Parable, 182

SUSANNE ANTONETTA   Rosette, 182

SANDRA M. GILBERT   Basil, 189

FLAVIA ALAYA   Love Lettuce, 190

ANNE MARIE MACARI   The Room, 198

DONNA MASINI   Hunger, 200

Part Six: COMMUNITIES

ROSETTE CAPOTORTO   Dealing with Broccoli Rabe, 205

ADRIA BERNARDI   Sunday, 205

ROSETTE CAPOTORTO   The Oven, 214

NANCY SAVOCA   Ravioli, Artichokes, and Figs, 216

MARIA MAZZIOTTI GILLAN   Seventeenth Street: Paterson, New Jersey, 222

Passing It On, 222

You Were Always Escaping, 223

DOROTHY BARRESI   Poem, 225

JOANNA CLAPPS HERMAN — Coffee an', 227
PHYLLIS CAPELLO — Jeanie, 235
— Working Men, 236
DONNA MASINI — Moving In and Moving Up, 237
MARY CAPPELLO — Fatso, 239

Part Seven: PASSINGS

SUSANNE ANTONETTA — The Lives of the Saints, 249
DORIAN CIRRONE — After We Bury Her, 252
MARIA MAZZIOTTI GILLAN — Ma, Who Told Me You Forgot How to Cry, 252
SUZANNE BRANCIFORTE — The Day Anna Stopped Making A-Beetz, 254
JANET ZANDY — My Mother's Career at Skip's Luncheonette, 258
— Secret Gardens, 259
ALANE SALIERNO MASON — The Exegesis of Eating, 261
DOROTHY BARRESI — The Vinegarroon, 269
ANNIE LANZILLOTTO — Triple Bypass, 273
JENNIFER LAGIER — Last Supper, 274
DORIAN CIRRONE — New Year's Eve, 275
KYM RAGUSA — Baked Ziti, 276

Part Eight LEGACIES

MARIA TERRONE — What They'll Say in a Thousand Years, 285
DENISE CALVETTI MICHAELS — Polenta, 295
LUCIA PERILLO — Lament in Good Weather, 299
SANDRA M. GILBERT — Mafioso, 299
MARIA FAMÀ — Picking Apricots with Zia Antonia, 300
ROSANNA COLASURDO — Mortadella, 301
MARY ANN MANNINO — Keep the Wheat and Let the Chaff Lie, 308
LUCIA PERILLO — The Northside at Seven, 310
MARIA LAURINO — Words, 312
RACHEL GUIDO DEVRIES — How to Sing to a Dago, 320
DOROTHY BARRESI — The Post-Rapture Diner, 321
LOUISE DESALVO — Cutting the Bread, 322

Acknowledgments

First, we would like to thank our contributors, who took our vision for this book, made it their own, and contributed poems, memoirs, and stories that far exceeded our expectations. This book is theirs as well as ours.

At the Feminist Press, we would like to thank Jean Casella, who responded enthusiastically to our idea for this volume, and who, throughout our work on the book, helped us refine our vision. Molly Vaux helped us turn the pieces we had gathered into a book, and assisted with the difficult tasks of editing and placement. Our many conversations with Jocelyn Burrell helped us see that we were on the right track. Heather McMaster's enthusiasm and hard work in publicizing our volume is much appreciated.

We would like to thank our husbands, Joshua Fausty and Ernie DeSalvo, who gave us excellent advice as our project unfolded, and who assisted us in many ways, including a few photo sessions (with food).

We would like to thank Cettina Minasola Giunta, Giuseppina Impiduglia, Liliana Zuppardo, and Diego Giunta for helping us gather the material on almonds that we have drawn upon in our introduction.

Edvige Giunta would like to thank Larry G. Carter, Vice President for Academic Affairs at New Jersey City University and the Separately Budgeted Research Fund for granting her release time to work on this book. She also would like to thank Barbara Hildner, chair of the Department of English, her colleagues in the department, the Memoir Faculty and Staff Group and Jo Bruno at New Jersey City University for their support. Louise DeSalvo would like to thank Jennifer J. Raab, president of Hunter College, Richard Barickman, chair of the Department of English at Hunter College, and Harriet Luria, deputy chair, for their support.

We both would like to thank Peter Covino, Mary Ann Fusco, Jennifer Guglielmo, Kym Ragusa, Daniela Spampinato, and Francesco Di Vincenzo.

Finally, we would like to thank our families, and especially the people to whom we have dedicated this book. We have drawn upon the inspiration of their lives and their support of our work in the making of this book. And we hope, of course, that it will enrich their lives as it has enriched ours.

Louise DeSalvo and Edvige Giunta
Teaneck, New Jersey
March 2002

Editors' Note

We have not standardized the spelling and syntax of Italian words in this collection. We chose instead to maintain the integrity of the language spoken by immigrants and/or to preserve the authors' transcriptions of the Italian language they heard in their families and neighborhoods and, in some cases, could neither speak nor write.

Introduction

. . . e la mandorla del dolore matura.
(. . . and the almond ripens with pain.)
ROBERTO ROVERSI

The Milk of Almonds was conceptualized about four years ago and gradually took shape when we talked on the telephone, as we always do, at the end of the work day, each of us making dinner in our own kitchens, one of us beating the ingredients for a *frittata* and the other stirring a *risotto con i funghi* made with ingredients—Arborio rice, porcini mushrooms, saffron—brought back from a trip to Italy. We spoke of the exciting burgeoning of an Italian American women's literary tradition to which we both proudly belonged. We had shared much wonderful food. At Louise's house, a beautiful veal, lightly floured, sautéed in butter, and finished with white vermouth and salted capers, hand-picked in Sicily, brought back to the United States by Mary Cappello, author of *Night Bloom,* and her partner, Jean Walton, and sent, as a gift, to Louise. And at Edi's, a parade of pizza—with tomato sauce, or with anchovies, or *capricciosa* style, with sliced hard boiled eggs, ham, mushrooms, artichoke hearts, black olives, and mozzarella—and *'mpanata,* a Sicilian focaccia, filled with sausage, spinach, potatoes, onions, and raisins, cooked for Christmas Eve and eaten with Daniela and Francesco, Edi's friends from Sicily.

Yes, we had shared food—planning meals, talking about where you could find the best produce and ingredients, exchanging recipes, cooking, and, of course, eating together. So, how could we not want to share a literary project about food?

Over the years, we had become avid and critical readers of each other's works-in-progress—memoirs, essays, poems, and literary criticism. Gender and Italian American culture were at the center of our work, and it had become increasingly clear to both of us that one of the ways in which we could explore, understand, and write about constructions of gender in the cultural context of our shared ethnicity was to revisit the history of Italian American women in relationship to food, the history of our mothers and grandmothers: our history. Food, we had come to understand, played a particularly important part in defining modes of power within an Italian American domestic context (as it also does for those in other ethnic contexts, though perhaps differently).

The Milk of Almonds became the book that we had to do because of our respect and love for the literature that our Italian American sisters and we have been creating, and also because of our common love and respect for food, our recognition of its cultural power and of women's historical role as food-makers, and our sensory and sensual ties to the recipes from a country to which we are both—differently—tied: Louise, as a second-generation American, whose peasant maternal grandparents came from Bari, in Puglia, and whose working-class paternal grandparents came from Positano, in Campania; and Edi, a first-generation American who came to the United States in 1984 in her mid-twenties from Gela, Sicily, to study English and American literature.

This book grew slowly, like a good pizza dough, rising in our minds when we allowed ourselves a break from teaching preparations or a current writing project. Edi was finishing a critical work on Italian American women's literature, *Writing with an Accent*, and Louise was revising her memoir *Adultery*. Those two books, which also deal with gender and ethnicity, inevitably shaped *The Milk of Almonds* in its planning stages, for we wanted to continue and extend our inquiries into the particular way in which women's writing emerges from an all too often ill-understood cultural context.

We would get together for lunch or in stolen moments in the afternoons—we live a mere five minutes apart—and as we refined our sense of our new book's subject, and as we began contacting writers and collecting pieces from Italian American women, we would sit across the table drinking espresso or cappuccino, or sipping cinnamon tea, and munching one of Louise's chocolate hazelnut biscotti (which her husband, Ernie, now makes because Louise has been busy working on this and other books). So, day by day, we collaborated on this book, pushing our empty soup bowls or pasta plates to one side of the kitchen table to make room for the newest work we had received from our contributors, which we would begin to read with great excitement. This, the work of women.

Because so much of the discourse surrounding the relationship of Italian American women to food was, to us, predictable, sentimental, and uncomplicated, we had conceived a revisionist volume that would collect fresh, new, complex, and significant work by Italian American women on this subject. We knew that it is impossible to talk about food without also talking about gender and culture. In our project, we were determined to avoid nostalgia, to strip the typical food narrative associated with Italian American culture and women of that sentimentality that has so long prevailed in the discourse that connects Italians with food, and, more particularly, Italian American women with food, and that deprives those stories of their complexity, conflicts, and contradictions and, ultimately, of their authenticity, beauty, and narrative power. By urging our contributors to demystify and demythologize those all-too-familiar spaghetti and pizza plots, and by encouraging them, too, to pen the unexpected food narrative, we knew that we could offer a collection that presented a fuller, more contradictory, and ultimately more satisfying perspective on Italian American culture and the place of women in it. All along, we envisioned a volume that spoke of food in a way that would be both a piercing critique and a loving celebration of Italian American culture.

From the beginning, we had writers in mind who, we believed, on the basis of their past work, would treat the subject of food, gender, and culture in challenging and different ways, and we invited these writers to contribute pieces especially written for this volume. We knew, too, that we wanted to include work by previously unpublished writers. We wanted fresh perspectives; we wanted to show how diverse and multivoiced our literature is. As we worked, we found that certain previously published pieces were necessary to the collective vision of our project.

Italian American women have long questioned their place within a culture that, while it can be a source of sustenance, can also represent a patriarchal force that often diminishes and silences women. And so we invited contributors to examine personal responses to food and how these have been shaped by the facts of our culture, ethnicity, and gender. And we encouraged contributors to think imaginatively about food, connecting it to gender, sexuality, ethnicity, race, class, power, the environment, health, immigration, politics, and culture. We hoped that works of prose and poetry would emerge in which food would appear, not as a tangential or accidental subject, but rather as its central, generating force, deeply interwoven with the narrative or thematic elements of the piece. We wanted pieces that would be provocative, questioning, and destabilizing of essentialist stereotypes about Italian American women and their relationship to food, even as they memorialize Italian American culture and life. We hoped the pieces we gathered would illustrate the multiple ways in which food could be contextualized within other, broader aspects of Italian American life and culture, such as birth, motherhood, family relationships, death, generational changes, gardens, rituals, and sexual identity, but also within aspects of Italian history, such as immigrant history; the condition of the peasantry in Italy; one's relationship to Italy, the country left behind; forms of homecoming chosen by these women writers.

We puzzled over the title of this collection throughout our work. We knew we wanted a title that was evocative, distinctly rooted in Italian culture and its rituals, and that captured our personal and cultural understanding of food as the embodiment of history, ritual, collective memory, and myth.

Gradually, we understood that the symbol of the almond had much personal resonance for each of us. Louise remembered how her maternal grandmother, as she worked throughout the day, would nibble almonds that she kept in her apron pocket. When asked why, she would respond, "For strength, and for remembrance." One of the Sicilian rituals that Edi misses most is partaking of *granita di mandorle,* almond ice, made with the milk of almonds, during summer. When Louise and Ernie were planning their first trip to Sicily (where Ernie's maternal grandparents were born), Edi insisted, "You must go to Aci Castello and have *granita di mandorle."* Edi's husband, Josh, enthusiastically agreed, describing the unparalleled experience of eating this simple, ethereal delight with warm brioche in the Sicilian bar facing the Church of San Mauro in the village guarded by the still surviving ancient Norman castle carved from the black lava of Etna.

In Sicily, where spring comes in February, as the almond trees blossom, they signal change, renewal, a rebirth greeted today with as much celebration as in antiquity. In the island's distant, mythical past, Persephone comes back in spring, although temporarily, to her mother, Demeter, goddess of Sicily, goddess of harvest and fertility. A daughter lost, found, then lost again: an endless series of departures and returns, the cycle of seasons, the rhythms of grieving and healing.

In ancient Eastern culture, the almond tree was associated with the cult of the goddess Astarte. In Christian iconography it is associated with Mary, mother of Jesus, a figure of ambiguous power, a woman who has survived the overwhelming loss of a child, a Christian goddess who embodies qualities of so many pre-Christian goddesses. Trees had been regarded as sacred throughout the Neolithic period, when they were believed to be the embodiments of goddesses. We imagine our ancestors—men, women, and children—in those ancient times, circling the almond tree, praying, singing, dancing, weeping, rejoicing, remembering, telling stories—stories of love, loss, grief; stories of hope; stories not to be forgotten; stories to pass on.

In Greek mythology, Phyllis, daughter of the King of Thracia, in love with Acamas, son of Theseus, believing him lost in the Trojan War, died of grief. Out of pity, Hera turned the girl into an almond tree, the tree that Acamas would embrace in anguish upon his return. And so, in the name of compassion and memory, the almond tree became the first to flower in the Mediterranean spring, its delicately shaded buds softening the still wintry landscape of late January.

In Agrigento, once an important Greek polis in Sicily, nine majestic temples still stand after more than two thousand years. These ghosts of antiquity watch over the valley and the nearby town, scarred by modernity, with its chaotic urban growth. Here, spring is welcomed on the second Sunday of February by *la festa del mandorlo in fiore,* the feast of the almond tree in bloom.

But the blooming of the almond trees is not always cause for celebration. In Alberto Moravia's novel *Two Women,* which describes the flight of Cesira and her daughter Rosetta during World War II from Rome into Ciociara, a poor mountainous region south of Rome, the almond blossom signifies near-starvation and despair. During the first days of March, through the mist one morning, Cesira sees the first of the white almond blossoms. To the evacuees from Rome, this had always been a joyful sign: spring was approaching. To the peasants, though, the flowering of the almond tree meant something completely different, for spring meant hunger, a diminishing of their provisions, and knowledge that their stores of food could not carry them over until harvest. Here, there was no cause for celebration, for they—and the evacuees, too—would now have to eat even more sparingly than during winter, and scour the countryside for any kind of edible herb, though their strength was already greatly diminished from hunger. The history of food in Italy is often marked by the intertwining narratives of abundance and deprivation.

In time, the blossom of the almond tree becomes a green, fuzzy shell hiding a delicious fruit: *la mandorla*, the almond, that exquisite fruit of Asiatic origin that, for thousands of years, has been so distinctly Mediterranean.

Crack the shell of the green almond before it hardens, and inside you will find a soft fruit: white, thin skinned, almost watery at its core. Edi ate this fruit during a summer she spent as a child in Piazza Armerina. In the hot August afternoons, she and other children would steal the not-yet-ripe fruits from the almond trees of the mother superior of the orphanage nearby.

You know that the almond is ripe when the green shell cracks. Inside, there is another protective layer, hard, brown, covering the fruit. And then, yet another layer, this one thin, almost papery. It takes hard work to get to the fruit inside. Some almonds are sweet; some are bitter and, although toxic, are still eaten at the Sicilian table, ground together with sweet almonds.

Sweet almond, bitter almond, source of pleasure, source of sorrow.

After they have dried, almonds are used as the basic ingredient for many Italian delicacies—the *sfinci di riso* (rice puffs) Edi's mother makes every time she comes to visit; *dolcetti di mandorle* (almond cookies); *torta mandorlata* (almond cake); *biancomangiare di mandorle* (almond blancmange); torrone; biscotti; and the marzipan fruits, called *frutta Martorana* (named after the Monastery of the Martorana in Palermo, where they were first made in the 1800s), which adorn the windows of pastry shops all year along, but are especially prominent in the weeks preceding the Day of the Dead, November 2.

On the morning of November 2, children awaken to find presents of sugar dolls of *paladini* (knights) and *principesse* (princesses), toys, and marzipan fruits in brilliant colors and the amazingly realistic shapes of walnuts, tomatoes, peaches, strawberries, pomegranates, figs, almonds. Children are taught that these presents have been left behind by family members who have died—grandparents, uncles, aunts. These are gifts from the dead, eagerly awaited.

Though it takes hard work to shell almonds, it takes even harder work to extract milk from them. Crushed almonds, sugar, water: the simple, delicious combination used to make *pasta reale*, almond paste—literally, royal paste— and used to make the milk of almonds, *latte di mandorle*, the ambrosia of the Italian south. Tradition requires that you put ground almonds in a muslin bag, soak the paste in cold water for at least an hour, and squeeze repeatedly until the water is, as Mary Taylor Simeti describes it in *On Persephone's Island*, "beautiful cloudy white swirls," like "a Tintoretto sky."

Drink *latte di mandorle* cold at a bar in Nicolosi or Palazzolo Acreide, or any Sicilian town where the makers—most often women—will neither part with their recipe nor sell a piece of their precious almond paste, although they will give you a *panetto* to take back home to make your own *latte di mandorle*, just because you are American. Drink a glass and you will feel refreshed, soothed, comforted. Or dip a soft, freshly baked brioche into a *granita* made with milk of almonds for breakfast or for a late afternoon snack in the summer at the Bar Viscuso in Aci Castello across from San Mauro, as Louise and her husband Ernie did last year and as Edi and her husband Josh did in the same place in years past, and savor the contrast between the warmth of the brioche and the cloudlike coolness of the *granita*, the brioche transporting the almond's exquisite bittersweet fragrance into your mouth. Heaven.

We took it as a good omen that on the very day that we completed this volume, Louise excitedly discovered that Fiordilatte di Mandorla was available in blue and white cartons in an Italian American grocery store in Ridgefield, New Jersey. And it was with glasses of the milk of almonds that Louise purchased there that we remembered the Italian South of our ancestors and that we celebrated the completion of this work, *The Milk of Almonds*.

Over the past several years, the study of food has been emerging as a cross-cultural discipline that brings together the work of sociologists, anthropologists, and cultural historians. In *We Are What We Eat: Ethnic Food and the Making of Americans* (1998), the historian Donna Gabaccia examines the complex interplay of ethnicity, food, and culture from the early immigrant experience in the United States to the present. Gabaccia demonstrates that a study of food sheds light on the development of American cultural and social history and she comes to a conclusion that has important implications for cultural politics:

If our food tastes good, gives us pleasure and connects us—if only commercially or sentimentally—to our neighbors, why not embrace those ties and the multi-ethnic identities they create? . . . As eaters, Americans reject uniformity or adherence to a single cultural experience. . . . Rather than dismissing eating as a trivial consumer choice, Americans might do better to take our eating choices very seriously. Then we could recognize and celebrate that we are what we eat—not a multi-ethnic nation, but a nation of multi-ethnics.(231–32)

In "'I Yam What I Yam': Cooking, Culture and Colonialism," an essay in *De/Colonizing the Subject: The Politics of Gender in Women's Autobiography*, a collection edited by Julia Watson and Sidonie Smith (1992), Anne Goldmann has written of women from U.S. ethnic minorities for whom cooking the dishes of their ethnic group "works to maintain cultural specificity in the face of assimilative pressures" (172). In "The Roots of Resistance: Women's Culture of Struggle in Italy" (part of a larger study in progress of Italian women and working-class politics in New York City, 1880–1945), Jennifer Guglielmo connects food customs and ritual with forms of social resistance among Italian women in Italy and those who emigrated to the United States in the early twentieth century, thus challenging the notion of Italian immigrant women as passive homemakers. This study demolishes the idea of immigrant Italian women as cut off from social and political activism. Guglielmo searches for those forms of political expression that are gender- and ethnic-specific; hence, she discovers the importance of food customs and rituals.

The new awareness of eating disorders, such as anorexia and bulimia, has triggered serious investigation of food in many contexts. Becky W. Thompson, in *A Hunger So Wide and So Deep: American Women Speak Out on Eating Problems* (1994), based on interviews with women of various ethnic backgrounds and sexual orientation, links eating disorders to issues of class, race, sexuality, and trauma. Louise, in "Anorexia," a chapter in her memoir *Vertigo* (1996), discusses the particular ways in which Italian American households dispose their daughters to a preoccupation with food, and also connects eating disorders to sexual abuse and historical circumstance.

In writing about food, contemporary American writers of various ethnic groups and writers from other nations have foregrounded the psychological, economic, social, and political implications of food-making and eating, while demonstrating the poetry of food-writing. Ntozake Shange's *If I Can Cook/You Know God Can* (1998), Elizabeth Ehrlich's *Miriam's Kitchen: A Memoir* (1997), Ruth Reichl's *Tender at the Bone: Growing Up at the Table* (1998), Margaret Randall's *Hunger's Table: Women, Food, and Politics* (1997), Betty Fussell's *My Kitchen Wars* (1999), Camille Cusumano's *The Last Cannoli* (2000), Joanna Kadi's *Food for Our Grandmothers: Writings by Arab-American and Arab-Canadian Feminists* (1994), Laura Esquivel's *Like Water for Chocolate* (1989), Clara Sereni's *Casalinghitudine* (1987), and Isabel Allende's *Aphrodite: A Memoir of the Senses* (1998) suggest that, at the close of the twentieth century, women writers viewed writing about food as a cultural and creative imperative. This is part of an ongoing project of cultural recovery and the reclamation of woman-made arts, as described by Alice Walker in *In Search of Our Mothers' Gardens*. And if the historical, cultural, and economic circumstances of women's relationship to food vary greatly, one must inevitably recognize the crucial role of gender in shaping that relationship.

In the anthology *Loaves & Wishes: Writers Writing on Food* (1992), edited by Antonia Till, a collection that includes writers from around the world (Sohaila Abdulali, Margaret Atwood, Rana Kabbani, Maxine Hong Kingston, Doris Lessing, and Virginia Woolf, for example), food is linked by a number of contributors to the enacting of power: providing food is often "the only kind of power women are permitted to employ" (X), even though some contributors emphasize the celebratory aspects of women's relationship to food. A special issue of the journal *TutteStorie* (2000–2001), titled "Bere, Mangiare," edited by Maria Rosa Cutrufelli, discusses the politics of food. In her introduction, Cutrufelli writes that in an age of biotechnology and genetically modified foods, the intimate connection of people with the growing of food, which translates into myth and a veneration and respect for nature, is in the process of being overturned. (To counteract these tendencies, each night Edi tells her son, Matteo, a story in Italian about the things his grandparents do in Sicily. The climax of the story—and the moment when he nods his head particularly vigorously—occurs when she tells him of the time he went to his nonni's garden and his nonna held him up so that he could pick oranges, lemons, and figs. Until Edi's daughter, Emily, was eight years old, she thought that lemons grew in the ground, like potatoes: Edi was shocked to realize how removed her daughter was from an understanding of how food grows that she herself, growing up in Sicily, had taken for granted.)

Food-writing and life-writing in Italian American culture are interconnected, for to examine our relationship to food is to examine ourselves, as well as the relationship between these selves and the family, the community, and society at large. This is one reason we believe that an anthology of writings about food by Italian American women is long overdue. As this volume attests, Italian American women see themselves and their relationship to food very differently from the media's often reductive, even derogatory renderings—the apron-clad mama in the kitchen happily feeding her family, empty-headed, selfless, eager to serve.

The voices of Italian American women in *The Milk of Almonds* are connected to similar feminist projects undertaken by our African American, Latina, Native American, Arab American, Jewish American, and Asian American sisters. Like these projects, this volume dismantles racist, classist, and sexist discourse—a process that, for Italian American women, continues to be a great struggle. This anthology illuminates many previously unexamined or little-examined facets of Italian American cultural history that must be understood in the context of poverty and prejudice and must be viewed against the waves of migration of the late nineteenth and early twentieth centuries and the mistreatment of Italian American immigrants in the United States upon their arrival—a hidden, often unacknowledged history.

Nick Mascolo, a friend of Louise's, once traveled with his father to Sorrento, the place from which his father's parents had emigrated to the United States in the early part of the twentieth century. This was an important pilgrimage for them both, and standing with his aged father, looking at the ranks of lemon trees in blossom, the brilliant azure of the water, Nick turned to his father, now a very old man, and said, "How could they ever leave here, it's so very, very beautiful?" "But you can't eat beauty, my son," his father replied.

There is, within every Italian American family, a story about why the family left Italy, why its members emigrated to the United States. And although many emigrated for political reasons, usually, at the heart of a family's emigration story, there is a story about food, or rather, about the lack of food, a story about devastating poverty, malnutrition, disease, starvation, famine. This leave-taking story is embedded in the history of the peasants of southern Italy, although it has not always been articulated and shared, for it so often involves shame—the shame of poverty, mistreatment, despair.

Louise's grandfather often described the pain of working as a young peasant alongside his father in the fields, knowing that a mere fraction of what was harvested would be available to the family for sustenance, and that whatever was provided would never be enough. This deprivation was the direct result of brutal, exploitative policies instituted by feudal landlords and the Italian government. And it was the day-to-day effects of social injustice—the inability of people to feed themselves and their families, the hope of a better life elsewhere—that motivated much of the great wave of Italian American emigration to the United States and elsewhere during the nineteenth and the beginning of the twentieth centuries.

This history is richly portrayed in works of Italian American literature. Many Italian Americans have written of the experience of migration, poverty, and cultural transition and the concomitant sense of trauma, shame, and loss—Pietro di Donato, Jerre Mangione, Mari Tomasi, Helen Barolini, Julia Savarese, Mary Cappello, Denise Giardina, Dorothy Bryant, Maria Mazziotti Gillan, Tina De Rosa, Gay Talese, and Mario Puzo, for example.

In the nineteenth century, "partnerships" between landlords and farmers and shepherds were an integral part of the feudal economy of the Italian south. A baron provided grazing land and flocks to shepherds and shepherds provided labor; peasants were completely responsible for the crops but gave over half of everything they produced to the landlord, in addition to paying exorbitant taxes.

The apparent promise held by the nationalists who had fought to expel foreign rulers and unify Italy did nothing for impoverished southern Italians. Italian citizenship (conferred in 1860) made little difference; the newly born Italian government failed to deliver the destitute from their oppression and suffering. In Helen Barolini's *Umbertina*, the situation is described in these terms:

> [It was a] thieving government . . . that took everything and gave back nothing—not a road, a school, or a sewer. . . . The *ladro governo* taxed the poor man's working mule but not the rich man's carriage horse. The *ladro governo* . . . made land distribution available only to those rich enough to buy great quantities. (29).

But for many who came to the aggressively modern New World, initially life was not much better. Although in the earlier part of the nineteenth century, immigrants came primarily from the north of Italy, toward the latter part of the century and into the twentieth century, more and more southern Italians left Italy because of exploitation and agricultural depression. The Italian state, moreover, according to Kathie Friedman-Kasaba in *Memories of Migration: Gender, Ethnicity, and Work in the Lives of Jewish and Italian Women in New York: 1870–1926* (1996), encouraged migration to the Americas, hoping that emigrants would return money to their households and to Italian banks (77–88). There was little difference between the oppression suffered in the south at the hands of the baron's *fattore*, and that perpetrated by the American bosses.

When Louise's grandfather, Salvatore Calabrese, described his privations as a railroad worker, it was always in terms of how little food was given to the workmen and how little money they earned after the *padrone* took his cut. But he also remarked upon how much wine was freely given, to keep them docile, Louise's grandfather believed. In an article that appeared in 1916 in the *Immigrants in America Review*, Dominic T. Ciolli describes how railroad men slept in their filthy work clothes—there was no place to wash—on vermin-infested bags of straw, covering themselves with discarded horse blankets, eight men to a roach-infested, windowless boxcar. They awakened at three in the morning, and worked from five until twelve "without rest," had a bread and water lunch, and worked again until four. Once, when a gang of laborers complained that they had no fresh water, the *padrone* remarked, "These dagoes are never satisfied. . . . They should be starved to death. . . . They don't belong here" (n.p.).

Eating well, then, in the context of the privations suffered by Italian Americans, can be best understood as a compensation for their forebears not having been able to eat well, and eating good Italian food can be seen as a way of dealing with the profound sense of dislocation, often remaining unarticulated, which is the product of any diaspora with roots in deprivation and mistreatment, such as that of Italian Americans. But the cultural narratives emphasizing the reputed abundance of the Italian American table have also done much to obliterate or masquerade that history of deprivation, the reason why so many Italian Americans came to the United States.

If the cultural memory and collective unconscious of Italian Americans is of a land that did not provide sufficient sustenance for those who emigrated, then, in the New World, the central importance of food in Italian American life and culture and in the works of Italian American writers becomes more readily understandable. For this is a people who have undergone the trauma of emigration, with its devastating—but also its creative and culturally productive—results. And though this preoccupation with food is often interpreted reductively by outsiders to Italian American culture (and by some insiders also), still, it has a politicized significance, for it counteracts those negative images of Italian American life—Italian Americans as mobsters, as uneducated dimwits—that persist in popular culture.

Cooking and eating—and also the processes by which recipes are transmitted and foods prepared, conserved, offered, or refused—are central to the work of Italian American women authors. Recipes and the stories that surround them represent occasions through which these writers explore their relationship to culture and through which they shape their creative vision. Many Italian American women writers and artists use food to tell old stories in new ways, and also to tell stories that have never been told before. Not only does food provide Italian American women authors with a language and images through which to express the ambivalent relationship they, as women, maintain with domestic space, it also becomes a way through which they can articulate the complexities of ethnic identity.

Although Italian American women's response to their culture is ambivalent—a simultaneous embrace and rejection—their work is ultimately transformative. For these works of art often reinterpret familiar Italian American cultural landmarks and touchstones—the kitchen, the stove, the refrigerator, the dinner table, the pizza parlor, the local store, and familiar foods, such as pizza, baked ziti, polenta, bread, almond milk—and tease new and often subversive cultural meanings from the simplest of subjects.

The writers in this anthology do not sentimentalize the lives of Italian Americans, the lives of working-class immigrants, or the cultural traditions of their people; nor do they render them through the lens of a reductive nostalgia. Instead, they illuminate how Italian American culture cannot be fully understood without a careful consideration of the vital place of food.

Redefining the role of food in the culture, then, is necessary if, as Italian Americans, and specifically as Italian American women, we are to free ourselves from the commodification and misrepresentation to which our culture has been subjected, and if we want to begin to trace and establish a sense of cultural legitimacy and dignity for ourselves, equivalent to that accorded to women of other displaced and oppressed peoples.

Still, as the memoirs, poems, and stories that we present here indicate, this work of reinterpretation and recovery, this assertion of our need for the recognition of and respect for our cultural heritage, is fraught with ambiguity and difficulty. What if the very act of emerging as a writer means to critique that culture for which we are trying to court respect? The celebratory, nostalgic mode is one that very few Italian American women writers are willing to accept. Instead, we seek authenticity, personal and political integrity, and an affiliation with other communities of women. Recovery of stories requires defiance and transformation, as well as the embracing of a tradition. The process of making a history involves the encounter with a world we love and reject simultaneously, a world we must come to understand and cherish on completely new terms. Writing has the power to accomplish this and so much more.

The Milk of Almonds: Italian American Women Writers on Food and Culture is the first major collection of Italian American women's writing in fifteen years, the first ever to invite major, prize-winning authors and emerging writers to examine our relationship to food, that topic so often treated stereotypically and reductively by observers of Italian American culture. This volume presents a drastic revision and redefinition of what it means to be an Italian American, one of the least understood ethnic experiences in the United States, and what it means to be a woman who calls herself Italian American and understands that appellation in the most deeply personal and political sense of the term. Here, fifty-four poets, memoirists, and fiction writers have contributed works that demolish essentialist views of Italian American culture. Together, they provide a powerful, richly textured, and nuanced interpretation of the authentic and extraordinarily diverse experiences of Italian American women.

Our contributors differ in their region of origin (both in the United States and in Italy), generational connection to Italy, age, sexual identity, class and ethnicity—some contributors are Irish American, African American, Jewish American, Caribbean American, Argentinean American, in addition to being Italian American. The work of these authors, we think you will find, is not only tantalizing, but also intellectually and politically provocative, for these authors revise, in often unexpected ways, any predictable notion of what an Italian American's relationship to food, her culture of origin, and the culture of the United States might be.

Although the writers' emphasis may be on food, they quickly take the reader on unexpected—and sometimes shocking—historical, personal, cultural, and emotional journeys. Food is the embodiment of cultural and personal memory, and these pieces show how we connect to and write of our loss and reclamation of our families and ethnic histories by meditating on the meaning of food. But food is also the locus of much deep pain and deprivation: others may use it to harm us, and sometimes we use it to harm ourselves.

In these pages, there are moments of celebration (though they are far from clichéd), but there are also moments that witness the historically unspeakable in the Italian American experience—anorexia, mental illness, physical and sexual violence, incest. Here the Vietnam War and its devastating legacy of drug addiction are described, as are AIDS, environmental politics, breastfeeding, illness, appropriation of old rituals for new situations, and the working-class experience. This is a multifaceted literature, recently emerging, written by women whose writings, unlike those of many other groups of ethnic women, have, for the most part, been overlooked. There is, in the culture of the United States, no general recognition that a tradition of Italian American women's literature exists.

The works presented here are written by women whose Italian American cultural heritage holds sacred the principle of silence and would prefer that the experiences of its members remain hidden, unexpressed. This is a literature that breaks that silence. This is a literature written by women whose lives tend to be stereotypically rendered and caricatured in the media. And yet this is a literature that radically transforms the view of what the experience of Italian American womankind is. It is a literature that is soul-satisfying and nourishing, though born of experiences that are often painful and difficult to describe.

Although writing about food can represent a cultural bridge to what has been lost, it also can become a cultural transgression. The works included here examine both possibilities. Here is a community of voices—loud, boisterous, savvy, sweet, tender, serious, sober, playful, desecrating, subversive, humorous. These are the voices of Italian American women writers at the beginning of the twenty-first century. Here we speak for ourselves as we have never spoken before.

Part One

❧

BEGINNINGS

Rose and Pink and Round

Carole Maso

The day is warm and beautiful. The day is also night—it is summer, I am putting the baby to bed 8 P.M., still light outside. The house is quiet. The world's spinning slowed up somehow, so that now it seems as if it is nearly perceptible. One can feel it—the rotation of things: planets, crops. Milky orb and globe and world. Lobe. Engorged. The hum and song of the nursery. The world is pink and round. In this delirium of hormones, dizzied, depleted, I turn. The chair's slow swivel. Bathed in an extraordinary glow. Outside boisterous life goes on: neighbor's children putting wood in a truck. Children fishing in the pond. At the window considerable birdsong still, the whole sky now pink as the sun begins to fall and darkness comes on. Universe of pure health and option. This irrefutable feeling of being at the center of one's life—with all the serenity and awe that comes with that recognition. This slow-moving liquid I am filled with. How to describe the feeling? The dream of these days—how unable to lift myself from it—this feeling of impossible fullness. Every motion, every thought and sentence is milk-inflected.

I pass her a perfect sphere of peace, health, well-being. Immortal life—nothing, nothing shall ever perish . . .

This mythic elixir—so elemental, so essential. At the center of our living: a fountain. The very essence of how we live—since we have arrived, since we have been asked to enter this pact: curve of world—earth-bound, earth-linked, the love we pass. I am drinking the stars, the little monk said upon his chance invention of champagne. I look at her drunken, pleasured face. That magic potion, her satiated face—a heady brew. With her small hand she pats my breast three times and she is at home.

And when the bough breaks? From time to time odd intimations enter this meditative space. Children walking an odd zig zag. The sound of a woman weeping. The liquid gaze of the cat. The baby's backward peddling in air. How utterly dizzied one feels, and opened up, and vulnerable. Filled up like this with milk. My heart bursting. My heart and body aching.

And I pass her perfect nutrition, immunization, long life, intelligence. One part dream, one part sacrifice, one part future, one part mystery, one part salvation.

Things that must have been inscribed in the cellular memory returning now: my mother coming into a room, and then leaving, and the way she brought light with her when she came and then took the light away. World dimming . . .

A beautiful, sad lullaby, sung in Sicilian. Unstoppable emotion. This feeling of nothing being held or holding back. The dam does break, the river overflows its banks—how can I describe this season of rain—plenitude—this fluid world where I am small like she is, and then a child, and then dead. And then alive again, at the center of my life.

The baby cries in the dark. Reaches for the milk she smells in sleep. Makes that little tonguing motion:

A cistern in France overflows.

My mother's hair escapes the pins.

A woman's eyes brim over as we move again tonight through that incomprehensibly sorrowful city of water.

A flood of memory—from the time before my birth. I feel overcome. A song played on a flute made of bone. A harp made of human hair. Animals gaze out of the ark.

In the elongation—day merging with night—where time and desire are dismantled, I carry a star, a cup, to her—the best part of me. Vessel for one instant of perfection. Rosebud lips of the child. Clear eyes of the child, as she nurses moving back and forth, back and forth, as if she were reading.

She sucks the world into focus—becomes so entranced by what she sees that for a moment she stops sucking, and the world blurs back again. I look at the place she is looking so intently. I think of what I see, and what I cannot see at all.

For those of us brought up on bottles, who never once tasted that charmed potion, there is a little moment for mourning now. The clear, the calm. In this space by the window the light gone to rose. The thing we cannot do without and have, already for so long. My own infancy comes back—and the woman I have become—the kind of peace that has eluded me—that missing fragment of living in me.

My grandmother singing a Sicilian lullaby—the sorrow and beauty and bitterness of the world gray—gives way to five children sleeping who once more, as they have done for all time, redefine the world, change the world with their dreaming. The child cries. Reaches out in the night.

And we pass the enzyme of sleep back and forth to one another. Dream. Deepest of privileges. Grace notes. 3 A.M. The chirping and burbling and tinkling things—the little toys and rattles and singing stars are now at rest. Only Rose and I awake. Now and then the sound of the cat's paws. Outside the whiteness of moon, and milk, and (winter arrives) snow.

Sometimes, delirious, a little saintly feeling comes—depletions—exhaustion, as if one were offering one's very soul. Heart's fire, devotion. This miraculous fluid. A squirt in a wound would heal—AIDS patients open their mouths to it like baby birds. The desire to live. Wish.

One feels marked by milk as if by visitation or vision. As the forest is marked by flame, or the forehead by ash, as each and every word I write is carved, engraved by ghosts.

Sometimes a vacant feeling comes—it stays at times a little longer than you'd like. Drunk up, emptied—you've lost again your train of thought—your ability to think precisely—what by now you begin to take as normal—the blur . . .

Flood of milk when the baby cries. My life is pure sensation. Rush and sound in my whole being it seems.

Mama, mammalian, mommy, mammary, the heart of the language world—the small mouth reaches for the breast, says Mama, Mommy, and minna minna minna, and begins to drink. Rose at one year old. The time I had imagined I would end this back and forth, this extraordinary cult of milk. But she is clearly not done. What to do? I think of all in this world that is arbitrary, senseless, cruel, stupid—and do not wish to be a part of it. I wonder why, since I have the luxury of the choice, would I for no reason take away something such as this? The world will begin its own inevitable subtractions soon enough. And so we go on.

Designed with utmost subtlety, there are enzymes to speed the digestion of the lipids, lactose, and proteins. I have decided to do a little reading. A complexly designed, ever-changing milk.

A truly living fluid in which antibodies and cells move about. The cells in mother's milk not only attack bacteria that could be harmful to the baby, but have the ability to produce antibodies that destroy bacteria and viruses as well. In the case of many viral diseases the baby brings the virus to the mother and the mother's gut-wall cells manufacture specific antibodies that travel to the mammary glands and back to the baby.

To protect directly from disease. I close my eyes. My body in front of the black car streaming.

Heightened, photographic flash before my vision field: the child inside the pure center of protection, a circle of always and forever.

This flexible fluid—the balance of nutrients adjusting according to the infant's needs—and continuing to evolve as the child grows. During a single feeding the concentration of milk even changes between early feeding and late feeding. Theories as to why suggest that the beauty of the design, the ability to shift, to change shape, to accommodate, is naturally inherent to the female body.

In a study in Bangladesh, breastfeeding was a protective factor for night blindness among preschool-aged children. In a study in Finland, in a study in. . . .

Breast milk provides softer curds in the infant's stomach than cow's milk and is more quickly assimilated into the system. While it contains less protein than does cow's milk, virtually all the protein is available to the baby. Half the protein in cow's milk passes through the baby's body as waste.

Researchers many years ago wrongly concluded that breast milk did not have vitamin D—but it was discovered that a liquid soluble D, formerly undetected and unique to breast milk, was present and completely met the infant's needs.

Iron and zinc are better absorbed by breastfed babies.

Breast milk lowers the risk of developing asthma, protects against diarrhea infections, bacterial meningitis, respiratory infections, childhood lymphoma and leukemia, juvenile rheumatoid arthritis, Hodgkin's disease, vision defects, and it goes on like this . . .

Breast milk is free. Breast milk is always the right temperature. It acts like a natural tranquilizer for the baby. The terrible twos do not arrive for breast-fed babies. And for the mother? Have I mentioned? The sleep inducing qualities of breast milk . . . as I drift off again. In this cloud of endorphins.

It tastes sweet and light.

Mother's milk is designed to build brains. It contains living cells, hormones, active enzymes, immunoglobulins, and compounds with unique structures that cannot be replicated. Its exact chemical makeup, still unknown.

Not to mention optimum hand-eye coordination, not to mention never spitting up, and it goes on and on: When the world was round and pink and she could drink everything she would ever need from it. Or so it seemed. And I could give something more precious and more valuable than I ever had before, or would again. And the way the gift passed back and forth so effortlessly with such ease and grace. And the person it made the one who did the giving. The gift that will last long after I am dead, the gift that might be passed to another baby—and from that baby to another baby . . . Someone had said to me that I when pregnant carried the life material for my own grandchildren—a girl baby whose eggs develop while she is still inside me. A tenuous thread, this fragile pearl string, a few drops—a connection with those who will come after—this trace of eternity. Sitting here barely moving, unable to lift my head from hers, I feel jettisoned into the future—the strangest of sensations.

And I feel more valuable and more precious than ever before, because I in all my ordinariness, and without any special effort, produced something this astonishing, this ideal—and the inevitable—that one day it would be over and I would have to give it up—and would once more become ordinary. No matter what else I did, or where else I went, I would never give something this whole, and wholly good again—it's a humbling thing—I feel humble in its presence—and in the dissolve.

She has made up little Mommy's Milk songs which we sing to the trance, the figment—butterflies as they flee. My daughter Rose, two years old rhapsodic:

"Mommy's milk in the yogurt, in the hat, in the trees, in the sky," a world shaped, defined by the places Mommy's milk touches in her mind—something so elemental like language.

"Mommy's milk in the meat sauce. In the pears. In the oatmeal. In the Cheerios, in the clouds, in the sky. In the blue eyes," she squeals. In all she sees and all that sees her.

"Matisse paints Mommy's nipples!" she says astonished . . .

"Mommy's milk is on Mommy's nipple. And butterflies," she says. "Butterflies?" She nods and pats my breast. "It's very pink. It's very beautiful. It's creamy. It goes round and round." And she makes circles in the air with her little hands.

The pink circles she describes begin to insinuate themselves behind my eyes. In all I see, circles now overflow, warm, radiating, aureole, the world is pure sensation, pure shape and pressure and trembling. These circles, a place of focus, brief moments of calm in the maelstrom. Still, it was not the duration that mattered, but the depth of the feeling, and because of the depth, an enduring quality came. I shall keep it with me forever. How everything in me has moved to gentleness, has conspired toward mildness. I can scarcely believe.

"Mommy's milk is sleepy, it grows and grows."

Other moments of serenity return: rising from a lover's bed and walking the unfamiliar streets alone, 6 A.M., day—the white page as it slowly gave way.

Rose, nearly three, nursing, looks up and in the hollow of my neck reaching says blue, she sees a blue, what Rose, she says, "ghost." "No butterflies," I say. "No, Ghost," she says. Emphatic.

Green gray blue of the hills out my window, gone to mauve to pink to pearl white and gray, then back to blue rose, the baby suckling. The gradual ending of this time as it comes on now.

Rose's lilting "Mommy's milk" can be heard more and more throughout the day, half reminiscence, half pure desire, still. Pale blue ghost of those last precious afternoons, when all was safe and warm and giving way to rose to pink, it goes round and round.

Now in the last moments of the miracle, as the milk begins to diminish, feedings only at night, as she begins to detect my necessary defection—all the things of this world—retreat. No. "It is pouring down," she says. Yes I see. "No, it is raining Mommy's milk on our heads. It is raining so hard." Enveloping everything now. The world, it grows and grows, it goes round and round. "Look." And I am holding life inside me. And she is holding life in her mouth. "Mommy's milk in the clouds," she reaches up to the sky, "Mommy's milk in the trees. Mommy's milk in the stars." It is pouring down on us, everywhere.

15 June 2001

∾

Aperitivo

Mary Bucci Bush

They named the baby Peaches because it was so sweet.

The baby was the size of a loaf of bread.

It was plump and brown like a meatloaf.

Its skin was soft as a perfect flan.

Its cheeks were red as apples.

Sweet strawberry tart, the father said, nibbling the baby's ears.

My little potato dumpling, the mother said.

She's so tiny, like a muffin, said the father.

Oh, peanut, mother said.

My little lemon drop, said daddy. Pumpkin pie.

We could eat you right up, mommy said, placing the baby's toes in her mouth.

The baby squirmed, its foot fell out of its mother's mouth.

I'm going to gobble you up, daddy said. He grinned and widened his eyes as he moved his big head close to baby's face.

The baby began to whimper.

See what you've done now? the mother said.

Don't cry, my little butterball, daddy said, sticking the baby's fingers in his mouth. Mmm, that tastes good. He smacked his lips.

The baby kicked the air with its fat legs. Its arms flailed above its face.

Look at the way her belly jiggles when she cries, daddy said. Bowl full of jelly, he said.

You're making her cry, mommy said, lifting the baby from its blanket. Don't you listen to him, she told the baby. You're my cinnamon bun, aren't you? All mine.

She buried her face in the baby's stomach. She blew air against the stomach, so that her lips vibrated and made a sound like a food blender.

The baby's eyes rolled. Its head lolled from side to side.

She likes that, daddy said.

The mother lowered the baby into the crook of her arm, then bent her head and nibbled at the baby's stomach.

I'm going to eat you! she said.

The baby's hands opened and closed. Its dark eyes floated from one face to the other.

Look there, daddy said, pointing to the kitchen counter. Your roasting pan. He laughed. Put her in the pan.

I'm not going to put her in the pan, the mother said.

Just for a minute, he told her.

I don't think so, the mother said.

I'll get my camera, he said.

He opened a drawer and took out his camera. This will make a great picture, he said.

Don't get too close to the stove, she told him. It's hot. I'm preheating it for dinner.

Do we have any celery? he asked. He took the baby from her arms.

Her blanket, he said. She needs her blanket underneath her.

Mother placed the blanket in the roasting pan. Like that? she said.

Daddy propped the baby in the pan. It stared up at them wide-eyed, its mouth round and red like a cherry.

They laughed at the sight of her.

Where's that celery? the father said.

I thought you said you didn't know how to cook, the mother told him.

Just for a little garnish, he said, placing tufts of celery leaves around the edges. The baby's hand closed around one of the tufts.

How about some of these cherry tomatoes for color? the mother said. Stay still, sweetie, she told the baby. You look beautiful.

Too bad we don't have any of those radish flowers, the father said.

He aimed the camera. This is great, he said, laughing. This is fantastic.

Oh, she looks like a suckling pig.

A Thanksgiving turkey.

I wish we had some parsley, the mother said. Instead of celery.

The baby was whimpering, and drool ran down its chin, and a bubble formed at its lips.

But I guess celery's better, the mother said.

How much does she weigh do you think, twelve pounds? Fourteen? She's really plump.

Look at her blowing bubbles, the mother said. She looks really juicy.

The father clicked away.

Is there film in that thing? the mother asked him.

The father lowered the camera, looked at it. I think so, he said. He moved closer and took another shot.

The baby squirmed and whimpered.

That's enough now, the mother said.

The father lowered the camera. They stood looking at the baby in the pan. Its knees were bent against its fat stomach. The pink feet stuck up in the air.

She sure looks good, the father said.

The mother nodded. She poked her finger gently into the baby's stomach.

Neither one of them moved.

Oh, the oven! the mother said. I forgot all about it! It must be hot enough
by now.

The baby screamed.

◈

Mother Hunger and Her Seatbelt
Dorothy Barresi

> *Things are more like they are now than they ever were before.*
>   Dwight D. Eisenhower

"When my first husband left me
I thought about forgiveness in ways
I hadn't before: I wanted to annihilate the bastard!

Pontiacs reminded me of him.
So did Robert Hass's poems, though not the one
about the gazelle watching his own entrails
being eaten pink by a jackal;
that one was safe.

I owned that poem for a while. And like drink
or pure selfishness,
it got me past those first, virtuoso weeks
of living my life in a provisional way,
not eating a full meal ever, or sleeping past noon

then getting up at 3 A.M. to watch *Amazing Discoveries*
on channel 13.
The one about knives. The one
about hair loss and yellow teeth turning whiter
under the pressure of oxygen.
And I was breathing, too,

coming up for air now and then.
Finally, when I spoke to Father Bentner about
this inability to find—in the face of the only

real injury I'd known not counting
childhood name-calling or petty

family squabbles—Jesus,
he stubbed out his Parliament in a teacup,
rubbed his raw
canonical jawbone, then spoke quietly—no, he intoned—
about the peace that passeth understanding,
Galatians and 'long suffering,'

as though a woman were nothing but a cold fish
and a bit of sourdough
about to undergo the long, late division
feeding multitudes. As though
I were dead already.
Then he asked me for a hug and good-bye, grab the surplice,

time to lead a rosary for Saint Lucy's Club.
A hug! Horny old fool.
That afternoon the sun fell
in slices through the trees, red birthday cake, and I
was famous with anger. Shaking.
The trees weren't the usual, Dutch-diseased elms

I'd grown up with,
but pestles grinding down some enormous
aspirin into the earth I couldn't take
for the headache starting
behind my eyebrows.
My Forgiveness Migraine, I call it now.

But back then, what did I know?
Indomitable self-love, city of scorn—any truth
is true enough in a pinch.
So when I saw *it*
flopping in the gutter by my car,
I got the message right away: curbside salvation

like a knock between the shoulder blades. Voilà!
A bluegill, I swear,
lost by an errant sea gull drunk on berries, or simply
blown off course
from Turkeyfoot Lake. Not a keeper, mind you.
Not enough to feed a family of one,

but a dirty four-inch fry the color of Mexican opal
dimming out on dry land.
A fluke, and a token of natural selection which says
the one who flies highest
without proper equipment
gets dropped, dropped, dropped. Just like that

I saw that I, too,
was one of God's poor dumb creatures
trying to make a go of it in the real world,
and death and suffering a factor
in making me feel better about living.
Someone else's death and suffering, that is.

At least that's what I thought then.
Call it my early conclusion.
Now I wonder with the rest, does innocence exist?
Is nature all fucked up?
Uncorrupted, we're worse than metaphysical;
we haven't got a clue. But that afternoon

I went away feeling
a whole lot meaner and better in this world.
Not special, mind you. Not asking
whyme, whyme,
because that's silly. I wasn't a me just then. I was.
Like a baby tooth left dangling from a doorknob,
or a half-sick tree,

or my seatbelt cutting bandolier-style across my chest
to keep me from sinking
into the wide, hot upholstery without recourse,

because *X* really does
mark the spot.

Then for five minutes, maybe ten,
I tuned in the heavy metal stations and drove
and knew where I was going.

Home to eat my young.
Home, where the heart hunkers down into the mud
with the rest of the bottom feeders, then all day,
baleful and sulky,
for what feels like an entire lifetime—guaranteed—
our blood gills work and blaze

and we never need sharpening,
though *blaze, blaze,* we wait also in a darkness
deeper down, like this entreaty
for the obvious miracle to come."

◆

Beer. Milk. The Dog. My Old Man.
Kim Addonizio

My old man used to take the dog
out to the garage
where the poker game was
and set down a bowl
of beer, that's the kind of thing
he thought was funny. He used to
give me some too and laugh when I
threw up or fell over
a chair. He taught me to fight
by smacking the side of my head
with his open hand, calling me
a pussy. Don't let them give you
any shit he said. When he smacked
my mother she didn't hit back,
just yelled at him. Once she threw

a glass of milk at his head.
It hit the wall and broke
to pieces on the floor.

I was ten when he died.
Too young to figure it out.
What I thought about was the milk
on the kitchen floor that time,
how they'd both
left it there and gone to bed.
The dog got to it and swallowed glass.
My mother said the dog
just got sick. The milk
evaporated she said.
Meaning it just
went into the air.
I thought, how could something
be there and then not? Milk.
The dog. My old man. He loved
a cold beer. Sometimes I'd sit up
at night in the garage and watch
how he drank it, tipping his head
way back, and I'd try to drink mine
exactly the same,
but quietly, so he wouldn't notice
and send me away.

∾

Our Father

Cris Mazza

Ours wasn't a family in public housing, not on welfare, not living in an urban war zone. Also not a destitute farm family in Oklahoma's dust bowl or a flooded plain beside the Mississippi. This isn't a story about victimization and deliverance. It's about a middle-class family that didn't realize it was middle-class, in any sense of the word. We just didn't know any better: that middle-class families ordinarily didn't cull the rejected vegetables left in a farmer's harvested field or eat what the fish store sold as bait.

But we'd never claim that a family living in a three-bedroom home in the semirural suburbs, whose main source of income was a father employed as a community college professor, was suffering or merely surviving. Even if the family numbered five kids. Even if a community college professor only made around ten thousand a year in the sixties. Even if new school clothes meant sneakers from FedMart plus bundles of hand-me-downs from cousins and older siblings. Even if going to the movies meant the drive-in with five kids in the back of a station wagon. And when our neighbors outgrew their bicycles, we used Brasso to make the chrome fenders and wheel rims sparkle. There were new toys—at Christmas and birthdays, never in between—board games and knock-off Barbie or troll dolls that wore the same size clothes. We always had books to read thanks to library cards and our mother's childhood collection. Of course the living room housed a black-and-white TV, until it broke down and wasn't replaced for over a year. Doesn't matter, we could only watch if our dad turned it on, and then could only watch what he chose. Also had to ask permission to open the refrigerator, never knew the (coveted) joy of individual chip bags or Twinkies in our school lunches.

But ours was not a family in poverty. Not in distress. Not in trouble. Just an ordinary family like millions of others, where dad had a job and mom was the Girl Scout leader, a family that might've eaten hamburger and tuna seven days a week without feeling deprived. Instead we dined on quail, rabbit, albacore, calamari, duck, eggplant, squash flowers, artichokes, figs, olives, natural honey in the comb, persimmons, even quail eggs. What might've seemed, had we recited these activities to a school psychiatrist, like an indigent family *scavenging*—going on weekend outings to gather abandoned or discarded, still living or freshly killed food from the countryside—was actually just *a way of life*, a relationship with landscape or region, possibly tacitly handed down from an immigrant father to son.

Eldest Son

Rather than the archetype ignorant peasant fleeing destitution in the southern regions of a newly unified Italy, bringing with him a family of uneducated children, our grandfather, Crescenzo Mazza, came to the United States around the turn of the century, after he finished high school in Naples, Italy. He came with his brothers, their wives, and his parents, and with money in their pockets—his father had recently sold the family's two Mediterranean shipping vessels.

Eventually our grandfather was married and working in Manhattan as a salesman for three or four Italian jewelry importers. With five children plus various extended family members, our grandparents lived rather well in a two-story house in Flatbush, Brooklyn. Our father played stickball in the street, rode the streetcars to Coney Island, and he used to get walloped for staying out late fishing and clamming near Flatlands Bay. The family then feasted on seafood cioppino.

As it would for so many others, everything changed in 1929. The stock market plunged and our grandparents eventually lost everything, including Grandpa's livelihood, so the whole family left New York and moved west, stopping for almost a year to sell baubles and pennants at the Texas Centennial in 1936. But California was their intended destination, and later in 1936—like tens of thousands of others in one of the biggest voluntary migrations in history—they arrived "home."

Our grandfather had brought enough leftover stock with him to open a jewelry shop in Long Beach's now-extinct waterfront amusement zone, a rinky-dink version of Coney Island. While the younger children attended school, our father worked in the store. When, serendipitously, the store failed, Grandpa was offered the opportunity to manage an Anaheim fish market owned by the DiMassas of the L. A. Fish & Oyster Company. This gave our grandmother the opportunity to prevail in her determination that our father's education should resume.

The Mazzas' San Pedro home was across the street from the temporary quarters of a private academy called Chadwick School, where our father worked part-time as a janitor, earning twenty-five cents an hour—and all went directly to the family's budget. Mrs. Chadwick, the founder and headmistress of the academy, discovered he was also a stellar student at San Pedro High School. The fledgling Chadwick School was striving for state accreditation and would need its first graduates to begin attending college immediately. So when her most advanced students were juniors, Mrs. Chadwick invited our father to be part of Chadwick School's first graduating class; then when the school relocated to its permanent (and present) site on the Palos Verde Peninsula, our father went along to board there with the other students, grades K–12, who lived on campus.

Chadwick School would later become home to the children of celebrities and movie stars. Among others, Jack Benny, Dean Martin, Edward G. Robinson, Jascha Heifetz, Sterling Hayden, George Burns, and Joan Crawford sent their children to Chadwick. Liza Minnelli attended classes at Chadwick, as did Jack Jones. Mrs. Chadwick's concern was that these privileged children might not be anxious to begin attending college immediately, and with an inaugural graduating class numbering around a dozen, she wanted to ensure at least one college graduate. That was our father's role.

Meanwhile, Grandpa bought the fish market, and he moved the rest of the family to a house he'd purchased in Orange County for around twenty-four hundred dollars. This was long before the period when some postwar subdivisions built in the area required prospective residents of Italian descent to *prove* they were Italian, and not Mexican. (Tensions between whites and Latinos had existed in California since the United States had taken over the Mexican territory; since American surveyors had lopped off large portions of old Mexican ranchos or had negated Mexican ownership of ranchos entirely; since former Mexican landowners had become the stewards and ranch managers for the new white landowners.)

Vine Street, where the house was located, was one block long, encompassed mostly by orange groves. The surrounding region also contained farm fields with lima beans, bell peppers, green beans, tomatoes, strawberries, and other produce. Every Saturday in the fish market our grandfather would prepare a big bowl of raw fish, and the field workers—Mexican and Japanese—would come in to get supplies for their weekend festivities. Our grandfather was not only acquainted with many of the farm workers, he also knew the owners of the produce fields. They gave him permission to come any time to pick his own produce. So Grandpa initiated the familial propensity to augment the family's lifestyle—or at least to procure food—in ways other than with money.

Our father's education at the University of California was partially sponsored by another of the private school's founders. Before he could finish his degree, however, our father's progress through college was interrupted by World War II. Four years later the new G. I. Bill allowed him to finish his education. Then—partially out of gratitude—he went back to Chadwick School as the chemistry teacher. There he met our mother, a new phys. ed. instructor fresh out of Boston University.

Homesteader

Our parents' little stucco bungalow on the campus of Chadwick School was rent-free, but when our mother had a fourth child, the house threatened to rupture.

When our father bought it, his new property in San Diego county had a long, low ranch house built on a three-quarter-acre lot on the slope of the hill. The front lawn on one level and back lawn on a lower level were both horizontal. The rest of the property sloped downhill at anything from a thirty to almost a forty-five degree slant. From the edge of the back lawn down to the property line, and continuing from there down to the bottom of the hill, it was all the natural terrain of tumbleweeds, rocks, lizards, wasps' nests, rattlesnakes, wild cucumbers, buckwheat, cacti, and rippling wild oats.

Our father looked around at his property and announced, "There's ten years of work here." Forty years later, he's still working.

It started with dynamiters who leveled out a place for an above-ground swimming pool. Then for several months our father (with a wheelbarrow), our mother, and all five of us (ages three to thirteen) picked up the rubble and made rock piles around the perimeter of the property. With these rocks, over the next thirty-plus years, our father has constructed walls—some as thick as two feet, ranging in height from two to six feet—which terrace the entire property into four levels.

These terraced levels have become home to a wide variety of fruit trees, including fig, persimmon, tangerine, lime, several varieties of orange, quince, avocado, loquat, pomegranate, plum, nectarine, peach, banana, apple, and apricot. Plus there are beds of rotating seasonal vegetables: lettuce, cabbage, Brussels sprouts, broccoli, asparagus, onions, garlic, herbs of all kinds, radishes, carrots, squash, pumpkins, artichoke, eggplant, spinach, Swiss chard, rhubarb, bell peppers, several varieties of tomato, green beans, strawberries, boysenberries, raspberries, and more. The property came equipped with two full-sized olive trees, so our father also cures olives. Our mother cans and preserves everything—strawberry, peach, plum, and boysenberry jam and mint jelly, quince sauce, tomato sauce, and boysenberry and pomegranate syrup. When we were young there were also rabbits, and under the rabbit hutches our father raised worms for freshwater fishing. We kept beehives for honey, chickens in a ten-foot-square coop, and quail in their own smaller coop—not for meat, just for the tiny eggs.

Twice our rabbits were used for school assignments. The first was tanning rabbit hides for a high school chemistry project. This project did not earn an A, but the only criticism from the teacher was that she couldn't stand the idea that the skins came from rabbits we'd helped slaughter. Later, that very wordless slaughter-choreography—featuring our father and one of us as assistant—became a photo series in a college photography class.

After helping him hang the live rabbit by the hind feet, the assistant turned away while our father dispatched a blow with a hammer to the base of the skull. The impact had to be clean—breaking the animal's neck instantly—or the rabbit would scream, but ears couldn't be plugged because as soon as the hammer hit and the bones cracked, the assistant had to be ready to take the hammer and hand our father a knife. Our father decapitated and let the blood drain from the twitching body into a bucket placed directly below. He then cut through the hide, down to the bone, in a ring around each ankle. The knife now held in his mouth by the handle, he began the removal of the hide. Since handing him the knife, the assistant did nothing except to get one of the hide-racks from where they'd been hung on the grape arbor before we started. Slaughtering took place in the shade of the arbor, surrounded on two sides by the rabbit hutches. This meant not only those destined for the meat freezer were witnesses, but also the adult breeding stock.

Meanwhile our father would be peeling the hide down the two legs. When the hide had rolled as far as the tail, he needed the knife again, one quick cut across the crotch. The knife back in his mouth, both hands back to gripping the slippery inside-out skin, he could now peel the hide quickly, in one motion, the rest of the way from the body, with a long sucking sound. Curiously, the hide would "pop" free of the front feet, leaving them still covered with fur, without further assistance from the knife. Our father held up the inverted tube of hide while the assistant threaded the stretching rack through it, fixed the hide with clothespins to the rack, then let it spring open and tight. It would hang in the basement to cure until the next litter of rabbits was ready for slaughter.

Dressing the carcass required one more slit from the knife, diaphragm to neck hole, then the knife handed off to the assistant—to be set on top of a hutch with the blade touching nothing but air. Next he needed the first cooking pot. This pot would catch the heart and liver as our father separated them from the viscera. The lid clamped on, that pot was quickly exchanged for the second one in time for him to drop the lungs and kidneys there. Those were for the dog. So now the carcass was empty, closely resembling a skinned cat. Once more with the knife, our father cut the front paws off and let them fall into the bloody bucket, then cut the body free of the back feet and slid it into a different bucket of clean salted water. Once each session, without saying anything, he would hold out his palm so we could both see the small heart still beating there—this was our proof of how quickly we were working, how quickly it would soon be over. How nothing was suffering.

None of us enjoyed killing rabbits. But the distasteful part of the process was, somehow, disconnected in our sensibilities from enjoyment of fried rabbit dinners. It was disconnected from the sublime phenomenon of the pink, blind babies that would appear, without anyone's help, the morning after the doe had lined her nest box with fine white fur. It was disconnected from blithe sunny mornings playing with six or eight softball-sized bunnies on the lawn. The slaughtering was somehow so disconnected from all the other care of the rabbits, that we felt true sorrow when roaming stray dogs came and bloodied the adult rabbits' feet through the bottoms of the cages; and another, more horrible time when the bees in the nearby hives became angered and attacked the first animals they found—the rabbits in their wire hutches. Rage at the bees and the dogs was useless—bees attack their enemies and dogs hunt in packs, and people all over the world raise their own food.

Hunter and Gatherer

From late summer, through fall and into early winter: this time of year was never called football season. This was hunting season. Dove, quail, and cotton-tail rabbit were all available and legal to hunt in San Diego County and even in undeveloped parts of the city.

A dove or quail meal was always a Sunday dinner with china and silver. Slow-cooked in a wine-based tomato sauce, the little bodies stayed whole but melted apart when touched; the engorged dark meat could be caressed from the fragile bones. Drumsticks smaller than a toothpick, wings the size of bobby pins. We ate with our hands, licked our fingers, dirtied cloth napkins, sucked the tiny skeletons dry. Quail—about the same size as dove but all white meat—was usually fried with oregano. Cottontail rabbit was stewed with tomatoes. Sometimes our teeth hit shattered bone and we would stop chewing, feel with lips and tongue, or use a finger to locate the tiny shot pellet that had been embedded in the muscle.

Pulled from sleep at 3:30 A.M.; the tranquil, liquid chill before sunrise and the swell of dusty heat as soon as a September sun rose; the soft traipsing in our parents' footsteps, trained to stay behind them and squat down when we heard the whistle of dove wings or saw a cottontail dart out of the brush; the retriev-ing, the decapitating, the defeathering and dressing, the cooking, the dining—none of it was experienced without a twinge of . . . not guilt, exactly. Maybe some sort of contrite sigh. As we helped our parents hunt (and thoroughly enjoyed the ensuing meal), as we bred rabbits for similar purposes, as we gave up pet adolescent roosters to the hatchet and burlap bag—none of these activities lacked trepidation during the volatile flash of death.

Near one hunting area, there was a farm packing house where truck farmers brought harvested produce to be shipped to grocery stores. Behind the loading docks they dumped rejects. We showed up with the back of the station wagon heaped with empty boxes, and from green-scented piles over eight feet high, we salvaged a cache of celery—taking only the hearts from the culls the farmers had cast out. There were also loose tomatoes scattered all over the ground—fully ripe, not squashed, but probably unable to travel to a store without bruis-ing. In a huge caldron on a Coleman stove outside, our parents turned boxes of tomatoes into jars of tomato sauce.

Another early hunting site was near the U.S. border in the Tijuana River val-ley, where now there are large parcels of park, some houses, and flood-threat-ened equestrian ranches. In the mid-1960s there was nothing but waist-high grasses, dry, sandy washes, native barrel cactus, fragrant sage and anise, coyote and foxes, rabbits, snakes, hawks, owls, meadowlarks, roadrunners, horned toads, wasps, and tarantulas. Here our father came across an abandoned farm. There was rusted equipment—a well pump, a hand plow—a dead tree near a house foundation, and one lone live fig tree. While we played below, he climbed the low, thick branches and filled a bucket with ripe figs. Our father eventually established three fig trees on his property. But in the mid-sixties, when any trees in our yard were mere sticks, this abandoned tree was like an island paradise for our parents. An island in memory too: we were the only people in a pristine prairie of brown, waving grasses, interrupted only by the dusty dark green dome of the old fig tree, no sound but the mournful cry of doves, intricate piping of meadowlarks, rustle of mice, wind chime of rattling leaves or creaking branches. Kids don't notice—and nobody remembers—stickers in socks, bug bites, or wind-tangled hair. That's what happens when things disappear, leaving us only with phantom-recollection.

A Patriarch's Vacation

Our father may have been a community college professor, but that doesn't mean he had the whole summer "off." Summer school and the flourishing backyard—always in need of weeding, spraying, harvesting, a new sprinkling system, usually a rock wall in-progress—easily filled the months of June and July. When August came, he gave himself two weeks "vacation."

Up in the eastern Sierra above a high desert town called Big Pine, there is a series of rustic campsites—no toilets, just outhouses—at altitudes from four to seven thousand feet. A glacier creek thunders out of the mountains, flowing into and back out of seven man-made lakes, formed in the early twentieth century to provide water for a developing town called Los Angeles. The state Fish and Game Department stocks the Big Pine Creek with rainbow trout, while brown trout—originally from Europe—live as though indigenous in streams and lakes all over the Sierra.

Packing boxes, duffel bags, ice chests, and tackle boxes; loading the handmade trailer; the endless testing of turn signals after hitching the trailer to the station wagon—these day-before preparations seemed to take long into the night. Departure was before dawn. But upon arrival at camp, after eight hours of driving, *no* one was allowed to immediately dip a baited hook into the river. Tents had to be pitched and rain trenches dug around each, gear stowed, empty campsites scouted for firewood. While our mother unloaded and organized equipment, our father packed his saw and ax into the woods to cut logs he lugged or dragged back to our site. While he chopped wood without a shirt, a muted shout was pushed from his chest, followed by the ring of the ax, but few words. His beard grew.

On a big rock between two trees, we wore out the knees of our jeans and got sap in our hair. It smelled thick and piney, turned black and tacky, and later our father would have to use gasoline to scrub it off. He walked back and forth, past the rock, gathering dry greasewood for kindling, a red bandanna around his forehead. We played with kids from other campsites, glancing up at him as he passed, and one little girl said, "I'm afraid of that Indian."

Our father spent more than one camping trip working with the creek itself. He moved rocks, some nearly boulders, into the cold, quick river, slowing the water just enough to make trout pools and places for fishermen to stand or cross to an opposite bank. He fished early mornings, then again at dusk, working both sides of the river.

Between ages five and seven, each in our turn, our father took us out alone to learn the finer arts of river fishing. Invariably in the first lesson, he hooked a trout and thrust the pole into our hands to land the fish, then he exhaled sharply, a nearly inaudible grunt, when we flung the fish out of the water backwards over our heads, tangling fish, line, and pole in the heavy brush.

At night when we sang with our mother around the fire, when we played card games by firelight, when we roasted marshmallows then burned the roofs of our mouths with liquid charcoaled-sugar, when we scalded our lips and tongues on hot chocolate in tin cups, our father sat quietly across the fire from us. His shoulders seemed to be somewhat hunched, as he sat on one of the logs he'd cut so there would be seven seats around the fire, cupping a plastic mug of thin hot chocolate and staring into the flames. Resting for the first time since he'd risen at four to go fishing.

Occasionally he came back to the campsite late, long after sunset, having been fishing miles from camp when it had finally become too dark to even see the river, let alone be able to flick his bait accurately into the riffle. He came in with fish to be cleaned. When we stumbled by flashlight to the outhouse and back, he'd be gutting fish in the glaring white light of the buzzing Coleman lantern, shadows of moths darting in and out of his illuminated circle. In the morning we would eat those fish for breakfast.

Another rite of passage was when we were considered old enough to hike with him to fish in the lakes. This meant hiking two or three thousand feet further up in altitude, three to five miles on the sandy John Muir Trail, carrying rucksacks packed with our lunches and long fishing poles.

Once we had traversed the alpine meadows and arrived at the lakes, once we baited our hooks and began fishing at a lake's inlet, he might make the familiar chest grunt, or even an audible "oh!" if we lost a fish we'd hooked, or if we had to go to him to extract a hook we'd oafishly allowed a fish to swallow instead of setting the hook in the lip. He would nod his approval for those we landed, or concisely notify us that the trout we'd just caught was a brookie or a cut throat—no hatchery-raised rainbow trout lived in the lakes. Before departing from the lakes to return down the mountain to camp, we cleaned our fish and buried the entrails a sufficient distance from water's edge. Again that exclamation from his chest if we didn't manage to extricate everything—gills, guts, plus pelvic and anal fins—in one swift movement.

Eventually we could hike further and faster and catch as many fish, and we were the ones staying out until long after dark, returning with trout to clean to find the card game in full swing, hot water simmering over the fire, packets of powdered hot chocolate waiting for us.

In times to come, our father would be going to our houses to pick oranges and tangerines, collect eggs, and gather walnuts. He would someday hunt duck around flat lakes on the Texas plain near a son's house and fish the Atlantic coast at another son's summer beach rental. He would inspect the banana trees and asparagus patches in his daughter's backyard, send visiting adult children home to Idaho and Illinois with bags of bulbs and waiting-to-ripen avocados and persimmons, help his grandchildren gather pecans in an abandoned grove in North Carolina, take visiting children and sons-in-law out in his boat to fish for albacore and bonita off the coast of San Diego, and return every year with one or two of his children and some grandchildren, to Big Pine.

Our father and mother now stay in a cabin. They haven't been up to the lakes in several years. The trout limit is five instead of ten, which makes fishing with barbless hooks even more necessary unless he wants to reach his limit before 9 A.M. That leaves plenty of time for playing cards, reading, and—finally—relaxing in the shade of the pines beside the effervescent glacier creek, still plunging, boisterous and cold, down the eastern Sierra slopes.

༄

Italian Grocer
Rachel Guido deVries

After he was produce manager for the A & P,
Pop opened his own store. He polished apples
to lay alongside sweet Jersey peaches all
fuzzy and gold, and sometimes got figs which he

held up like gems. Bread and baccala, olives
in a big brown barrel. Provolone, locatelli,
Genoa salami, prosciutto behind a gleaming
case. Each morning he donned a white coat
like a doctor, marched the aisles, and watched.

He hired Angie the dyke to keep things neat.
She fed me cherries when I was three. Mamma
worried I'd choke. Pop and Angie laughed
and Angie said I'd learn what to do with those pits.

When the store burned, Pop went mad and wept
all over the street. Angie vanished from me, and
the queer man upstairs lost all of his drag. White
people in the neighborhood said Pop the Wop
torched his own store for insurance. He had none.
His white coat, smelling of cheese and fish,
was gone.

Smoke and Fire
Mary Saracino

Daddy charges upstairs. His footsteps rattle the ceiling. He runs into the bathroom, and the whole kitchen shakes below him. I think about getting up and grabbing the broom and dustpan, sweeping away the salt and pepper still spilled over the table, but I can't move. Mama gets up, but she doesn't pick up the mess. She grabs a cigarette and lights it. She leans against the kitchen sink and looks down at the dirty floor. Above us, the ceiling shakes with noise.

"Get the hell out of my way. I've got to go to work." Daddy's voice rumbles through the walls.

"Dad." Joey's voice tumbles down the hallway, like he's being pushed from the bathroom. A door slams. I hear running water. A pause. A knock. Another pause. Joey's voice, again. He hesitates this time. "Dad, I gotta pee."

"Hold it," Daddy orders.

Quiet fills up everything for a second, then the bathroom door squeaks open. "OK, hurry up." Daddy's voice is nicer now.

Down the hall, the boys' bedroom door opens. Feet shuffle, and the floor creaks. Another knock on the bathroom door. Danny's voice this time. "You gonna be long, Dad?"

"For cryin' out loud, what's wrong with you guys?" Daddy booms.

The bathroom door slams. Daddy comes crashing down the steps. He plows through the living room, sending the Venetian blinds rattling. He opens the front door, then slams it. The car peels out of the driveway. Gravel hisses in the cold air.

"I wish they'd all just shut up, for once," Mama says. Her voice crawls out of the quiet and startles me. I turn and watch her without saying anything. "Why'd I ever have so many goddamn kids?" Mama complains. She blows her thoughts into the room with her cigarette smoke.

I stare at my saddle shoes. I might need boots today. I glance out the kitchen window to check if it's snowing. It's ugly gray November outside. Clouds and trees and ground all the same ugly color. Even the maple tree in the side yard looks cold. Snow collects on its branches. I close my eyes and think about snow angels and making snow forts. Soon. It will only be a little while longer before it really starts to fall. When it's thick and heavy, everything gets real quiet. That's the kind of quiet I like best of all—when nothing moves. It reminds me of the back of my closet. I hide there sometimes, under the skirt hems and pant cuffs dangling over wire hangers, and nobody can find me for hours and hours. I take a box of vanilla wafers with me and suck on the cookies until they melt on my tongue.

I stare at the cupboard and wonder if Mama bought vanilla wafers at the store yesterday. I want to grab a few, forget about school, crawl into the back of my closet and eat them right now. Mama flicks ashes into a metal ashtray and pulls a small saucepan out of the cupboard. She crosses over to the stove, and I follow her with my eyes. My heart pushes against my ribs. It rushes into my lungs, up through my throat. It beats in my chin, my cheeks, my forehead.

Mama covers the pan and pulls out the toaster. She mumbles, "I'm a good mother. I make them breakfast every morning. Toast the bread. Make the cereal. Pour the juice. I love them all. They just never let me alone."

Mama cuts a piece of toast and lays it on a small plate. She drops the butter knife onto the floor. It clangs and splatters oleo onto my clean shoes. She stares at the floor, then she looks at my laces and finally right into my eyes. Her eyes are empty, like a dark and dangerous room. I look away, so I don't have to go inside.

"It's OK, Mama. I'll clean it up."

I grab a rag from the sink and wipe the oleo from my shoe and the floor. Mama nods a thank you, then sits by the window and lights another cigarette. She coughs, taps her fingertips on the table, takes a long drag off her Chesterfield, sighs and rubs her belly.

"Dear God . . . I won't. I can't," she mumbles. "Patrick, what are we gonna do?" She looks right at me. "Peanut," she says. She wants to say more but Danny and Joey and the girls rush into the kitchen and her words disappear.

"Mornin', Mama," they all say. Mama closes her eyes as they kiss her, one by one. I hang back, watching. I don't want to kiss her this morning. Danny and Joey grab a chair and reach for some toast. The kitchen is noisy again.

"What's burning?" Danny asks, sniffing the air.

"Mama! The oatmeal!" I yell.

She doesn't move. I rush to the stove and turn the burner off. Mama takes another drag and watches. The smoke spills out of her mouth. I grab a pot holder, wrap it around the pan handle and dish hot cereal into Rosa and Winnie's bowls.

When I get to Danny's bowl he shoves my hand away. "I don't want any crummy burnt oatmeal," he snaps. He hogs three more pieces of toast. I want to slam the pan on his greedy fingers.

"Mama," I start to complain, but she's not listening. Her head's turned away, and she's facing out the window again. Smoke floats around her hair.

It's useless. She's not gonna help. I put the pan back on the stove and sit next to Rosa. I stab my spoon at the glop of oatmeal in my bowl. I don't want to look at Danny or the others. They act like nothing's wrong. They pretend they didn't hear the fight this morning, the awful shouting. Even if they were dead, they would have heard it. It would have shook the dirt off their graves.

My eyes slide back and forth between the table and Mama, checking to see if she's stopped staring out at the clouds. She's going away again. I'm afraid she'll burn a hole through that window, with all her looking, and slip away into the sky. My stomach is a bowl of small, twisted knots. I open my mouth to scream, but nothing comes out.

Mama stays like a statue all through breakfast. After we eat, I clear the table and put the dirty dishes into the sink. "I'll wash them when I come home for lunch, Mama." I don't know if she hears me or not. I send her I-love-yous with my mind. She doesn't say a word. She just keeps staring out the window and rubbing her stomach like she's gonna throw up again.

The boys grab their jackets and head for school. "See ya later," they call as they race out the front door. Rosa and I walk to school, too. Every day we pick up my best friend Amelia, who lives three doors down from us. Before we go, I wipe Winnie's face and hands with a dish rag and lift her out of her highchair. "Go in the living room. I'll turn 'Romper Room' on for you," I say. I pat her head thinking that will make her feel better. Winnie tugs at Mama's bathrobe. "Come on, Winnie, leave Mama alone," I order.

It's getting late, and I worry about making Amelia have to wait for us. After Winnie's settled, I grab Rosa's winter coat and bundle her up for our walk to school. I tuck her mittens in tight around her wrists to keep out the cold, just like Mama taught me. I pull out her red rubber boots and push them over her feet. Then I put on my own coat and boots and grab my book bag. I take one last look around the room to make sure I've got everything.

"Make sure Rosa keeps her coat on today," Mama calls from the kitchen. "It looks cold out."

"OK, Mama," I say.

She's come back. I peek into the kitchen to say good-bye, but she's lost in the window again. I wave to the back of her droopy bathrobe, grab Rosa's hand and head for the front door. "Let's go," I say.

Before we leave I give Winnie her raggedy blanket and kiss her forehead. "Be a good girl, now," I say. "We'll be home for lunch. Don't worry."

Rosa and I rush down the steps, down the block. The cold air slaps my skin. It makes me think of Daddy cracking his belt against the kitchen table. I squint as we turn the corner and head straight into the wind. I squeeze Rosa's hand.

"Come on. We're gonna be late."

"Ow! You're hurting me," Rosa cries.

"It's too cold to dawdle," I say. "And besides, Amelia's waiting."

Amelia rushes out of her front porch and waves hello as we get closer to her house. Most of the time I'm happy to see Amelia. Next to Zoomer, she's my best friend. I like her soft eyes most of all. They're blue-green, like a clear, clean lake in summer. But today I'm grouchy, and not even her summery eyes will make it better. All I can think of when I see her is how her mom and dad never fight. I've slept overnight at her house lots of times. I've eaten breakfast and dinner there, too, and never, ever, have her parents screamed at each other.

"Morning, Regina. Morning, Rosa." Amelia's lips are purple from the cold air. "What took you so long?"

I nod hello without answering. Her round pink face sticks out of the white flaps of her hat like carnival cotton candy in a paper holder. Sweet as candy, that's Amelia. She bounces along next to me and starts talking.

"What's wrong, Regina? You're so crabby. Are you hungry or something?" Every time I'm grouchy, she thinks it's because I'm hungry. That's the only time Amelia's crabby. She can't imagine any other reason for a sour mood. Amelia's silly like that. "Didn't you eat breakfast?" she asks. "My mom made me waffles. She said it's what you need on a cold day like today."

"I ain't grouchy," I snap. I don't want to hear about Amelia's breakfast or how sweet her mama is. "We're just late, that's all," I snap. I walk faster. "And we got to get to school."

"I'll say," Amelia huffs. It's as close to mad as she ever gets. "We got that math test today. Did you study last night?"

"Yeah," I lie.

Amelia wouldn't understand if I told her about having to babysit Rosa and Winnie while Mama went off to see Patrick. She's the youngest one in her family, and she never has to watch anybody but herself. Besides, I can't tell her stuff about Patrick, anyway. I promised Mama. Amelia buzzes on about our test and the *Sound of Music* record she wants for her birthday. She says it has lots of great songs for us to learn. When she grows up, she's gonna play Maria von Trapp on Broadway. It's what she's always wanted. Her yakking is starting to bug me. You'd think she'd see that I'm not really listening. I say, "Uh-huh" and "Yeah" sometimes, just to throw her off, but she doesn't notice. She's too busy loving the sound of her own voice.

The snow falls hard now. The wet flakes land on our heads, the backs of our coats, the tops of our boots. We've got five more blocks until we get to school. I wonder if Amelia's gonna shut up before we get there. The cold air stings my ears. It feels good, like saying Hail Marys when you feel sad. My fingertips are numb from holding my book bag. All those heavy books I have to lug back and forth to school. I didn't hardly open them last night. I'm worried. I'm worried. I'm worried. The wind kicks snow in my face. It sticks to my hair and ices over. The cold starts to pile up in my lungs. My insides are cold now, too. Everything is frozen solid, like a pond. Amelia's voice slips off my ears. I grab hold of Rosa's hand to warm my fingers, but it's too late. My stomach rumbles. I think about the salt and pepper spilled over the kitchen table. I think about Daddy's voice hissing mad and Mama's face, cloudy as the snowy sky.

Two more blocks and we'll be at school, far away from the screaming yellow kitchen walls. I'll sit at my desk, pick up my pencil, answer my test questions and push everything else away. One block from school now. I can see the big red brick building from here. I can read the letters, tall and friendly like a guardian angel: St. Joan of Arc Parochial School. I count my steps. One, two, three, four, five, six, seven, eight, nine, ten. And again, one, two, three, four. . . . When I step off the curb my knees buckle. I drop my book bag and fall back onto the sidewalk into the snow.

"Regina, are you OK?" Amelia cries.

"I gotta sit for a minute," I say.

I concentrate on the front door of the school. Five, six, seven, eight, nine, ten. Rosa starts to cry.

"I don't feel too good, Rosa."

I pull my mittens off my sweaty hands. My fingers are white, as white as the wet, heavy snow falling all around. I think about Amelia's mom making waffles for breakfast. I think about Amelia's dad taking them sledding last week. I think about the lost baby, the one who died when she was being born, the one that broke Mama's heart and makes her stare out the window like she's waiting for her dead daughter to come over the hill. That baby's eyes are probably green-blue like Amelia's, always happy, always warm. I stare up at the tree branches. I want to climb to the top branch and jump off, fly away, never look down, never look back. Something funny pushes from inside. I drop my head between my knees and throw up.

"Regina," Amelia rushes to my side. I count the buckles on her boots. "You better go home and get into bed."

"No," I shout. "I'll be OK. Really."

I wipe my mouth with the edge of my mitten. "We're at school already. We've got the math test, and—"

"No," Amelia says. "You should go home. Let your mama take care of you."

I shake my head. "I'm going to school, and that's that."

Rosa cries harder now.

"I'm OK," I try to reassure her. I pull myself up, wipe the snow off my butt, pick up my book bag, reach for Rosa's hand and stare right into Amelia's stubborn face.

"You're crazy, Regina Giovanni," Amelia says. She shakes her head. "Sometimes I just don't understand you."

Sometimes, I want to say to her, sometimes I don't understand you either. You never want to scream until your head flies off. I stare at her pink, round, little kiss of a mouth. Maybe I could go to her house instead, have her mother tuck me in, read me a story, make me hot chocolate. Sing me to sleep. I can't stand it anymore. I wish I was a million miles away. I wish I was as big as a house and as loud as thunder. Sometimes, Amelia, I shout at her with my thoughts and burning eyes, sometimes I wish I was you.

❧

Outside

Kim Addonizio

Still on probation,
he's careful,
won't touch anything that looks
like it might break bad.
He gets a job
washing dishes.
The guys he works with
are all right—Mexicans, Salvadorans.
Their English is bad. He likes
picking up words, teaching them.
Pussy is *coño*, he knows that
from prison, and like prison they say it
fifty times a day.

The kitchen is steam
and scalding water, yellow gloves
for his hands. On breaks
he sometimes stands
just inside the restaurant,
leans against the wall
by the swinging door.
White tablecloths, bottles
in silver buckets,
fresh flowers everywhere.
No one looks at him.
He thinks about sitting there,
holding a menu. Then goes
out back to the alley
where he can smoke,
look up between buildings
and not be bothered.

Sacred Hearts and Tar

Donna Masini

They say I dreamt it,
the tunnel behind the oak chest,
a passage through the building
out to the street.

Nanna. The oak chest. Hermits in the cookie tin.
I tell my sister the raisins are waterbugs
then crush them to show her: farm mud, the spicy dark
Italian fall, terra cotta statues

on a ship from Italy to Brooklyn.
Guarda piccolina. Che cosa fai?
Chestnut smells deep by the doorlight
to the cellar, the padlocked bins

mice and spiders and washing machines
the wet smells of drying sheets.
In the back, behind black bars
the boiler thrums like an iron heart.

I grab my sister, run to the courtyard
caught between the buildings. Clotheslines
crisscross up the four stories,
Rose Velotta reeling in her husband's shirts.

The rusted pulleys shriek, resist, and the clothes
look dirtier after they're washed.
Upstairs Michael Pergola's trains loop all day
around a braided rug—nowhere to go—

as Mrs. Pergola slides another angel
food cake into the oven. *Walk softly, lightly.*
There I bit a glass ornament, the tiny silver
manger scene shattered and Jesus in pieces in my mouth.

The sky pressed down across the building tops
like a giant Tupperware lid, sealing
the cooking steams that rose up kitchen walls:
spaghetti, cabbage greens, the thickening pies.

We counted twelve windows up the side of each brick wall.
Forty-eight windows, the sill soot like smeared mascara.
But mostly we followed the ground, trapped
ants in paper cups, covered them with holy cards.

Grandpa's cards. The sacred heart of Jesus pointing
to the arrows, bars across his heart.
I am the way, Jesus said.
Suffer the little children.

Blotches of tar, scars across concrete.
Grandpa wandered from crevice to crack,
stooped over holes. With a pail of hot tar
and a flat doctor's stick, he filled and scraped.

When he left we dug it out.
With spoons and sticks, rocks, toothpicks,
and broken toys, we tore, we scraped,
we ripped out the tar.

Part Two

❧

CEREMONIES

Kitchen Communion
Camilla Trinchieri

Mama has been cooking for a solid week. The food we eat during this week of mourning must be hers only. When Sal tried to go down the road to get doughnuts, Mama stopped him at the door. "I'll make you doughnuts that'll make your belly sing. No hole, that's a waste of good dough. If you need the hole, cut it out yourself."

She is grieving, she is not herself, we, her three children, tell each other with glances behind her back. We sit at the round kitchen table by the bay window for breakfast, lunch, and dinner, like in the old days when we were still a family gathered under one roof. Foods that marked the Sundays of our growing up, that came from every region of Italy: *calamari in umido* from Campania where Mama was born, *maccheroni con carciofi* from Calabria, lamb *alla bolognese* from Emilia-Romagna, *capretto* with fava beans from Lazio.

We eat; we thank her for the bounty of her table; we think we know what she is up to. Mama is weighing us down, hoping she can anchor us to this house, bring us back to filial duty, to respect, maybe even back to loving our father.

Her back to us, Mama stands on the solid wooden box Papa made for her so that she can reach the sink and the stove. She has just come home from Mass and is still wearing her blue straw hat with the veil pushed up as high as a crown. I rub Mama's back, tight with unhappiness, as she shucks the peas.

"Let me," I offer. Mama elbows me away and wraps the sheet of newspaper around the empty pea shells. Beef broth is simmering on the back burner. Diced onion and pancetta wait on the cutting board. Today we will lunch on *Risi e Bisi* to honor the trickle of Venetian blood in Papa's veins, a Northern heritage of which he boasted to every Italian American he met.

Mike, the oldest, the one Papa hit on the hardest, lights a cigarette. "So what are we going to do with Papa?" After lunch we are heading home— me to Brooklyn, Mike two roads down from Mama, Sal way across the country—each of us back to our own hideout, away from the shrinking walls of this house.

Mama turns around to face us, the glasses she needs for her nearsightedness still in place. We are blurs to her. She has not taken off her glasses since Papa dropped dead last Saturday, fitting an Armani suit at Garden City's Saks for an old customer of his.

"Burning up your father!" She is still on her box with her fist buried between her breasts, as if she'd grown a hole there. Her eyes are fixed with a new determination—eyes that can turn sweet at a sudden memory, at a kindness or a touch from one of us. Radiant eyes when Papa was anywhere near her. "You're real happy about that. You think you're clever ganging up on me."

"We didn't twist your arm," I say.

"We've been over this a thousand times." Mike opens the window wider. I hand him a small coffee cup to use as an ashtray. Outside in the vegetable garden Mama has cut down the row of Easter lilies. The stubs look hacked.

"The Vatican says cremation is okay," Sal says. He opens the refrigerator, which is filled with Mama's leftovers. The food the neighborhood women brought the first few days Mama made me take over to Our Lady of Divine Grace.

"They're doing it in Italy now, too." Sal helps himself to a cold slice of eggplant from yesterday's parmigiana. "I guess they ran out of room, huh?" He pops another slice in his mouth.

"Wait for dinner, Sal." Mama's words come out weary from having been repeated for most of Sal's life.

"Cremation is what he wanted, okay?" Mike blows smoke toward the open window. "He told me he didn't want a fuss."

Mama hunches her shoulders, drops them suddenly, as if their weight has caught her unawares. "He said nothing to me."

"He didn't always tell you everything. I'm his first son. I'm the one he told."

We got Mama to agree to cremate Papa with a lie; he didn't tell his first son, second son, or daughter anything. Papa wasn't a communicator. Cremating Papa was our decision. It seemed simpler, more cost efficient, the American thing to do.

"We executed his wishes." Mike's voice is loud now. The only other sound is a far-off mower. "That's what we did, and all you do is lay down the guilt trip."

"Hey Mike, control the foghorn, okay?" Sal says. He looks as if he's ready to give Mike a fast kick in the pants. Sal, obedient, respectful, was Papa's golden boy until he exchanged the sun of Long Island for California's Silicon Valley and forever happy skies. He can do no wrong for Mama. "And no smoking in this house, okay?"

Mike drags harder on his cigarette between swigs of his beer.

Mama gets off the box and kicks it closer to the stove to swirl butter in the hot pan. She adds a little olive oil. "To stop the butter from burning," she used to tell me when she was still trying to teach me what I refused to learn. "Cooking, that's how you hold a family together," she'd add in hopes of snaring my interest. It was the first disappointment I gave her.

I watch her throw in the onion and pancetta and wonder if she has seen through our lie. "He loved you, Mama," I say. "He didn't want to keep you tied to him after his death." No headstone demanding weekly visits with flowers and prayers, as if it were some altar.

"You," Mama sweeps the handle of the pan across the room to include the three of us. "You don't want to come back to pay your respects!"

I say, "Remember Rita Cerani's husband dead three weeks, she put her head in the oven and turned on the gas? That night at the beach after her funeral? You remember that?" It was a summer night, the kitchen too hot to cook in, and Papa had come up with the idea of dinner at the beach. While the boys and Papa gathered driftwood, Mama and I unpacked the pots and the dishes from the trunk of the car.

"When I die, don't do anything crazy," he said, shaking the skillet closer to the fire to nudge the clams open. "And I want no black, you hear, Connie? Wait a couple of months, then dress yourself up and catch yourself a new young man. To hell with what the neighbors think."

Mama laughed and hugged his arm. "If you go, I'll decide what to wear, not you." She kissed him then, on the lips, the firelight licking their joined faces, leaving a glow. When they parted, the tip of Mama's tongue disappeared back into the darkness of her mouth as if it was a candy she was eager to suck. It was the longest, most embarrassing moment of my ten-year-old existence. Later I asked Sal if it was the mention of death that sexed Mama up. He said dumb questions didn't deserve answers, but I swore to myself never to bring up the subject of death anywhere near a boy.

"We could borrow Vito's boat and scatter Papa in the ocean," Sal says. "He might even float all the way to Italy and get to visit finally." Papa felt there was never enough money for them to go. When the bank promoted me to assistant treasurer two years ago, I offered to pay for them to take the trip. Papa was too stubborn and proud to accept.

"They don't scatter in Italy," Mama says. She hands me the knives and forks for me to set the table. She shakes her head when I hand them over to Sal. The same thing happens when I hand over the dishes, her good Sunday dishes that have to be washed by hand.

"We can bury the urn in the rose bushes," Sal offers. "Papa can stay in one place, if that's what you want."

"He loved those roses," I add.

"Is this a religious thing?" Mike asks, his elbows rooted to the table Sal is trying to set. The tablecloth, Papa's wedding gift to Mama, has been in place since our first meal together after the funeral. White linen with white roses embroidered in the corners, it comes out for special occasions, and she has never let a stain stay on it for more than a couple of hours. Now it's covered with this past week's food spatterings. I offered to pay for a trip to the cleaners more than once, but Mama insists it's just fine the way it is. She won't even let me change the napkins, Mama who was called Santa Nettezza by Papa, Saint Clean. "She wants to make that tablecloth unrecognizable," Sal said this morning when we cleared the breakfast dishes. "She's hell-bent on destroying it. I bet you the next time you come she'll have thrown it away."

I scratched at the crust of a tomato stain with my nail. "Maybe she wants to keep a record of this week. The three of us with her, eating through her grief."

Mike scrunches his cigarette down into the coffee cup. "Are you worried about the Second Coming?" he asks Mama. "The resurrection bit, the body has to be whole to make it to Heaven. Is that it?"

"You don't even respect your father after he's dead and can't do you any harm." Mama's body shakes as her elbow rises and falls with each stir of the rice. "You wanted to make sure there'd be nothing left of him. Whatever he did, he didn't deserve that." She steps down from her box and pours the *Risi e Bisi* into the Capodimonte tureen Vito Marinucci brought back for my parents after a trip to Naples. Vito was Papa's best friend and offered the luncheon after the funeral at his restaurant, the Sea Palace, with its three banquet halls dripping glass from the ceilings and a view of the Sound from the ladies' room. Mama invited all the old timers in the neighborhood and the salesmen from the men's department at Saks. Mike was angry at her for accepting Vito's generosity. "We aren't beggars," he kept repeating during the luncheon. "We could have had it at the Plaza." Mike does handiwork for a living and barely scrapes by.

Mama takes off her apron, makes her way to the table, holding the tureen. Mike gets up to get another beer. Sal pulls out the chair for her.

"Don't worry about your father," Mama says. "I'm taking care of him."

"Your hat," I remind her as she's about to sit down. She takes it off with a shaky smile, the first of the week, and hands it to me.

"It's been ten years since we sat together, all of us at one table," she says. It's a statement of fact. She is done with reproaches.

Mike sits back down and glances at his watch. "It's been four and a half hours. At breakfast."

"That's not what Mama means," Sal says, sitting down next to her.

"He knows what I mean," Mama says.

My place is next to Papa's empty chair, which I don't take because suddenly I don't know what to do with my feet or Mama's hat. I'm back to being twelve, at another Sunday lunch in this kitchen.

"You've got a wife and three kids," Mama says to Papa's stony face. I'm the only kid there. Sal and Mike are at the beach. Papa's long hand twirls spaghetti around his fork. His thumb is covered with needle pricks from sewing. Thimbles are for sissies. He works the fork so quickly that bits of sauce fly out and spatter on my blouse.

"You've got a wife and three kids," she repeats.

"What are you talking about?" Papa asks.

"You know what I mean."

Papa's fingers don't stop turning until he's got every strand tightly wound. Nothing else is said.

After an afternoon spent working on his roses, Papa moved out. He came back three years later, while I was painting my nails fuchsia at the kitchen table and Mama was cooking dinner. Without even looking at him Mama said, "Hurry and wash up. I just threw in the pasta."

I still have the bottle of fuchsia nail polish.

Mama takes off her glasses and waves her hand at me. "Louisa, just put down the hat and sit down."

We shake out our napkins in unison. "Get ready," Papa would say as we sat down at the table, our napkins in our fists. "Get set," he continued to say after he came back. "Go!" And we, his kids, continued to play along, allowing him this one family game. Unfurling my napkin is as familiar and unconscious a motion as crossing myself when I walk into a church. A commemoration of sorts to a man I'd stopped believing in.

Mama's head barely clears the reclining figure of Neptune on the lid of the tureen. Our plates are piled next to her elbow, waiting to be filled. She clasps her hands. For a second I think she's going to pray.

"Family stays with you," she says, "even after you go off to lead your own lives, even after death. That's the way it is, like it or not. You think you're better than him, that you're not going to make any mistakes in your life. He's dead and you've gotten rid of him, dust to dust and all that baloney. Wrong! Your father's in your blood and he'll be in your children's blood if you should be so lucky to get married and have some. And you're the better for it." She lifts up the lid of the dish. A veil of steam covers her face. "It's you he came back to. He loved you with everything he had and I want you to keep that love. It'll make life good for you, believe me. A mother's wish. Now *buon appetito*."

"*Buon appetito*," we repeat together, our amen of the table, as she ladles out the creamy rice. The steam has evaporated and the air now smells sweet of peas and butter. White ocean light reaches into our corner snatching the gloom from our faces. I flatten the rice into a circle and start from the cool edge of the plate. It's delicious, as always. Vito claims Mama's the best cook this side of the Atlantic. I think Papa came back for her cooking.

Sal watches me eat and laughs. "The map, Mama. We can't eat *Risi e Bisi* without the map."

"Right behind Louisa."

I turn around. The boot of Italy stares back at me, each region crayoned in a different color by me more than twenty years ago. Campania is yellow because Mama claims that is where the sun shines brightest. She remembers the light even though she left when she was three years old. The light of Long Island comes closest, she says.

Through food we discovered the old country. Every Saturday morning, while Mama cleaned the house and my brothers played baseball with the neighborhood boys, Papa would take down the map of Italy and put it out on the table between us. I would close my eyes and let my finger fall on a region. Sometimes I cheated and kept one eye half open to make sure I didn't pick last week's place. For the next half hour before Papa had to leave for work, we would go through cookbooks and recipes Mama had gotten from neighbors or copied down from books in the library. At Sunday's big meal, while we ate the region's specialty, Papa or Mama would give us a little history lesson.

I recite what I remember. "Venice was built on 117 islands by people fleeing the barbarians. During the Middle Ages and the Renaissance Lombardy was important for banking and today it boasts the largest production of silk. Apulia is famous for its pink Baroque buildings and the strange white *trulli* with conical roofs no one can explain."

Mama nods her head in approval. She is filling our plates again.

"I remember the food," Mike says, leaning back into the window, letting the sun relax his face. "Duck stuffed with chicken livers and mushrooms."

"Calabria," Sal says. "How about those fried cookies? *Panelle?*"

"From Sardinia. Made with chick pea flour." My favorite region was Sicily. Pasta *a sfinciuni* followed by swordfish *rustutu cu' sammurigghiu'*, the words as exotic as the tastes were strong.

Mama looks into the Capodimonte tureen. It is empty and her face folds in, like those flowers that close up at the end of the day. "*Risi e bisi* comes with a poem Papa wrote. Who remembers it?" She keeps her head down, as if expecting the silence that follows.

I get up, taking Mama's hat with me, and walk to the hallway. I hang the hat on a peg next to her coat while my eyes travel to the door of my parents' bedroom. Papa's urn is in there. I walk on tiptoe, an old habit. The door is locked. Never in all those years growing up did they lock their door. I used to think, when sex grew heavy on my mind, that the unlocked door was the reason Papa left. I tiptoe back to the front door and get Mama's keys from her coat pocket.

Papa's urn is resting on the bedside table that Mama has moved to the foot of the bed directly in line with her pillow. Surrounding the table, the lilies from the garden, each in its own vase, look like wobbly candelabras. Their perfume is overpowering. I feel like a gag has been pressed against my nose and mouth. I want to get out of there, but instead I sit down on the bed and stare at the copper urn, burnished so that fingerprints won't show. "So that faces of ungrateful children will not show either," I imagine Papa saying. I'm not proud of myself.

After Papa came back, Sal and Mike were old enough to be able to ignore the rules he tried to reinstate. They tolerated him for Mama's sake, without showing either anger or love. I became ashamed of him, the feeling growing stronger every day, making me leave home a month after I graduated high school. I told myself I was ashamed of finding him hunched down on a kitchen stool in his long-sleeved, woolen undershirt, soaking his feet after work. I was ashamed of the way he'd take out his measuring tape in front of my friends to make sure my skirt was two inches below the knee, of the way he'd lift the lids off the pots cooking on the stove to taste Mama's cooking and tell her to add salt or water, to lower or increase the flame, as if she couldn't perfect a dish without him. Above all, I was ashamed of myself for not being able to keep Papa home.

I tap the urn's lid, a friendly pat like the one Papa used to give the top of my head as I'd fly across the room on the way to school, to friends, to the beach, his way of registering my passage through his space. Now he's the one who's flown through my life in what seems a blink of the eye. I guess he was a good man. Mama says he loved us. I don't know. I'd like to believe it, but I'm scared of the grief that would come with that. I give him another tap. It's the best I can do for now. I've been unable to cry.

The lid shifts under my hand. The urn has been opened. My eye catches a trail of dirt on the crocheted cover of the table.

Lifting the urn, I find it much lighter than the five pounds I carried home from the funeral parlor. The dirt on the table disintegrates into silken ash when I dab it with a finger. I open the urn slowly, afraid Papa might still spill over me. It's half empty. I put the urn back at the center of the table and screw the lid on tightly.

What has Mama done with him? She hasn't stepped out of the house since the funeral. In fact, she's barely left the kitchen. The week's litany of food comes back to me, her insistence that we stay the week, that we let her cook all our meals. Slowly, unbelievingly, I get it.

In the bathroom I try to throw up, but nothing comes out and I sit on the toilet bowl and wait, in case my stomach changes its mind. I lean back against the cool porcelain of the tank and debate telling my brothers. I can see Mike sticking his finger down his throat, his face flashing the anger he can barely contain under any circumstances. He would never forgive Mama. I can see Sal laughing. "Holy Communion," he might say. "This is his body. This is his blood. Cool."

As the minutes pass I realize that dusting our food with Papa's ashes makes a crazy sort of sense, Mama's way of keeping the family intact.

"You fall in?" Mike asks when I get back to the kitchen.

"How could you forget the poem?" Mama is asking Sal as he makes espresso on the machine he and I bought our parents for their fortieth wedding anniversary. The house is filled with the presents of our collective guilt at having walked away. "Your father wrote it for you kids."

He didn't write it; just translated it from the Italian he found in a cookbook at Vito Marinucci's house. I have the same cookbook; that's how I know. I drop Mama's keys on the table. She casts her eyes down, then lifts them to search my face, with the same look of worry she had when we came home from school, always on the lookout for a fever or a humiliation on our faces. I kiss the top of Mama's head and start reciting.

> To bless the holy spring
> That makes a garden nice
> All I need is a bowl
> A bowl of peas and rice.

Mama's eyes turn sweet. That's when I ask her if there are any leftovers for me to take home.

❧

Dizzy Spells
Dorothy Bryant

In the kitchen, my father and I put the groceries away: relish in the refrigerator, bread in the polished steel bread box, cookies in the tallest of the matching can-nisters. The house is quiet.

These walls are closing in on me.

I feel as confined as I did forty years ago in our house on the wrong side of the tracks that used to run through Sequoia Park, a house half this size, a kitchen half this size, three or four steps from sink to stove to table, my tiny cor-ner of the table where I ate, did my homework, read, listened to the radio. In that house, too, the front rooms existed only for cleaning—daily dusting, weekly vacuuming and polishing. Even the tiny bedroom my sister Flora and I shared was forbidden during the day; our beds, the only place to sit, were expected to retain the smoothness of regulation army cots.

Our home was no different from Aunt Eva's, no different from many other proud, home-owning immigrant families'. Some even covered sofas and rugs with sheets before they closed the doors and huddled in the kitchen, servants to their own houses. Some built a room in the garage, moved in a stove, an old round table, scuffed old chairs and sofa. They added shelves of playing cards and board games, a radio, a sink, a toilet, a sewing machine. Such a family might spend easy convivial days in the garage; late at night they re-entered their house, tiptoed past the shrouded emblems of their prosperity, and went to bed. Our garage contained a wrecked car or two my father repaired and sold, but it would not have been converted to easy living space in any case. My parents spent their time working, at the shop or at home.

This image of our home life is incomplete, unjust, not What Really Happened. There were frequent family dinners, festive birthdays, anniversaries, holidays, when we spread throughout the house. There was my tenth birthday party, more lavish than any of my friends' annual ones. There was a piano bought for me with Depression-scarce dollars, and daily practice in the otherwise forbidden front room, and sometimes my mother listening through the open door to the kitchen while she ironed. During my year at the junior college, before I married and left, my books and papers covered the dining room table, where I studied.

But memory is never fair. These relaxations of rules fade beside images of my mother's fury at a scratch on her hardwood floors (the floors were "hers," just as the shop and the money were "his"). Any lapse, a careless word, a spill or a scrape, a forgotten step in our cleaning ritual, might trigger a long, enraged lecture ending with the reminder that I, who had never known what it meant to begin life on a dirt floor, would never comprehend the sacrifices made for me.

This was not the woman who died last year. That woman spoke gently, bore her suffering quietly, smiled her gratitude for my infrequent visits. The whole truth can be a mistake, a distortion of the here and now. I saw her, not as the weak woman she was in those last years, but like an image in a photograph obscured by multiple exposures over time: the young woman furious at the mess I was making on her floor; the middle-aged woman stricken by the mess she feared I was making of my life. My vision was always blurred by images of a relation that existed forty years ago.

One day in particular stands in my memory as symbolic of that relation. I was bathed, combed, dressed in my finest; we were going . . . somewhere, to Aunt Eva's for a holiday dinner, perhaps. Our house had been scrubbed to untouchable perfection. Even my corner of the kitchen table was forbidden. I must vacate the pristine house while my mother dressed. No, not out to the street where I might run off with friends. No, not to my toy shelf in the garage, where I would get dirty. No, not to the shady back porch, where it was cold and I would get sick again. To the back yard, but not among the freshly planted vegetables and flowers. The only place left was the foot-wide concrete walk bordering the planted beds. How long did I pace the prisoner's walk, round and round the tiny square of forbidden soil? Surely no more than half an hour.

I hate that scene, not just because it happened, but because I never forgot it, let it swell up to a symbol of my childhood, a symbol that reeks of self pity. Must the child in us remain so unforgiving?

"Well, now, what's for lunch?" asks my father, opening the refrigerator with cheerful foreknowledge of the answer. "What's this?" He stares into the refrigerator, nearly empty but for the aluminum plate I brought.

"Captain's Plate," I remind him. "You know, that fish you like."

"Oh, yeah. Want some for lunch?"

"Let's save it for dinner."

He nods. "Plenty of other things for lunch," he says as we view the nearly bare, white spaces of the refrigerator. I look at the gleaming, empty shelves gratefully. A friend's mother shops every day like my father, but lavishly, pushing and piling new containers of food onto the rotting, wilted, rancid accumulation regularly cleaned out by her daughter. Another friend (another daughter, never a son) finds colonies of mice multiplying all over her mother's house, following the shifting caches of food she hides in new places after her daughter discovers and removes them. For once I appreciate my father's frugality. I help him draw out his usual lunch food: the head of iceberg lettuce, gutted, washed, drained, and sitting whole on a plate; small, wrapped pieces of salami and cheese on a saucer; the jar of sweet pickle relish.

While I wash my pear and get the bread, he reaches under the sink and lifts out a bottle of red wine, decanted from the gallons delivered too often. He puts another paper place mat on the table, and I set out a plate, glass of water, knife, and fork for myself. Paper napkins are bunched into a metal rack on the table next to the toaster and his bottle of pills. He pauses and looks at the table, nods with satisfaction, pleased that it is properly set, pleased that it is set for two instead of only for one. We sit down.

"Want some?" he asks as he pours himself a glass of wine.

"No thanks, Dad. Too early for me."

He notices the bottle of pills, picks it up, slowly reads aloud as if for the first time, "Diaboneze. One before each meal." He nods, opens the bottle, shakes out a pill.

Until he turned fifty, my father ate hugely, sugared his wine, grew rounder and rounder. Then, diagnosed diabetic, he amazed us by his total conversion, turning forever from rich pastries and sauces, a born-again nibbler of spare, bare portions. He even quit smoking. He lost fifty pounds and never regained an ounce. Of course, it was my mother who studied the diets, weighed his food, balanced the portions, but it was his will—the iron will I have only recently realized—that made him shed his favorite indulgences when their threat to his well-being was made clear. He controlled his disease by diet alone until a few years ago. When my mother died, we worried that without her constant reminders, he ould forget to take his Diaboneze. But he never forgets.

am rising to get him a glass of water when he pops a pill into his mouth and s it down with a gulp of wine, a health contradiction, a new development.

Not so new. My mother began to complain five years ago, but I could not believe her. I still cannot believe the telltale signs, the red lines radiating from his nose: he drinks too much. Two glasses of red at lunch. Sherry before dinner "only one glass, *un dito*," but he forgets, pours that "one glass" again and again. Two glasses of red at dinner. So he says. I have seen him at his most clear and rational. From noon until bedtime at eight, he becomes more and more muddled.

He unwraps the cheese and salami, cuts a thin slice of each onto his plate, peels one leaf from the head of lettuce, pushes a dollop of relish onto his plate, then half rising, leans forward and drops two slices of bread into the toaster. He sips wine while he waits for the toast and urges me, expansively, "Help yourself, have some cheese," pointing to the withered white cube on the saucer. I'm not sure when he began buying bargain wheels of white jack, cutting it into wedges, wrapping it, freezing it. The first few wedges are not bad, but later ones, like this one, thaw out dry and hard, with half an inch of gray near the skin.

The toast pops up just out of his reach. He spears it with his cheese knife, drops one slice on his plate, one on mine. The toaster sits at the exact center of the table. Once I moved it a few inches, to put it within his reach. Next time I came, it was back at the center of the table. Spearing his toast must be fun for him, or maybe more comfortable than touching hot toast with fingertips, or . . . whatever the reason, I began to learn my lesson: let him do what he likes if it does no harm. He has rights that do not depend on my understanding.

I cut myself a piece of the dry, tasteless cheese, and I think of the cheese that hung over the wine barrels in our cellar, filling it with strong, musty smells.

I remember my mother, Saturday noon, home from the shop alone, waving Flora and me off to the four-hour matinee at the local movie house. She sat at the kitchen table with a loaf of sourdough French, a thick red salami, a high-smelling gorgonzola, the newspaper, and a smile of blissful contentment as she anticipated an afternoon of solitude.

A month after her death, when the real shock set in and I was frozen in unanticipated grief, a friend counseled me, "Think of her during a happy time." I tried. Not the harried sessions of housecleaning. Not the anxious hours behind the counter at the shop. Not the evening bookkeeping across the kitchen table from my studying, biting her lip until she "balanced." Not the festive family dinners where, exhausted after a week of preparation, she waited apprehensively, almost resentfully, for the favorable verdict on her always superb cooking. This Saturday noon scene at the kitchen table was the best, the most purely happy picture of her I could conjure up. I am not in it.

My father eats silently, neatly, precisely—a bite of cheese, of relish, of brea a nibble from the lettuce leaf, all washed down by a sip of wine. He measu his bites so that he will "come out even." If I offer him half of my pear, he refuse, disdaining any fruit he did not grow, stew, freeze himself. But if I sil put a piece of my pear on his plate, he will eat it with pleasure, provided I have peeled it, a typically Italian requirement. What about the lost benefits of eating the whole fruit, all the fiber and nutrients in the peeling? He would point out, justly, that he never catches cold, never has a stomachache.

He pours another glass of wine.

"Dad, do you think you ought to . . . ?

"What? What's the matter?"

I look silently at the wine.

"A glass of wine with meals is good for you. Not too much. Wine is a food. Take it only as a food." He recites this explanation in the same measured tones he used forty years ago when he condemned our neighborhood drunk. He takes another sip, closes his lips delicately over a burp.

"That's your third glass."

"No! Second. Two glasses at lunch, two at dinner, never more." Is he right? Maybe it is only his second. But what he eats with it would hardly fill one glass. His face is flushed, his speech already blurring. "Got no use for people who drink too much. Drown their sorrows! Huh. Make their sorrows. Like the family in the old country when I was a little kid. Ever tell you about them?"

Yes, but I encourage him to tell me again and again. The further back he goes in memory, the closer he gets to What Really Happened. Like a car with a faulty transmission, his mind works best in reverse. Besides, I like these stories. I should bring my tape recorder next week.

"They called those years *la miseria*, the factory shut down for months at a time, my father gone to America. My uncles sat around, drank wine, slept, woke up and started drinking again. While they slept, I used to drain all the glasses. Six years old, an alcoholic at six, it's the truth. We'd have starved if it hadn't been for Magna Pina."

Here comes the part of the story I like.

"My great-aunt. She used to go out every morning before dawn, all bent over, this sack on her back. Dry goods, thread, pins, lace, anything she could scrounge from the mill when it shut down—bits of cloth, ribbon. Walked the roads, past Lanzo, through all the villages, peddled whatever she could. At night 'he'd come home and scratch her marks on the fireplace stones. She couldn't ⌐ or write, but she kept her accounts straight, on those stones, right down to ¿nny. She put food on the table for all of us." He stops, looks at me, frowns, ˙ait eagerly for his closing line. "You know, as you get older, you're start- ok like her."

ᵉ. I can't remember the last time he paid me such a compliment. If t it is.

more years of that. Then my mother and I took the boat. She didn't didn't want to leave the family. She cried and cried, and as soon as the ship left the dock, she got sick. She was sick the whole crossing, three weeks, lying there. I thought she was dying. I kept trying to tell them, my mother is dying, but no one understood Italian, and they just smiled, and I thought, my God, these Americans, they are monsters. When we finally got here, another week on the train, and what did we find? My father drinking hard, too. It was the mines, killing work. No money for food. He spent it in the saloon before he got home. Or there'd be a layoff and no money except what my mother got cooking and washing for other miners. All the men drinking even more from nothing else to do. Your Aunt Eva was born nine months after we got here. I didn't know anything. I came home from school one day, and there she was. You know what I did? I started to cry. I said, 'We don't even have enough to eat, and you go out and buy a baby!' What a thing for a boy to say the first time he sees his baby sister! We used to keep a little *grappa* in a trunk in the closet, for sickness, a teaspoon for upset stomach, for the flu . . . and my mother was so weak and white as a ghost, so I went to get some out of the trunk for her. The bottle was empty. My father had even drunk the medicine! Ten years old, I looked at that empty bottle, and I said to myself, I'll never do that. After that, I never drank, only when I eat, use wine as a food."

True, I have never seen my father drunk. I never saw him do more than nurse a drink politely at a family dinner or a wedding while the other men downed glass after glass. But the incredible is undeniable. His drinking has been slowly but steadily increasing for years. Now that he is here all alone without my mother to nag restraint . . . I tell his doctor, who gazes somewhere above my head and murmurs, "Make sure he eats." How?

"Time for dessert." He gets up and goes to the sink, opens the cannister and takes out one cookie. He offers the cannister to me, but I shake my head, and he returns it to the counter. Back in his chair, he splits the hard disk exactly in half and dips one half into his wine. Silently he nibbles and sucks the wine-soaked cookie. When he starts the second half, he murmurs, "Didn't come out even," and pours more wine, peers at the bottom of the bottle, then empties it, filling his glass. "That reminds me, I have to call Bertini and order more wine."

"I thought they delivered a case just over a week ago. Don't tell me you've gone through four gallons."

He raises the glass to his lips, drinks, sets the glass down. About an inch of wine, clouded with cookie crumbs, remains.

"Dad, four gallons of wine in less than two weeks—along with sherry—that's too much for . . . "

"No, only three gallons."

"A different-sized case?" I hadn't noticed that. "Only three gallons to a case? I thought there were four."

"One was empty."

"They delivered a case with one empty gallon? Someone made a mistake?"

"They do it all the time."

"You mean Bertini is charging you for four gallons and delivering only three? How long have you been buying his wine, thirty-five years? I can't believe the old man would . . ."

"That's the way it is."

"But that winery is a huge corporation now. They only deliver to you for old times' sake, more trouble than it's worth. Why would they short you a gallon?"

"It's those new kids who deliver here on the way to the restaurants."

"You mean the trucker steals a gallon?"

He shrugs.

"Did you complain?"

He shakes his head.

"You want me to complain? I'll call them."

"No, no." His voice is panicky. "They'll take it out on me. They'll stop delivering."

"So what? There are brands of good, cheap wine on the shelf at the supermarket."

"Forget it, forget it. That's the way they are now, that's all."

How can he accept being cheated this way—after calculating every penny of change due him from every purchase at the store?

"What time is it?" He takes a toothpick from a cup beside the toaster and begins to pick his teeth, another Italian habit. Is that how he has kept all his teeth? He glances at his glass, picks it up, finishes off the remains of the wine.

Suddenly I realize what has happened. I have witnessed the birth of a new confabulation. The wine disappears more and more rapidly. My sister Flora notices. I notice. We warn him, we nag, we say the unspeakable, the incredible: he drinks too much. Since our conclusion from the evidence is not acceptable, he has invented another. Empty gallons are none of his doing; they come to him already empty.

Wait until Flora hears this one. Should I forewarn her? I feel an odd impulse of mischief, to let him spring this one on her as he did on me, see what she makes of it, how long it takes her to catch on. I want to laugh. I want to grab him and shake him. I want to scream at him that old age should bring wisdom, dignity, should at least retain self-respect. Oh, is that so? Who am I to prescribe how he should face his final losses, his end? When I face mine, not so many years from now, maybe I too will decide that "wine does more than poets can to justify God's ways to man." Or is it "mead" does more than "Milton"? Is misquoting familiar poetry a sign of incipient memory loss?

He strokes his toothpick across his paper place mat, already stained and streaked with crisscross tracks of food from how many toothpicks, how many meals? Years ago my parents began using these thin paper place mats, discarding them with their paper napkins after each meal, or at least by the end of the day. Since my mother's death (and how long before? was this a minor queerness she didn't bother to mention?) he keeps the same paper mat day after day, fighting our attempts to change it for another from the hundreds stacked in the drawer.

I get up and begin to clear the dishes. I wait for the moment when he leans back in his chair, ready to get up, his hands off the table. Then, in one fast, casual sweep, I pick up his plate with one hand while, with the other, I snatch his place mat, crushing it into my fist so that, even as he twitches his hand forward to stop me, he sees that he has lost it to the garbage can. I feel a cheap thrill of victory over him.

But he wins the battle of the dishes this time. I don't even put up a fight. In my kitchen, plates and glasses sit all day in the sink, waiting for hot, soapy water after dinner, a practice unthinkable in my mother's kitchen. When there are too few dishes to fill the basin with hot soapy water, he insists on a tepid rinsing under the faucet. There are never enough dishes anymore for hot soapy water. Gradually the dishes, glasses, spoons, and especially forks are acquiring a dull film. One of these days, Flora says, when we are both here together, we will take piles of plates out of the cabinet and wash them properly.

He holds a dish under the tap, then hands it to me. I wipe it. Suddenly he clutches the edge of the sink, swaying.

"What is it, Dad?"

"Oh." He shakes his head. "Sometimes I just get these little dizzy spells."

After wine at lunch. After sherry at four o'clock. "Want to sit down? I'll finish."

"No, I'm all right now." He hands me the forks and knives to wipe. "You know, after we retired from the shop, your mother and I used to do this together. I miss her so much."

"Yes, Dad."

"We were so happy. Why did it have to happen? Just when we could . . . just when we could begin to take it easy and enjoy life . . . "

"You had some very good years after you retired."

"And then all of a sudden, just when we were starting to enjoy our house, our garden, our leisure . . . "

"Mom had been sick a long time, Dad."

But he refuses to respond, refuses even to hear me speak of his wife's long, painful decline. It is one of the cruel facts erased from his memory.

As I put the last dish in the cabinet, he takes one out, setting the table for his next meal: fresh paper place mat, dish, glass, knife and fork. While dirty dishes never remain on the sink, a few clean ones stand on the table ready for his next meal, day and night. He seems anxious until all are in place for the future.

❧

My Children's Names

Janet Zandy

(for Anna and Victor)

My children have heavy names
Thick sliced, roped and braided names
Old world names
Names reeking of steamer ships,
close quarters, and shadows.
Names of heavy black cloth
and stiff, sweaty secrets.

Names that plunge
Deep into the earth
Caked dirt under the nail names
Pungent names, kneading and scrubbing
Simmering and boiling over names
Names that mean business:

Josie, Carlos, Hannah. Albert, Sylvia, Jenny, Herman, Amelia.

My children want names that climb
and cling to the sun
Diaphanous names
Clear pools, clubs, and right-school names
Names whose sails billow out
White and clean
American names
Names that sound like something you buy.

Heather, Brittany, Amber, Tiffany, Bunny, Lance.

Not Rumpelstiltskin, but Snow White names.

Later in the afternoon he told her to suck him while he did the crossword. When he got stuck on a word she would stop sucking him, if she knew the answer, and help him out. She sucked him for seven days while he came and grew soft and hard and came and slept and woke up hard, and at the end of the seven days he had finished the crossword and said, Now you can rub yourself against my leg until you come. Once again she rubbed herself against him and came almost immediately, and then licked his palm. He slapped her away, got up for a beer, and was gone forty days and forty nights. When he came back she had chewed up the couch cushions and gnawed on the coffee table and was lying on the floor with her tongue out. He expected her to be angry with him, but she only looked at him with large sorrowful eyes and begged to be fed. He gathered the newspapers spread on the floor where she had shit, and the potted plant where she had pissed, and after cleaning up and throwing out the cushions and turning the coffee table around so he couldn't see the gnawed leg, he ordered Chinese takeout and they ate together. When they were finished he cleared the empty cartons from the table and had her lie down on top of it. For the next thousand years he went to work and came home and each night they ate Chinese food; then she lay down on the coffee table and they watched TV for the rest of the evening. During the commercials he would lean down and suck on her breasts or put a finger up inside her, neither of them taking their eyes from the screen.

One night during a Toyota commercial, as he was moving his finger in and out of her, she came, closing her eyes during an orgasm. When she opened them she was alone. The chain and collar were gone, and she was lying in a bed on top of a white sheet, naked, a ring of bright lights around the bed blinding her. Frightened, she curled into a ball in the middle of the bed, but after a few hours when nothing else happened she grew bored and curious, and sat up. She crawled to the edge of the bed to try and see who or what was on the other side of the lights. Out there it all looked black; she couldn't see anything so she stuck out one hand to feel for the floor. Cautiously she slid her hand farther and farther down, gripping the sheet with her other hand, then lying down on the bed to explore as far as the whole length of her arm, but still she couldn't feel anything solid. She imagined falling, into that black space where she would be swallowed up, hurtling through the darkness alone, and she drew up her hand and crawled back to the middle of the bed and lay there whimpering, waiting for the man to come back with the newspaper and the Chinese food, for she was suddenly very hungry, starving in fact she realized, and when he didn't arrive and didn't arrive after years and years and years she began to eat herself, starting with her hands and feet, and when she had devoured her legs and arms and cunt and belly and breasts, she started rocking back and forth on her head. Faster and faster she rocked, until at last she rolled off the edge of the bed, falling through the blackness and then the galaxies and finally the solar system, and when she got near earth she settled into orbit around it, waxing and waning and weeping.

❧

The Seven Sacraments
Mary Beth Caschetta

Last Christmas, after Maria Salerno and I cooked a different fish for each of the seven sacraments, I started believing in God again. Maybe it was my friendship with Maria and her sister, Jannette, their loud conversations, their insistence on tradition, their cheerful faith and careful food preparation. Maybe my past came back to claim me: Baptism, Confession, Eucharist, Confirmation, Ordination, Matrimony, Extreme Unction. It's hard to say for sure. I used to pretend I wasn't Italian.

The First Sacrament: Baptism (Linguine with Clam Sauce)

Although I grew up eating pasta every Sunday and Wednesday, I never felt as ethnic as the Salerno sisters. I came of age in a wealthy suburb in Western New York, along the Erie Canal, where being Italian meant your father was a doctor.

As a kid, I knew enough to stick to my own—the other sons and daughters of Italian doctors—and downplay the nagging feeling that, outside of this small circle, I didn't belong. We gathered in our front yards, outside Catechism, pretending that going to church several times a week, cursing in Italian and English, and having grandparents argue loud enough to suggest a fistfight, was what everyone else did too.

As daughters we were policed by unreasonable curfews, hemmed in by history and the threat of pregnancy. Our brothers were the preferred ones—a fact we managed not to notice. When we were old enough to date, we preferred blonde boyfriends, who didn't look like anyone related. As if we might marry ourselves into a polite first-class citizen status, we tried on new names: Mrs. Antoinette Brown, Mrs. Fatima Winston, Nunzia Appleby III.

"I always forget you're ethnic," a boyfriend once told me proudly. "Like you're not really Italian or something."

I was flattered. Outside my neighborhood, I worked hard to master the whispery murmur of Protestant girls, to control my hands, to refrain from giving the evil eye—or the finger—to someone *stoonad* enough to get in my way. I wanted to be a nice girl, not an Italian one—just the sort of person Jannette Salerno described as an utter disgrace.

"What's the matter with you?" she said the first time we met. We were standing near a buffet table, spread as long as a football field—stuffed shells, cinnamon raisin meatballs in red sauce, chicken piccata, escarole. (Funeral food.) For months, I'd been getting to know her sister, Maria, my new boss, who was a lesbian. Eventually, she became my new best friend.

"Sorry?" I said, straining forward.

Jannette grabbed my shoulders and hugged me hard to her chest. I had been eyeing a plate of rice balls. "Jesus Christ," she said, "you can pretend whatever you want, but you're as Italian as I am—pretty fucking Italian."

We were at a Salerno family gathering, my first invitation into Maria's life. I had gotten to know Jannette by report; she phoned in her opinions about my life from New Jersey.

"My sister says, 'Go to graduate school,'" Maria announced. I was trying to decide whether to take the GRE for the third time. "'You can never be too educated,' my sister says." I followed the suggestion. "My sister says, 'Come out to your grandmother.'" Again, I took the advice, and felt closer to my family for having taken the risk.

For a married woman with four children—Sofia, Little Tony, Frankie, and four-year-old Vinnie with the face of a priest—Jannette was uncannily accurate about what a woman like me should do about her life.

Jannette started calling me The Third Sister, The Little Sister. "I don't know much about sisterhood," I said, deflecting. I was embarrassed to recognize myself in her strong-willed ways, her confident gestures, her exasperated martyrdom. The idea of getting trapped inside another Italian family, rife with disappointment and with sexual and emotional demands, scared me.

"We're not asking," she said. I was willing to be brave to belong again to something.

"My sister says there's nothing to it," Maria added. "It usually happens over the phone."

"What usually happens?"

"The menus," she said, "the meal planning."

"Menus?"

It turned out that sisterhood with the Salernos was mostly about food.

The Second Sacrament: Confession (Shrimp Scampi)

After a few months, my friends complained. "What's the big deal about food? You never cooked before."

"I used to make lasagna," I protested.

"One dish." They knew me well.

"It's the Salernos," I said. "Cooking's a thing with them."

Sisterhood was easy. A phone call once or twice a week. Conversations about dinner, lunch, occasionally brunch. Once in a while I showed up at their place to cook, help cook, or pretend to help cook for a family party.

After a while, like magic, my writer's block lifted. It was no small thing: I'd been blocked for half a decade. And once, when we were at Ellis Island, I saw a ghost, which Jannette later called an angel. They were always seeing angels, the Salerno sisters.

"What about us?" my friends wanted to know. "We're your sisters too—your lesbian sisters."

Maria had taken to leaving her secret cooking tips and best recipes on my answering machine at home, or taped to my desk at work. "It's different," I said. "She's Italian."

You can call an Italian sister before 7:00 A.M. knowing it's an acceptable hour for conversation, or you can call for a predawn consultation, even when you have nothing particular in mind. It was part of the deal. It felt good to be Italian, to have sisters who expected so little.

Usually Maria's lover, Nan, and their daughter, Mae-Mae, were sleeping when I called. Maria was cleaning the oven, or meditating in the living room, planning a meal.

Once, when her favorite aunt died unexpectedly during surgery, Maria was up at 4:30 in the morning, making a three-bean salad for pot roast. "I think eggplant would have been better for grief," she said, "but I just don't have the heart for all that chopping."

"I've been thinking a lot about veal," I told my other friends.

"I know! The cattle industry!" they shouted. "Terrible, what they do to those little baby cows. It's torture."

I had meant parmigiana.

The Third Sacrament: Eucharist (Garlic Filet of Sole over Lemon Risotto)

When I was seven, the face of Jesus appeared to me in a glass of orange juice. I was already a damaged kid, hypervigilant, one of God's self-appointed civil servants.

I thought a miracle might follow from this vision, but instead my brother drank the holy juice, which I'd carefully placed on the top shelf of the refrigerator.

A few years later, I had a second vision. This time it appeared in a spot of rust on the hood of Sal DaSilvo's Mustang next door: the vague outline of a skinny Christ, arms stretched out on a cross. Sal wrapped the dark gray Mustang around a telephone pole a few days after his sixteenth birthday, destroying in a fiery crash not only himself and the rusty crucifix, but also three of his high-school buddies.

"That kid was a hoodlum," my father said, breaking into his runny eggs. "Probably driving drunk with those derelicts."

It was a well-known fact—to everyone but me—that Sal DaSilvo's father had connections with the Mafia. Years later, after college, a childhood friend told me that an organized crime crackdown was the reason the DaSilvos moved to Cincinnati in such a hurry. "You were Rosa DaSilvo's best friend," she said. "How could you not have known?"

Little Rosa, tiny and wild-eyed, younger than me by four months, ran around topless, dropping her panties for any boy who wanted a glimpse. Once, in her basement, we played "Hug Like a Husband" and she bit my shoulder so hard that I bled on her mother's coffee-colored carpet.

"I didn't mean to hurt you," she explained when I was allowed to play with her again. "It just came over me, like God pressing down. Like love."

I touched the place where her teeth had made their mark. "No more biting," I warned, secretly flattered. "I don't care *who* presses."

All the years Little Rosa was my best friend, I never slept at her house and I only ate dinner with her family once.

It was a few weeks after Sal died in the miracle car, a quiet gray afternoon; the shades were still drawn, shutting out the first big thaw of spring. Though it was Thursday, Little Rosa's mother cooked a Sunday kind of meal: baby potatoes with parsley, an entire rosemary chicken as if relatives were coming, my favorite green beans, iceberg lettuce with grape tomatoes and Italian dressing made right in the vinegar bottle.

Mr. DaSilvo arrived home with fresh bread from the bakery, but before we had a chance to slip off the warm white bag and sneak a bite, Little Rosa's mother got mad over something.

"Son of a bitch," she said. "You're not the king of this household."

Little Rosa held her breath.

At my house, my father was the king of everything, and we knew better than to challenge him, especially at a meal. Dinner was a nervous affair.

The DaSilvos ran things differently. Little Rosa's mother was the opposite of mine: temperamental and demanding, nobody's pushover. To punctuate her point, she turned the salad bowl over onto her husband's head and stormed out of the kitchen.

At the dinner table, Mr. DaSilvo sat brushing tomato and vinegar off his shirt. Little Rosa and I looked down at our plates. When nothing happened, she whispered, "Aren't you mad at all?"

Mr. DaSilvo started to laugh, placing his hand on his daughter's head, like a priest blessing a child. At his son's funeral, Mr. DaSilvo cried like a baby for

having bought Sal the dark gray Mustang. The facts of Sal's death were differ-
ent from what my father had surmised: the brakes in the car were shoddy, the
night was stormy, and no one in the car had been drinking.

Little Rosa's mother returned from the bedroom where—from the look of
things—she'd been crying.

"Take that bowl off your head," she barked. Her voice was no longer a threat.
Refusing to look at her husband, she served each of us a pile of tender white
meat.

I thought of Sal DaSilvo, the first boy I knew who died—the first human
being—his mortal body floating out a windshield. I thought of God and how
impossible it was to believe He could hurt us this way.

The Fourth Sacrament: Confirmation (Mussels in White Wine)

If I had mentioned that rusty Jesus to someone, I might have saved Sal DaSilvo's
life. I repented with vigor.

By the time puberty came, I planned on joining a convent instead of going
to college. I spent months imagining myself in a little stone chamber with stern,
dowdy women who believed in the merit of study and silence, who had simple,
austere meals at regular hours, who might someday kiss me in the passionate
name of the Lord.

Instead, I went to Vassar.

Vassar was strange and beautiful, with clusters of rich, handsome students
who had a sophisticated sense of the world, but extremely crude taste in food.
I stood on line at the Campus Dining Center, listening to their rave reviews of
the food, as if they'd never had a meal cooked for them before. The food was
downright bad, especially the ketchup pasta mush they passed off as Spaghetti
Marinara. It was rumored that President Reagan had left a broccoli endowment
to the college, evidenced by the broccoli omelets, broccoli quiche, broccoli
almondine, chicken and broccoli, broccoli cream soup they served.

Others shared my distaste—starving girls on the margin of every meal. They
dressed in gossamer dresses, hair piled impossibly high, bones jutting, smiles
strained. I'd grown aware of anorexia, finding myself precariously perched on
its thin edge. Unnerved by their sunken eyes, I felt dangerously close to the
truth about food: one day I could wake up and simply refuse.

At Vassar, too, though, I learned a vocabulary that helped my life make sense:
depression, scholarship, homosexuality. There were interesting texts to replace
the old familiar one about Jesus and his cross—complex stories by Milton and
Shakespeare, Brontë and Tolstoy, Virginia Woolf, Luce Irigaray, Francis Bacon,
Margery Kempe. New characters to envy, new writing styles to emulate.

Keeping secrets came naturally. I carried around small piles of bad poems and a private novel I had written in four spiral notebooks about a gynecologist who kept jars of dead babies in his basement.

At Vassar I also contributed to a literary magazine, took fiction writing workshops, and generally went public. I wrote a novel about an Italian American woman who ran away from her husband and children and returned to Italy to kill her father for sins committed during her childhood. It was stagnant and stale, but everyone praised it anyway. People were eager to convince me I was smart and a writer. This was new, and I was tempted to correct them: "I have three older brothers." In some way, going public with my writing replaced my childhood need for secrets and God. Or revenge against my father. I began to write the way I prayed —constantly and passionately—hoping I'd be able to find a forgiving listener.

I was 24 and three years out of college when I met the Salerno sisters. I was lonely, single, depressed, an atheist by default, and as much estranged from the notion of God the Father as I was from my own father, on whom I blamed most things. The Salerno sisters, though, seemed to be firmly planted in the world of answered prayers. They spoke a lot about their father, a schoolteacher with a big heart who loved them. For a while, I thought that explained the difference between my life and theirs.

It's not that Maria and Jannette were raised by saints. Their mother refused to speak to them during long stretches of their childhood. This made life confusing and unpredictable. And she was a staunch traditionalist, unfortunate for Maria, who fell in love with Nan.

Maria found her path in life *with* God, instead of finding it, as another lesbian might have, *despite* God. After I knew Maria for a few years, she got called. The instructions must have been explicit, because she told Nan they had to move across the country. They packed their things, moved from Manhattan to Berkeley, and found a suitable kindergarten for Mae-Mae, the daughter they had adopted in China.

"It never rains in California," Mae-Mae announced on the way to the airport. She'd just learned enough English to mix song phrases from English into her constant chatter in Mandarin, which none of us understood. When she leaned against me in the car on the way to the airport, I realized how much I'd miss the salty smell of her hair.

Maria enrolled in graduate school to become a Unitarian Universalist minister, and Nan took a job as a landscape architect.

After the move, Jannette and I carried on limpingly. She cried at the thought of her sister on the other side of the country, and I avoided visiting for two years. Eventually, we established a new rhythm, conducting our relationship over the phone, visiting each other on holidays.

Jannette maintained a position of resignation. "When God calls," she said, "you pick up the phone. You don't leave the answering machine on. I mean, who's going to argue with God?"

Certainly, I was in no position.

The Fifth Sacrament: Ordination (Shredded Ginger and Scungilli Salad)

When a visiting priest from Rome tried to seduce me and my roommate at an off-campus rectory one Saturday afternoon, I resigned myself to atheism. We'd been helping him get oriented when he came up with some excuse to drive us back to his place, a few miles out past Vassar Farm.

At the rectory, he built a fire in the fireplace and offered us a drink. He suggested that we take turns rubbing each other's backs while he drank wine and watched. He said whenever two or more people gathered in His name—while massaging, apparently—he could feel the hand of God on his heart.

"An adult form of faith," he said, holding up a bottle of Merlot. "I can draw you a warm bath. Would you like that? In Scripture, baptism is often described as a bath. Wash away your sins."

We sat on a little wooden bench in the foyer of the grand old house, staring up at the priest, who was still in his robes. He was smiling, white teeth against olive skin.

"No," my roommate said quietly, snow melting in a puddle at her feet.

"You gotta' be kidding, right?" I asked the guy. My roommate shook her head and turned to me. Something about the look in her eyes made me laugh, a release of fear and indignation.

"Beautiful laughter," the priest said, lifting his wine bottle higher. "Also a form of prayer."

I clapped the priest on the back, as if we were sharing a really good joke. "C'mon," my roommate whispered, grabbing my hand. "Let's get out of here."

It was a long way back to campus. In the dusk and cold, nothing felt funny anymore.

"Maybe it's because he's European," my roommate said, meaning *Italian*.

"Or maybe it's because he's an asshole."

About halfway home, it started to snow. "The Church is filled with hypocrites," I said. "With humans, anyway," my roommate said.

I got the idea that emptying my bookbag would lighten my load, get us home faster. "I'm not going back," I said, leaving my faith on the side of the road with yesterday's campus newspaper, gum wrappers, and my half-eaten lunch.

About halfway to campus, my roommate suggested the plan: "I vote we repress the whole thing." We managed to disremember the night of our escape completely until spring semester, when another freshman who sang and played guitar at Saturday Mass went public with her charges. *Assault,* we heard. *Endangering a minor.*

"My feet are frozen," I complained. "I can't take another step.

"See that light up there?" My roommate pointed. "That's the campus." I could see the outline of the place we suddenly came to think of as home. I was wearing one of her mittens and had started to think about crying.

"Come on," she said, grabbing my hand. "We can run the rest of the way."

The Sixth Sacrament: Matrimony (Clams Casino)

The Christmas Maria and I decided to cook the fish, we'd been friends nearly seven years. I'd flown out west, leaving behind a desperate feeling of barely being alive. I was a few months out of a six-year relationship that had been difficult and deceptive. I was tender, sensitive about being alone. I had no idea I was waking up into a new life, where love and happiness would make sense.

I saw my future on the pullout bed in Maria's apartment, watching Oprah Winfrey. It was 2:00 A.M. I was jet-lagged, too tired for a late movie, and when I flipped through the channels, I landed on a writer friend of mine casually chatting with Oprah about her new book. I didn't know that life with this friend was where I was headed. I remember being tantalized, though, and wanting to wake someone up.

"I know her," I said to myself, and it turned out, I really did.

In the morning, I didn't mention I'd seen someone I knew on TV. I sat with Maria in her very small campus kitchen in Berkeley, drinking coffee, filling her in on my life and work, listening to her talk about Mae-Mae and Nan. We tried to come up with a suitable menu for Christmas Eve. That night, Maria was going to preach and sing "O Holy Night" at an early service. After, we planned to rush home and have a dinner party.

"We always had seven fish on Christmas Eve," I said. "Fried smelt, red sauce with scungilli, lemon filet of sole, Clams Casino, shrimp cocktail, and this weird octopus thing. Lobster Newburg was the highlight."

"We did too," Maria said. "No Newburg, though. What's that? The American sacrament?"

"I didn't really get that it was seven fish for the seven sacraments," I said.

"The sacraments stand for signs of divine grace," Maria told Mae-Mae. "Signs that God exists."

That night, Maria sang "O Holy Night" to a crowded church. All day she practiced, and all day Mae-Mae teased her. "Puhleez, for an end of this Holy Night." It was the last Christmas of the twentieth century, nearly a year from the day Maria, Nan, and Mae-Mae had nearly died when a truck hit them head on. Nan was still suffering from a broken sternum, trauma hanging palpably in the apartment. Mae-Mae held her head over Nan. "Look," she said. "I'm healing the sick."

"Let's throw out the Eucharist," Maria had said, when we could only settle on six complicated recipes. But Jannette talked us out of it over the phone from New Jersey.

"What, are you crazy?" she asked. "Body of Christ? It's the flesh we were raised on."

The Seventh Sacrament: Extreme Unction (Lobster Newberg)

The day of the seven fish, Mae-Mae helped us shop, carefully prying her fingers into the mouths of the uncooked clams. "It must be hard to breathe in there," she said.

Maria and I cooked for nine hours, using recipes from our relatives. We used memory and our taste buds to guide us, paying homage to our grandmothers, each of whom had cooked a variation of this meal throughout her life.

Maria raised her glass, "To my grandmother, may she rest." At her funeral, Maria had preached the sermon and sung "Bread and Roses" in honor of her grandmother's work in the labor movement.

Dinner was served at the table of the motherless at eight o'clock sharp. It went like this: Nan's mother had died at fifty-seven of breast cancer. Maria's mother had turned away from her when she came out. Mae-Mae's mother had left her at the market. And there was me. My mother had abandoned me simply and without fuss; she turned a blind eye when her husband and son came to my bed at night to sin.

"I don't believe in true love," I told Mae-Mae later that night, after she climbed in bed with me. We'd just come back from sprinkling oats for reindeer on the front stoop. I had no idea how close love was.

"Maybe you should try wearing a skirt," she said.

"Do you ever see God?" I asked her.

"Oh sure," she said, pointing to heaven. "He was here tonight."

"Tonight?" I asked.

"In the Clams Casino," she said, and dropped off to sleep in the crook of my arm.

❧

Kissing the Bread

Sandra M. Gilbert

1.

and the fields inside it.
The winter of the crumb, the iron
hoe hacking the furrow,
the hiss of grain in the wind.
The priest in the crust
says *kiss,* says
In nomine Domine,
bless, kiss.

2.

My mother in the four by seven
yellow kitchen in Queens,
pressing her lips to half a
loaf of day-old challah, the food
of someone else's sabbath,
before dropping it into the red and white
step-on can:
her mother the Sicilian midwife
taught her, taught all nine,
to kiss the bread before you
throw it away.

Why?
Non so. You kiss it, like
crossing yourself before a crisis, before
the train leaves the station,
before the baby falls,
startled, into a sudden
scorch of air.

3.

No. No doubt
not that. But instead
Dickinson's "the Instead."

They were full of terrible
accurate sentiment,
those old Italian ladies in the kitchen—
crones, with witch hairs haloing
their chins, with humps and staggers
and nodes of bone ringing their fingers.

Kissing the bread was kissing
the carrion that was the body
of every body, the wrist
of daughter and husband, the crook'd
arm of the mother, the stone
fist of the father.

Kissing *goodbye,*
saying the daily
goodbye, the skeptical
god be with you
as the long loaf sank into ashes,
as the oven sputtered its
merciless complaint.

4.
They were kissing the corn god, you say?
Kissing the host, the guest,
the handsome one who grows
so tall and naked
in the August grove?

But what if they were mocking him,
mocking the crust that stiffened, the crumbs
that staled and scattered?

> *You thought,*
> *bread, that your magic*
> *salts were eternal, that your holy*
> *taste was your final shape,*
> *but see, you were wrong:*
> *I bid you goodbye, my tongue*
> *gives you a last touch, my teeth*
> *renounce you.*

5.
But no again: my mother's kiss
was humble, the mortified
kiss of guilt—*I can use you*
no longer—and the kiss
of dread: *what will I do, challah,*
pumpernickel, rye, baguette, sweet white,
thick black, when you
are gone?

And the kiss, I think
I thought she meant,
of sorrow, as if kissing
the bread is kissing
the crows that fly low over
fields we never saw in Queens,
the blurry footprints
between long rows of wheat,
the blank sun roaring overhead.

We stood in the Jackson Heights kitchen.
The white 1940s Kelvinator
whirred, no comment, and strips of
city snow crisscrossed the window.

I was eight and baffled.

If an angel should be flying by
when you make that face, she said,
you'll be stuck with it forever

❧

Pomegranate
Lucia Perillo

How charitable to call it fruit, when almost nothing
inside it can be eaten. Just the gelatin
that thinly rinds the unpalatable seed.
The rest of it all pith, all bitter,

hardly a meal, even for a thin girl. But food enough,
at least in myth, to be what ties Persephone
half the year to hell. Thenceforward her name
makes the corn stalks wither: that's why
the Greeks called her *Kore,*
just Kore, meaning *the girl* or *the maid,* the one

who because she was hungry stood no chance against even
the meager pomegranate—though it's never clear
this future isn't the one she wants,
her other choice being daylight, sure,
but also living with her mother. In some versions

she willingly eats the plush red seeds, signing on
with the underground gods and their motorbikes
and their dark shades. Oh . . . all right—
no motorbikes. And *eat*'s not right either.
But what, then—"sucks"? "Strains the seeds against her teeth"?

Of course it would have made more sense for Hades to tempt her
with something full of juice: a grapefruit, say,
or a peach. But maybe these
would be too close to her mother's feast.
And only a girl like Eve could be so blank a slate

to ruin herself with a meal as salutary as the apple.
Give her instead the kind of nourishment
that takes its own hydraulics to extract,
like the pomegranate or the spiny
asteroid of the Chinese chestnut. Or the oyster,

from which, between the riffled shell and shucking knife,
there is no exiting unscathed: a *delicacy,* we say,
whenever the hand hangs out its little
flag of broken skin.
But doesn't the blood that salts the mouth

somehow make the meat taste sweeter? As when she turns
toward us in the moonlight with the red pulp
mottling her teeth: don't our innards

—even if to spite us—start to sing?
I know that's what mine did on those nights

when our girl got called from the junipers
where the rest of us hid her—all it took was his
deep voice, and she stepped out.
Then came sounds that, instead of meaning
carried all of punctuation's weight: the exclamation

when she had her air knocked out, and the question
that was her sudden, inswept breath.
And the parentheses when time went on forever,
when there was no sound because he'd got her by the throat.
He seemed to like our watching, his imperiousness

saying books about how much we didn't know: the jelly
sluiced inside the mouth or the seeds rasped
back and forth across the palate,
until it came time for her to hide behind her own hand
when she had to tongue them out. Sometimes

it would end when the boyfriend strolled her off,
steering as if she were the boat and her skinny arm
were its tiller. But just as often
he'd have somewhere to get to, or lose interest,
as if so much activity had pushed him to the brink of sleep,

and that's how she came back to us kneeling
in our moonlit patch of stunted trees
whose evergreenery wove our hair and pressed
its crewelwork in our haunches. In the half-dark
it would be hard to make out what he'd done: lip pearled,

her chin gleaming like the hemisphere of a tarnished spoon.
But didn't the leaves seem brighter then,
if it can be said that junipers have leaves?
As our hard panting rattled through
. . . but no. Stop here. No of course it can't be said.

∽

The Anthology Poems
Mary Ann Mannino

*Anthology and Anthology 2 are about my mother. The meaning of anthology is
a bunch of flowers and my mother used to wear crocheted handkerchiefs that
looked like flowers. When she died, I was eating food that tasted like flowers.*

Anthology

My mama wore white oxfords
and hand crocheted hankies
in the pocket of her uniform
over her heart, all puffed out
like flowers, pink, orange, blue.

Summers, she walked to work.
I watched from the kitchen window.
Her starched white cotton uniform
stood out like the dresses
on my paper dolls.

When she came home for lunch,
she made us hot dogs,
so hungry she ate hers raw.
She liked angel food cake
which she served with tea and
embellished stories, better than
the movies, about the lives of
ladies whose hair she had
washed and permed that day.

Anthology Two

The night my mother died
I ate Indian food
that tasted like
roses smell
in someone's house
not a friend.

The phone call from
the sitter came in
the middle of the
chicken dish.

∾

The Prodigal Daughter
Dorothy Barresi

If a daughter bent on pleasing
turns her knives
inward, then the salad plate goes

to the left of the glassware,
the cup aligned
with the soup spoon—where were we? Oh, yes,

the prodigal daughter
did not return.
She never left home in the first place.

And if the fatted lamb is brought to the spit & fire
in her honor,
his black head split jowl to jowl

so that the jewels of his brain
are sizzling, for pudding,
the snout a gourd scooped out

for pomegranate wine,
then she has made that dinner
and that unending drama.

In the gray hierarchy of cook smoke,
let her symbols go up:
ash and amaranth,

the ankle bracelet off at the stump.
This is not the story
of the water in the well,

but of the dutiful woman who might throw herself
down any moment
just to hear the splash,

then refrains. (Refrain)
This is not the new dispensation.
This is not the different earth.

Her old mother is crazy; she's smearing
roast garlic on her cheeks and reading
the riot act to the chickens

with a paring knife.
Her father? He's not gone yet, but he *needs*
her so—who will take care of him

in his early retirement?
Mutiny. Even the least fallen angels
take a dive sometimes. But that

she will not do.
There are dishes to do, and bread
to pound senseless, and dancing classes, and all those

damn sparks to contend with
around the fire pit
clicking its castanets. So what if she caught fire?

What if she who gave herself away so lavishly
in the interests of others
were sent up in a whippet of smoke

to signal the tribes: here is a woman
who was granted mastery
of one thing, herself,

good-bye!
Outside, the road lays down
its dusty hammer and tongs,

field mice nest in the skulls of wolves,
and worms eat their way toward God
through dirt, or vice versa.

But who is this woman of blank hosannahs,
this genteel, wellborn
woman bound by pity or mercy or self-spite

to spin at the wall, plotting: and who, in any case,
will protect her if she leaves
from all the prodigal sons hitchhiking

like so much unclaimed freight by the side of the road,
sticking out their spoiled thumbs?
They have a lot of living to do

before they settle down
and marry that
cute thing next door, this

dervish in suspense, in tears.
Quick, someone sing a cheery song
about disgrace

and many veils.
Someone count the silverware.

❧

The *Giara* of Memory
Edvige Giunta

The snails on the asparagus plants stared at me from forests of thick and lus-
trous leaves, some so tough and sharp that they pricked me when I parted them,
as I searched for the slender stems of the asparagus. The plants stood in lines,
circled protectively the small yard outside my window. Occasional weeds

peeked through cracks in the stone walls. The small branches of the asparagus pushed up proudly: the effect was that of a dwarf forest where the vegetation was so intricate that one could not distinguish tree from tree, plant from plant. And the eyes of the sun could not penetrate, only warm it to its depth through the heat that the external branches filtered.

The snails dragged their soft bodies, partly hidden within the delicate frames of their shells. I watched their quivering antennae, fascinated by the tiny spirals of their "homes," and followed their slow journey through the leaves for hours. Sometimes we collected the snails that lived on the asparagus leaves and my mother fried them with garlic and oil. We pulled the wrinkled bodies out using safety pins and ate them, our tongues clicking and slurping. I felt a slight revulsion for this meal, but relished the smell of the snails frying in the black pan and the job of inserting the safety pin into the shell, digging it like a minute dagger into the soft body of the snail, dragging it out gingerly. I watched it dangle from the tip of the pin, then put it in my mouth cautiously so that the pin would not pierce my tongue. My mother used to buy large snails called *'ntuppate,* which vendors sold at the corners of the narrow streets that cut across the Corso in Gela, their raucous voices calling out to the women with chanting rhythms like Arab songs of courtship. The *'ntuppate* were much bigger than the snails we gathered in the garden, and the openings of their shells were covered by a white layer, a protective door they had pulled shut between them and the world. For my father, the *'ntuppate* were a delicacy only for feast days. When I got older, during my late adolescence, when so much would change, I stopped eating snails, later disdaining even the escargots on the menus of fancy restaurants in the United States.

My older sister, my brother, and I searched methodically, patiently, through each of the asparagus bushes that lined the paths of our garden in Caposoprano, a twenty-minute walk from our home on the Corso. Caposoprano, the archeological area of Gela, is close to the walls of the ancient Greek polis. After more than two thousand years, the Greek presence is still tangibly felt in our town, not as a sophisticated and inaccessible culture, but as a simple part of our lives, written on the white strips naming the streets, written in the faces of the townspeople, and in the stories mothers and grandmothers tell and the lullabies they sing.

It was tempting to move quickly from one plant to the next. It would have been much easier to pick only the asparagus stems shooting out from the green thicket. But then we would leave behind all those other hidden stems. Later, my mother would prepare a delicious *frittata* in the same black pan used to cook the snails. The stems of the asparagus would soften into the beaten eggs, except for the tips. I loved the bittersweet taste of my mother's *frittata,* which we ate between slices of day-old bread, the tips of the spears shooting out erratically from its compact texture. The asparagus of my Sicilian childhood were thin and tender, so different from the huge, thick, leathery American version of this vegetable, its dull green contrasting sharply with the bright green of the asparagus from the Sicilian garden in my memory, radiant with color, alive with flavor.

Picking the asparagus was a job requiring attention, and we did it with care, slowly, like picking snails or wild strawberries. The tiny red spots of the wild strawberries winked invitingly, while the nearby purple and yellow violets trembled under the gentle pressure of the summer breeze. My father planted these delicate flowers next to the wild strawberries deliberately. This was the place in the garden where we had to move gently. We had to tiptoe, and our hands had to move lightly, as if touching butterflies. Our hands plunged deep into the foliage, parting the leaves, so we did not damage those frail strawberry plants that did not have the resilience of asparagus.

It was easy to recognize the ripe strawberries. They let your fingers know that they were ready to be picked. They let your fingers know that they were ready to leave their home.

My small fingers touch each strawberry and turn it gently, ever so gently. If it doesn't come off immediately, I know better than to force it. It's not yet ready. With the asparagus, I bend the stem. When it's not too stiff, too hard, I know it's too late.

Each of us children carried a small bowl of freshly picked tiny wild strawberries back to my mother, who would fix them with lemon and sugar, macerating them for hours in the refrigerator. We savored them after lunch, leaving the reddish syrup to sip for last. My mother's strawberries, their sticky sweetness, the *giara* of memory.

The garden was full. Grapevines, zucchini, lilies, mint, citronella, basil, lemons, potatoes, carnations, roses, figs, pears, and, when the weather got cooler, pomegranates, mythical fruits of fertility and death. In the summer, we picked peaches, grapes, plums, then walked to the back and plunged the aluminum *cannata* that hung on a nail in the large *giara*, the old, big-bellied clay *giara* that my father filled every day with fresh water from the well, since we had no running water.

I waited anxiously for the apricots to ripen. When I pressed the apricots against the stems that connected them to the branch, the ripe ones could not resist the pressure. As I relaxed my hand, if the apricot was ripe, my palm would be full of the yellow-orange flesh of the fruit of my favorite tree. The tree where the swing hung. *L'altalena*. Such a beautiful word. *Swing* is not at all right. It's too quick, too sharp, too cutting. Swing. Say it loud and you hear a blade cutting, a whip flogging. But *altalena—altalena* is smooth and musical and takes me, rocks me between the *l*s and the *ah*s. Altalena, altalena.

Il giardino, the garden, we called it, a term that included it all. The old house with the red roof. The storage building attached to it that we called *il magazzino,* where we trod around gingerly, watchful of the fearless country mice that came out of hiding. The stable by the gate that we rented out. The trees, the neat paths where industrious ants dug their living quarters. The plants, the flowers, the well, and the Greek cemetery below us. We also called it *'a casina,* a Sicilian expression that means "the small house," a preposterous term to describe the place that takes so much space in my memory.

The apricot tree has been gone for years, killed by lightning or time. I am always shocked by the heavy sight of its absence. The strawberry plants, too, have been gone for years.

My mother still goes to the garden, tending it as best she can, with the help of Cuciuzzo, the gardener who has helped my parents take care of the garden for thirty-five years.

We left. We have all left in one way or another. My older sister Ortensia lives in Rome with her husband and their three children. My brother Diego lives in Catania, but often travels to Czechoslovakia, where his girlfriend's family lives. My younger sister Claudia and I came to America, far away from the garden.

We left. We left for reasons we know and for reasons we do not yet fully understand. We left like some of our ancestors did. Like my grandfather and his brother, who emigrated to Argentina in the 1920s in search of better economic prospects. My grandfather would come back, but always longed for those missed American opportunities. We left because we are Sicilians. So that we could miss our island, and always try to go back, knowing that we never, ever fully can.

We started to leave when my sister Ortensia and I entered adolescence. We no longer enjoyed the long summers at the garden in Caposoprano, too far from the excitement of town life, with the evening *passeggiata* on the Corso, ice cream at the Torrefazione, meeting up with friends, sneaking to a party without my parents' permission, or a ride on the back seat of a motorcycle, equally forbidden, equally delicious. How could the garden and its fruits compare to such exhilarating alternatives? So we stopped spending summers at the garden.

We started going just for the day, on special occasions. Pasquetta, Ferragosto, the first Sunday of spring. My mother would roast peppers, artichokes, and *sarde.* Not small sardines, but *sarde,* large fish about six inches long that my mother would sprinkle with plenty of salt and roast on the fire she prepared at the back of the house. While we were eating, the onions roasted in the ashes. We would eat them later, at home, dressed with vinegar. There would be no pasta on that day and that day only. If you had *sarda 'rrustuta,* you did not have pasta.

Sarda 'rrustuta was my father's favorite. We ate *sarde* with our hands, a primitive feast, and each of us ate ten, twelve of them. They were salty on the outside, tender and juicy on the inside. I remember my father ate the whole thing, including the head, picking uneaten heads from our plates, scornful of our disdain for what he regarded as the best part of the fish.

The artichokes, blackened by the fire, were crunchy and salty. My mother insisted that we eat everything she had prepared because it would all be inedible the following day or even later that evening. Everything had to be consumed then and there. Nothing would taste the same later. Later it would all taste old and stale, dry and cracked like the pages of a book left in the sun for too long.

I don't remember when we stopped going to the garden altogether. There were no more *scampagnate*. Going to the garden became a chore, my mother's chore. At times, one of us would accompany her, reluctantly, only after she promised that we would stay for no longer than half an hour. Once there, we watched my mother rush around picking parsley, basil, and *sparacedda*, a vegetable I have never seen in this country. American broccoli seems a pale, tasteless substitute for the leafy greens and tender florets my mother would use to make soup with pastina in the winter, or that she would dress simply, with olive oil and salt for dinner.

One by one, my siblings and I moved to Catania, a two-hour bus ride through the hills and plains of the interior, to attend university. We only went back for brief visits during the summer, Christmas, Easter, the Day of the Dead. With the exception of my brother, we moved away from Sicily and settled in different geographies.

Then my mother would go alone to pick whatever fruits and vegetables still grew in the garden. Everything that had once flourished diminished in number and variety. And my mother's dream of a house, a real house in the garden, built where the old house with the red roof stood, my mother's dream started to vanish and she grew sadder for it, sadder every day.

My mother started to buy fruits and vegetables at the *fruttivendolo*, something she never, ever did when we were children. And she no longer went to the garden for the tomato ritual, for the making of *astratto*. The making of *astratto* was midsummer work, women's work. The making of *astratto* so distinctly captures my Sicilian childhood that I approach this writing of it with *timor reverentialis*, the reverent fear of the sacred. While many different tomato products would be the outcome of the ritual, in Sicilian, the whole ceremony was referred to as *fari l'astrattu:* to make extract, to make tomato paste. In Italian, *astratto* is called *conserva*. Conserve. *Conservare*. To maintain. To keep alive. To remember.

The tomato ritual took place primarily in the gardens and orchards on the periphery of the town, but it was performed even in the dusty streets and narrow alleys of Gela, a stubborn clinging of townsfolk to a vanishing agrarian past. It was a collective enterprise: working-class and middle-class women came together for this work. It was exhausting physical labor that started in the early hours of the morning and continued under the boiling Sicilian sun until the early evening, only to resume the following morning.

The women labored for days. They started by gathering hundreds of glass bottles for the sauce and jars for the *astratto*. They thoroughly washed and dried them, aligning them in rows on tables covered by plastic cloths that had been wiped clean with sponges. They left them there waiting, without caps and lids, like hundreds of children with their mouths open in expectation.

Because gardens could not produce enough tomatoes for *astratto*, they were communally purchased in large quantities from tomato purveyors in the countryside. Dozens of crates overflowing with ripe tomatoes were brought to the garden. The women washed the old wooden boards on which they would spread the warm, liquid sauce. After a few days of relentless sun, it would turn into the creamy *astratto* used to make *ragù*.

Ragù is different from tomato sauce, *salsa*, which you use for plain pasta, with some grated *caciocavallo*, or in the summer with fried eggplant and ricotta salata, that simple, exquisite dish known as *pasta alla Norma*. *Ragù* instead is that sauce made with ground beef, chicken, or pork: you sauté onions and meat in olive oil, then add a few tablespoons of *astratto*, diluted with water, and let it simmer for long hours until you get a thick and creamy *sugo*. My mother always adds peas, and so do I. Lasagna, *cannelloni, arancini, involtini* all demand *ragù*. *Ragù* is more complex and richer in taste than *salsa*. When I was little, *ragù* was the condiment for Sunday meals, or special occasions. The plain tomato sauce, or one of its numerous variations—with garlic for pasta sauce, with onions and oregano for pizza sauce, both sprinkled with a little sugar to take away the sour taste of the tomato—was for the everyday meal.

Like the other women, my mother wore an old, stained, flowered housedress that would soon become splotched with red. She covered her hair under a faded kerchief. Carmelina, Cuciuzzo's wife, was always there, as was her mother and sisters, Rita and Margherita, some neighbors, and at times my maternal grandmother.

They prepared huge fires upon which black cauldrons boiled for hours, days it seemed. The mechanics of the ritual still escape me. As a child, I took part as a spectator, then gradually became involved, doing the easy tasks, like turning the *chiappe*, the tomatoes cut in half and left in the sun till the skin became as wrinkled as that of old people. When the *chiappe* were completely dried, they were collected in *mappine*, large kitchen cloths. My mother would fill glass jars with *chiappe* and cover them with olive oil. In the winter we would eat them between slices of firm *pane di casa*. (A few years ago this traditional food of the poor appeared on the shelves of American gourmet stores. Now you can get them at Pathmark and Shop-Rite. They call them sun-dried tomatoes. When I buy them at Buon Appetito, my favorite Italian grocery store in Bayonne, New Jersey, the English words struggle to come up, pushed back by the Sicilian *chiappe*, a slightly obscene words that means cheeks, buttocks, just what a sliced, ripe, round tomato cut in half looks like.)

My older sister and I helped out by doing other small chores, such as washing the tomatoes, stirring the *astratto* bubbling under the sun with a wooden spoon, wiping counters, bringing the wooden boards inside at night.

The men stayed cautiously away from this world ruled by women. The small children, boys and girls, ran around, sometimes helping, sometimes getting in the way, occasionally shooed away by a mother, aunt, or sister, who would wave her hands impatiently, like she did at the greedy flies that threatened to assault the fruits of that communal labor.

If one of the women had her period, she was not allowed to get close to, let alone touch, the tomatoes, the tools, or the products of this summer ritual, lest the sauce would turn sour and vermin grow in the midst of the paste. My mother, an educated woman, an elementary school teacher, was a stalwart supporter of this superstition. "Don't touch a plant while you are menstruating, don't touch the sauce," she warned, like a powerful priestess teaching her acolytes about the dangers of desecration.

Until a few years ago, every time my older sister would go down to Sicily from Rome, my mother would send home, for my nephew and nieces, the chicken that Cuciuzzo's wife roasted at the garden. Crunchy, juicy, cooked to perfection, with a lemony taste softening the touch of the fire, it's the best chicken I've ever had, but there's no recipe you can use to duplicate it. My sister's children simply called it *il pollo di Cuciuzzo*, and so did we.

So my sophisticated sister, my sister the doctor, my sister who has Valentino tiles in her bathroom, carries juicy chicken legs, bottles of tomato sauce, jars of *astratto*, roasted peppers, and *pane di casa*, to her home in Rome in her elegant hand luggage. She dutifully places it under her seat, in compliance with airline regulations. The aroma of still-warm food spreads incongruously in the Alitalia plane.

The garden has been stubbornly resisting, resilient like my mother and father, but now it's giving in. It is tired, old. Like my parents. It is dying of solitude and defeat, of loss and regret. My mother still goes to the garden where thirty-five-year-old trees are dying from lack of care. Cuciuzzo is sick. He might have cancer, my mother tells me. She speaks of these trees and Cuciuzzo in the same breath, in words full of sadness, grieving multiple, incipient losses. "'Ncuscenza!" she says.

The literal meaning of the word is "lack of conscience, or responsibility." But in Sicilian dialect it means, "What a shame! What a loss!" When she talks about the trees, my mother speaks Sicilian, not Italian. Sicilian: language of intimacy, love, and death—language of origins. *Arbuledda*, she calls them, the same word used by my father, a word filled with affection: tender, little, beloved trees. It would be a shame to let them die, she tells me. My mother's tenderness and compassion towards the trees does not surprise me—she has seen them grow; she remembers them slender and fragile, babies, *criaturi*.

The people in my town have been dying too. People in their seventies and eighties I have known since I was a child. *La comare* Formuso died; she was in her nineties, godmother to one of my mother's siblings and very close to my family. My maternal grandmother used to visit *la zia* Formuso daily: "Cummà, ch' si ddici?" they ask each other, holding hands lovingly. My grandmother cries, telling me she feels guilty because *la comare* got sicker and died after my grandmother left town for a few days. She thinks *la comare* felt alone, abandoned, and gave up. After her death, my grandmother, whose appetite for life has always sustained mine, who survived losing an eighteen-month old daughter, who stood strong while nursing my grandfather through the cancer that killed him in 1989, says to me, "A dirti la verità, questa morte è stata assai pesante. Mi sento sola e stanca"— "To tell you the truth, this death was hard to take. I feel alone, and tired."

But it's not only the very old people who are dying. People in their forties and fifties and sixties are getting sick and dying too. It seems that most of them are dying of cancer. A childhood friend, a schoolteacher, a shopkeeper, a neighbor, an uncle, a friend of my mother. Cuciuzzo is dead now, too.

I was an adolescent when the leaves of peach trees started turning black, sucking in the poison from the oil plant that invaded my hometown in the early 1960s. One more conqueror in the land of many conquests, this last one would bring nothing good: no new customs or aromas of exotic spices or unknown delicacies, not even new gods. No cult of Demeter and Persephone, no *kore* statues to grace the houses, no temples, no castles, no medieval turrets. This invader erected its own gray towers near the sea, directly across the single surviving column of the Greek temple of Apollo in the ancient acropolis. This is where lovers meet to avoid the indiscreet gaze of a town eager for gossip.

Antiquity and modernity stare at each other above the heads of these oblivious lovers. Which one will yield first? The solitary Doric column or the gray factory, with its toxic fumes insidiously rising from the towers and settling into the heart of the town, into its people, its fruit trees, its tomato gardens, its strawberry plants, its asparagus patches? The peach trees were the first to give us warning. Now it's the insides of people that have been corroded by the fumes of progress they have been breathing for far too long.

My mother perhaps knew that in my adult life I would not be going to the garden to fill hundreds of bottles with tomato sauce. Sure enough, cans were making their way, slowly but surely, into Sicilian kitchen cabinets, even, eventually, my mother's. And I, like my sisters, was meant for other work, other places. We were meant for fast-paced lives, for homes far away from the Sicilian garden, its rhythms and its rituals. So my mother never taught me how to perform the summery miracle of the transformation of tomatoes into the sweet condiment of winter days.

The tomato ritual, the garden, stand precariously on the edge of memory. And I, I watch from a distance, trying to evoke a world that is passing. Fragments of these summer days flicker, linger flirtatiously, but vanish when I try to grasp them, leaving me empty-handed and alone.

The *giara* is gone, stolen. The house in the garden is falling to pieces and it is dangerous to go inside. There is no roof at its center. You walk inside, look up, and there is the blue sky staring back at you. Vegetation has sprouted from the ruins, wild and thick, embracing a broken chair, the leg of a doll, a rusted pot. Part of the house is gone. The room I shared with my older sister, the living room, my parents' bedroom, the kitchen. But the hall and the dining room are still there, and my mother still stubbornly goes inside, despite the danger. My younger sister, when she visits, yells that she is crazy, but follows her nonetheless.

Back in the garden recently, I snap pictures with my camera, its miniscule, phallic zoom shooting out. I try to be an observer, a cautious, respectful, distant observer, but the garden overtakes me. I linger at the back of the house, by the wall of what used to be my parents' bedroom, near the window that was always kept shut to keep out the heat. The window looks at me, sad and disconcerted by its own aging and disintegration. Rusted nails hold the corroded pieces of wood by a stubbornness so old, so familiar. My fingers caress the rough, cracked surface. I want to kiss it, kneel down. I want to pray. *Mea culpa.* So sorry for your death. So sorry I left. *Mea culpa, mea culpa, mea maxima culpa.*

I press my palms against the wall of the house. I scratch its stone surface. The dust gets underneath my nails, settles into the crevices of my skin. I am treading on my own bones.

Part Three

∿

AWAKENINGS

Go to Hell

Nancy Caronia

It wasn't until Grandma was in her seventies and Grandpa too old to hurt her anymore, in and out of hospitals, that she decided to leave him. She could take his beatings, but she couldn't take his helplessness. She went to her sons and asked them to take her in. But it was too late, or was it merely revenge for all those long ago years of abandonment? All her sons had excuses, the most famous being, "my wife, she just can't handle it right now."

I saw Grandpa for the last time in a hospital bed. He was a stubborn son of a bitch, held on for eight months when other people would have just gotten it over with and died. I went to the hospital with my godfather, Daddy's brother Uncle Ed, and his wife, Aunt Mimi, a born-again charismatic in the Catholic Church, and their daughter, Bernadette, the one they said would be a beauty queen, but wound up marrying a womanizing salesman instead. My two sisters looked like Bernadette as little kids. It was remarkable when you put their three photos together, anywhere from the age of six up until about thirteen they all looked exactly alike, but how come she was the only one that was beauty queen material, that's what I'd like to know?

Grandpa was curled in a fetal position, his arms wrapped around his head. He was sleeping when we first walked in. Aunt Mimi and Uncle Ed went up to him and kissed him on the head. Uncle Ed spoke loudly to him, "how ya doin' Pops?" Grandpa woke up from the sudden noise, "what, what, I can't hear ya, what are ya sayin'?" Uncle Ed laughed and said, "The old man's deaf," and walked out of the room, left the three women alone with his father. Bernadette went up to Grandpa then and put her arms around him and kissed him hello, all gentle and soothing-like. Me, I hung out in the background not wanting to get too close, pissed that his son left us alone in the room with him. Grandpa must have noticed my separateness because he shouted out to me, "yer Frank's daughta, ain't ya?" "Yeah, Grandpa," I replied as Uncle Ed walked back in the room. "C'mere," he said, "I wantcha to tell ya fatha somethin' fa me, I wancha ta tell 'im. Hey, c'mere, I wanna talk ta you," he shouted across to me when I didn't make a move. Uncle Ed stood next to me and suddenly pushed me forward, taunting me as he pushed. "Well, go ahead, don' be afraid, he's not gonna bite you." I went to Grandpa's bedside, glaring at Uncle Ed. I put my face close to his, smelled the death on him, and was glad—glad he was almost gone, glad he couldn't hurt any of us anymore.

When I was about seven years old, my cousin Maddie burned herself on my grandparents' barbecue grill at a backyard party they had at their house in

Woodside, Queens, late sixties suburbia. Some of us were playing tag and she ran right into the hot grill that Grandpa had placed in the middle of the driveway after he'd cooked all the sausages on it in the backyard. The kids had been playing in the driveway the entire day, but he'd insisted on placing the hot grill in the middle of our playing field even after our fathers, his sons, told him it wasn't a good idea. "What the hell do any of you know anyway?" he shouted at them. "Leave me alone and let me do what I want. It's my house," he proclaimed. His sons shrugged their shoulders, walked to the small backyard, and opened up fresh bottles of Rheingold.

Grandpa laughed when Maddie ran into the grill. She was running backwards away from our other crazy but cute cousin, Joseph, who was "it" in our game of tag. Grandpa cornered Maddie between the grill and the house, teasing her, "serves ya right for playin' rough, ya wanna play rough ya gonna get burned" and he laughed louder as he pushed against her arm where the second degree burn was beginning to blister. All the cousins were yelling at him to stop, but Maddie was defiantly silent, not shedding even one tear as he taunted her.

Finally Aunt Helen, Maddie's mother, came running from the kitchen where all the women were washing the dishes and pulled Maddie away from him. "Leave her alone Pops. Jeez, she's only a little girl." Grandpa reached out for my aunt and said, "don' talk ta me that way, I'm not yer husband, I'll smack ya." And he picked up a nearby broom and tried to swat her with it while his sons drank their Rheingolds and watched from the backyard.

I was about to walk away from his hospital bed when Grandpa placed his arm around me in a chokehold, a position he enjoyed administering in my younger days. He was too small now, too weak, but his arm lay heavy on my back. I gave into his weight and leaned in closer. I waited for words that would change the way I thought of him. Words that would erase the past.

I turned to look at Uncle Ed and Aunt Mimi, hoping for some help. Grandpa wasn't speaking, just looking at me, and he began to caress my hair. I felt suffocated. It felt familiar, and my impulse was to bolt from the room without looking back, but it was more important at the time to stay and get the message for my father—the message that would make sense of my grandfather's cruelty. I would be the receptacle, tell my father Grandpa "didn't mean it, he never had."

I tried to cut off the death that surrounded him and waited for the sacred message. "Grandpa, what do you want me to tell my father? You said you had something you wanted to tell him. What is it?" He stopped playing with my hair. "Tell ya fatha," he started, then stopped, hesitating for only a second. "You sure yer Frank's daughta, right?" I was losing my patience with this old, smelly man, and my voice came out short, "yes, Grandpa, what do you want me to tell him?" And then he spat it out, surprising us all. "Tell ya fatha go ta hell." He laughed loudly,

"Tell 'im go ta hell." He repeated it over and over, singsong, like a nursery rhyme. "Tell 'im go ta hell. Tell 'im go ta hell." I lifted his arm away and stepped back across the room. My Aunt Mimi shook her head back and forth. "Pops don't mean it. He don't mean that." Uncle Ed said, "you'll have to tell ya fatha."

I remember sleeping at my grandparents' house only one time in my life. I'm sure there must have been more than this one incident, but it's the only one I have any recollection of, and I didn't even remember the whole picture until after that last time I saw him in the hospital. My grandparents had an apartment in Coney Island, on Avenue U, after they sold the house in Woodside, which means I had to have been about eight years old. My sister, Stephanie, and I slept over on a Saturday. We were supposedly helping Grandma do the shopping for the big Sunday dinner she cooked in those days. The menu consisted of antipasto, soup, macaroni, roasts of lamb and beef, lots of fried vegetables like zucchini, sedano, or cauliflower, and salad with fruit, cheesecake, and cannolis for dessert. We shopped all day, walking up and down Coney Island Avenue, the deli men giving us slices of salami and the bakers handing us cookies.

That night after dinner we sat in the kitchen, asking questions on how to make the sauce and what did she put in her meatballs that made them taste so different from our Irish American mother's. "Well, yer mother, she jus' don' know how ta cook. She won't listen ta me, so you two betta watcha good so you canna teach her." I don't understand people who exchange written recipes. All I ever needed to learn about sauce I got from watching Grandma. "Throw alittlea this an' do this," she always said when I wanted to know how much of something it needed. And then it was always, "but it changes wid how many people ya are, so ya jes gotta do ita fer yourself. Eacha time ya make somethin," she advised.

That night, Grandma put the two of us to bed in their extra room, where we'd have dinner starting at noon the next day. "Be good and go ta sleep. We gotta get up early to geta ready for evabody," she admonished as she closed the door. Stephanie and I were squished in the same bed, something we didn't like, and were talking to each other when Grandpa came in later that night. He came over to us, and since I was on the outside of the bed—I was older and less likely to fall out—he grabbed my arm and said, "ya wanna play?" I told him it was too late, but he didn't hear me or he didn't care, I don't know which, and next he unbuckled his belt and opened his trousers. Stephanie tried to get him off me, but she was just a skinny little kid then, and no matter how hard I kicked him with my legs he held my arms above my head with one hand and pushed my head into his crotch with the other.

Finally, Grandma heard the noise and opened the door, yelling at Stephanie and me, "I tole you to go ta sleep. Whatsa matta wid you two?" She screamed

Grandpa's name when she saw what he was doing. He pushed me away fast, buttoned his trousers, and the two of them started yelling at each other in dialect. Grandma sighed and called to me. She wanted me to go to her, but I couldn't move. I didn't want to go past Grandpa. Stephanie took charge and pushed me forward, squeezing the two of us past him. The three of us went into the kitchen and Grandma wiped my arms and face with a dishtowel. Stephanie sat at the other end of the table and made faces at me to try to get me to laugh. When I didn't have any reaction, she became antsy and said she needed to go to the bathroom and that she could do it by herself. I screamed out no, and she plopped back down into her seat. I was, after all, still her older sister.

Grandma looked upset. "What's wrong, you wan' somethin' to eat maybe? Yeah, that'sa good, I'll make you somethin' ta eat." I nodded my head yes. I didn't want to disappoint her. She took out a saucepan and pulled out a box of farina from one of the cabinets over her head. I didn't pay close attention to what she was doing, but when she took the pot off the stove and I saw the white stuff in it I started to choke and said I wasn't hungry. She threw up her hands. "Wha'sa matta' wid you? I made this fa you and now you don' want it? You kids. What am I gonna do?"

After the hospital visit, Uncle Ed drove us back to my grandparents' apartment. I sat silently in the back seat, next to Bernadette. My father greeted us at the front door. I hadn't seen him in about a year. He looked older and heavier than I remembered. He also looked worn out, something I never remembered about him. Grandma yelled from the kitchen, "what kep' ya so long? I ben waitin' ta put the macaronis on."

Uncle Ed made a beeline for my father. True to form, first thing out of Uncle Ed's mouth was, "Frank, ya daughter has somethin to tell ya." "Jeez, Uncle Ed, can't you even let us say hello." I kissed my father on the cheek. "Grandpa didn't say anything. Don't listen to your brother. He's as crazy as your father." "What did he say? C'mon." My father rubbed the back of my neck as he questioned me. "What did Pops say?" "Nothing," I sighed, "you're all crazy, you know that?" Uncle Ed laughed. He knew he'd aroused my father's curiosity. "Pops gave a message to you through yer daughta." I shot Uncle Ed a nasty look and didn't look at my father when I said in an angry voice directed at my godfather, "you don't want to know. Trust me." I wanted to protect my father the way he never seemed capable of protecting me or my siblings. "What was it?" he asked. I was silent as I turned toward him. My father looked down at his feet, rolled back and forth toe to heel, his hands deep in his pockets. He broke the silence by saying softly, "my fatha' tol' you to tell me go ta hell, right?" I looked directly into his eyes. I was surprised, and nodded my head in assent to the truth he already seemed to know. My father blushed. He knew the joke was on him again and he had to play along.

As the youngest, my father was the brunt of their jokes for years, but he learned to see where the next assault was coming from and always beat everyone to the punch. His nickname from birth was Chubbs, and that was usually where the abuse began and ended. My grandmother fed him proudly when he was a child. She made him eat and eat and eat. Her baby, the youngest, would prove there was no poverty in their house. Where there was girth there was wealth. "Eata somamo, ya so skinny." I still hear Grandma's voice accusing my mother of not feeding him, always telling my father he was too skinny even when he was too fat, always measuring how they were doing against his size.

I stood in Grandma's kitchen, watching my father's face go through the same fight for control that mine does when I try to ignore a hurt. It's this look in his eye that says, I know, I want to kill, but instead he eats another piece of roast beef, another plate of pasta. His weight is no longer a sign of their wealth, but of a rage unexpressed, violence committed, poverty of the soul and ignorance of the heart.

"I know, he says it ta me all the time. Everyday I go ta the hospital, he tells me go ta hell. It's like a joke," he laughs to accentuate the last point. His laugh turns to a shrug when I don't join in and look like I'm going to cry. Uncle Ed laughs with my father, pats me on the back. My father rolls his eyes toward me as I slink away from my uncle's hand. He picks up a cookie on the countertop, puts it in his mouth. My grandmother yells at him from her place at the stove, "Frankie, we gonna eat now, wha'dya doin'? Yer not gonna have an appetite. Lookit all the food I made fer you." He picks up another cookie, pops it quickly in his mouth, and says, "don't worry, ma, I'll eat. You know me. I always got an appetite. You don't gotta worry about me."

After that hospital visit to my grandfather, my memory was jarred but good. I could never look at any of my relatives the same way again. And once I remembered about him, it was like the floodgates opened onto the memories that had kept me frozen inside my own life for so many years. My therapist said to me, "would you want to sit down with your rapist and try to reason with him if he was a stranger?"

When my mother called to tell me Grandpa was dead eight months after I last saw him, I whispered "good" into the receiver, not sure if I wanted my mother to hear me or not. She either didn't hear me or didn't want to hear me. "Well, he's bein' waked on such-and-such days and I'm goin' on this day and the funeral is on this day, you better plan with work—" I cut her off. "I'm not going." She let out an impatient breath. "Whadaya mean yer not goin'? Oh my god, how can you not go? It's yer father's father, for chrissake." "Listen. I don't care. He wasn't a nice man and he made a lot of people miserable." I was tired from the conversation. She changed the subject when she realized I wasn't going to join in the adrenalin rush of her newest drama. I could hear her taking a puff off her cigarette as she said, "well, do ya wanna at least talk to yer father?" "Is he there?" I asked. "Yeah, I'll put him on." She was curt. "Well, no Ma, I don't. Not right now. I gotta go," I stammered out and hung up the phone.

Funny, but no one called to find out why I didn't go to the funeral. No one ever said anything. It was like this wall came tumbling down, only they continued on as if the wall was intact, and for them, I guess, it was. At least that was what I believed until Aunt Mimi wrote a note to me a year later begging me to reconcile with my immediate family. "Everyone misses you. Jesus loves you and so do we." She sent a religious greeting card along with a green plastic rosary and a bunch of prayer cards with saints' pictures emblazoned on them. I wrote her back and told her I had nothing to reconcile, and for the first time I let a blood relative know what my grandfather had done.

Aunt Mimi and Uncle Ed surprised me by calling and inviting me to lunch at their house in upstate New York. "We'll have takeout, praise Jesus," she says when I surprise myself by saying yes and ask for directions to their home.

The three of us sat together around their white formica 1950s kitchen table, Chinese take-out spread before us. Uncle Ed barely touched his chicken and broccoli, and tears formed in his eyes as I recounted as much of the story about Grandpa as possible without giving them a heart attack. He looked at me. "Is it true?" I wasn't angry when he questioned me, simply answered, "yes, Uncle Ed, I have no reason to make any of this up." "We always knew Pops was crazy, but this, we never thought he was sick. You know we asked Betsy"—their oldest daughter, not beauty queen material—"and she says it never happened to her," his voice pleaded with me. I kept quiet, because I thought, well, she just doesn't remember, that's all. My uncle said, "well, look at me, I'm fine. He beat us, you know, but I'm okay. Well, I am afraid of the dark, but I have Aunt Mimi stay up with me at night until I'm ready for bed. If the hall light's off I won't walk to my bedroom. I get scared. So yer Aunt Mimi stays up with me until I'm ready for bed." I listened silently to this sixty-five-year-old man with two daughters and four grandchildren. I have my answer.

We sit quietly until Aunt Mimi breaks the stillness by gathering up the left-over Chinese food and packing it away. "Lunch tomorrow, praise Jesus," her voice tinkles through their kitchen, "praise Jesus."

∽

Motherlove

Mary Jo Bona

For a Friend

When I said you had love in your eyes,
they were filled with it, twin moons
pulling your face toward my ear while lips

sang Sicilian nursery rhymes,
I imagined love in early June:
Mother kneading dough for bread, her

hands and brow wisps of white;
a look of consternation narrowed her eyes,
burrowing deep into her own mother's

failing heart. Hurt as a deer, her mother
lay dying in a white room, with the old
moon hanging down, weeping

*swing low sweet chariot, coming for to carry
you home.* The cart, smooth ice in the night,
glimmering against ceaseless black

skies. *Oh, where did she go, moon?*
Pull me to her with
your voice low and faint:

that way you will know
desire, how killing it is. . . .
I remember my mother's faraway

eyes, when she looked up from her biscotti
dough, goulash dumplings, matzo-balls
and jelly rolls; while she stared

at me, eyes brimming
with motherloss, her mother's
hands warm at her cheek.

When you hummed your mother's midnight songs,
I hear a long-ago wooing,
and feel again my mother's eyelashes

flutter upon my cheek,
her lips crooning love songs,
her eyes soft as dusk.

∾

We Begin with Food
Rosette Capotorto

my grandmother's
arms rolled five pounds of flour
into *cavatelli* on a Sunday morning

labor & love &
the planting of
flowers and fruit

I see your hands she says
the night we meet
a woman who is a contractor by trade
an artist by desire

          then   we are able   to talk

black   italian
  motherbrothersister

food
              taste this

tender long green
           bean
kitchen whistle clean

              knuckles

nails
skin   sun
   texture

learned how to cook from my father
the hard way

wooden spoon
red touch of tomato
borough accent specific
as a dime

rooftops come in handy
on hot summer nights

love is thick
       and painful

fingers   forearms   fists

slap   throw   punch
working hands
       sometimes
              gentle as an egg

mortar   brick
    concrete

plaster mixed like dough
       dry white circle
       a simple board   water

toxic she says
I know what I'll die of

   callous   cramp
       muscle

armload of wood

crown of barbed wire
    girl jesus
black and beautiful

rock me in your
arms of stone and steel
let me eat and drink of you

∾

Breakfast in My Seventeenth Year
Rosette Capotorto

the morning of
the first day of my
post-high school job
in the accounts receivable
department of Union Carbide
on 47th and Park my mother
got up and made me   (to make me)
breakfast   it had
been years since my mother
made me breakfast
not because she was lazy
she was not that never that
my mother
she was tired oh
so tired and she craved sleep
and rest and sleep rest and sleep

she worked hard my mother
oh yes she worked hard   she had
several jobs and they were all
on call all the time jobs none
of these nine to five five to ten
jobs no
she was still raising little kids
then five, six, ten whatever
wife mother wife   cooked all meals
made all lunches   lunch was still a meal then

washed all dishes all clothes all floors
she was the wife of a construction worker   wife
of a pizza maker   wife of the eldest son

italian wives like other kinds had to

for a long time I had been
the one to make breakfast
for the others get them out
the door for school

but that morning
the first day of my
post-high school job
way downtown on 47th and Park
my mother got up
to make me
breakfast.

Bone, Veins, and Fat
Cheryl Burke

They must have thought I was a junkie. What else could explain my gaunt face, sallow skin? It was 6:00 P.M. rush hour at the supermarket. The needle marks on my inner arms flashed prominently under the fluorescent lights. I felt translucent, as if the people who stared at me as I walked through the aisles of Pathmark with my mother could see through me. The glazed-over look on my face did not help with the staring, and despite my mother's commands to smile and look "normal" I couldn't help myself. The nurse at the pediatrician's had turned me into a human pincushion earlier that day as she prodded my arm.

We stopped in front of the meat section and my mother picked up two varieties of Italian sausage, one hot and one sweet. She placed the plump packages in her cart and grabbed my arm, the one with the good vein and the Band-Aid. I flinched. I looked down into the refrigerated case. The fluorescent light reflected on the shiny plastic that was tightly wrapped around the meat, exposing bone, veins, and fat.

"What do you want to eat before your father beats the crap out of you?" I picked up a package of flank steak, held it in my hand, felt the gelatinous pull of the meat under the plastic and watched the blood that pooled around the edges of the Styrofoam tray. The woman next to me looked at me and then looked at my mother with contempt. I was fourteen, angry, and I had just been diagnosed with anorexia nervosa.

A few days before, my mother had walked into my room and gasped. There was no lock on my door; it had dislodged when my father knocked the door down a month earlier, during an argument. Nor was there any privacy in my house. The walls and the doors might as well have been transparent. I had been standing in front of my mirror in my panties, studying the ripples on my stomach, the soft skin that hung like old drapery from my skeletal frame. Watching the flesh Jell-O about as if it were disconnected from my body.

"My god," my mother said. She grabbed me by the shoulders and shook me. "What are you doing? What's happening to you?"

I grew limp and looked at the statue of Mary my grandmother had placed on my dresser. Mary always looked serene. She was the perfect model of suffering. I looked back at my mother and smiled, the grin spreading from the corners of my mouth like a slow-burning fire.

"Nothing," I said. "I feel great." She began to cry.

We were a fat family, always looking for solace in a heaping plate of food. My father would eat an entire kielbasa with cabbage after work, before dinner. The sausage coiled like a snake on a bed of grass on his plate, and I sat there, watching him eat it section by section, slathering it with mustard, his ruddy Irish complexion growing redder with each swift bite, his stomach, a bulbous orb of flesh, hanging over the top of his jeans.

My Italian mother prided herself on her elaborate meals. She used only fresh ingredients and shopped at Cangiano, an Italian specialty store in Staten Island. She forbade me to eat junk food but had no problem when I helped myself to a large plate of lasagna with sausage after school. My thin friends ate candy and cookies that made them hyperactive; I ate entire meals that wore me down.

My parents were children of working-class immigrants. Female worth was measured in beauty. It amazes me that a family so centered around food was also obsessed with how its women looked. Whenever we went out, I was instructed to don every piece of gold jewelry my parents had bought for me. By the age of twelve, I was also required to tease my hair to my parents' liking and douse it with hairspray to keep it just so. My mother picked out my outfits. Her gaudy taste, suitable for an older woman, often made me look middle-aged.

Once, as she oversaw my dressing, she grabbed at my torso. "What a shame you have so many stretch marks!" she exclaimed, staring at my middle. Embarrassed, I pulled on the shirt and buttoned it up. I checked out my reflection in the mirror. I looked like a freak.

"Why do I have to wear this stupid outfit?" I asked. My mother had forced my chunky twelve-year-old body into a pinstriped pantsuit meant for a woman four times my age.

"Because nothing else fits you," my mother answered.

Despite the family's eating habits, my parents often asked how I got so fat.

There is nothing quite like Sunday dinner in an Italian American home. We started at noon, directly after church. We would arrive at my grandparents' house, the elastic of my plus-size dress tight around my waist. Both Nanny and Grandpa cooked. Grandpa browned the meats that were to be added to the gravy—sausages and meatballs, pig's knuckles and braciole, rolled into cylinders and cut into pinwheels. The oil from the meats added a golden sheen to the top of the sauce, an iridescent halo of grease.

My grandmother made everyone's "favorite." For my father, ziti with sauce, ricotta cheese, and an assortment of meats on the side. For my brother, spaghetti with butter and fresh grated cheese. For me, a Pyrex dish of the most delicious-smelling chicken parmigiana, the perfect blend of hearty and sweet. There was always antipasto and sometimes a lasagna or baked ziti too. This was followed by a roasted chicken with potatoes and peas cooked in the trench of fat that surrounded the bird. For desert there were pastries, cakes, pies, and candies. During each course, my mother would remind me, "Don't fill up on this. Wait for the rest of the meal." But "filling up" was never a concern for me. I didn't know what "full" was, and the tempting cornucopia did not help me learn.

There was much ado about serving the men. My grandmother would say, "Make your father a plate, Cheryl." My mother would say, "Make your brother a plate, Cheryl." When I refused, my mother would purse her lips and say, "This one is going to be a problem." During the meal, my father would point at what he wanted and I would have to spoon the food onto his plate and pass it to him. My mother served her father. My grandmother served my uncle.

During the meal, various arguments would ensue, between my mother and her younger brother, me and my younger brother, my mother and my father, my grandmother's two sisters, who lived in the upper portion of their two-family house. I would say that my brother was spoiled, that the family spoiled the boys. My mother would say that she treated us both the same. My uncle would say that he wasn't spoiled. My grandmother would ask us if we wanted more food. My grandfather would demand an end to the fighting. My father would get up when he was done eating and fall asleep on the big chair in the living room.

By the time we were done, it would be about four. We would all sit around the living room, comatose, our legs splayed out. The men would unbutton the top buttons of their pants, shouting about whatever sport was broadcast on the TV screen. I could feel the elastic band of my dress, pulled to maximum capacity; I knew it would leave a red indented mark around my middle. I would go to the bathroom and find some relief in removing my tights.

At about seven, Nanny would ask, "Who's hungry? Should I make sandwiches?

"Oh God, I'm so full," everyone would moan, but the sandwiches appeared and we would all eat again.

On a family vacation when I was about ten, at a campground in Maryland, we had a hearty breakfast of pancakes, bacon, and eggs. After a swim in the pool, my parents picked up a box of fried chicken. Then my father, remembering we were in Maryland, a state famous for crabs, got in the car to go for a bucket of the crustaceans.

Earlier that day, my parents had gotten into a screaming fight at the pool. My father called my mother a "jackass." My mother called me a "little bitch." I called my brother a "jerk-off." But the food calmed us down and brought us together like nothing else could. With our pudgy legs stuffed into shorts and sneakers, our mouths sucking on the chicken bones and crab legs, we looked content, almost normal. With our fingers oiled and slick, our dysfunction was masked in the slovenly gratitude of overeating.

The day after my mother barged into my room, I was taken to the doctor for some tests. I sat on the examination table as the nurse slapped the crook of my arms to find a vein. I watched my blood fill vial after vial, a defiant shade of crimson. I was amazed at how easily it poured out of my body.

The questions the doctor asked sounded more like accusations than inquiries. A whirlpool of phrases—pregnancy, liver disease, IV drug use—resounded in my head. My mother had answered the first one for me. "No, she couldn't possibly be pregnant. She doesn't even talk to boys." My not flirting had always been an issue for her. I was a quiet girl, different from the other women in my family, who were needy and controlling in their loud, self-appointed martyrdom.

"Well, how is her relationship with her brother?" the doctor had asked, then added, "or her father?" I overheard this as I peed into a Dixie cup in the adjoining bathroom. Was he suggesting that my father or my brother had impregnated me?

Embarrassed, I became speechless when I returned to the examination room and I could only grunt an answer his questions, "Is there any chance, that you could be pregnant? Do you know how you get pregnant? Are you using drugs?"

My only sexual encounter had been that past summer, a messy, unfortunate petting session with an older boy who came in his pants. And it would be a few years before any narcotics would enter my system.

As I shed the pounds, I gained the fascination of my classmates, who couldn't believe their eyes, and the skewed respect of teachers who had previously pulled me aside to tell me that if I were to lose a few pounds, my grades would miraculously improve. I started the diet in the middle of seventh grade, at five foot four and close to two hundred and thirty pounds, healthily enough on Weight Watchers. Then I whittled my food intake down to four-ounce burgers severely microwaved to render all the fat, steamed broccoli, and milkshakes consisting of ice, one small banana, skim milk and several packets of Sweet & Low.

On my fourteenth birthday, I watched three of my friends polish off the ice cream cake my parents had bought for me.

"Aren't you going to have any Cheryl?" my friend Lisa asked, scratching her flat stomach with one hand and eating with the other.

"How can you sit there and watch us eat?" asked April, who always seemed to be sporting a bikini top and cut-off shorts.

"You can break your diet, it's your birthday," said Anita, her jeans sitting low on her slender hips. *They can eat that cake,* I thought to myself as I sipped a Diet Coke. *They're so skinny.* I had spent most of that morning in front of the mirror, fantasizing that I could cut off the skin that hung from my abdomen with a large pair of shears. I was five foot six, one hundred ten pounds. I had lost a lot of my hair. The rest I doused daily with Sun-In, which promised to add blond highlights but which turned my hair purple. A thin layer of hair now covered my body like a microorganism. My complexion, at one time enviable and compared with bisque china, now looked yellow. I was sensitive to light, cold, and noise, and never left the house without sunglasses and a sweater. I jumped when I heard the bass-thumping sports cars that frequently sped down the street. My period, which used to arrive like clockwork, hadn't stopped by for five months.

After the diagnosis, my mother watched every forkful of food that made its way to my lips. She watched me chew and swallow. Someone would stand outside the bathroom door, listening to make sure I wasn't forcing myself to vomit. My grandmother would say, "Eat. Be a good girl." That's all I was really trying to do. My father showed his concern by whipping up vats of mashed potatoes infused with whole milk, butter, and sour cream and broiled thick sirloin steaks, formerly my favorite meal. When I refused to eat, he turned a violent shade of red and slammed his fist on the table. "You want us to put you away? Is that what you want?"

These were the same parents who used to take food away from me. The same mother who would grab a roll of my fat and shake her head and say, "What a shame." The same father who flew into a rage when he found a Planter's peanut bar in my back pocket after he forbade me to eat candy in the fifth grade.

They desperately wanted me to be thin, but on their terms. Food had made me the way I was, caused me the misery of self-hatred, and now my revenge was not to allow it to pass my lips. I had taken my rage at the hypocrisy of my family and my society and turned it against myself.

In school, my anorexia was viewed as an oddity, worthy of freak show reverence. One rumor circulated that I had had my stomach stapled. Another said I had a rare "disappearing disease." A lot of the girls wanted to know my dieting secrets and said I was lucky to be that thin. Boys would ask me, "So when you lose weight where does it go?" or, "What's it like to look in a mirror now. Do you like think you're somebody else?" Some boys, who would never talk to me when I was fat, became flirty and attentive. I was proud of my protruding collarbone, my size-five stretch jeans, and proud that I could touch my forefinger to my thumb when I wrapped my hand around my upper arm.

I had fought with anorexia for a year and a half when I began to put on weight. At first I appeared healthier and I received praise.

"You look good Cheryl. You have more color in your cheeks now," my English teacher said.

"You look better with a little more weight on you," said my friend Lisa.

"Let's go try on some clothes at Mandee's," suggested Anita. "I'll bet you'll look great in a pair of tight jeans."

My mother said, "I'm glad you're healthier. Just don't get fat again."

I had no idea why I was putting weight on. The thin milkshakes and hard-as-pucks burgers still made up most of my diet. I ran eight miles a day, did two hundred sit-ups, three hundred leg lifts. Somehow, though, I grew larger. My period resumed; my hair grew back; the fuzz on my body disappeared. I was almost normal.

Then it happened.

I woke up one day and I was fat again. Not as fat as before, but definitely larger. I stood in front of the mirror, turned to my side, and saw that I had grown wider. I faced front; I was definitely bigger. I didn't know what to do.

I went to the bathroom, washed my face, brushed my teeth, did my makeup and fixed my hair, hoping that when I returned, my reflection would be different. But it wasn't. I squeezed myself into the loosest of my denim miniskirts and went downstairs.

My father was at the kitchen table reading his paper. He looked up at me. "Are you sure you should wear that?" he asked.

I grew larger still, and found myself back on the examination table; the accusatory questions, the blood-letting. This time I was told, "You've managed to get yourself a thyroid problem," as if it was the result of some indiscretion on my part, or as if I'd failed to use a condom or consumed an entire sheet of acid.

I soon ballooned back to almost two hundred pounds. I watched my failure take over my body with each glance in the mirror and each trip to the scale. I heard whispers behind me in the hallway at school as the kids tried to figure out what had happened to me. Some said the staple had fallen out, or I had extreme gas, or I was pregnant, or I was retaining enough water for three people. I was called "Fatso," "Fat Bitch," "Porky," names I'd never been called as a child. Being a fat fifteen-year-old was a greater sin against femininity than being a fat twelve-year-old. If "normal" working-class adolescent girls were good only for sex, then I was good for nothing. And I was reminded of that everywhere I went.

Anita, Lisa, and April sat on one side of the booth at McDonald's with Big Macs, shakes, and mountains of french fries. I sat on the other with a Diet Coke.

"Aren't you hungry, Cheryl?" Anita asked.

"No," I answered. Of course I was hungry; I was just too embarrassed to eat in public.

"At least have some fries," Lisa said. I reached over and grabbed a few.

Three boys walked by. One of them said, "Wow, did you see that fat chick?" We could still hear them laughing after they left the restaurant.

"You'll lose the weight again someday. Don't worry. We think you're beautiful," April said. I got to the point where I couldn't stand to be around them in their miniskirts and half-shirts. I grew reclusive, almost never leaving my room. At lunch, during the school day, I sat in a corner and read magazines and books. I fell in love with Holden Caulfield and Sylvia Plath's fictional persona, Esther Greenwood. I realized what I really craved was not edible, but intellectual. I became obsessed with escape. College would be that escape. My rebellion would be to get a college degree.

Education meant very little to my blue-collar family. My mother was the first in her family to graduate from high school. My father never went beyond eighth grade. My guidance counselor told me I was setting unreachable goals, I was being overly ambitious, and suggested I go to "beauty culture training" or secretarial school. When I talked about college, my relatives would say, "Whaddaya tink, you better than us?" or, "You ain't got nothin' we ain't got."

I am reminded of my maternal grandparents, of a time in my life when food still courted innocence, before it became the familiar harbinger of fear and failure.

Years before, in Rosebank, a predominantly Italian American section of Staten Island, a provincial enclave that prided itself on its ethnic heritage and paying respect to that heritage through food, I spent many summer days in the warm sunlight of my maternal grandparents' kitchen, helping them jar tomatoes for the winter. My grandfather grew the most delicious tomatoes, the kind that remind you that tomatoes are indeed a fruit, bursting with sweetness and juice.

After breakfast, I would follow him through the garden, holding a basket into which he had placed what was needed for that day's jarring. The tomatoes were brought back to the pantry, where my grandmother and I washed them and pulled away the vines and leaves. Then they were placed in a machine that deseeded them. I was allowed to crank the lever that pushed them through.

The result was a rich, velvety red puree, which was then placed in a pot so large it took up two burners on my grandmother's giant white stove. There the tomatoes would meet with olive oil, garlic, rosemary, oregano, and black pepper. As the ingredients simmered together, rich smells filled the kitchen, smells of comfort, home, and love.

It was not until I was in college that I was finally able to lose weight and acquire healthy eating habits. During my sophomore year at NYU, I dropped fifty pounds, almost effortlessly. When people asked me how, I wasn't sure what to tell them. But looking back, I can see that I was finally in a place where I was respected, fat and all. I was mentally active, intellectually engaged. When I walked down the street, I received the cat calls every woman receives on the streets of New York City. Bizarrely, even this helped me to feel "normal."

I am in my late twenties now, have managed to keep the weight off, and still love the healing power of food, its comfort. At the moment, I have a container of homemade sauce in my freezer, like my grandmother made those summers in Rosebank, ready to be thawed when needed.

∾

Big Heart
Rita Ciresi

He came out of the back, his apron bloody. The butcher Mr. Ribalta had the biggest belly I had ever seen. When he leaned into the case to grab a handful of hamburger or lop off a rope of sausage, his stomach grazed the meat. I wanted to poke his fat, to see if my finger would sink into it like pizza dough, or press my ear against him, to hear his insides sloshing and grumbling. But I hung back from the meat counter until he crooked a plump finger and beckoned me forward.

"Oh, Swiss Girl," he called. "Yo-do-lo-do-lo-do-lay."

I always eyed his Swiss cheese. I wanted to take a chunk of it home and slip it between a wedge of sharp pepperoni and a slice of salty prosciutto on a seeded roll. But Mama refused to buy it. "I don't pay good money for holes," she said. She frowned when Ribalta reached into the case to cut me a sliver.

People said Ribalta had a big heart, but Mama was convinced that heart longed for only one thing: to turn her into a big spender. Every Saturday morning before we left the house for the market, she armed herself with a black plastic wallet stamped with a picture of the Leaning Tower of Pisa, a shopping list, and a green pencil stub she had pocketed after playing miniature golf at Palisades Park. Since my sister Lina thought she was too old for such outings, Mama took me—a mere nine-year-old who didn't yet know how to protest—as a witness. I was supposed to make sure Ribalta didn't try any monkey business, like doubling the wax paper or pressing his thumb down on the scale. Although Mama had patronized Ribalta for years, she still didn't trust him. "It's not like he's family," she said.

The market stood on a corner, the front windows lined with white paper, lettered in blue, that announced the weekly specials. Above the shop, behind windows hung with yellowed lace curtains, Ribalta lived with his mother. Mama called her Signora. For years I thought that was her first name.

In cold weather or warm, Mama and I found Signora out front, sweeping the dirt and litter off the sidewalk with a ragged broom that had lost half its dirty bristles. She held her broom still just long enough to peer at us through her cat-glasses. When she was satisfied she had recognized us, she resumed sweeping.

Ribalta's shop officially opened at nine, but we always walked in a little after eight-thirty. Brass bells clattered as the door swung behind us. Mama headed down the first narrow aisle, stopping once or twice to inspect some canned goods that sat on the high wooden shelves. "Cheaper at the A&P," she announced loudly.

At the back of the store stood the gleaming white meat case, lit with fluorescent tubes that made the unit hum and vibrate. Behind the case was a swinging door, and behind that, the mysterious room where Ribalta butchered his meat while Radio Italia played. Mama went up to the counter and hit the silver bell on top with the flat of her hand. The radio went dead. We heard water running. Then Ribalta came out of the back, his breath heavy as he wiped his hands on a clean white cloth. He pushed his gold wire-rimmed glasses up on his nose. He was the only shopkeeper in our neighborhood who ever smiled at Mama.

Mama nodded back, her eyes on the case. Ribalta stocked it so the contents ranged from the reddest and rawest meat to the cleanest, tidiest rolls of processed food. First came the organs—bloody bulbs of liver, tough-looking necks, and limp hearts—packaged in clear plastic containers. Then came ground beef pressed in an aluminum tray, rump roast and flank steaks, coils of sausage, and a quilt of overlapping bacon strips. Cuts of pale pork and veal were followed by moist chicken breasts, and piles of stippled yellow legs and scrawny wings. In a separate section of the case, Ribalta kept logs of ham, coppacole, Genoa salami, and blocks of cheese.

Mama checked each item on her list against Ribalta's prices. Then she placed the list on top of her wallet and firmly crossed off some items with the pencil stub. "Here's what's left," she said. It always took Ribalta a long time to fill the order. Mama made him display each cut of meat, back and front, before she allowed him to put it on the scale. And when she said she wanted half a pound of something, she meant eight ounces, no more and no less. Ribalta patiently lifted chop after chop onto the scale, while Mama watched the gauge waggle back and forth until it settled as close to the weight she had asked for as it would ever get.

After Ribalta had wrapped the meats in stiff white paper, tied each bundle with red and white string, and marked the price with a black wax pencil, he crossed his arms and rested them on his big belly. He knew exactly what Mama was going to ask for next.

"Any scraps today?" she said.

"For the dog, eh?" Ribalta disappeared into the back.

He came back balancing a pile of metal pans. He displayed the contents to Mama and the haggling began.

"Veal bones," he said. "With plenty of meat. Chicken necks, close to ten of them."

Mama rejected the necks and offered fifteen cents for a bag of bones.

"Make it a quarter," Ribalta said.

"For those sticks?"

"These are beautiful bones. Juicy. Tender. Flavorful."

"Twenty cents," Mama firmly said.

They went back and forth like that, until Ribalta ran out of scraps and Mama was satisfied she had bled him for whatever she could get. Ribalta stacked the white packages in a box. Then he winked at Mama and peered over the case at me.

"Oh, Swiss Girl," he said. "Yo-do-lo-do-lo-do-lay!"

He turned, wiped off a cleaver, and reached into the case to whack off a hunk of the cheese. He handed it to Mama. She frowned when she gave me the cheese. "Say thank you," she told me. To Ribalta she said, "You're too generous."

"Why not?" he replied as he wiped the cleaver. "Life is short." Then he came around the side of the case, carrying Mama's box. We followed him up the aisle. The strings of his apron stretched tightly across his broad backside.

Up in front, behind the squat glass counter, Signora now sat on a wooden stool. Ribalta lowered the box onto the counter and left Signora to figure the bill with a pencil and paper.

Mama left the market with a satisfied look on her face. But after a block or two, when the box grew heavy and she switched the weight from one hand to the other, she bit her lip and wrinkled her brow, convinced that Ribalta had gotten fat off her business and hers alone. "*Grassone!*" she said. "Thinks I don't notice that diamond ring."

On his right pinky, Ribalta wore a thin gold band studded with a diamond. Mama often remarked on it. "Who else do you know owns such a swanky thing?" she asked me. I shrugged. No other man I knew wore jewelry—not even a wedding ring—except the archbishop, who came to our church once a year to give Confirmation.

Ribalta didn't go to church. Sundays, my mother and my aunts gathered together on the sidewalk after Mass and stared after Signora, who hobbled home alone. Then they turned back into a circle and began their attack against the butcher.

"What does the man eat, *pasta e fagioli* six times a day?"

"How can he breathe with a belly like that?"

"How does he move his bowels?"

"The size!"

"The smell!"

"Fat as an opera singer."

"He's a bachelor."

"That's his problem."

They blamed Signora. They said she spoiled him, babied him, cooked him whatever he wanted. They said that after she died, he would lose a little weight. Find himself a girl. Get married and have children.

Every afternoon when I fetched the newspaper off the front porch, Mama paused a few moments from her housework to scan the obituary page. One day she snapped the newspaper open and pointed to a picture with triumph.

"Ribalta's mother," she said.

"That's not her," I said.

"Stupid," said Mama. "It's an old photograph."

"The name's wrong too."

"What? Gelsomina Ribalta, that's right."

"But you called her Signora."

Mama laughed. She spent the rest of the afternoon on the phone, repeating the story to my aunts.

For three days after the funeral, the shop was closed. A black ribbon hung from the door, and upstairs all the shades were drawn. I made a sign of the cross as I passed on my way to school.

On Saturday morning I stuck close to Mama on the walk to the store. When we arrived, the front door was locked. Mama pulled at the handle to test it again. Then she peered through the door. A boy stood in the front aisle, stacking loaves of bread on the shelf. He turned. Mama rapped at the glass. The boy held up his wrist, pointed to his watch, and then went back to stacking the bread. Mama was astounded.

"The sign says open at nine," I pointed out.

"That sign has hung there for years. Signora always opened."

"*Aspettino*," the boy called out.

"A real *paesano*. Speaks no English. Lazy."

We waited two or three minutes in the cold before the boy came to the door. He was older than he seemed at first, about twenty, and short and erect, with muscled arms and a firm chest that swelled beneath the bib of his clean white apron. He had close-trimmed black hair and dark, liquidy eyes with long black lashes, high cheekbones, and a moist, pouty lower lip. A gold medal hung on a chain around his short, solid neck. I fell in love with him instantly.

Mama strode past him without even a nod. "Off the boat," she muttered, as I followed her down the first aisle. I turned back to look at him. He stood with one hand on the counter and watched as Mama hit the bell on the meat case. Ribalta came out slowly, wiping his plump, squat hands. Radio Italia continued to play.

"You forgot to turn off your radio," she said.

"My cousin likes the music," Ribalta answered.

Mama looked back down the aisle at the boy. "That one there is your cousin? Funny, I don't remember him at the funeral."

Ribalta hung his head to show his sorrow. Then Mama got a hold of herself and rolled out her standard sympathy speech. "The flowers were lovely. I've never seen so many in my life. Sent by relatives?"

"I ordered most."

I could tell Mama was racking up the price of that in her head, adding it to the cost of the fancy coffin Signora had been buried in, and the white headstone that had an angel with outstretched wings.

She scanned the meat case. If she was hoping Ribalta would be running some specials to lure his customers back into the store, she was disappointed. "Start with the hamburger," she said. "That's fresh, I hope."

"I always sell fresh."

"Three-quarters of a pound, then."

I stood with my back to the front of the store. I felt the cousin's eyes on us. I was embarrassed by my childish red earmuffs and red wool mittens, by Mama's flat black boots and shabby wool coat. The haggling was long and intense that morning. I stood there awkwardly. Mama's undisguised astonishment at what she found on the counter mortified me. Ribalta's cousin stood behind a cash register.

"What's this fancy machine doing here?" Mama said.

"We're joining the modern age," Ribalta said.

Mama looked dubious. "Pencil and paper was good enough for Signora," she said. She watched the cousin carefully as he sorted through the box and rang up the paltry sums scribbled on the packages. When the insubstantial total popped up on little silver tabs in the window of the cash register, I wanted to die of shame. I turned my back as Mama drew the bills out of her Leaning Tower of Pisa wallet.

"Slow as molasses," Mama said after we left the store. "And sloppy, too. Packed the bones on top of the meat."

Just as Gelsomina Ribalta became known simply as *Signora*, the boy became known as *Cugino, The Cousin*. "So what do you think of Cugino?" my aunts polled one another, with little smiles on their faces. Too many muscles, they decided. Too long nails. He took forever to figure out the total and too long to pack the box back up. He was too handsome for a man. Good looks spelled trouble, you better believe it!

"Heartbreaker," my Aunt Fiorella pronounced him, nudging me. "Look out!" Then all my aunts cackled. I turned red, both from the shame of knowing that Cugino would never be interested in a silly girl like me, and from fear that Mama and my aunts would guess my secret. I had never been in love before, and I was sure it was written all over my face. But if Mama caught on to it, she said nothing. She was distracted by other things at the market. She made it her business to find out more about Cugino. The more Ribalta refused to be pinned down, the harder she hammered him.

"So where is this cousin of yours from?" she asked.

"Calabria."

"I thought your family was *napoletana*."

Mama hesitated. "I hear you sing in a band," she said.

"That's right."

"Your *cugino*, he's in show business too?"

"He plays horn, yes. We'll be giving a concert downtown. For *Carnevale*. Come hear us play."

Mama was taken aback. No one ever invited her anywhere. I imagined us standing in the square, bundled in our winter coats. Cugino stood up from his folding chair, lifted his gleaming trumpet to his lips, and staring me soulfully in the eyes, played a lilting solo that sent the audience into a frenzy of applause.

"I don't go to *la festa*," Mama said. "Your *cugino*'s parents, they'll be there?"

"They're dead."

"Orphaned so young. "

"Nineteen."

"He'll be married soon," said Mama. "He has a girlfriend, I guess?"

"Not at the moment."

"You should fix him up. There are plenty of nice girls in the parish."

"We don't go to church."

"You should."

"What for?"

"To find God."

"God is in our hearts," Ribalta said.

"He's at Sunday mass," said Mama. "And you should be there, too, with your cousin. Who knows? You both might meet a nice girl."

"We already have our favorite," Ribalta said, and smiled at me. "She's called the Swiss Girl. Yo-do-lo-do-lo-do-lay!"

I prayed I would be Cugino's favorite. In the middle of a spelling bee at school, or during the Eucharistic prayer at church, I would feel warmth envelop me, and suddenly Cugino would be by my side, his thick fingers clasping my upper arms. We were rolling over and over again in a bed of grass, lying together on the beach as the waves lapped in on the sand. We kissed and embraced. . . .

I desperately wanted to impress him. On the way to the store I tried to convince Mama to spend more money.

"Let's get some Swiss cheese today," I said.

"It's cheaper at the—"

"Stop talking about the A&P!" I said. "Especially in the store."

"Who can hear me?" Mama asked. "Ribalta's blasting the radio in the back and Cugino *non capisce.*"

"He understands from the way you say it."

Mama sniffed. "I've got nothing to hide from his type."

"Why don't you put your wallet in a purse?"

"Because I've got two hands."

"Don't you want a new wallet for your birthday?"

"This one works just fine."

"Aren't you tired of the Leaning Tower of Pisa?"

"When it falls over, you can buy me a new one."

I tried to wean Mama from haggling over the scraps. But the bargaining grew even more intense as the weeks went by. Mama insisted on leaving even earlier for the store to make sure Cugino didn't let anyone in before us. She stood outside the shop door, talking about him loudly as he stacked the bread.

"It's that cousin," she said. "He probably steals the scraps and gives them to his friends."

"Ssh," I said. "He does not."

"He's taking Ribalta for a ride, believe you me."

"He is not."

"One of these days he's going to clean out that fancy cash register and be long gone."

"He won't leave."

Mama snorted. "That would break somebody's heart."

"It would *not*."

She looked at me. Then she laughed. "Oh, so you're wild about him, too?"

My face felt warm. "Am *not*," I said. I looked down at the dirty sidewalk. The word *too* resounded disagreeably in my ears. "Who else likes him?"

Mama snorted. "Are you thick in the head?" She gestured with a limp wrist toward the store. "*Tutti frutti* in there," she said.

I bit my lip. *Tutti frutti* was a phrase my father used to describe that strange, grinning man in the sparkling cape who played the white grand piano on Sunday night TV. I couldn't believe that Ribalta—and Cugino—were of the same ilk as Liberace. But when Cugino came to the door and Mama pushed past him, I noticed he wore something gold and sparkling on his finger—Ribalta's ring.

I kept my eyes on Mama as she marched down the first aisle, her fingers tightly clasped around her wallet. I hated her. She had killed my dream of being with Cugino as neatly and cleanly as Ribalta chopped the head off a chicken. I'd get her back. My heart pounding, I waited while she made her selections. When she was through, Ribalta folded his arms over his belly.

"Any scraps today?" Mama asked.

"For the dog, eh?" Ribalta answered.

My blood raced. "We don't have a dog," I announced.

Mama gave me a murderous look. Ribalta opened his mouth and nothing came out. He swallowed. In a sad voice that showed his disappointment in me, he said, "I know that," before he disappeared through the swinging door.

The moment he was gone, Mama smacked me soundly on the back of the head with her wallet. "That'll teach you," she said. "I'll never take you here again."

I turned and walked halfway down the soup aisle. The black letters on the Campbell's cans blurred. I was crying. Mama had put me to shame. Cugino, fortunately, was nowhere in sight. I went out the front door and around to the side of the store. The yard behind the market was blocked off with a high wooden fence. I peered over the gate.

Through the back window of the shop, I could see into the room where Ribalta did the butchering. It was illuminated with long fluorescent tubes that gave off a bluish hue. A huge refrigerator—five doors long—lined one whole wall. Above the triple sink hung knives as long as swords, cleavers that looked like they would fell a tree, and an assortment of scissors to trim and snip the meat after it had been sliced and gutted. From metal hooks on the ceiling, slabs of meat hung like punching bags waiting for someone to pummel them. On a wire stretched across the room, plucked chickens dangled, long, skinny, and naked as Mama's bras hanging on the clothesline. Radio Italia was playing opera. Cugino moved around the room, then came out the back door carrying a bucket. He held it above his head as he came down the stairs. Then, from the back of the yard, trotted three lambs, their coats gray and covered with bits of grass. Their hooves sounded sharp on the frozen ground. They nuzzled up against Cugino's white apron, licking him and looking up at him with glassy, expectant eyes. Cugino waited until he had gotten to the center of the yard before he dumped the bucket. There, on the ground, lay beet stalks, shredded turnips, carrot and potato peels—and what little of Mama's coveted scraps that Cugino hadn't seen fit to put into a soup or stew. The lambs crowded in to feast on the mess.

Cugino looked up and saw me. He said something in Italian, broke it off, then beckoned. He came over and unlocked the gate to let me in.

Cugino gestured toward the lambs, then smacked his lips and rubbed his stomach. I screwed up my face to show I didn't understand him.

"*Per la Pasqua*," he said.

"Yes," I said. "Easter pets."

He smacked his lips and rubbed his stomach again, smiling. I noticed his teeth were crooked and his stomach was a little bit flabby. He looked like an actor in a silent movie trying to get a laugh. I wondered how I ever could have loved such an idiot.

"*Capisci, capisci?*" he asked. When I kept on staring at him, obviously not understanding what he was driving at, he grabbed one lamb by the fur on top of its head, held out one finger, brought it up to lamb's neck, and dragged it across, in the gesture of an executioner.

I took my hand away from the lamb I was petting. I couldn't decide who was more evil, Ribalta for butchering the lambs, or Cugino for telling me he was going to do it. Tears welled up in my eyes. Cugino looked confused. Then he reached out and took my hand. After all those weeks of dreaming he would touch me, his grasp felt tight and cold. I was about to pull away when Mama appeared at the gate, against the broad white backdrop of Ribalta's figure.

Mama tried to open the gate, then rattled it. She began to sputter incoherently. *What was this? Crazy nut! Drop her hand! Disgraceful! My daughter! He'd go to hell for this! Sick turkey!*

Ribalta's fat seemed to quiver as he gestured at Mama. "Calm down," he said, reaching over her to fumble with the lock. "Please be calm, Signora."

Mama made a fist and shouted something evil-sounding in Italian. Cugino dropped both the bucket and my hand and raised his fists at Mama. When Ribalta finally popped open the gate, she marched in and dragged me out of the yard. "Family business!" she said to Ribalta as she pulled me down the sidewalk. "More like *funny* business you've got going on here. And you'll pay for it, just you wait and see."

On Easter, I refused to come down to dinner. I lay on my bed, trying to recapture the feeling of being in love. I tried to melt into a dreamy state, to smell the meadow and hear the waves. But it was useless. I couldn't get it back, no matter how hard I tried. I had lost Cugino, the same as Ribalta.

For Cugino was gone. They said Ribalta stuffed his pockets full of money and sent him packing. The butcher had his business to think of. Mama talked loud and word spread fast that something just a little bit fishy was going on over at that meat market, and never you mind what, although you could take a guess.

Knowing she wouldn't meet up with Cugino at the market ever again, Mama returned to Ribalta's on Holy Saturday and acted as if nothing had happened. She came back with a boxful of packages and reported, with satisfaction, that a very nice older woman—perhaps a relative of Signora's—sat behind the counter. She was quite pleasant and spoke good English, too.

As I lay on my bed, trying to block out the squeak of knives scraping against the plates, I heard Mama telling my aunts, for the umpteenth time, how she had bargained Ribalta rock-bottom low on the lamb. It was such a good deal she even bought some mint jelly. Why not? Life was short. "Try it," she urged them. "I got it on special. Delicious."

∽

The Origins of Milk
Daniela Gioseffi

Mushrooms grow in my thighs
to spite the frenzy I've offered as love.
Faces explode my albums
with sighs that shatter gravestones.
Torn up for confetti, I'm showered
on the celebration winding in the streets below.
Another man is elected to rule the flow of milk.
I look for my mother copulating among sheep
in a dream field. A haze floats in over my head,
a long cold shore of sand.

I ask a genie waiting to be born
in blue smoke from my navel if
she has heard my magic words and knows
I, too, wish to see beyond the lamp.

All the telephone booths are out of order
in the soup of the city. Strange voices,
shells from unknown seas sound in my ears.
Stray dogs wander in gutters, nipping
at my toes. Abandoned children sit on curbs.
Panhandlers replace clowns on every corner.
They do not smile or dance, but simply ask
for money to be dropped in empty cups.
I ponder coins, weather maps, rubber stamps, newsprint,
white bread, false hair, plutonium.
Stranded in a society of abstracted men,
I am made of primal customs practiced in varied tongues.
I gather water, try to chat with you amidst flower-boxes.
Fumes clog my throat; machines follow me down the street,
grinding gears against flesh. Grey dials turn. I try
to call you whom I met by the accuracy of chance.
The telephone receiver is gone.

It's stuck to my mouth. My eyes
are dimes caught in my hair.

Blood I left on your sheets
came from moons of change hidden in my belly.
When we part, are you still there, are we
lovers as we were?
Curdling time gives us up to decisions.
Kettles whistle for morning coffee
and we mourn our dreams. I want
to bottle wind, drink it for cola. Instead,
I lose you among strange hands, open mouths,
wiggling buttocks, umbrellas.
I would have been what you were searching for
with sheer will, if you could decide
what sleeper you resemble and which of your dreams
struggles behind your eyelids.

I hardly bear the hollow music of a tubular life.
Birds in my inner ear batter wings to get out.
I have no names to call them to open windows.
The artful lover lacks artless feeling.
I knew when you touched me where your thoughts were.
I can't be fooled into orgasm, but I can pretend.
Into my chest, I follow birds, trying to sing
proper notes to the moon, mirroring the sun,
to the darkness in me, nothing without your light.

Perhaps the finest language is silence in its glory.
I long to be an apple tree standing in your garden.

೧

Cracked

Loryn Lipari

I grab the handles on the sink, turn them on; the water here at home feels softer, warmer. It looks clearer as it slides off the top of my hands and trickles in between my long, skinny fingers. My cuticles are puffy with redness. They glow under the heat of the water. I've been biting them since I was a kid. Whenever I watched television, read a book, went to school, took a drive, tried to lie, I always had my fingers in my mouth. I would look for the dangling piece of skin and trap it between my front teeth, pull it away from my finger, and nibble on it. I have spent the last twenty-eight days in East Strousburg, Pennsylvania, trying to get rid of a drug and alcohol problem. Gnawing on my fingers is all I have left.

Once upon a time, not so long ago, January 28, 1965, around 8:18 A.M., I am born. About nine months before this date, Vinny and Ginny were drunk, and were tumbling off some couch somewhere, maybe in North Bergen, or Teaneck, New Jersey. Vinny was from North Bergen and Ginny says she's from Teaneck. Not that it mattered anymore, where they were from, just that they were together and building a family. Ginny is German and Vinny is Italian. Ginny is Protestant and Vinny calls himself a Catholic. Ginny puts those things aside and becomes whatever it is that makes Vinny happy. Whatever happy is. Ginny meets Vinny's family. Ginny cooks their foods. Ginny and Vinny create me.

Twenty-nine years later, my reflection catches me unguarded in the mirrored medicine cabinet above the sink. My face is drawn. Still. My cheekbones jut out of my face as the skin stretches across the bones. My eyes sink into their sockets with deep, dark circles around them; my skin is a bloodless gray mixed with yellow, no longer the olive complexion I inherited from my father. I gained only one pound in rehab. Not because I didn't eat. I did. I just didn't gain any weight. My metabolism is very high. The nurse marked the chart just before they released me with some remark on an eating disorder. I didn't think I had an eating disorder. I just didn't know how to eat. I forget to eat.

Chinese food used to make me sick. I still can't eat it. In a feeble attempt to nourish myself, I would order Chinese takeout, some numbered dinner combo that came with pork fried rice and an egg roll. I'd do this on Fridays, after work, my paycheck feeling heavy inside my pocket, order General Tso's chicken. (Who is General Tso?) Is this the food they eat in China? If I went to Sicily, could I ask for those little potato things Nanny used to make on Sundays with leftover mashed potatoes or those bite-sized meatballs she served at room temperature? In Italy, do they have carts like the ones in Central Park or at San Gennaro's Feast that sell sausage and peppers? I know nothing about people in other countries, or about my own family, even less about me. I do know that I am twenty-nine years old and thought I'd be dead at thirty, that I made attempts to eat before I smoked crack, and that I wasn't much of a cook.

Vinny and Ginny are both on the couch, next to the kitchen. The recipe to make me is unclear—they are both guessing. They know the basic ingredients are: two cups him, to maybe one cup her, and that's all they know. The rest, they think, must be in the baking.

The intercom from the lobby below buzzes by my front door. It is the delivery man with my dinner. At the door, I grab the brown paper bag (the receipt stapled to the top, greasy on the bottom), and pay the guy a dollar over the amount of the check. I open the bag on the cherry wood dining room table. The beige tablecloth is not open to its full size; it rests in an uneven folded rectangle between two silver candlesticks. The table is hardly used, more a mass that fills the room, but it is the only table in the apartment and serves its purpose on nights like tonight.

I slide onto the beige cushioned chair, pulling it closer to the table. My body leans forward, hunched over, not touching the high back of the chair. I drag my fingers along the edge of the aluminum tray and free the plastic cover. I fill my fork with rice and shuffle around the oversized pieces of chicken souped together in a thick orange sauce. Cat. It's not chicken. It's cat meat. I'm not sure if that's why I never eat much of my Chinese takeout. I never made a dent in anything I ate, cat or otherwise.

The Chinese food ends up on the kitchen counter. Maybe later that night, inside the refrigerator. Maybe a week later in the garbage.

Vinny and Ginny left me raw. A recipe gone bad, somewhere an ingredient was left out, the original recipe altered, changed, lost in the move.

Me

1 Serving

Combine:
1 big part Vinny
to
Some parts Ginny
*Cooking instructions may alter

Crack made me rise. It processed through my body the way food is broken down and digested, except the order was changed. My bowels emptied before it entered me. My desire for it grew with every foiled package that I stretched and smoothed out, inspecting it for more. It didn't fill me up like Nanny's Sunday meals. Antipasto, olives, Italian bread, the potato things, meatballs, anchovies, pastina soup. That wasn't even the main course and I was full, stomach bulging over jeans, breathing slowed down. I'd sit at her dining room table and unbutton the top button of my blue jeans. I was far from overweight: sixty pounds. I wasn't tall, not even four feet at the time. It didn't take much food to feed me. I would spend most of the time detaching my forearms from the clear, plastic tablecloth, shifting in my folding chair, waiting to go home.

The more crack I smoked, the more I wanted. No leftovers, no getting up from the table before dinner ends, no pushing away the plates or asking to be excused, no crumbs left in this piece of foil. On my hands and knees, I frantically search for more. I smoke dust particles that I grab from the carpet, pieces of things that collected themselves at the indentation of the bed's legs. Crack that perhaps slipped or fell from the vial, the package, the pipe, the stem. I would mistake lint, salt from a pretzel, a fingernail, probably even a cuticle, for crack. I'd mix it with ashes and try to smoke it.

After smoking for hours, I would dry heave over the toilet, stretched out on the cool bathroom floor with my arms wrapped around the rounded, smoothed edge of the bowl. When I puke, it is like a contraption attached to my toes with two rollers and a crank. Every time the handle turns the rollers squeeze and push their way up my body. I become a tube of toothpaste with nothing left inside. My mouth is corked, closed, and the pressure collects inside my body, two inches below and behind my belly button. The crank shifts position and the air pushes higher into my chest bubbling like a volcano's lava inside my throat. It enters my head, behind my eyes, blinding me. A jerk reaction forces my mouth to open. The few bites of Chinese food dislodge grain by grain, by now mostly stomach acid. Despair strains the muscles in my lower back unlike any puking that had substance to it could. My body convulses, trembling at my fingertips, bouncing off the hollowness of my empty stomach like a house cat outside in a snowstorm, balling itself inside a damp corner, attempting to stay warm. On the floor, I warn anyone smoking my crack to save some for me. After, when I wipe my mouth, catch my breath, I blame the Chinese food. As I take another hit of crack, mix it with the bile on my tongue, I swear never to eat Chinese food again.

I looked for crack. I waited for crack. I sacrificed everything to digest crack. It was my missing ingredient. I started making my own cookbook, variations on recipes for crack. Nothing Vinny or Ginny could ever imagine making.

An empty Methadone bottle with foil wrapped around its top sits on the aluminum heating/air conditioning unit in my room, just below the Manhattan skyline. A rubber band coils around the screw top, holding the foil tightly to the bottle. I use a straight pin to puncture holes through the foil. The same pins my grandmother used to hold patterns together for my aunt's clothes. My fingertips are clean, for now. My thumb and index finger are not the dirty, blackened tips they usually are when I'm smoking crack. I twist a flat-head screwdriver against the side of the bottle until it breaks through the plastic, peeling away the shavings like a coconut shell. Slice a straw down to the size of an uncooked ziti and insert it into the hole on the side of the bottle. Scoop the ashes up with the hollowed filter of a Parliament cigarette and mix, like a Caesar salad, the ashes with chunks of crack on the top of the foil. Cook it with the flame of a fifty-cent lighter, a fluorescent, clear, purple, plastic device. Its flame, uneven and high, jets up towards the bangs of my hair. My thumb is dirty from ashes and callused from sliding it over and over again against the silver sphere that ignites a spark. I inhale deeply.

Where do I get the instructions for preparation, the measurements of crack to ashes, the cooking procedures that make sure I get a good hit? Not in my great-grandmother's collection of recipes, in between pizza dough and butter cookies. Her daughter, my grandmother, Nanny, didn't write down for me, in her slanted script on loose-leaf paper with the corner torn off, olive oil stains at the bottom, with instructions to knead, the number of handfuls of crack to use.

Crack

Preheat mental state to 450°
Prepare pipe for smoking Crack (see pg. 136,
	"Pipe Making Techniques")

Combine:
	2 to 3 Parliament filter-sized scoops of cigarette ashes (preferably whole)
	2 or 3 small rocks of Crack/Cocaine
	(May have to break down by hand)
Heat:
	Using a lighter for best results
Inhale slowly
Repeat as needed
*Hint: re-use foil package

Ginny stays and Vinny leaves. Ginny leaves and Vinny comes back. Neither one leave an impression me.

I cup my hands and allow the water to collect in my palms. My hands are small and smooth on the inside. They don't look like they've been worked much, but they have. The index finger of my right hand is bent. The second joint is bloated and painful. It was built up to be this shape, like biceps or a calf that's been worked, pumped every day by a Nautilus machine, except my machine was not in a gym and the joint is not a muscle. Instead, it is an arthritic mass caused by repetition. Twelve-inch scissors rested heavily in this hand for over ten years. Made from steel with black painted handles, these scissors were the tool of the embroidery industry, the bread and butter of my family. Every day I would slide my index finger and thumb into the oval handle that I padded with embroidery scraps. So many years of sliding (it is an art to slide the blade) across a 45-inch-wide, 15-yard-long piece of embroidery, my index finger cramped and swelled at the second joint. It stiffened from repetitive movements. Sometimes I had to cut hundreds of these pieces in a day.

I work with Vinny. I drink with Ginny.

It's three o'clock and I have some crack in my pocket. I know that if I smoke it at work I'm going to regret it, but it's not that easy to rationalize. The "afters" don't really exist. Desperation steals all logic and I smoke the crack.

Nanny is in the kitchen. A counter separates the dining room from the kitchen. It's not very big, so everyone stays away from her cooking space. I make my way in the hopes of getting a black olive or two. The bowl is resting on the counter next to the stove, by the empty can with its lid still up, ragged edges where the can opener chewed itself through the edge. As her aged hands cup a few of these, Nanny warns me that if I eat too many olives, I will get a fever. I like the thought of something so small and tasteless having so much power. Picture this: Black olives can give you a fever. I eat the olives.

Nanny dies of cancer.

I open the bottom right-hand drawer of my desk. A few empty hanging folders cover the bottom. The folders shift and tangle themselves with the metal hooks as I feel toward the back of the drawer for an empty soda can. I'm careful not to grab the can in the middle, using my thumb and forefinger to find the opening one drinks from. The center of the can is pushed in on one side. Pin-sized holes are punctured at the base of the indentation. Old ashes and resin stiffen around the inside of the holes. I stand at my desk and slide the can into the front pocket of my jeans. It slides in with ease, bulging against the fabric. I pull my sweatshirt down over my waist, covering most of the bulge, and make my way into the bathroom.

The sun cuts through the window and onto the pink, white, and beige tiled floor. I glance at all four stalls and choose the last one, by the window. I push the window open and am startled by the brightness of the afternoon, the alley in between our building and our neighbors, the noises of the birds that draw me outside. Clumsily, I pull the can out of my pocket, place it on the ledge inside the stall. I need to smoke a cigarette to get fresh ashes. I flick some ashes into the indentation, but they are carried by the breeze and fall on the radiator's ledge. When I try to pick them up, they charcoal into the flat, pink paint and onto my fingertips. The next time, I am more careful and the ashes land in the center. I slowly press them down and spread them over the holes. I sprinkle a few rocks on top. Carefully balancing the can with one hand, I search for the lighter with the other. Just for a moment, right before I light it, my body weakens. It shivers and my bowels cry softly.

"Variations," "Other Techniques." The substitutions that are passed on from lack of a) utensils, b) ingredients, c) time, d) a better recipe.

It's ten o'clock and my father calls me into his office. He nibbles on a buttered roll and sips from a blue paper coffee cup. His desk is dusty. He sweeps the crumbs and the lint away with a dustbroom made of straw. The specks fly in the air around us.

"Uuuh . . . aaah." My father could never get to the point without a series of *uuuhs* and *aaahs,* as if I am supposed to know what he is trying to say. Like it is easier for me to say it than him.

"Don't forget, you got a doctor's appointment today. Uuuh. Here's da form for the dee insurance company. You bring dis wit ya when you go."

The form is from his old insurance company. The doctor I'm going to see is my father's private physician, but I take the form, nod, collect my coat and go to my car. Did I drive that day? Make any stops? Smoke crack? Drink? Go home? Visit friends? I know for sure I didn't go to my father's doctor's office. He wasn't changing insurance companies. There was no physical I needed to go to. The blood tests were for drugs. My family wanted to know what it was that sucked the color from my face, the brightness of my eyes, and the flesh from my bones.

Vinny is scared for me. Ginny is scared, too. They try all the old ways first. They throw me against the wall to see if I will stick, to see if I am ready. When they find me soggy on the kitchen floor they are forced to abandon the old recipes and look for new ones.

When I come back to the shop, hours later, I walk across the parquet floor, around the machines, and straight to the tables in the back and start to work. My father comes to the back and I pretend not to notice him. The scissors slide across the fabric. I grab the cut end and flip it into the box of garbage next to me.

"Uuuh . . . aaah . . . ummm, so, what'd he say? Anything?"

I stop for a moment and look into the distance as if I am taken by some deep thought, a revelation. I look my father straight in the eye and say, "Yeah, Dad. The doctor told me I have three months to live. I should be dead by June."

I return, mechanically, to my work and leave him, my father, there. Alone.

I turn the water off and shake my hands. I grab for the towel and dry them off.

Original Recipe

1 Full Serving

Combine:
One full cup Loryn (sifted)
A dash of Vinny
A dash of Ginny
Add:
2 tablespoons Faith
1 tablespoon Wisdom

*No pre-heating necessary
*Knead gently by hand
*Artificial ingredients not recommended

∾

Broke

Rosette Capotorto

when you're so broke that
    they've turned
    off
    your phone
and in the kitchen
    cupboard   is
a can of corn and some
kinda pasta you don't remember buying
and in the freezer a plastic container
marked stock 95 and your
kids' icicle experiment
            and
    one already-been-cooked
    steak bone

and you don't cry
you don't scream
don't rant rave buck
  stomp snort or crack

you hold a strange blue calm inside

then
    you have reached
        the   eye
                        of the storm

you tell yourself change is good
change is god the godhead

and though your shoulders could
give you away
hunched up tight as a soldier's
someone   would have to
touch
     you
  to know that

and because you are in the
eye of the storm
you can
write this poem
  instead of slitting your wrists
    jumping from the bridge
       into cold cold water
and you recall the saying
  in Sicilian
    one mother can take care of a hundred children
    but a hundred children cannot take care of one mother
and you laugh
grimly
as you call up your strength
the way your great grandmother
must have laughed
as her children
      departed for America
          because she had only dirt to feed them

and she never saw them
again
         her children

and a friend died
  three weeks ago
and she was your age &
it could be you   and
her daughter is eighteen
  and yours is only seven

but you are in the eye of the storm
and you did cry as your friend's
ashes were scattered in the
        churchyard
        and those few tears you
                cherish
because your tears   like
perfect sunsets   are seen
        rarely

and then
        only at the edge

                    of the world
    at the edge

Part Four

❧

ENCOUNTERS

Other People's Food

Pamela E. Barnett

Mama Zarifa starts a lipstick passing among her many daughters, including me, her *binti Amerikia*. My husband, Andrew, is taking photos, recording a May 1994 visit with the Hourani family, who live in the Palestinian refugee camp Qualandia, which lies minutes northeast of Jerusalem. We are on the concrete patio, underneath a slatted roof of grapevines. In one photo, eight girls and women with olive skin and hair dark as Turkish coffee smile. I nestle into the picture inconspicuously; I could be a sister.

Indeed, many Palestinians suspect I am kin. Though Andrew, an anthropologist, speaks Arabic, Palestinians address their comments to me. I am a graduate student in English, finishing a dissertation abroad rather than learning this language. Yet, despite my stilted conversation and his fluency, Palestinians still look into my eyes to ask their questions. They tell me my face is familiar; they have seen it before. Maybe I have a family name that they know? "Tarrifi" is easily placed in Ramallah; "Algibrini" is as easily placed in Hebron. To illustrate: my friend Maha collects traditional Palestinian embroidery, mostly ceremonial dresses. Each village has its own specific pattern and design—Bethlehem's purple cloth dress with its detailed breastplate is the most elaborate—and Maha aims to have a good representation of each village's art in her collection. One particularly fine wedding pillow is, unusually, signed. Maha went to the village outside Hebron where this pattern and family name exist and immediately found the granddaughter of the artist. The name and the art are not personal. Generations of women with the same last name make, over and over, the bands of color and geometric shapes that indicate who they are and where they came from. This tapestry of connection has deep meaning here and Palestinians generously try to stitch me into it.

When Palestinians ask the inevitable question about my ethnicity, I tell them only that I am Italian American. I tell them I look like my grandmother Lillian Murillo, whose parents were born on the Italian island of Capri. They smile, gesture broadly, and say, "The Italians and the Greeks are the Arabs of Europe!" The women hug me; the men nod. My face is familiar, they say, because I share their "Mediterranean blood."

But I do not look like Lillian, who dyed her dark hair blonde and protected her skin from the sun lest she look like an "Italian peasant." Rather, the extended family has long marveled at how closely I resemble my Jewish grandmother, Rosalyn.

I do not say this in the Palestinian homes I visit, certainly not in Qalandia, where nearly every male over age sixteen has been imprisoned at least once for offenses like burning tires, throwing stones, or writing anti-Israeli graffiti on the refugee camp walls. I do not say this in Qualandia, where sad old men still carry, in their pockets, the keys to their homes in Ramle.

When I visit Zarifa's sister Salwa in Hebron a week later, I drink thimble-cups of coffee laced with cardamom and eat from endless trays filled with watermelon, cucumbers, and *kofta* meatballs. We are comfortable together, cracking salted seeds between our teeth and talking about green cards, when Salwa's husband arrives home. He looks at my Western dress, so rarely seen in Hebron, without smiling, and neglects the comfortable exchange of greetings. His wife and daughter-in-law look at each other, embarrassed, as he brusquely asks if I speak Hebrew. Only three months before this visit a Jewish settler named Baruch Goldstein heard the muezzin call to prayer and walked to the Hebron mosque, where he murdered twenty-nine men kneeling on prayer rugs, twenty-nine men who died barefoot, their dusty shoes left at the door.

I feel a cool flash of sweat under my unfamiliar, exceedingly modest clothes, and for once, I am afraid: "No, I'm American." Knowing that I could pass for an Israeli, I add, "My family came from Italy."

This is the first and only time, during my thirteen-month stay, that I have felt uncomfortable in a Palestinian home, and the only time a Palestinian betrayed a discomfort with me. I have been in countless Palestinian homes, and in each I was hugged and kissed and stuffed with food, always the best on the table. Mama Zarifa would yank the most succulent parts off the chicken in the table's center and hand them to me. Noticing my tentativeness with a condiment called *zatar,* a mixture of ground thyme, salt, and sesame seeds, another hostess put a hunk of pita bread in my hand, took my wrist, and led me through a generous dip, first in olive oil, then in the spice. Palestinians eat intimately, dipping bread into shared bowls of *hummus* and *ful* and tomato salad dressed with lemon and mint. One common dish, *makluba,* consists of saffron rice and chicken cooked in a round baking dish, often as large as two feet in diameter. *Makluba* translates roughly as "upside down," and when it is ready, the baking dish is covered with a huge platter and then flipped to create a spilled mountain of rice and chicken. It is spectacular, brought to a table where everyone claps at this lovely everyday accomplishment. To eat it, you lean in with the others, grabbing the meat you want, then pressing handfuls of rice into small grain sausages. I had to collapse my own boundaries at Palestinian tables. I took food from people's hands; sometimes, like a bird, I opened my mouth for food that someone wanted to feed me.

Such physical intimacy with eating was unfamiliar to me. And yet, I was struck by how easy it was to engage in these social scripts, how familiar their way of being together was. The clatter and din of eating with working-class Palestinian families reminded me of the Barnett side of my own family.

Children circle our family table, climbing into different laps; we reach across each other to grab bowls of things we want to eat; we talk loud and use our hands. Like my Aunt Gale, Palestinians coached me in the kinship relations, making sure that I understood that Lucy was Zarifa's daughter and Liana's sister and Maha's mother. But this familiarity can't be because I am an Italian "Arab of Europe." Indeed, I have little idea what it means to be Italian or Italian American because my grandmother Lillian spent much of her life consolidating her identity as a WASP, bleaching even her eyebrows and affecting an upper-class Boston accent. If I learned how to be "Mediterranean," I learned it from Ashkenazi Jews.

Though my paternal grandparents' families are from Austria and Romania, Herman and Rosalyn Barnett often playfully claim to be "Italian Jews." This identification begins on the block in Brooklyn where my grandfather grew up surrounded by mostly Jewish and Italian neighbors. His Jewish and Italian friends learned how to box by beating each other up; they swam naked in the East River; they ate dinner at each other's tables. The neighborhood adults shared similarly. My great-grandmother would make gefilte fish on Friday and exchange some of it for Mrs. Battistone's Friday dish of baked oysters in garlic. Grandpa was always proud to be Jewish, but he incorporated something of his Italian friends as he ate what they ate. When he claims to be an "Italian Jew," it is a joke that bespeaks his love for the friends and neighbors he grew up with. It is a name that represents some of his earliest identifications, his sense of belonging when he was in other people's homes.

With my grandmother's help, he reproduces the tables he has known. "Italian Jews" get the best of both worlds. Grandma makes us *matzo brei* for breakfast and Grandpa makes us *zuppa di pesce* for dinner. For Thanksgiving, we eat platters of eggplant parmesan, spaghetti in clam sauce, veal marsala. (As Uncle Harry puts it, "Why eat a boring meal just because everyone else in America is?") When the expressions of astonishment start rolling in, someone says the food is so fabulous because we're "Italian Jews." With an anthropologist's curiosity, Andrew asks what they mean by these idiosyncratic ethnic claims. The evidence accumulates: Grandpa only drinks espresso and one of his favorite stories is of publicly savoring, with grunts of pleasure and kissed fingertips, pasta in black squid ink in a Sicilian restaurant where they warned him, an American, against this local dish. We love Italian food, but the identification has more substance than that, albeit that substance is culled from a host of Italian stereotypes. We are Italian Jews because we laugh loud and eat too much, because we sing at the dinner table. Grandma and Grandpa are "practically from the motherland" because they love nothing more than having all of their children, grandchildren, and great-grandchildren in their home at one time. They assure

Andrew that he can be an honorary Italian Jew because, like all Barnetts, he is always "either starving or stuffed"!

I spent a year denying my Jewishness on the West Bank, and yet it was understanding the cultural codes and, more significantly, cultural fantasies, of my Jewish family that enabled me to so successfully "pass" as Italian American.

My grandmother Lillian grew up in Darien, Connecticut. Her parents, Antoinette and Frederick Murillo, owned a grocery that supported the family with five children, but not especially well. As a young child, my grandmother would make money by pulling patron's groceries home in her red toy wagon. One day, she pulled home groceries for a childless, aristocratic white woman who then made a routine of meeting her at the store and then inviting her in for lemonade after the groceries were put away. She invited Lillian to help her around the house and then increasingly kept her there to have her company and mother her. This is the story that defined my grandmother's life, a story about a lifelong identification with a woman who was everything she was not. Lillian entered that woman's home—first as servant, then as guest, then as substitute daughter—and she learned how to "pass" as this woman by cleaning the way she cleaned, grooming her body in her image, eating the food that she ate.

Anytime my grandmother weighed in on a matter of taste, she invoked the woman she knew as a child, "a wealthy professor's wife" who "always knew the best in everything." I don't know this woman's name, but I am linked to her by a host of rituals for living. I learned her lessons: "fold towels in thirds, not halves," "rub glycerine and rosewater into your feet and elbows every night if you want to be beautiful," "scrape every bit of brown skin off a potato."

But if I am linked to this woman, it is by a thin string of imagination, because Grandma did not share her memory with me. It is a story in which my grandmother was vulnerable, and she only told it to my Aunt Cynthia the night before her surgery for the colon cancer that would kill her six months later. This woman actually wanted to adopt Grandma. One evening, accompanied by her husband, she went to the house adjacent to Murillo's grocery and asked my great-grandmother Antoinette to give her a daughter. Antoinette accepted the value in what was offered— piano and ballet lessons, summer at the Cape, private school—but she argued that the oldest daughter must leave the family first, whether it be for marriage or for such unusual circumstances as these. She offered Barbara, who was just as pretty and smart. The woman did not know Barbara. She was shocked that a mother would substitute one child for another. She wondered what kind of people could debase a loving request to this sort of transaction. The woman abandoned my grandmother to the Murillo clan. Lillian was called "dago" by children who had nicer clothes than she wore.

Lillian was embarrassed by her parents' accents. She grieved over never entering the professor's beautiful, and familiar, house again.

I think now that Grandma must have pinned on Barbara every lost night sleeping under those perfectly laundered sheets. She consistently expressed absolute contempt for her sister. I still feel guilty that it was Barbara who pureed Grandma's food in those last months, Barbara who changed her colostomy bag and who, on that very last night, rocked my grandmother's rattling body. My grandmother was incoherent and weak and could not protest. But when Barbara tearfully, and with gratitude, told me the story of that last embrace, I winced, imagining my grandmother's rage. She did not want to be held—not by anyone, and certainly not by the sister whose very existence meant she never became the rich, white daughter of a woman who smelled like roses.

My grandmother never again wanted anything over which she couldn't have complete control. Not even relief from pain. Her hospice nurse told me that though she wanted to alleviate her suffering, Grandma refused pain medication. The nurse said she was traumatized by my grandmother's agony and needed her supervisor to counsel her through the process of letting Grandma have the control that she wanted more than the relief. When the couch that she died on was moved, a revolver was found underneath it. Cynthia speculates that Lillian meant to kill Barbara; I know that my grandmother wanted the power to die if she decided to.

The control my grandmother had over her dying was consistent with the way she lived her life. She always did what she wanted to do, regardless of the impact on others. When she wanted to spend the summer alone with her second husband, she threatened her four-year-old stepchild into lying about her age so she could attend sleep-away summer camp. If Grandma wanted to move—and she did, frequently, traversing the entire country—she moved. If my grandfather didn't want to move, she packed up the house anyway. (He would eventually follow, even though she would often return him to the previous state of residence within two years.) She had an amazing capacity to bend others to her will. A mechanic who knew the problem wasn't in her car's radiator would capitulate and painstakingly examine the radiator. A pharmacist would give her penicillin without a prescription. Certainly I could not resist her: I let her send my food back to restaurant kitchens even though I thought it tasted good; on shopping trips, I tried on pleated pants that I knew would make me look fat.

Of all the things Grandma bent to her will, her erasure of her Italian American identity was the most thorough. It was accomplished against rather substantial odds. After an early marriage to a boy from a "better family," she worked as a housekeeper, then as a cocktail waitress in the fancy hotel bars where she served the people she wanted to be. She would not tell about her own classic immigrant struggle—working-class jobs, saving money, buying a

duplex in Boston and renting out the other side, buying more rental proper-
ties. She would not speak of those years, but she was an ardent proponent of
the American Dream. Anyone could do anything if they put their minds to it,
if they were willing to work hard, to sacrifice. Some people display themselves
as evidence. But my grandmother's dream was not to "pass" as a WASP, but to
have been born a WASP. She understood that all the capital in the world could
not buy her the symbolic capital of the right birth. So she advocated the
American Dream for the unfortunate and obscured her own origins.

My grandmother spent her life becoming the woman who almost adopted
her. She bought St. John's knits; she traveled to England and France, but never
Spain or Italy. When I studied Italian in college and asked her to practice with
me, she denied memory of the language and advised me to learn French
instead. Grandma remembered, in detail, anything she learned about a person
from a "good family" (even if she met the person on an airplane), and repeated
their stories for years as evidence of her intimacy with people who went to
Andover, people who had weekend houses at the Cape or who auctioned their
parents' estates at Christies. She cooked pot roast; her marinara sauce came
from a jar. She liked to go to Italian restaurants, but as a tourist enjoying "eth-
nic" food. I only learned that she was Italian American as a teenager when she
betrayed pride in some uncles who, the story goes, started the first Italian
American newspaper in New Haven. I asked her in the last year of her life
whether she experienced discrimination when she was young and she asked
me, utterly confused, "What are you talking about?"

She never spoke of those years growing up at the grocery with Antoinette and
Frederick; she gave me a contained genealogy, one that began with her and ended
with me. Only as I write this do I understand something that governed our entire
relationship. She loved me so much that she was going to turn me into that aris-
tocratic white woman's daughter. Whereas my brown skin was cute as a child, as
a teenager she tried to literally bleach me out. She would take me into the bath-
room and try to pumice the dark skin off my elbows and knees. She bought me
cases of Jolen cream bleach so that I could keep my fuzzy brown upper lip fuzzy
and blonde. She advised that I would have to "go blonde" in my forties as "all rich
women do." She advised me against sunbathing. How could I be accepted by
society if I looked like an Indian! Like a black! Didn't I know that dark skin was
the skin of peasants who worked in the fields? Now that I was growing up, near-
ing college and courtship, I had to protect my skin, especially my face. The debu-
tantes in *Town and Country* magazine were summoned as evidence: their skin
did not contrast dramatically with their white dresses. I also needed a new, less
prominent nose, and got one two weeks after I turned sixteen.

My grandmother bought me the things that the professor's wife had wanted to
give her, and in the process of transforming me, she performed her own fantasy

of self. She insisted that I have cardigans in every color available at Brooks Brothers; she sent me to Europe for the summer; she went into a debt she never came out of to send me to Barnard College. From here, I see these as acts of loving generosity, but also of self-abnegation.

One of the stultifying things about Lillian's identification with the professor's wife was her relationship to eating. In all the years we ate out in New York City, we ate only at Gallagher's steak house, and we ate only filet mignon. Grandma insisted there weren't any other good restaurants in town. She knew the play she was in when she went there and paid thirty-five dollars for a steak with some creamed spinach on the side. Rather than being liberated by eating other people's food, Grandma was afraid to actually taste her food. Who knows what she really liked to eat?

This is an astonishing thing to realize, because we talked about food *incessantly*. I would often hold the phone receiver away from my head while she made, yet again, lists of the things I should eat to be healthy and beautiful: grapefruit for breakfast, fresh fruit cup and cottage cheese for lunch. I should have a little piece of steak. Go light on the bread. Go light on the butter. A little pat on the broccoli wouldn't kill me. We talked a few times a week, and she routinely asked me to list everything I'd consumed in a day. Of course, I never learned. "Beans and rice? Guatemalan peasant food!" "You need to have meat. If you don't get that blood in you, you become weak and sickly." She was convinced that I was a vegetarian because I didn't have the money for lamb chops. When I got my first apartment after college, she would visit me with a cooler of filets and stuff my refrigerator before taking me shopping.

She dressed me correctly, fed me correctly, oriented me toward worthy goals. When Grandma encouraged me to become a professor and "write books," I felt that she was recognizing something in me; and indeed, this career choice seems like a "calling," and essentially my own. Yet, I can see, as I tell this story, that I became what she wanted me to become. She remembered the professor she knew as a child, and as a young woman she worked briefly as a housekeeper for the American literary critic Van Wyck Brooks. These professors' homes were the most sophisticated she had ever seen. These professors' families traveled and had rooms designated as libraries and they sometimes conversed in foreign languages. The professor's wife always lingered in her psyche as the good mother she was meant to have. The professor's home was one where desires were satisfied, where children born in the wrong home to the wrong parents could finally become who they were meant to be.

In the Palestinian village of Kobar, Hanan wraps my head in a scarf, takes my hand and introduces me throughout the village as *okti,* "my sister." She insists that we are related: what runs through our veins gives us dark eyes; it makes us good cooks and dancers; it makes us smile easily. Hanan explains that the blood also accounts for my dead-on reproduction of her accent as I speak Arabic words. It tells her why I eat everything she puts before me with such pleasure. She speculates that she is feeding me familiar things, the food my grandmother made for me as a child. But I know that Lillian would shrink from Hanan's newly plucked, succulent pigeons and her thickly spiced lentil stews. Grandma would deny any capillary that linked her to these dark people living among olive trees.

And I wonder what Hanan would see in my face if I were to tell her I am Jewish. The idea of "Mediterranean blood" helps Palestinians express their feelings of fondness and connection to me. But it is also an idea that could be used to explain what is alien about me or anyone else: "You are not one of us." Blood is culture's most dangerous fiction. Belief in "blood" naturalizes our socially instantiated differences into insurmountable barriers. It has, historically, buttressed genocide.

As I let Hanan place the spicy *kofta* on my tongue, I am sure that this intimacy could not withstand a confession. But this is not the world I want to live in. I want to tell Hanan I am Jewish, and yet also an *okht.* I want her to believe me in a place where there are no words yet for this kind of kinship.

When I eat other people's food, I metaphorically collapse boundaries. I have done this before: opened myself up to others, identified with new families, repudiated the tenaciously policed identities that keep us from one another. I am a "white" professor of African American studies, a Jew who feels kinship with Palestinians, a Jew who was raised by Christians and whose four siblings identify as such, a straight faculty advisor for my university's bisexual, gay, and lesbian association. This is the world I want to live in: a world where we acknowledge our differences *and* affirm our human and glorious capacity to understand and love across these boundaries. As a child I was told that my Romanian great-grandmother was a Romany gypsy, and while this is an unlikely story, it is the one I like best. If I've inherited anything, it is a story that tells me that I, too, will go anywhere, that we've already been in spaces that weren't strictly our own. That those spaces became ours when we sat down at the table, took what was offered, and passed on our own bowls brimming with what we knew how to give.

❧

What I Ate Where

Diane di Prima

the first i remember to tell of was the food on east fifth street. all kinds of food on east fifth street but the kind i'm remembering now to tell of we called menstrual pudding. it wasn't so bad really, was merely potatoes in tomato sauce and that's all no spices even and no no meat. but to pretend there was meat and that we were eating stew we put the tomato sauce. the potatoes were just potatoes which are ok if you like potatoes. some people i notice are crazy about potatoes. i'm not and never was, i can't say menstrual pudding turned me against them, i just plain never liked them to start with. not mashed not homefries not even bakedidahowithbutter.

how come we called it that was this cat jack who was staying there at the time, he had that kind of mind, i mean he called things things like menstrual pudding. we ate it for three or four days as I remember, i was going to say for breakfast lunch and supper, but that wouldn't be true because we just gave up on those three, on breakfast lunch and supper i mean, and ate when we couldn't help it, and after a while the potatoes got mushier and mushier and finally the whole thing was almost only mush. we added water too at the end if i remember.

it wouldn't have been so bad, menstrual pudding, if it weren't for the color of the walls, taupe, which just didn't go with tomato sauce, no, and especially not on grey days. how come the walls were taupe was we wanted to paint them beige, that is i did, cause almost everybody else said why not leave them grey in one room and pale yellow in the other and not too dirty why paint them at all. but no i thought beige and black would be very chic and i wanted a very chic apartment especially for this very chic girl i knew who hardly ever came down there anyway but. so but to save money we bought white paint which is the cheapest, a dreadful grade of it that rubbed off like chalk when it dried but it was the cheapest, and we bought four gallons of it and with it a tube of paint tinter whatever you call it. i figured to get beige what you needed was a light off-browninsh color, so i figured burnt sienna which i'm fond of anyway, a little of it in white would make beige. it didn't. it made pink. now pink walls (i tried it out) are not chic and they make you want to vomit, and besides i hate pink anything almost there are a couple of things pink which i don't hate but we won't mention them shall we, and they are anyway not walls. so we went out again to the paint store to figure out what to do with these four gallons of something what was it pink light-burnt-sienna which we had rashly mixed all of in a big pot-thing saying if we add a little more it will turn beige until it had become pink indeed and i mean it. and in the paint store we looked at the colors, all of us dancers, writers, folk singers, none of us painters in the least, looked at them and looked and tried to figure what mixed with this pinkstuff would make beige and finally settled on raw umber, which when we added turned the whole thing taupe. and we gave up and painted everything taupe by candlelight so we wouldn't have to see too much the color, and it was within these taupe walls which rubbed off like taupe chalk and were all runny different shades of taupe that we ate our menstrual pudding on those four grey november days that year and how many of us there were i don't remember.

the next i remember is the hapsburg house oddly enough, but then again not so oddly either cause wouldn't you want to remember the hapsburg house after you remembered a thing like menstrual pudding? or don't you go in for extremes. I remember sitting there with this cat who was half cherokee with a spanish name, a beautiful cat with those cheekbones and lovely eyes, sitting there with him and ordering shrimp and wildrice in a cream sauce after first downstairs the martinis and the second one drunk in such a way that it was settled what we would do that night. and i was radiant very high with the early spring this was many years later, and pregnant but not knowing it yet, not even suspecting till the following week, and that night occupied simply with being beautiful and the talk which was if i remember of classical chinese how to study it and the cape in the winter.

and after the dinner we went to henri quatorze and the cherokee cat showed me off to some of his friends and i was courted and drinking pernod and water. the tablecloths i remember were red and white check very corny it was dark and downstairsy and there was that in my stomach. i mean that feeling that happens when you are about to go to bed with a cat for the first time, the sense of adventure the quick in the air, and i drank pernod being unconsciously pregnant and knowing how another winter chalked up. . . . we went home i remember to high ceilings and the firelight and he was the only cat i've ever known who could be sexy in his underwear even in his underwear there was something fey about it i still remember.

in the morning he left for the cape to go back to the cape and the next week the bad times began there began to be rats in the kitchen. . . .

i remember the winter the january i ate nothing but oreos. if you know what oreos are, they're those chocolate cookies two of them at a time stuck with sugar in the middle, and very addictive. i mean i really got hooked on them. there was this low armchair in my pad and i would sit in it and eat oreos and read and sometimes drink a little milk or water cause oreos in large numbers they tend to stick in your teeth.

when i wanted company i would go upstairs and visit these two girls who were my neighbors. they were a little crazy. they liked oreos too but not as much as i did, i mean not three or four packages a day, but anyway they would sit there and eat them with me to keep me company, and they washed theirs down with ale. ale and oreos i didn't dig too much, together like that. but boy, to hear the wind blow and all that awful january rain and a bunch of windows looking out on old crumbling filthy brick walls, and to sit in the middle of all this eating oreos and reading was—well anyway it was a way to get through january. to get through january in manhattan is hard, to get through january and february the same year almost impossible.

one of the best ways to get through i found was this eating oreos. except that it makes you fat. really fat. even if you don't eat anything else and you think, shit, how can i get fat i haven't had breakfast or lunch or anything like that, but don't kid yourself. OREOS MAKE YOU FAT.

or maybe it's just me. the girls upstairs ate a lot of them, but i couldn't tell if they were getting fatter or skinnier because they never got out of bed. that was a weird pad. the bed was in the center of the center room and they were in the center of the bed. the edges of the bed were for ashtrays and beercans and beercan openers and pastels and oreos. and they had these red lights that they turned on all the time with that grey outside it was too much, and dust over everything like you read about in biographies of proust and try to imagine but you hardly ever encounter it. real genuine dust-from-not-moving, from not capering about, not the kind of dust you'd 'raise' the kind that drifts slowly, settles in through a whole grey winter. we would sit and eat oreos and drink ale if there was any and sometimes one of them would draw in a black book with pastels and everytime it rained we would talk about the fallout.

and one day the girl who never drew said she would draw too, it was snowing, and she got out the other one's watercolors, and while the other one drank ale, and i did terrible abstract pastels, she carefully like a child drew an apple and a pear each two inches above a wobbly perspectivy table and carefully like a child she filled them all in with color, the pear yellow the apple orangy-red and the table brown and it was very beautiful. and she said There that's my still life what else is there to paint? and we said Landscapes. and so she drew a tree with a bird in it and a very tall flower stem and the flower on top of the stem was also the sun and it was like blake or rédon but much more childlike and lovely, and she said There, that's finished what else is there to paint. and we said People. and she drew and painted all in one color a grey blue a very all wrong lumpy dispro-portionate person who was not beautiful at all, and then she said There i have finished, i have mastered the art of painting. and we said to her No you haven't because your people aren't right yet. but she said That is how they are, and if they are not right i will be known as a painter of landscapes and still lifes.

and then i went out and brought back from the snow pastrami sandwiches and yes more oreos and we waited for it to get dark.

.... there were dozens and dozens of family dinners that happened to me after i left school, and they were all alike and all of them different. they have all of them run together in my head with no separations and that is how i will tell them now, with no separations. mostly they were the dinners of holidays, of thanksgiving and christmas and easter and birthday parties. some of them were weddings and one that i remember was a funeral but i won't tell about that not this time.

on the days of family dinners you would come back to the house after not hav-ing been there for a very long time. you would come back in bluejeans with holes in your sneakers and everyone would look sadly at you. one time i remem-ber, an easter, not having the carfare to take the subway and walking in from manhattan over the bridge, from washington square with a friend who was hungry over the manhattan bridge and into south brooklyn. i didn't tell them we walked, i stole some change for carfare back to the city.

they would look sad but they would be glad to see you. you would eat some meat from the sauce while it was still cooking because of course you would have had no breakfast, and then you'd go up to your room and look at it, the things in it untouched since your last visit, except the furniture escaping one piece at a time and going to make up the furniture of other rooms. and you'd putter with papers and old letters and take out your files, just to see how they were all there, to know it. it gave you a good safe feeling that there was a place to send papers, a place to leave letters and books that you wouldn't be reading.

and after a while they'd say Diane come down to dinner and i would come down to a house now full of aunts. there would mostly be little aunts, and one or two bigger, coats in two closets and on my mother's bed, and all my cousins some grown a good bit but no different, some a good deal different and that always happened fast. i had seventeen cousins in all, first cousins, i don't know how many aunts and uncles, and there were always the second the third and fourth cousins who just came over from italy and the great aunts. of them all i remember a few, aunt-olga because she cried a lot, her white hair curled and she had a nogood husband; aunt-julia who talked the most but was very lovely and young; aunt-jenny who always sang and was happy and happy. her husband was happy too, my uncle-larry, but he was more quiet about it and didn't sing much. i remember him well from the earlier days when he would be the one to give me books, cyrano i got from him, and penguin island.

we would start with the antipasto, the aunts would bustle. there would be dishes coming and going always and they would bustle. some would be washing things between the courses, others getting the salt or the vinegar for something, and all the time we'd be eating we ate all day. when the eating slowed down the kids would put on the phonograph and they would lindy and the older folks would wait and wait their turn and play a foxtrot. i learned to dance from them first, it took a long time to get rid of the way they danced. they danced like the twenties or thirties i don't know which, i guess it's thirties, they danced like, the twenties movies i've seen show nothing like it. they danced without moving the upper part of their bodies, nothing moving from the waist up like on ballet dancers. the result on some of them was a really great tango, on most of them it was just ridiculous.

so i'd eat and eat and dance with the kids and with the older folks, i was sort of in the middle, and they would look sad, the older ones, and ask me if i was going back to school. and if i felt good i'd be honest and say no. they would ignore my bluejeans all of them except my mother and she would have taken me upstairs first thing to put on a dress, one of her dresses or one of the ones i'd left home, and i would say no, the hell with it and we'd go down again and join the others.

mostly it was good and not unpleasant. the evenings were good when we went back for seconds, the lukewarm meats when it got dark, the black coffee we drank with anisette, the fruit and nuts. my brother would play the piano and we would all sing, we sang the old songs left over from the war: bongo bongo bongo I don' wanna leave the congo, maria elena, and symphony of love. and then we sang older songs than that even, for the grownups. just a song at twilight, and desert song.

it would be really dark, and my mother would wrap up some meat and some italian food that i'd never cook for myself, and the bag would still be warm. i'd pick up the change i could find in the kitchen, and all the aunts would be in the process of leaving. then i would say some cool things to my brothers, take the food and go back to my part of the world.

❧

The Stereotype
Rosette Capotorto

Tomato
tart
red
round
red
sweet
red
tomato

❧

My Grandmother, a Chicken, and Death
Regina Barreca

The miracle of death I first had the privilege to witness when I was about five years old.

My grandmother and I, along with a dozen other females of diverse ages, had been waiting about six years for a bus to come down Avenue U in Brooklyn. We'd been marketing—as people then referred to the process—and now stood in vigilance alongside our string bags, which were lined up next to us on the pavement as if on parade. In addition to the bags of flour, boxes of salt, and cans of olive oil bought for convenience, my grandmother had purchased a live chicken, which she held under her arm. This was a Big Deal, this particular purchase. Relatives were coming all the way from New Jersey and the big chicken was a special treat. I had never seen her buy a real live chicken before and although I knew this practice was not actually unusual, I was fascinated by the entire ritual: the selection process, the holding of the bird, the fact of the creature's vitality.

The bird was in her embrace, nestled in the broad expanse of her black cotton sleeve. It seemed calm enough. Resisting the temptation to ask my grandmother if I could try to hold it, I settled for sneaking looks at its eyes. The bird seemed to look back at me, and I rather fancied that we had built up a bit of a friendship. I felt sort of proud of the bird and of my grandmother's ability to control and deal with the creature on this warm morning. Other people waiting on line

also looked at it and commented on it, some speaking Italian to my grand-
mother and smiling at me.

Finally, the bus arrived. Other people got on first; we waited until they were
seated. My grandmother, in her seventies at the time and a slow mover, took her
time in moving everything into the vestibule of the vehicle. Only after we had
dragged our parcels up the few steps to the little entry platform did the driver
notice the chicken. "Lady," he said, with some impatience, "you cannot bring a
live bird on the bus. Sorry. I gotta ask you to leave."

I stood, ashamed and shocked, not knowing what to do, afraid of what
would come next. We were holding up the bus; other people had important
places to go, and there we were, standing not quite on the bus and not quite off
of it, with bags and bags of food and a big live bird. My grandmother had never
been questioned to her face before, at least not in my presence. Hers was the last
word on anything; she wielded an authority so supreme it went unquestioned.
And the bus driver had the courage to issue a command! What could possibly
happen?

Without a word, and without diverting her eyes even for a second from the
face of the driver, my grandmother put her right hand into the cleft of her left
elbow and deftly twisted the chicken's neck. It took maybe one and a half sec-
onds. The chicken no longer filled her arm with its vitality; it was just another
grocery item, merely one that had not been packaged at the market. Nothing
was special about it anymore. Then my grandmother raised her eyebrows, cock-
ing her head towards the man, as if saying, "Now is there a problem?" and the
driver shook his head no while motioning for us to pass through. Nobody on
the bus said anything. My hands shaking, I put coins in the metal and glass box
for our fares. We sat down. My grandmother put the chicken into one of the
larger bags and brushed off her dress. She looked straight ahead, but she also
stroked the back of my neck, as if to reassure me. I loved my grandmother but
I was far from reassured by the gesture.

Don't think I didn't eat with a full appetite that night—I was as appreciative
of a good meal as ever. The relatives from New Jersey were treated like royalty
and everybody had a good time. The next day my aunts made chicken salad for
sandwiches with the leftovers.

So much for the miracle of death. One minute the chicken is nestling and
making eye contact and small noises and the next minute it's just an ordinary
chicken for dinner, head flopping to one side and silent. Death was easy, it
seemed; one moment and the whole business was completed.

The miracle of birth would be explained to me only much later and treated
with far more shame.

◡

"No Thank You, I Don't Care for Artichokes"
Sandra M. Gilbert

"No thank you, I don't care for artichokes,"

decreed my mother-in-law as my husband
passed the platter of inward-turning
soft-skulled Martian baby
heads around the table,

and they were O so shyly slyly
jostling each other with their boiled-
green sardonic gossip
(what was the news they told?)

when he sharply answered, "Mother,
have you *ever*
eaten an artichoke?"
                    "No,"

she said, majestic, "but I just know
I don't *care* for them, don't
care for them at all"—
for truly, if they weren't Martian,

they were at the least Italian,
from that land of "smelly cheese"
she wouldn't eat, that land of oily
curves and stalks, unnerving pots

of churning *who knows what,*
and she, nice, Jewish, from the Bronx,
had fattened on her Russian-
Jewish mother's *kugel*, kosher

chicken, good rye bread. . . .
Bearded, rosy, magisterial
at fortyfive, he laughed,
kept plucking, kept on

licking those narcissistic
leaves, each with its razor point
defending the plump, the tender
secret at the center, each

a greave or plate of edible
armor, so she smiled too,
in the flash of dispute,
knowing he'd give her icecream later,

all she wanted, as the rich
meal drew to an end
with sweets dished out in the lamplit
circle, to parents, children, grandma—

the chocolate mint she craved,
and rocky road he bought especially
for her, whose knees were just
beginning to crumble from arthritis,

whose heart would pump more creakily
each year, whose baby
fat would sag and sorrow
as her voice weakened, breathing

failed until she too
was gathered into the same
blank center
where her son

at sixty bearded still, still
laughing, magisterial
(though pallid now)
had just a year before

inexplicably settled.

༄

Hot Peppers
Rina Ferrarelli

Bright red
and pointed like horns
weapons against the evil eye
antidotes against decay
lean and dry, ascetic
extreme like saints
revolutionaries
that set everything on fire.

If You Were a Boy
Rosette Capotorto

If you were a boy
I would keep my knife
under my pillow
ready
to cut your heart
at the slightest move

if you were a boy
I wouldn't trust you
further than I could
push you

I would run out the house
when Sunday wrestling
came on the tv

but you
strong armed
smooth skinned
coil haired
beauty
are a woman

saltysweet
chocolate & tomato
big black she wolf
tiny baby girl
la diavola
with pointed tail & high heels
come
give me those
soft sweet breasts
and your smell of
pink

❧

Tridicinu and 'Mmaculata
Gioia Timpanelli

"*Hunger,*" *she said,* "*is very personal. At first, it even tricks you into feeling guilty over your own misery, guilty for your lack of human grace. It holds your wrists tight in its bony fingers, it breathes its foul breath into your gaping mouth as you sleep.*"

"*But wait,*" *we said,* "*this happens in the story Ovid tells. It's an old story.*"

"*True, true,*" *she said,* "*but why do you insist on being literal to time? You see, time changes the details but the story of greed and retribution or, as you moderns insist, of 'cause and effect,' is essentially the same. Why do you believe hunger could never happen to you, not where you are, and not now among your people? You think you are too well off for hunger to find you. Ah! My friend, we, too, thought exactly the same.*"

PIETRAPERZIA, SICILY, 1886

My name is Tridicinu and this is the story of what happened to me when I was twelve.

In half an hour I left the carriage road to Vittoria and got on to an old foot path up the mountains, the mayor's message to the bandits burning in my pocket. After a two-hour climb I found what we call the "Cat Boulders" and turned for the old farmhouse, which I had not seen in years. In ten minutes the footpath ended, but I kept walking. The sun was hot, and after a while I realized I had been walking for a long time. When I saw the land change and that I was climbing again, now past some small, tough caper bushes, I felt I was finally heading in the right direction to the stand of chestnut trees. Sure enough, there before me was the clearing where I once spent the afternoon filling my sack with some good healthy stalks of young *carduna*.

But instead of the old place, all I saw now was a dried and dead field and ahead of me a huge pile of rubble, dust, and fallen rocks from what must have been the old farmhouse. There was nothing but ruin. No house, no garden, no vines growing, not one bit of green anywhere. Nothing. All the chestnut trees except one had been cut down. It was a pretty pathetic place. Were the bandits really living there?

All the while I kept looking around, but I didn't see or hear anything so I walked quickly to the one chestnut tree still standing. I had planned to find a borderline, the right place where I would sit and watch patiently, and when I became sure that the bandits were not there, I'd hang the mayor's message on their falling-down door, maybe look around and then leave. Although I knew these borderline spots are not usually obvious to strangers, here at the large chestnut tree I felt I had found my hiding place.

I was elated, for now I could discharge my messenger's duty and yet save my own skin. I was going to get away with this after all. My brothers would lose again. They would be angry if against odds I could make it back alive. But since I always did better not planning anything too closely, I didn't think more about it. And after relieving myself, I felt happy and satisfied and I sat with my back against the tree as if I owned the place.

But I should have remembered my Mother's saying, "*Cu vidi chiu di lu patrunnu è urvu*"—"Who sees more than the owner is blind." Just as I was feeling comfortable in my perfect hiding place, something moved not twenty feet from my head. A woman, who must have been standing perfectly still for as long as I had been in the clearing, walked right up to the tree and stared down at me.

"Get up!" she said. "What are you doing here?"

"I'm just carrying a message to some new workmen around here," I said. Standing and feeling like a real fool, I added, "I was told by their friend, the mayor of our town, that they might be living near here. Maybe, *Signura*, I could just give you this note and then be on my way."

"What are you talking about? Are you crazy or just *babbu e fissu*? Now that you've found this place you can't just go back. Bad luck that you found us. And what kind of 'friend' sent you to these 'workmen'?" she laughed. Not expecting an answer, she added, "Come on, let's see what we can do. Follow me." She was the most fierce woman I had ever seen. When she looked at me I felt a shudder go through me. Her eyes were burning steadily, like a ferret whose eyes once fixed me with a feral stare so that by just looking into my eyes one minute, it transfixed me, and in the next second it was gone. Later I would learn that she had this ferret trick and could be someplace one minute and then suddenly not there. It was then that I saw a pistol in her hand, which as she walked moved in and out of the folds of her skirt.

When we got to the pile of stones, she opened a door that I hadn't noticed before, and suddenly I could see that the farmhouse, although a wreck, was still on its feet, maybe more on its knees. The place was no more than a hovel. It was dark and cool, and I smelled something familiar boiling on the stove. I stood there thinking, "Boy this dump smells like heaven."

"What are you doing?" she asked.

"Nothing. I'm just standing here," I said.

"What do you mean you're just standing here? You're not just standing here; you're smelling the air like a fox. Do you want some of those chickpeas?"

"Yes, I wouldn't mind tasting a little, thanks," I said, a bit too quickly.

"Good, that's what I like, a person who doesn't stand on ceremony when he's starving."

She brought me a small pot of chickpeas in one hand and a huge spoon, dangerously held by her thumb against the most falling-apart chair, in the other. I took the spoon and chair and then the bowl, sat down carefully on the almost nonexistent raffia seat, and right there in the middle of the room dove in with the big spoon. The chickpeas were good. The taste of onions was so sweet. But before I could take another mouthful, she came back from the stove shouting in her gruff voice, "Wait a minute," as she made a thin cross over the chick peas with olive oil; "Wait a minute," she said again as she threw a pinch of coarse black pepper over it; "Wait a minute," she said under her breath, as she handed me a thick slice of good Sicilian bread from her pocket. "Now it's about right and you can eat!" Well, thank God, I thought, since I hadn't eaten since the day before, unless you count the small cactus pear I had picked on the way out of town. On this score things were looking up.

The fields and mountains became another home. Whenever I wasn't acting as lookout, or fixing things at the farmhouse, or cooking with Immaculata, I was out walking. Even at siesta, "*l'otta di lu caudu*," I didn't go back to the house but slept instead against the old chestnut tree where she had first spied me hiding. The neutral trees, beautiful and indifferent to my human fate, gave me another chance at life.

If I wasn't fixing all those broken-down things like that old raffia chair, I was helping 'Mmaculata prepare the daily meals for the two of us. The men did not live with us. Their hideout was a secret, which I had not yet discovered. Rarely and at erratic times they showed up for a meal and she was always able to put something together. In my whole life I had never eaten as much as I did in those months. She loved to cook, and in helping her I learned something new every day.

Once we had nothing but a pile of lentils in our jars. "Prepare them," she said, so I threw the lentils into a pan, ready to ladle water over them. "Haven't you ever seen your mother prepare lentils?" she asked with an alarmed look on her face. "You're always in a hurry! Forget that. It's sometimes attention to the smallest stone that will set you right. It isn't always the 'big shot' move that saves you; sometimes it's the million and two small moves that sustain you every day that can be vital. Of course both kinds of actions, Sonny, are essential. Sit down and clean the lentils." She pulled the pile of lentils in front of her, and with her crooked finger went through every single lentil, pushing aside the pieces of dirt and all the little stones. We sat together quietly cleaning lentils in an enormous sense of peace. When we were done we had a real pile of stones. "Look at what you were going to cook; even if your tough stomach digested them one of them could have broken your teeth. Then what?"

We baked bread twice a week and sometimes roasted meat, which the bandits had stolen from both the rich and the poor, paying no attention to consequences. "That's going to matter to them some day. They are going to make an enormous mistake right in that detail there and pay for it."

Each meal that she made for us was a surprise. I ate things that I had never eaten before, cheeses that were tastier than anything imaginable: ricotta salata with little oranges, *mandarini,* and sweet, small black walnuts that we ourselves had gathered. I got to be able to judge good provolone, which we ate with onion bread and little cured, black olives; and for the first time I ate baked fish with pine nuts and currants and grated bread crumbs with dried herbs, but we also had a penny's barter of tuna under oil or Christmas dry cod made in four or five different ways. She could make anything out of anything. You'd think I would be so worried that I couldn't eat, but that wasn't the case. Maybe I was too young to be a worrier, but that's not true because I have seen babies that were worried before they could even crawl. Whatever the reason, I enjoyed every meal we made, beginning to end.

Sometimes I would see a change in her face at table. Something was troubling her, but she wouldn't discuss it over food. ("It's not the time for misery. Never talk misery or argue at table—it's more than bad manners! Only good talk and thanks!" she said again and again.) But once when the last mouthful had gone down and she got up to put away the bread, she turned and looked me in the eyes as I was going out the door and said, "Well, they're looking to kill you as soon as it's convenient. What are you going to do about it?"

"You're a magician," I said. "Why can't you prevent it?"

"Listen, kid, I've already saved you a few times with Gino and once with the 'Pazzu,' but that's not what we're talking about here. It's you who has to figure it out. Like all kids who have 'real trouble,' you've got a limited course of action: you're going to die, crumble, or meet fortune halfway. I'd say at the moment you're up for grabs. Sometimes I see you definitely leaning towards the strange and possible solution. I hope you make it. There are no written lessons, Sonny, only tests."

Once, when the provisions were low, 'Mmaculata caught a rabbit, which she marinated in vinegar for longer than I wanted to wait, so I asked her, "Why don't you make a pot of those chickpeas again?"

"Don't get sentimental on me, you can't afford it," she said. "There you'd be feeling all good about those old chickpeas and not paying attention, and someone might have just sneaked in here and 'adjusted the taste' so that you'd never eat chickpeas again. As it is, your future is being cooked in a leaky pot."

"I can fix leaky pots," I answered cockily. She gave me that oh-you-pathetic-kid shake of the head.

"I hope so," she growled, "I really hope so."

I had been there for eight months when one beautiful morning 'Mmaculata woke me by bringing me *caffe latte cu li fidduzzi*, the usual big cup of coffee and hot milk with broken pieces of nice, two-day-hard bread in it with a heaping teaspoon of sugar over it.

"Get up!" she shouted in that raspy voice. Her rough dog hair was standing up in its usual morning places. "Get up, get up! Do you know what wild asparagus looks like? Today you're going to find them in the fields up there," she pointed. "This is the right time for them on the mountainside. I can feel them growing out there."

I knew asparagus, but not really well. I spent hours searching for them up in the mountain meadows, climbing higher and higher, leaving a part of my life below. In the middle of a field I found some old dry asparagus plants, and then seeing the mound of sheep dung scattered here and there around some old last year's dried stalks reminded me of something I had half-seen once before. This made me look closer and there hidden was a thin, thin, dark green asparagus spear. Once I found that one stalk I found others easily. And just as I was adding the last one to my collection, I heard a beautiful shepherd's pipe. I followed the music until I saw the shepherd wrapped in his large cape, playing his pipe, sitting on an outcropping below, with his back to me. I walked out of sight and lay on the blessed ground, and for the longest time listened to the music. I can't tell you how long I stayed there, for time was lost. And when suddenly the music stopped, I heard a great rush of *tlee tlee* tlinging of tiny sheep bells. I stood up, picked up the asparagus, and saw, below, the shepherd and his flock now moving down the mountain.

By the time I came home I had two beautiful bunches of wild asparagus, which I had tied with thread into bouquets like flowers. They were thin, thin and very dark green, their wild fragrance like nothing planted in human rows. As I handed them to 'Mmaculata I bowed and she said, "They deserve the best cheese and garlic, but first we have to make the dough for the lightest *lasagneddi,* the thin pasta goes with the freshest olive oil, garlic, and cooked asparagus. To begin, you must make the dough from fine flour, feel this through your fingers; good water is next, but the real secret is in your hands and how you handle the knife while cutting the dough. If it is right you will always hear the same music: *tsikita, tsikita, tsikita.*"

"Tsikita, tsikita, tsikita," went the kitchen knife, cutting the folded dough into perfect flat noodles. "*Tsikita, tsikita, tsikita,*" went the morning, and in the end we had a long string of not-too-thin and not-too-thick pasta drying. Later, we boiled a whole pot of them and ate them with the freshest and nutty tasting olive oil, a good taste of garlic, topped with the right number of thin dark asparagus, on top of which we grated coarsely ground *pecorino,* topping it off with a pinch of coarse pepper. Beautiful thin asparagus growing on the mountainside with all that human evil. Asparagus were among the first green things I saw there in March. March when everything has hope but is holding danger as well. My father used to say each year, "March sits like a knife, bitter winter on one side and spring on the other." '*Tsikita, tsikita, tsikita*' went my twelfth year.

❧

she's doing the dishes
Vittoria repetto

> she's doing the dishes
> that's the deal
> i cook she washes
> and i watch her
> she laughs
> winks
> and wiggles her ass at me
> so   i go behind her
> press myself
>   into her
> open her 501's button flys
> trace my fingers down
>   navel to mount
> she stops washing
> i say
> no   keep on washing baby
> i part the hairs
>   the lips—major—minor

circle her clit
when she comes
she loses her grip on the chef's knife
almost breaking my favorite blue bowl.

❧

pasta poem
Vittoria repetto

l'americana is talking
complaining
yuppies say pasta
instead of spaghetti
she looks at me
hoping to prove her point
i smile
say
when i was a kid
i ate linguine
lasagne
ravioli
cappellitte
capelline di angeli
ziti
fettuccini
tortellini
and gnocchi
all pastas
when i was a kid
spaghetti was what americans ate
over   cooked
and out of a Chef Boy-ar-dee can
l'americana shuts up

❧

Breakfast, Lunch, and Dinner

Agnes Rossi

Food was there at the start. We met when he asked me to pass him a basket of cheddar cheese Goldfish. I was happy to do it because before he'd sat down I'd had those fish all to myself and had fallen into a rhythm of taking a sip, eating a fish, taking a sip, etc. I didn't want to give them up altogether, though, so I slid the basket along the bar until it was equidistant between us. He took a handful and said he hadn't had any dinner. I smiled and nodded as if to say I know what that's like, even though I didn't and don't. He put a couple of fish in his mouth, then shook the ones left in his fist like they were dice he was getting ready to throw.

After more nods and smiles from me and more fish rattling from him, he turned to get the bartender's attention. I selected a fish from the basket. Before I was able to put it in my mouth, he asked if he could buy me a drink. I said yes, using the hand that held the fish between thumb and index finger to gesture. I don't remember why a simple yes needed gestures—I was either thanking him excessively or taking a roundabout route to yes by way of no. I didn't put that fish in my mouth until he turned to pay for the drinks.

Our conversation moved by fits and starts through the better part of an hour. When I got up to leave he asked if I would meet him there the following night. I said I would and did. That second night, as it came to be known, we stayed until closing time then went to a diner where he ordered sausage and eggs, so I did too. He had his eggs up. I had mine scrambled. I didn't think I could handle all of that gooey yolk attractively.

He drove me back to my car and we kissed for a good long time in the parking lot. Driving home, I sat up straight and wished there were more cars on the road. I felt alert and outgoing. Driving, especially on the deserted road, didn't seem like enough to be doing.

He called me early the next morning and said he was tired but happy and asked me to dinner. In the restaurant, rubbing my knuckles with his thumbs, he said, "I don't want to scare you, but I think I'm falling in love." I said I thought I was too. That's when I started to cook.

I was unemployed so my days were spent getting ready. Like a European, I'd go to a butcher for meat, a fishstore for seafood, a vegetable market for produce, a bakery for bread, and—very important, we were new and nervous—to a liquor store for wine. I'd get back to my apartment around noon, deposit the various paper bags on the counter, then stand in front of the refrigerator and eat a half a tomato as if it was a cupcake, biting around the edges then popping the center in my mouth whole. I was too giddy to want to eat, and too concerned with how my stomach would look later in bed, but I didn't want hunger pangs interfering with my ability to concentrate on my cooking.

The recipes I was going to use had, of course, already been selected from the fat *Joy of Cooking*. I'd read through them to determine what needed to be done first. Veal might have to be submerged in marinade or chicken rinsed in cool water and set, uncovered, on a plate in the refrigerator. If I was making Caesar salad—he loved it and would eat even the soggiest leaves—olive oil (*none other*, the book warned) had to be poured into a glass jar with a clove of garlic. The jar had to be covered and set in the sun on the kitchen windowsill. Several times during an afternoon, I'd pick up that jar, turn it over in my hands, and watch the garlic move through the oil.

I'd do everything I could except set the table—there is something sad about a table set for dinner at one-thirty in the afternoon—then go and take a long shower. I'd rinse determinedly until the hot water gave out because I'd read enough women's magazines to know the importance of rinsing. (Vidal Sassoon thinks you should rinse your hair until your arms ache. I think I was about ten when I read that interview.) When my water was colder than I could stand, I'd step out, wrap my head in a towel, then rub the bargain body lotion I was buying to counterbalance the expensive groceries, into my skin. Still moist in creases, I'd dress carefully but casually—I didn't want to look *dressed*—then it was back to the kitchen to turn the oil-and-garlic jar and wait until I could start cooking.

By the time I'd hear his car, everything would be just on the verge of readiness. I'd go and stand at the top of the stairs. As he'd make his way up we'd smile at one another, a little embarrassed but also genuinely relieved to be together again, as though each of us was afraid that the other had had a change of heart during the course of the day and decided to call the whole thing off.

As he'd pull me close I'd be aware of things bubbling and needing basting behind me. He'd sit down at the table. I'd show off at the stove. The final stages were flashy. I knew I looked like an expert, doing several things at once, all of them aromatic.

He'd pause after nearly every mouthful to tell me things were delicious. He'd have seconds, sometimes thirds. I'd been intensely involved with that food all day—inspecting, selecting, paying, washing, tossing, sautéing, serving—and was tired of it. With him there, handsome and husbandlike in front of me, it couldn't get my attention. Anyway, not eating meant more prominent hipbones for later.

As the weeks passed it got easier to be with him. We moved through our meals with just the sounds of forks against plates and wine into glasses. Touching him, a finger on his forearm, a foot on his chair, seemed to complete the sensation of good food in my mouth.

No longer cooking with win-or-lose urgency, I was less familiar with the food by the time it made the table. I ate as much as he did. My stomach wasn't a factor any longer. However it was would be fine.

We went to restaurants a couple of times a week and ordered with complete abandon. We had appetizers, bottles of wine, and when the dinner plates were cleared, we had Grand Marnier with our coffee. There was an unspoken financial agreement: I bought the fixings for elaborate dinners and he picked up eighty-five-dollar checks.

We took the security we'd found at the table with us when we got up. After lunch one Saturday, we went shopping for a pair of shoes together. Looking in the store window, I leaned back and felt his belly in the small of my back. In a fit of contentment, he bought a pair of black shoes he was never going to put on without first saying he didn't know why he'd bought them. I'd see him reach for them and wait for him to say what he always said, "I hate these shoes."

Gradually I stopped using serving dishes. Food went from the pan to the plates. With an eye on my grocery bill, I cut out the wine. We drank iced tea or water. I no longer needed recipes. I knew about how long it took to cook a chicken or a chop and was confident enough to experiment with seasonings.

I began having to send him to the store for things I'd forgotten. He spent twenty minutes walking up and down supermarket aisles looking for capers. "Are they fish or vegetables or what?" he snapped when he got back.

By then he'd all but officially moved in. One morning we were up and getting dressed, not realizing the severity of the snowstorm outside, when his boss called him and told him not to bother coming in, the roads were a mess. My mother was next. "You're not even thinking about driving are you?" I waited for my boss to call—I'd gotten a job answering the telephone in a doctor's office—but he didn't. I left a message on his answering machine.

We got undressed and took our coffee back to bed with us. We thought we'd spend the whole day there, but in an hour we were up and hungry. We put on all the snow clothes we could find and walked the six blocks to the A&P. We bought eggs, cheese, English muffins, Canadian bacon, and a coffee cake. On the way home we passed one of those square trucks that deliver potato chips to people's houses. It was stuck in a driveway. He wanted to ask the driver if we could buy a tin of chips. "No," I said. "Come on. We have enough."

He spread a blanket on the living room floor while I went to work in the kitchen. We turned on HBO, ate, snoozed, fooled around, and watched movies all day and into the night. At three o'clock in the morning we were wide awake watching a movie about a couple who did nothing but go for walks and talk. These two walked through endless parks and down city streets. They walked alongside rivers that blurred and became crowded outdoor markets. Most of their conversations were about dreams one or the other had had, long dreams that sounded like they were being made up on the spot. When I found myself waiting for the "and thens"—"and then, suddenly I was in hell . . . and then a girl I secretly loved in high school was there . . . and then I knew they were going to bury me alive"—I got up and turned it off. We crawled into bed to sleep some more.

When the alarm went off the next morning, I was already in the shower. He opened the bathroom door and asked me to please hurry up. I stayed in longer than I would have if he hadn't emphasized the please, then went into the kitchen to make coffee.

There were dishes in the sink and on the counters. The spatula was face down in the frying pan, bits of cheese on its edges. The milk had been left out and smelled sour, which put an end to the coffee since neither of us would drink it black.

In the living room, the blanket was still on the floor and the television was not in its usual spot. I didn't touch anything, didn't even throw out the sour milk.

When I went back into the bedroom, he was pulling on his pants. As I buttoned my skirt, I had the sense that we were competing to see which of us could get out into the responsible world first.

He stopped volunteering to go to the supermarket without me. The tomatoes he'd brought back were always too soft, the pork chops too thick, anyway. We started food shopping together. My spirits would lift as we'd pull into the parking lot. I'd get to buy things I wouldn't have if he wasn't there to pay the bill. Like artichokes. Yogurt-covered peanuts. Spring water. He'd push the cart and I'd dart off and back again. When it took me a while to decide on something, he'd catch up to me. I'd know he was behind me because he'd tap me softly on the rear end with the cart.

Since he was paying for the groceries, dinners out became something I had to press to get. I knew as I opened a menu, large and leatherette, how to make trouble if I wanted to.

Towards the end of one scratchy Saturday afternoon, I gave him an ultimatum. "I want to go out," I said. We went to a gaudy twenty-fifth-anniversary kind of place where I, pushing hard, had ordered a second bottle of wine by the time a white-haired lady came to the table and asked if we'd like to have our picture taken. When he said no I said yes. She took it, six dollars was added to our bill, and he was furious.

I found his tightfistedness so unattractive. The financial finagling that I was doing, the transfer of the grocery bill from me to him that I'd engineered, seemed somehow feminine and so my birthright.

A week later I got the picture in the mail. Our faces look fleshy and fixed, his in anger, mine in drunken I-dare-you.

We began to take food with us in the car. Like an alcoholic husband and wife with their mayonnaise jar of gin, we had our hard pretzels and Kit Kat bars.

We were getting ready to drive to the shore for the day—the shore meant sausage and peppers, clams on the half shell. He was sitting out in the car waiting for me. I was on my way out the door when I realized we had no food for the way down. Nothing. I was in the kitchen putting pears in a plastic bag when I heard the car horn. I went to the window and looked out. He saw me and changed from one long blast to a series of short toots. I stood and listened. He leaned out of the car and shouted, "What's taking you?"

"Snacks," I shrieked back, stretching out the middle of the word so that it lasted for several seconds.

The end came when he had the courage to say out loud that all we shared was appetite. I knew he was right, had even tried to justify the situation to myself—other couples had the opera or the New York Mets—and failed. But there in the serious afternoon light, it was too humiliating to admit.

I tried to dislodge food from its spot at the top of our agenda. I checked the "What's Happening" column in Friday's paper. On Saturday morning I asked, "What do you want to do today?" as though we generally did things. I'd already chosen an antique auction, though neither one of us knew anything about old furniture beyond that we liked it in a vague sort of way.

He agreed to go immediately and said seventy miles wasn't too far to drive. There was a lot of chirpy conversation in the car. We commented on things as we passed them, deer and factory outlets.

After two sets of directions from pedestrians, we pulled up to a field that had rows of folding chairs on it. There were clusters of people in the first couple of rows only.

"Hasn't it started yet?" I asked one of two young men who were loading a bedroom set onto the back of a pick up.

"You kidding?" he said, slamming the gate of his truck closed. "It's in full swing."

The other guy seemed to understand how important the auction was to me and said, "Most of the dealers stayed away. The organizers are demanding too high a percentage."

We stayed for a little while, sitting side-by-side in the otherwise empty fifth row.

On the way home we stopped and bought a pizza with extra cheese and mushrooms. I insisted on setting out plates and napkins before we opened the box.

We each had one piece pretty happily, but halfway through the second I was trying not to cry and having trouble swallowing. There seemed to be dry space in my mouth around the bite of pizza.

He looked at me then stood up. He tipped his plate over the garbage pail, put it in the sink, and said, "I'm going, okay? I'll call you." I nodded and kept nodding while I listened to him go down the stairs.

Part Five

TRANSFORMATIONS

I Can Be Bread
Anne Marie Macari

It was him with his fear of swords.
It was him with his cold skin,
his sunken eyes, his crooked smile,
his love of honey, anything
sweet, really. Anything fragrant.
Who else but the celibate could show
the way. It was him naked,
frail, his body worn, eaten by pain,
his body ecstatic, its thick
hairs holding the light.
Him with his arms out, his eyes
oozing, the light killing him.
Him with his puckered penis,
his bare feet in the cold
stream where he relieves himself,
O lion barking back. O
bloody hand on my breast.
The light has many names,
many dreams, he steps farther
into the water. Light
side-stabs him. I offer my mouth.
I offer my spread legs. I
can appear or disappear
in the water. I can torture
him with honey. I can be
bread. I can kneel. I can
carry my own bed. The light
has many names. I can
be naked, unafraid. I can be
in the same stream or I can
walk away, a lion
barking back, squatting, dripping

my bloody wine, bearing
up in that light,
bearing the light.

Finocchio

Sandra M. Gilbert

> *"Add finocchio seeds to your pasta sauce for that real Sicilian flavor!"*

Its humble gray-black kernels
nubs of the taste of what *was*
jostling in a jar
on the shelf of the *alimentari,*

        tell me what Proust knew,
        and Persephone,
        how history can
        shrink to a seed:

the enormous stalking
light, the feathery
evanescent green of let's say
just outside Agrigento

        packed into a tiny
        stageset—gesturing tenors,
        little flares of
        the tarantella—

at the wrong
end of the opera glass . . .
But O but drop just three
seeds into the pot

        where beef blood broods
        and olive gold, and red and green
        of the garden,
        and out bloom all the giants:

the histrionic cousins
stamping in the kitchen,

the mothers
railing or weeping,

and the broken ones—
Cristoforo deported, dying
alone in Rome,
mad Liborio who put his fist

through the window
("*Finocchio!*"
"He thought he was a girl!"),
and Eddie, back from the Great War,

who saw his mother
wrapped in black that said
"Your papa's dead"—
and "groaned and fell to the floor in
a faint"—

and behind them the long steep street,
Strada del Purgatorio
in Sambuca di Sicilia,
just another outpost

of the past inside
the seed inside
the sauce, the wine,
the bread, beside

the tall ruins
of the Temple of Concord,
the Arab traders, the faint
mysterious uncles.

∾

Pomodori

Adele Regina La Barre

My nonna's breasts were like tomatoes—juicy and round at ninety-six, so many many years after eight children had sucked them out. In this miraculous longevity, as in all things about my grandmother, I took great comfort in her example, for I am the only one of her grandchildren to be named Adele after her. She in turn took comfort in my name—although she called me Regina as my mother cannot, for that is the name of Mamm'Adele's second daughter, my mother's most beloved sister, dead two weeks before I was born. Mamma still goes quiet at her name.

Among my mother's four elegant sisters, Regina was the plain one. Cecilia, Vera, and Lilia were dark-haired, ivory-skinned creatures who swayed like Loretta Young in impeccably tailored suits they designed themselves. They spoke softly and carefully to disguise their Italian accents. Regina had unruly red hair and long limbs with too many elbows and knees. Worse, she had an accurate, mordant tongue. But after her death she was beatified into a saint of ardent hair and dulcet voice. I inherited the gangliness, the reddish gold hair, the freckled skin, and the charmlessness from Regina. No matter. From Mamm'Adele I might inherit the long, embarrassing life and tart breasts.

My names gave me permission to touch my grandmother's antique body so that when my mother, exhausted by the burden of her own mother's exhaustion, would leave her for a day or two (I can't say to rest), I would come with the only other hands licensed to touch. At first she wept. *Che vergogna*, that I should know that the diabetes had taken her sense of touch and she could no longer be sure that she was cleaning herself. Oh yes, my hands could pet her. We were all allowed to pet her—in fact, required to pet this woman, whose own hands had always been too busy with scalding chickens or attacking dough or quelling rebellious hair into braids or stabbing the vast linen canvasses on which she embroidered her epics in Sulmonese cutwork to have any tender touches, any petting for us.

My Zia Vera, her own skin barren of maternal tendernesses, was triumphant that her mother's hands no longer worked. "It's disgusting," she said. "She takes these stingy little shreds of toilet paper and wads them around her finger, then misses. The shit's all over her hand and under her nails." My aunt spoke in English. I glowered silent *state zi'* at her. "Oh, she doesn't understand," continued Vera. The next day Mamm'Adele said she'd rather it were I who came to care for her.

Care for her? Care for the body too holy for even my blacksmith grandfather to break? "Adele, Adele," he petted after her softly in his wine-sodden self-pity, terrified that the terrors that he wreaked every day on the house, his children and grandchildren, might drive her for one minute out of his sight.

"Don't touch don't touch," she would say in the voice of an oracle, but grinning. Later I would try to press against her laced corsets. She didn't grin for me.

From this I learned that tendernesses are to be meted out like punishment, the due only of those who have earned them, and perhaps not even then. After my nonno died, Mamm'Adele was spirited away to her eldest daughter, Zia Cecilia, born when my nonna was only sixteen. Maybe it was at her daughter's that Mamm'Adele found herself fifteen again, a girl even, still flirtatious and affectionate. As her eyesight deteriorated she remembered the poetry she'd learned in school and recited Leopardi by heart without my nonno interrupting to deliver himself of a more grandiloquent version. The masterpieces in thread continued under fingers that had eyes of their own. White-on-white, plump-bellied putti dove; shy lovers courted; swallows darted; snub-nosed masks spat symmetrical garlands of baroque fruit and blown roses. She dispensed the embroidered *biancherie* to all the *nipoti* who, struggling with the language for thanks, would pet her instead.

My mother and her other sisters watched their mother hold court at her favorite eldest daughter's and were relieved they need be no more than ladies-in-waiting. My uncles discharged their duties as ministers of finance and could afford to be wistful. Then Zia Cecilia died. It was the spitefully dutiful turn of Zia Vera, Mamm'Adele's least favorite daughter, the *puttana* smoking and drinking in her toreador pants. I visited more often and on each visit listened to recitations from Vera of the indignities old flesh could heap ungratefully on a daughter. The shared girlish gossip at Zia Cecilia's was replaced by querulous tyranny at Zia Vera's.

It was my father who in the end told my mother that their turn had come. Pop flattered his mother-in-law with serious conversation and indulged her swooning over records of Vittorio Gassman reciting Shakespeare's soliloquies. My mother bullied her mother back to a semblance of strength, forcing her down to the kitchen to knead bread she couldn't see and out to the garden to pinch vines she could no longer smell. Mamma listened with her to tapes in Italian of Judith Krantz's bodice-ripper romances and shook her head along with Mamm'Adele, who proclaimed each evening, "*che porcheria*"—nevertheless listening to each book to the end because the rental should not be wasted. Such unmentionable subjects as impotence and variant gratifications seemed to crop up in the advice columns in the Italian papers my mother read out loud to my nonna's outraged glee. Sometimes Mamm'Adele would shyly ask questions about the *schifosi* acts shameless persons performed on each other's bodies. Only then did I notice her own ancient body, and I was ashamed—of my body.

Okay. Flesh is like bread dough that has risen too far and deflated. Don't get sentimental over it. If she groaned with the pain of forcing turds out her brittle *culo,* I would come behind the commode like my mother and punch at her shoulders and knead them down. Having my hands on her already would make it easier to lift her and lean her against the bed so I could wash her. The canal through which we all passed was now extruded in corrugated swags, little spikes of hair remaining clotted with tiny pieces of toilet paper. Oh, the folds to be washed—lifted like sheets from the furniture.

But the linen sheets she had woven herself as a girl have gone thin with use. Worn out down the middle, split, then the outer edges brought in and joined with feather stitches, they stay crisp even as the last threads go; the cotton sheets she had made from bleached feed sacks, elegantly joined by the same stitches, remain rough even after years through my mother's dryer. Mamm'Adele was comforted by their familiar harshness against her rapidly numbing diabetic fingers. I would have been comforted if the wrinkles festooning her slack belly were sharp like creased sheets, but her skin was as soft as a mouse.

And her breasts were like tomatoes. After her rosary she would call to my nonno, "Cherubino, Cherubino," twenty-five years since last he'd touched her. He must have answered because she'd talk in the dark to somebody in a voice that mixed flirtatious lilt and oracular exasperation. "Come for me," she'd coyly command.

After Mass when my nonna died, Pop said lightly, "We'll put her ashes in the garden with the tomatoes. Ashes make good fertilizer; she wouldn't want to go to waste." Mamma said nothing. I looked at her compressed lips trying to gauge whether this was my father's sardonic joke and, if it was, did she actually think it was funny. Perhaps, in the tradition of my nonno, my father was thumbing his nose at the church and the pious hypocrisy of the Mass for the Dead. If he were, would my mother rush to join his infidel's nonchalance? Mamma said, "You know how she loved the garden. You know how she loved my tomatoes."

Well, Mamm'Adele didn't love that garden. She never saw it because she had gone blind before she moved in with my mother, and when she was forcibly led into it for some fresh air and distraction she whined the whole time at my mother's bullying and at the inadequacy of her crops and at her failure to be the gardener all my genius uncles found the time to be. Great leafed chard and chicory and their Lucullan tomatoes. . . . To tell the truth, my nonna was right. Mamma is a grudging gardener—parsimonious with seed and with manure and with planning—stingy with affection for the earth though dutiful to it. Eventually duty took my nonna's ashes and patted them into the faraway earth of my nonno's grave. Not into the garden, of course. Nothing special, according to my father. My mother has never talked about that journey.

The garden was neglected more than usual the last year of my grandmother's life, then neglected more still the next year as my father almost immediately passed into his heart's last clutches. Squares of soil where Pop could no longer do the deep spading went fallow. Stakes were left tangled in their strings. Arugula behaved like the predatory weed it is. In the house, Pop hovered adoringly behind Mamma, seldom leaving her alone—though soon he too would leave altogether. My mother, her hands as occupied as her mother's and as embarrassed by petting, sent up more clouds of flour for too much pasta, dug more furrows than she planted, and made more dresses than her granddaughters could wear so that my father wouldn't see her fear as he followed her feebly from room to room, touching her arm and delivering himself of learned lectures on obscure subjects too recondite for my mother to understand—though Mamma often mangled them later on and represented them as her own at the Sunday table. In her telling, the periodicity of sunspots obscuring global warming somehow became lunar, causing environmentalists to suffer from PMS. My father beamed indulgently, glad to have our exasperated attention deflected from his purloined cigarettes and his failing heart.

"Oh, just plant me under the tomatoes," said Pop to stave off the terror. "I owe my ancestors." The August before, he'd gone down to Salem, New Jersey, for the Great Tomato Festival, where each year the town commemorates some remote progenitor of my father who had proven tomatoes edible to the whole world, not to mention Italy, by stepping out on the courthouse steps and, before all the astonished colonial yokels, consuming the fatal flesh of the fox apple—thereby dooming his family ever after to mixing their blood with the true and faithful gardeners and eaters of *pomodori*.

The March day my father died, my mother came back from the hospital and grimly set to work breaking up the frozen earth in the garden. She worked until dark. My youngest brother, Paul, had flown nine hours, hopscotching from New Mexico to the Garden State, to be with Pop, but arrived twenty minutes too late. At the hospital they allowed him to sit in the morgue. Paul was cold and starved. He came into the house and foraged in the freezer for some tomato sauce from last summer. When he found it, he heated it and poured it over leftovers which Ken, my next younger brother, and I ate from the same plate.

By the following morning our sister, Christina, had arrived with her daughters. Christina wandered wordlessly to the sink and started washing vegetables. Soon after Zia Vera and Uncle Dick (who is also my father's brother) arrived with our double-first cousins. Thicker blood. When we were little kids, we thought that meant our blood was like tomato paste, while all the rest of the *cugini* had thin sauce in their veins. Then came Pop's relatives and all my mother's *parenti*. Our own children milled about, embarrassed by our grief and bored and hungry. Container after container of sauce was taken out of the freezer and defrosted. Who knows what was cooked to go under it.

"This is from last year's crop?" Zia Vera asked to distract Mamma.

"I didn't get them in until late, but still I had too many."

"Don't I remember. I told you that you shouldn't bother, that I'd start the seedlings for you, but you had to plant anyway, stupid wop. First spring gust blows in from the east and we think we can smell the Adriatic. Then every guinea who can find room for a number ten tin can on his fire escape or knows how to knot a handkerchief on four corners for his head is out there setting tomato flats like a *contadino*."

"Oh come on, Vera," said my mother, glad to be angry at her sister's usual alcoholic diatribes of ethnic self-loathing.

"It's true, it's true," crowed my Zia, giving my mother a punch in the arm. "Early last summer you had so many seedlings you told me you were bringing me a carful of flats. I told you I had already set out my tomatoes, but no—you said you couldn't let them go to waste and that you were bringing them anyway. I had a picture of great squirming vines heaving through the windshield, strangling you until the leader of *The Revenge of the Killer Tomatoes* took over the driver's seat, but you arrived with an empty car and not a tomato in sight."

"Vera, you always have to exaggerate."

"So what did happen to all the tomato plants?" asked my brother Paul.

"Well, Vera said she didn't want them, so one night I took them down the hill to Marzullo's Nursery, squeezed through the fence, and mixed my flats in with theirs."

"Why didn't you just throw them out?" My brother Ken hews closely to the paternal line, *nonno papà e figlio*, of pragmatic blasphemy in the face of anything sacred, anything sentimental.

"Throw them out?" My mother was deeply offended. "Throw them out? That would be wasteful. I figured they'd blend in and somebody would adopt them."

Paul guffawed, choking on a spoonful of polenta. He looked down to see if he had sputtered any sauce on his shirt. "Aren't you worried that twenty years from now some orphan tomato will have gotten into Marzullo's locked files and will show up at your door asking, 'Are you my real mother?'"

For a moment we thought Mamma might cry. But she didn't. She said she had to go out to the garden for something—probably to see how many of last summer's stakes could be used for this year's tomato vines.

∽

lovers and other dead animals
Vittoria repetto

> she said lobsters don't die easy
> they scream
>   &
> you have to
> hold the lid down.

ᑎᐧ

Tripe
Lucia Perillo

> We were never a family given to tongue or brains.
> So the cow's stomach had to bear her last straws,
> had to be my mother's warning-bell that chops and roasts
> and the parched breasts of chickens, the ribs and legs
> and steaks and fish and even the calf's sour liver
> had become testaments to the monotony of days.
> Since then I have understood the rebellion hedged
> in its bifurcated rind, its pallor, its refusal
> to tear or shred when chawed on by first
> the right then the left jaw's teeth—
> until finally the wad must be swallowed whole.
>
> The tough meat meant life's repertoire had shrunk
> to a sack inside of which she was boxing shadows—
> kids and laundry, yes, but every night the damned
> insistence of dinner. And wasn't the stomach
> a master alchemist; grass and slops and the green dirt
> transformed into other cuts of bloody, marbled beef.
> Times when she wanted her own transformation
> the house filled with its stewing, a ghastly sweet
> that drove us underneath the beds. From there
> we weathered the bomb-clouds rising off her range,
> blowing the kitchen walls as wide as both Dakotas.

And I pictured her pale-faced & lustrous with steam
as she stood in that new open space, lifting
the hair off her neck as the stockpot billowed
its sugary haze like the sweat of a hired man.

∾

Let Them Eat Cake

Anne Calcagno

Until the other day, I did not know my feet had become so crookedly misshapen and wide. I told myself my socks were unnecessarily thick; the weather was too hot; it stood to reason my shoes were squeezing me. That wasn't true. I had changed without knowing it because I hadn't looked my way for a long time. With my eyes focused away from me, I've lived out my days in an interlude. Because when I suddenly saw the width of my warped feet, my eyes next traveled up the length of my legs, noticing mottled bruises like disheveled leaves rotting on my legs—I have distractedly smashed into things. I moved to cover them, saw the back of my hand, vein-swelled and colorful, too, like a cabbage leaf. In surprise, I touched my face, the skin slack as silk. I was stunned; as if it all happened in one day, the pieces lined up: I am not young.

It feels as if I have always been fat. I married twenty-three years ago, have been overweight for twenty. Over time, I lost all personal perspective, grew overwhelmed in reaction to wide-eyed glances: when you're fat you're a focus. In public places, like the supermarket, they observe you until you can't get away from being your own prisoner. Wheeling my cart around, I peered as much as I could, before fleeing. I've been an exaggeration of cells, and a reduced woman. My short blonde hair curls into squat corkscrews, tips up; sometimes, when the perm is running out, I look bristling. Yet, when the harried supermarket cashier glances up, I'm the one whose eyes roll into her lap. This is how it is to be an anomaly. Yet the point is, the other day I looked at my feet, which are garbled by widening corns, and it became terribly clear: like other women, conclusively mortal, I am going by degrees. No one is a constant picture.

My disfigurement was a private affair. I ate and many things became mine. My consumption accumulated, giving me the appearance of having more years than my actual age. For many years, with a lot of effort, I still could have peeled off those layers and reached a young person. But it is too late. Time went ahead and did some real altering. I am forty-one and have come to look like hell. But my feet, the other day, weren't a continuation of this exaggerated flesh that haunts me. They were life and the broad response of time. I don't know why I saw this.

Age is an invisible train charging through the dark, wearing down the rails. Gradually, I'd been feeling in need of repair. I grew to have more bent space inside. I thought: what should I call this? what have I done?

My husband, perhaps two weeks before I looked at my feet, became aware of his own wearing down. He began to feel his life erasing, tried to leap back from the movement of the train, the foreshortening of horizons. He grappled to stop losing things, saw me. He remembered me differently: supple, eighteen, my eyes on the gravel lifting up very quickly to notice he was there. I was like a leaf. He could have picked me up and taken me anywhere, kept me in his pocket or pressed in a book.

So, a martini in his hand, he said, "You were sweet and your ankles were thin, hon. Now you're close to a heart attack."

"What's happened now?" I asked.

"For Chrissake, Susan, you're wasting your life. Listen, I won't watch you do this anymore. Lose some weight. I'll buy you dresses. We'll make you into a star, the star of my life, Susan. We've waited too long for this."

"Isn't this coming out of the blue?" I ventured.

"Don't you understand what I'm saying?" he replied.

Harry is almost bald, and his remaining disconnected hairs stood straight up with the lamplight gleaming behind them. He had finished his drink. He stared at me. We were in the middle of a movie episode and I was a girl in bright dresses, and he was a young dapper ready to love. But he was catching on fire with the lamplight gleaming around his head and shoulders.

Harry invested himself in this rejuvenating idea, and became insistent. He had not talked to me much in a long time, yet now he repeated himself. "You lose some weight. I'll buy you dresses. What about the good old days?" These must have been the beginning of our marriage. Being a salesman, he started going away. Absence became a pattern. I sought company in food. I grew into a wide plateau, crushing the good old days, he says. I can't remember the good old days.

Five years ago, I started working. The newspaper ad looked for someone "willing to learn." I am a secretary for an escort service, on the top floor of an old undecorated building. They call it a modeling agency. This is the way it's done: hidden and glorified. I believed the disguise for a long time because that's what you see looking up at you in the Yellow Pages. You have to read the fine print to figure out the code. And I didn't see. Strangers in town get lonely and greedy. They call my boss, Rose, willing to pay. I file their accounts. An array of girls in tight colorful dresses and hose, with foreign accents or long hair, always in high heels, come to the office, dependent and warm, wanting more than they have. I give them applications and they preen themselves in front of me as if I am neutral practice for a man. I watch silent but accustomed. I keep thinking I'm to give them something, but I can't find it. I have come to believe in the heart of every woman there is a secretary; she wants to assist. These women are so different from me in their way of serving; each is a bird full of plumes and her red fingernails hand me back the forms. But she is a secretary. As I am.

I tried to explain this idea to Harry a while back. "Hell, call them something better than secretaries. Can't get help like that from Kelly Girls!" His hand slapped his knee with gusto. In the beginning, I remember I was happy because of the way he enjoyed his own jokes.

"It's serious," I said. "So many servants in the world."

"We all need to rely on each other, sweetcakes. That's what you forget when you shut yourself tight as a rock."

When I found out the girls were not models, I was amazed. Thereupon, Harry visited me at the office to peek at photos. "Pretend I'm an important account," he said.

In the meantime he had been having a few salesman's affairs, things in motels of which he lately informed me. He was explaining his decision to help me regain the shape he first met. Upset, he confessed, he could not make love to my shapeless flesh; he pursued women with angles and curves until it bored him. "I can't remember one face," he said. "That's pretty sad."

"Why did you tell me that?"

"You need a confidante, to understand yourself. When you tell someone else your sins, you've got a responsibility to change. Now you'll make me change, hon."

"I never wanted to know everything about you," I said.

"Can't you see what I've done to keep myself protected?"

Harry wanted the woman he loved to be so riveting that the envious stares of others around him would, like a magnetic force, keep him gravitated toward her. I grew into a monstrosity. Precisely the fact that they stared at me spun him away.

After Harry confessed, I couldn't get rid of what he had told me and how my weight had ruined my life. Two weeks later, on a glazed-flat day, my swollen feet caught my attention. I stared. Minute by minute I grew amazed, because my realization was unprecedented. Looking at my feet, I saw that age had bitten into them with all its crookedness. It didn't appear hesitant to finish its meal. And I don't know why, but then I knew that my hands, my eyes, my cartilage— all of me—was tied close to the same sounds and ways of others, held to the globe. I am what always happens in time, and it's so magnanimously unlike my own failings. Now, the only thing is: I do not want to become the shape of a woman Harry chased.

If I am ever thin I will not have thrown off dead weight; my husband will have pressed it into a thin red lining right under my skin, that is what memory is like. Harry stormed into our house with yesterday's picture of me in mind, hoping to peel me back out. I am very full but he has decided I could just as well be beginning. No one can be emptied out. Never before has my aloneness been made so clear. There are other fat women like me; I see them in the pastry aisles. But I am in myself alone.

Harry has been out of town, on a job, for three days. At lunchtime, I went to the Red Cross shoe store and selected bright green comfort-fit pumps. Their sharp little heels protruded like horns from cocoons. It was me and the geriatric ladies all belonging in the store together, relishing our colorful spoiling of our troubled feet. Things have blown open around me as if I suddenly stepped over the horizon into a rushing wind: it lifts my hem, pulls my hair into disarray, swirls up my sleeves. Walking to work in the pictured disorder I've realized I want someone to talk to, to explain this. I feel newly in existence, terribly sensitive, sick of confinement. What is this? An older woman. Unlike before, I'm impelled to watch myself as a part of everyone.

I know the women Harry slept with were likely to spend an hour getting ready to go out for coffee. He looked for this, having found me incapable of it. It wasn't for him to see that their ardent self-description is an embroidery of hunger. When these women are as young as the escorts I work with, they feel the pulse of their generation clicking in their heels, and they toss and turn looking for something. They stretch into life like branches, to grow. My husband, I am sure, never sensed this feeling in them; instead, felt out his advantage. Their limbs were octopus tentacles he could feast on. And when they were older, didn't the women still seem to be looking for an answer? By habit, they allow their men to imagine that they are waiting to be shown life. The men become accustomed mostly to devouring them blind. The women don't ask for change. They don't like change. They want to remain beautiful and wanted. Over the years it takes more and more time.

Today, a girl walked into the office, tallish, in a red coat. Her hair bleached, curling down her shoulders, her nose pointed, her mouth plump and nubile as a rosebud. She reminded me of a picture of the women at Louis XVI's court in France, women in high hair and lace, with red cheeks, women decadent in their life, who at the end of the world said: "Let them eat cake."

I wondered if she knew any of this. "You think women understand the world less than men?" I asked.

She looked at me, her eyes compressing very thin. "Are you kidding? Every one of those men had a mom, and if those moms hadn't been preparing men for the world the men wouldn't be able to handle anything." She looked at her red fingernails. "It takes a woman to know." She leaned close, "I know how to baby men, too."

"Don't do it," I said.

"Shit. I don't have much time. Is this an interview?" She hiked up her hose, tugging at her ankles, clamping her thighs.

"They look at photos before the interview," I said.

"I look good," she replied. Rose called the girl into her office.

I made a sudden collect call to my friend Rema, who I've know since childhood. She listens without needing preliminaries, though she lives far away. "Rema, thank God you're home. Can you listen now?"

"Well, tell me."

"It just hit me like a ton of bricks that I haven't given myself a look in years. Who've I been?"

"You've been living, honey," Rema says. "Where did you get the idea that you have to stare at yourself all the time, to live? That can hold you up. Plenty of people go nuts like that."

"No. We don't have this idea straight, most of us; you have gold running in your veins, rising up to your heart. If you *see* that, you begin to catch it."

"Some people might feel that way," she says. "Sure, some do. What's been happening?" Her voice is patient as lake water.

"I can't understand myself why everything has changed," I say. "Everything seems on fire. It makes me so nervous." I just looked at my feet.

Rema says, "That's how it is; you can't tell when the next thing is going to happen."

After work, to see the world a little, I walk a few extra blocks to the bus stop. People are so busy running home, I'm not noticed. Today, the yellow leaves were falling and breathing themselves into the wind, mingling up a bitter scent of regret. I've noticed each winter comes by advance of many tantrums; the trees toss their heads, the grasses shake, disheveled, blown up, turned brown. Today, the leaves scurried over, wildly dancing between my feet while an endless blue blanket looked down, self-contained. All at once, something alive darted at my feet. I flung myself back, against a wall. My heart nearly leapt out of my mouth. It was a squirrel, now staring at me, a yard away, flicking its tail, raising itself on its hindquarters. It began to gesture at me by way of masticating, though it had nothing in its jaw. Two others ran up and all three performed this communication, chewing a mock meal, understanding that I had something to give them. And I do understand hunger. But I had nothing for them. On the bus going home I saw animals in people's faces: a lynx, goats, a flamingo, a saddened spaniel. But these citizens won't show their hunger.

It saddens me to know I walked around for years in trepidation of myself without knowing or remembering this hunger in others. I tried to hide my own, but it spoke on my body. I peered out a small window that never opened. Every day circled me like gauze, and I was mummified into the years. My husband called it a disgrace. My heart closed like a little stone. Harry is ravenous for taut flesh, yet now age flicks him around in its large jaw, tugging at his skin, decomposing his bones. He is amazed, denying time's hunger.

I never had this brazen confidence to deny life's big appetite, but I never thought I'd understand it either. Yet life and time are always tapping inside your ear to confide in you. Occasionally, I would be startled by sounds like a foreign song: vague, remarkable music. I placed it far away. But chords were rising through me, to describe me. This is how potential approaches you: in no one else's language. If you grasp it, other people sense it. It begins to announce itself. Like a song, you can't exactly say you see it. Mine rose up through my feet.

I looked down at myself and saw the silent onslaught of years, the wide general thing represented in my feet. This isn't my failure. I have a double dimension of weight: one fat made me hide, but this can have grace because it's everyone's mirror.

The night before Harry left on his present trip, he visited the supermarket. Lettuce, trim-fat dinners, broccoli, tomatoes, celery, and crackers returned with him. He looked as happy as an auctioneer. He slapped his hands together, grinned: "Here we go! We're ready, aren't we?"

It is as if a beetle begins crawling inside my stomach.

"The thing I want to tell you, honey, is that this isn't just about taking off pounds; it's about building a whole new love. A spic-and-span streamlined one, Susie. I can hardly wait."

I looked him straight on: "I'm concerned with my spirit. And you can't get that with celery. How could you go looking in the supermarket?"

Harry's pupils retracted quick as crabs. "So you're a coward?" he asked. "Are you? Shit, you're the biggest disappointment of my life." He turned to the kitchen sink and spat. He grabbed the porcelain edge as if he was saving it from falling off the wall. "You're going to ruin our life!" he shouted.

I have my age. It climbs around my hips and pulls them down into more and more chairs. All my veins are pulsing fiercely, and this work, through time, has slackened my skin, interspersed it with magnets and marbles. This is an accumulation I must tend to. Life surreptitiously crowded in me. I want to walk through my markings, to pick them up as on a cafeteria line, to have so full a dish I'll be stunned by it. Age is a sort of overeating.

Many of the escorts from my office fear life will pass them by. They fling themselves into the world to be touched. Life has walked through me and, like a town square, I have been mute through the walkings, have been the vessel not the subject. I see that though I did not pay attention to the way life was changing me, I cannot say it passed me by. It passes no one. I must try to tell them this. Age draws itself on the flesh and time becomes palpable. You can tell yourself certain things did not happen and let your mind become a blank slate, but the flesh won't play chameleon. It stabilizes you, and imprints the artifacts of your route: they're yours.

I am rising, heavy and powerful as an old seal, independent in my digestion, awake.

∾

Parable
Anne Marie Macari

The parable of the pears was the one never repeated
because it had to do with sex, and more than sex
it was Jesus at his best showing them secrets
about the different kinds of love. There was a pear
whose brown skin had the whole rough hillside in it,
but inside so sweet he had to lie down to eat it,
and a more rare, red-skinned pear. It had no shame.
The harsh Jesus of the figs and vines
was undone, thankful, he was brimming,
in his mouth that taste he could never confide,
they would never believe him, they still wore
the dullness, they still thought day to day,
something simple might change their lives if only
they listened, if only they forgot everything
they knew, something of heaven would sprout
from their mouths if only they were ready for its flavor.

∾

Rosette
(*St. Thérèse of Lisieux*)
Susanne Antonetta

The Zepherine drouhin's impossible to grow—
a martyr to rust, my mother said, when she weighed
eighty-five pounds & her cough rasped,
grinding her bones together. I imagined her
inside, full of a fine white meal. The fierce
chlorophyl of morphine. She had had her hair done
before going in the last time, a head of fat pubic
curls. *Make it last this time,* she said.

When the Zeph. bloomed three weeks in that wet winter
I knew Therese held us in her hands.
I began piping perfect shells. The saint
worked with me. The shells
hard white, spined, perfectly articulate.
Impossible for me before.

It's something I can only tell
to her, how much I think about cakes, about frosting
the white solemn surface—
not wet, not dry, this blank
moisture my hand feeds—
my bud roses, drop flowers, floodwork,
weave, & figure piping, & stars.

A martyr to rust, my mother said of the Zeph., like she
was not the concern.

•

Sometimes I mix my colors, do flowers
in black gray olive, inner-ear, inner-flower dark.

For my mother's wake: a garden of mudbrown grass
black satin apple blossoms on black stems, slate roses.
I held a wedding woman to a gas flame, bent her double
& robed her in black buttercream (my sister
took her off) still the cake sat there, a sheet cake,
& a mourning-garden, like what
the vague blue hand of death would grow.

Why shouldn't we take what we can & leave our mark?
God did that, I'm sure, in Genesis
found out what he was
& what he didn't want to be any longer.

I border with rosettes, there, where one universe ends
& another less
personal one begins.

•

Saint Thérèse
on her own photograph: *yes that's the envelope. When*
will anyone see the letter?

Though it's the envelope we love: a salt-cellar
reliquary of femur, pinch of hair on a cross. At Carmel
the other nuns
crowded her cooling body. A dead virgin, a bellpull
to the Lord! Whether they liked her or not they cupped her feet.
Sister St. Vincent found herself cured of a sucking anemia,
her blood plush as ocean.

If I'da been a saint, my mother said, coughing
(pointing to the tucked skin where her breasts had hung)
you could make a fortune off these . . .

                                        •

I put a cake in the car when I went to see her.
White, with pink roses, a true pink you get
with just a toothpick-tip of Christmas Red.
Fingertip scatter of apple blossom. White rosettes
marking the border. Her relics delivered
from place to place, I expected
a brilliant white limo with rearview rosary dangling
instead she came in a blue stationwagon, New Jersey plates, bare—
the church calls it the Thérèsemobile.

Her riding in the gilt & jacaranda bonebox (Rome won't say
how many bones we got)
plexiglass & under it, rosettes
on the gothic spires. At Our Lady's
they had six little girls with America roses
throw petals in her path.

The long wait in line
& the woman I stood behind tubed
in Ralph Lauren jeans, with gray-blond
cocker spaniel hair. She held two fists full of rosaries
touching them to the box in practiced turns—

each side of the crucifix had to touch—
& when she caught my eye she squinted
in a shrugging, humorous but not sorry way . . .

Doing it to sell, I thought, *she must be*, the way
she glanced at the box, the saint's photo
suspended there, without interest.
Rosaries dripping like kelp from her hand.

Won't do anybody any good, my mother said, *not blessed
that way.*

Thérèse's mother like my mother followed her breasts to heaven
but when Thérèse was four not forty, too young
for sponging off bedsores, turning
& turning a body, the letter
slipped halfway out.

•

I don't use butter in my frosting. Only Crisco. Powdered
sugar, for the whitest
white, of mountaintops & ravished souls. Too sweet

Paul says. Said. I have a theory that if the world hadn't fallen
we could love that sweetness. How could any joy
be too much?

I used to think I made my cakes
so the eater could know God's glory here on earth,
the beauties earthly things can reach for.

Then my mother died, I couldn't conceive. Paul left
by printing out an e-mail he wrote a friend
where he said I had no heart, & bad thighs. He knew,
he said, everything in the past was wrong . . . I believed
I could only give a moment's sugary numbness
to a life pointless & without pleasure.

Finally I found
both reasons true—

•

Thérèse in my cottage garden, Thérèse
on the freeway
in a box on the backseat, like a cake.

We live in an age of inventions. And I was determined
to find an elevator to carry me to Jesus.

What I keep regretting isn't Paul
or the death of my mother
but being a woman who can't keep roses alive—
who prunes in spring, won't deadhead, won't feed
or give weekly water, who might plant thyme
& mow it down with the lawnmower, half careless,
half cruel
getting disgusted finally in August & putting down
diazinon & Miracle-Gro.
The deaths of small things
barely worthy of anyone's forgiveness.

•

Jesus isn't doing much to keep the conversation going
Thérèse said once, a woman who spoke in rose petals.

If she comes to you, you get roses somehow
like my friend Ruth whose tubes ruptured.
Out the ambulance window she saw Thérèse, smiling,
& when she came to
a silk shock of petals in her palm.
Fell off something the nurse said, *here have it*
—a white rose—
& now Ruth calls the saint *Terry*, like they've been to lunch.

Father said, *She makes sainthood real*
to people like us . . . the mundane, almost
profane martyrdoms & ecstasies

Giving herself, at Carmel, the rustiest spoon
the coldest piece of omelette, offering herself

as a *victim to Merciful Love,* detailing
The Anguish of the Parlor Visits.
Before that at age 14 her Christmas conversion, Jesus
filling her soul as she started to scream
about wanting Christmas presents in her shoes.

The sweet flower of passion she squeezed
from the bag of ordinary life.

.

Paul wanted me to *want*
more for myself, my own shop, a life
with something in it that could pass for glory.

Always beside me at my dinged spot in the kitchen, butcher block
hovering above my pleasure.
Always taking my tips & spinning them on his thumb.

If I got sick enough of him I snapped the TV on.
Once after my mother's
cytoxin drip (enough to kill
a swarm of locusts, the doctor said,
beyond tact) & my mother probably still vomiting
back there at the hospital, thumbing her
Combatting Cancer with Potent Potions handbook—

Paul & I stood & watched a show on marsupials
me squeezing out budroses & Gerber daisies
Paul spinning, me piping, & between us
the invisible ink of thought . . .

Once in evolutionary time
everything was marsupials, but the earth broke up,
so they survived in Australia—kangaroos, wombats,
koalas—but died everywhere else.
Still giving birth to embryos they carry in pouches like letters,
too weak, wiped out
on other continents by newer stronger species, & a mother
kangaroo will throw her babe
to the revised, mammal
body of a dingo, rather than die herself.

(So this is the world You made the first time, You
who feel so unsurprised by it all!)

And I stopped to watch while my #77
star tip went clattering across the floor.

How could this be enough?
That's what he said to me.

                                    •

Scraps, Orts, & Fragments

Thérèse—named after a dead child, mother couldn't nurse because of breast
cancer (tumors), sent her away for a year to a wet nurse.

The Anguish of the Parlor Visits. Doctor Night. Virgin statue smiling.

What an interesting study the world makes when you are about to leave it.

But Pauline, I am the Child Jesus' little ball, if he wants to break his toy, he is
free.

Lent 20 francs to Celine. Oh! Jesus, you alone, and that is enough.

The terrible disease of scruples. You would have to endure this martyrdom to
understand what it was like. It would be impossible for me to say what I suf-
fered for eighteen months. (aunt described her at the time as "delightfully
happy," playing in the Normandy countryside)

                                    •

I will return. My heaven will be spent on earth.
fingertip thrill

Thérèse of Lisieux—Christmas present in the shoe, near tantrum, realization
of grace

I will send down a shower of rosepetals from heaven

I will spend my time in heaven doing good on earth.

people looking at her like "a string of onions"

mother died of breast cancer when she was 4—my dog Lummi dying, that floppiness

receiving roses

cake decorating & needlework—decorator's rosette; the border, the boundary, the edge of the physical world

windstorm—rose petals flying

∿

Basil
Sandra M. Gilbert

> A question the box of earth
> still asks the kitchen,
>
> *as in* green blades
> of Liguria, green
>
> spears of the watery
> forests of Thailand,
>
> peppery keen
> airs of August
>
> *as in* wise king
> do not fade,
>
> *as in* a pot of,
> where the lover's head
>
> explodes into new
> ideas, *as in*

chop the loss finely,
add salt and stew

and halo the old charred
grandmother stove,

as in what to do
with the last

three stained tomatoes
hung on the vine.

∽

Love Lettuce

Flavia Alaya

It must have been the zucchini soup. He sat down at my table—exactly where he sits to this day—his pale eyes widening at the chartreuse velvet vision on a soup plate. Then he spooned it in and smiled. This was a happy man.

He was proud of his own cooking. "I make a very good lasagna," he told me, and promised to bring me some. And it *was* good, I discovered later, but by then he'd had my *tortellini in brodo*, those lovely little "Venus-navels" shimmering in a gilded broth laced with the driest of dry marsalas. And possibly a stuffed roast chicken I remember favoring at the time, the bird expertly deboned and then plumped back to fullness with a savory stuffing of semolina bread and sausage, a few caramelized shallots, the faintest hint of clove, and it might have been then he decided his lasagna could wait.

My kids called him my Hardware Man even before they met him, and since they no longer lived at home I suspect it may have been meant to sound protective as well as sexy. After all, I'd discovered him when I went to order replacement glass for a back window somebody had smashed breaking into the house. Of course, considering that Neil Hardware is in a pretty hardscrabble Paterson neighborhood, Eighteenth and Tenth, opposite a crumbling nutmeg-colored old textile mill and only a block from the bar where they pinned the murder charge on Hurricane Carter, maybe I was the one discovered. Because little as I expected to find true love at the hardware counter, I think Sandy expected even less to see it come through that old bevelled-glass door, past the sidewalk bar-ricade of six-foot aluminum ladders and galvanized garbage pails and into the dimly lit funk of what had been a man's world for the past fifty years. Let alone in the shape of a lady professor with a smoky voice and pretty good legs.

He insists (which I think makes it OK to repeat it) that he was a goner almost from the moment I signed the credit card slip with my exotic, belly dancer name and a hand as smooth as a girl's. But *I say* it was the soup, because while I may at the time have been in that last rage of a woman's lifetime quota of estrogen and still looking pretty good, as they say, I wasn't looking for love, believe me. Nor was he, he says, and I believe him.

Why should we? Till that moment, life seemed to have been a chain of bummers for both of us, mostly for love or what had looked like it coming down the road, and it still almost scares me, the *mystery* of it, how we could have met ourselves, in a way, in that queer jumble of a store and that awful junkshop place in both our lives.

First he made excuses for turning up at the house, my needing a special bucket for the city's new recycling program, for instance, so he dragged an empty nail bin up the steps to the front porch one day, Neil's big white van parked down at the curb just ahead of the fire hydrant, and rang the doorbell, scaring the bejesus out of me. But the first time he came by *after* work was to install a towel rack for the new top-floor bathroom, one of those odd bits the carpenter had left unfinished, and that was when I invited him for zucchini soup. My old three-story Queen Anne had already seen a lot of quirky carpenters, but so had he, and I liked that he had something pithy and dry-witted to say about every one of them from his side of the hardware counter. So as fall turned to winter, more and more things seemed to need doing around the house, and chances were, whenever one of my kids visited, I'd be headed down to Neil's. "Ma's gotta go to the *haaardware* store," they'd say with those wiseass, grown-up-kid smirks. "*Again.*" But maybe they were thinking I'd done the lonely widow thing long enough.

Sandy is a pretty tight-lipped Dutchman and would never be telling you this himself, not the way I am. Even then it took me weeks to learn how he'd left a bad marriage in Illinois and come back to Pines Lake, just north of Paterson, to live with his parents again, the job at Neil's thrown in via his brother-in-law. His dad had just had a triple bypass, and it wasn't long before his mom got sick and things went into serious crisis. Not that he was much of a nurse, but what was a lonely guy to do, living on Heartbreak Hill and Harry Chapin tapes? At least

he could handyman the rambling ranch-style he'd grown up in, though it was
a lot to keep up with—the job at the store, the caregiving, the cooking, market-
ing, housekeeping, plus mowing and raking the yard, not to mention conquer-
ing the force that wants to turn every scintillating in-ground swimming pool
on earth into a slimy, algaed pond.

The house itself was simple enough, a hunkered-down white-and-brown frame
set back from Mohawk Trail, one of those sidewalkless, bungalow-dotted little
roads all named for Indian tribes that wind their steep and mazy way down to
Pines Lake. It was set on such a sharply sloped lot, front to back, that it took
three stages of huge, well-engineered deck to get down to the pool level from
the kitchen door, the ivy and rosebushes woven into its latticework making a
kind of dark pueblo for wild raccoons. Back of the pool, the ivy clung like wiry
dark hair along the fence, tangling itself at the far corner of the yard in the
hooves of a big plaster deer, who looked so mournful down there you could
almost hear him cry, lifting his throat and antlers out of the dark.

Sandy'd lived there for about a year and a half when I met him. It was obvious
that he'd been doing his job. The entropy of the place was under control: the
lawn, his pride and joy, was smooth as a putting green, the pool utterly clear and
blue and inviting. And he thought it had also been good for him—not just
physically, though it was that, making him feel a different kind of fit from the
straight, iron-pumping work of heaving fifty-pound bags of cement off the
delivery truck and onto the loading dock at the store—but good for his soul,
especially those late summer twilights after a swim, sitting out under the drop-
ping tulip trees, making pets of whatever raccoons he could coax up on to the
top of the deck to take M&Ms out of his ears.

He'd be the first to admit that he'd made that lawn an obsession, the kind of
thing people do when they feel a little guilty about what they're doing—and
what they're not. Neil's had everything to feed both the obsession *and* the
lawn, of course, not just the hoes and rakes but the electric shears, the power
mowers, the hedge trimmers, the walkway groovers, the bug sprays, the
weedkillers—nothing to keep him from total investment till I came along.
And even after that he had me out there, alongside him, yanking up any
feisty little knobs of dandelion and purslane and chickweed with the nerve
to survive.

I resisted. I've never been a lawn purist, anyway, and I said that if he hadn't
already poisoned this stuff we could be eating it. I still nurtured girlhood mem-
ories of outings with my Sicilian mother, traipsing around Van Cortlandt Park

behind her, learning to pick the first spring dandelions for a tonic *insalata*. For a bit after Harry died, I'd had a little escape-place in New Hampshire, ensconced in a sloping meadow that had stirred my old mother-love and opened a whole new universe of weed-lore. I can bring dreamy tears to my eyes just picturing that lemony sorrel poking up between the patches of gravel in my yard, those long tender shoots I'd turn into a lovely sour soup that seemed to fit my melancholy at the time.

That first summer with Sandy, I gave him an obscure little Emerson satire I'd chanced on about the silliness of lawnmaking. But Sandy is a deep man. He merely glanced at it and smiled with that still certain blue irony in his eyes, and left it lying exactly where I'd put it down for him.

Meanwhile, my kids had read the signs of things warming between us. Alert to this little space of contest between us about the lawn, which I still thought jolly enough, they followed up a typical perverse-kid impulse and put a green fridge magnet in my next Christmas stocking. It read: "*I fought the lawn and the lawn won.*" Sandy and I both laughed out loud at the Clash take-off. But by then we were madly in love, indifferent to minor differences. Indifferent to kids. I slapped the magnet up on the fridge, where it has been ever since.

And now I wonder, did that little message grow out of touch with reality—or was it really an uncanny predictor of surrender?

•

But I am ahead of myself.

Because I must tell you that back at my old Queen Anne in Paterson I'd achieved the kind of utterly secular humanist landscaping program to make a born-again lawn zealot weep: plain concrete driveway, woodchips under the front juniper bushes, a layer of gray gravel over the backyard maple roots where the grass wouldn't grow, a bit of flagstone here, a bit of stone wall there, the stray hair of ivy at the lot line. A few remaining square feet out of the city lot the house sits on, lying beneath an immense and beloved beech tree, was my lawn, my crabgrass, as green and trimmed as I could make it or anyone else could who'd do it for me for money.

Barely past the stage of *tortellini in brodo,* Sandy was bound to change all that. First he tossed a little seed under the beech and nursed along the resulting straggles of new grass. Then one spring day I found him digging up a ten-foot patch near the backyard patio. There we planted red and white peonies together, ringed with orange and pink and purple impatiens, and I admit it was very pretty, like those colorful flower rings hugging the roots of the Pines Lake tulip trees. Times I've missed that blazing flower cluster, the way it turned our humble little flagstone patio into a place to be—a place to *eat*. A big glass table, complete with striped umbrella and cheap garden chairs, and there we were, doing ever more sumptuous gourmet parties al fresco—homemade breads, chicken with rosemary on the grill, seared fresh salmon with *aioli*—most of which I'd prepare in the kitchen and he'd carry out to the patio on trays in a perfectly coordinated frenzy between the two of us.

I guess for some time now Sandy had stopped describing himself as a good cook and taken happily enough to the role of sous-chef. We got to bringing our coordinated catering skills up to Pines Lake in a fine duet of meals-on-wheels. Classic favorites, naturally—London broil, steamed lobster, roast potatoes, corn on the cob—but it was really less about eating than as a way for us to be with Ed and Eleanor and still be together. Of course, *they* weren't quite sure what to make of all this *food* suddenly vrooming into their lives, like some Annette Funicello pool party. Ed was appreciative, brightening at certain touches, like that hint of fennel on his broiled sole; not that Eleanor wasn't, just that she ate like a bird, poking around and leaving food on her plate. Maybe she just didn't like sharing Sandy with me just when she thought she'd got him back to herself.

And then Ed died, and things began to come undone in Pines Lake. Sandy started his divorce, while his brother, who'd just got married, moved into the house next door on Mohawk Trail. As these things happen, *he* began to be Eleanor's *good* son. And as these things also happen, the seesaw between Sandy's place and mine began to tip. More and more as the weather turned and the days got short, we ate at my little round kitchen table again. Inspired by a tender passion I could express no other way, I made him fresh pasta on my precious *machinetta*. I even turned out my own ravioli. And alone together in the purple light, the sun fading over the backyard fence, he still in his everlasting soup spot, we'd sit holding hands, love and pasta, pasta and love, more intertwined than ever, more than the ivy in the low rock-walls at the edge of my yard, which we could just see from the kitchen window.

And which Sandy couldn't wait to tear out.

It was as if that ivy stood for the memory of anything in my life before he'd come into it. As if it stood for memory itself. So at last I said yes, he could tear it out, *if* he planted daylilies, which he did, and *if* he put comfrey along the new fence my good neighbor had put between our yards. And spring onions. Which he also did.

Ah, but the lawn. At first, he simply mowed it in a dutiful way—what was left of it after the impatiens and peonies—not letting on, perhaps still unsure himself, what he would do with it. On the north side of the house, just beyond the beech and square in the shadow of house and tree, it was, after all, nothing more than a somewhat arable patch. Not really fit for gardening.

And yet gardening there must be. Even as we began to talk about getting married and staying on in this old house (which he loved), Sandy seemed to become slowly possessed with a kind of madness, a kind of holy *gardening* madness. Not to be wasted on this inconsiderate arable patch, he announced one day, determined to set tomato and pepper pots on the roof of the Victorian veranda along the driveway, a roof, wide and ample, that lies just outside my den windows and sits, day-long, smack in the southern sun.

The summer blazed hot and dry. The planters grew bigger and heavier. Sandy ran home from work several times a day to climb out my window and water them, needing, by late July, to run a hose from the bathroom. He disrupted my writing. He left a trail of muddy footprints down the stairs. His roof-garden began to demand more and more attention, more and more water, in a spiralling cycle like an unsatisfied fisherman's wife. And yet the madness seemed to go on growing in him, and not just *in* him but *out* of him, *pouring* out of him, flooding over him. An urgency to create. An urgency to create *food.*

•

It comes to me now that the real onset of this possession (no other term will do) was the trip we took to New Hampshire together to see my old haunts and visit friends from the days I used to go up there to write. Rick and Geri especially, two of the gentlest, happiest, funniest, earth-eyed, back-to-the-land dreamers who ever invested their savings on a cantle of old farmstead on the Blackwater River, to "grow dirt," as Rick said, for an organic farm. But they were growing crops, too, and harvest was in full blaze when we got there, the whole miraculous works of it, canning in full tilt in the summer kitchen, herbs and flowers everywhere, that grooved landscape just radiating Earth Mother energy. And I think as he took in all that succulent ripeness something in Sandy seemed to fall into its sacred place, *fruit of the earth and work of human hands,* like a piece of liturgy.

We learned then that Rick and Geri got their seed from an organic cooperative in Maine called Fedco. The sixties had never died in Fedco-land, a place with a heart and a dry and witty Yankee catalogue-writing style to keep it from going soggy. We pored over their catalogue that winter like Paolo and Francesca over Camelot adulteries. How do I explain it—that something *erotic* for us about the whole thing? The most luscious bits of all, best read in bed together, were the descriptions of lettuce, divided with delicious whimsy into sections entitled "Lettuce Begin," and "Lettuce Continue," just so novices like us would know that lettuce has at least two seasons. So what, if our first crop degraded in July into a forest of seedy perdition? As soon as the summer heat was gone there'd be another crop, its heads just as round and sweet, its leaves just as lusciously green and pink and purple and gold. We might gather us greens and go right on gathering them, long into the shortening days, till the cold that had first braced their leafy shoots in the spring finally struck too deep in November and froze them translucent.

The very *thought* of lettuce so tender and near-sempiternal seemed to raise Sandy to new heights of gardening passion. He finally tore up the entire crab-grass lawn on the north side of the house. And I was glad to see it go, if only to envision in its place our own North Country, perfect for lettuce—the slant sun in the morning, the cooling shade at the hottest part of the day, the mild final rays cutting deep into the yard over the housetops to the west, toasting the tips of the red hiver.

At last, as his nascent new seedlings transformed the side lawn, Sandy took the last plunge and, defying the maple roots, dug up the gravel in the back to build raised beds for herbs. The birds and bees thought they were in the same paradise of sage and mint and oregano and chives as I was. He even built out the arable patch to grow zucchini, filling and leveling the slope against the front sidewalk, tilling and turning it by the sweat of his brow. Until finally the whole garden was alive with color from April to October, from palest green lettuce and deepest green spinach through bushbeans and pole-beans and *haricots verts* and red-stemmed beet-tops to yellow squash and purplest egg-plant, until that last rush of profuse citrus gorgeousness in the tangled multi-colored tomato crop of high summer—and all of it so perfectly synchro-nized in this tight little space that as one crop vanished another seemed to take its place as if by miracle.

And what a stupendous first lettuce crop that was, growing in bouquets like cabbage roses, better than roses. Sandy would crowd the heads together in a basket and present them to me as if they could be carried down the aisle. And if we hadn't got married in August, between crops, I think I would have.

Who would not marry such a man?

After the wedding, we partied on our own patio, and cut the cake, dotted with edible flowers, together, beneath the mingled shade of the maple and the beech. And almost apart from the trees, you could barely remember what had been there before.

•

Now for six months of the year my cooking was ruled by his garden. When we added wild arugula, brought like treasured contraband from a friend's place in South Jersey, the salads of June, with a new white *balsamico* dressing I invented to sweeten without smothering them, became a sighting of heaven. That first spinach *frittata*, after its last pass under the broiler flame, looked like an edible Mondrian. A few weeks more gave us *frittata* of beet-tops, vermilion stems staining luminously through the golden eggs like a dye. And the green beans! For weeks we'd blanche them by the mountains, touch them with salt and a hint of extra virgin and lemon, a grinding of black pepper to finish, and *basta*! If we couldn't eat them all (and we never could, alone) we'd fight over who'd have them cold the next day.

Ah, and then, in the superabundance of August, the zucchini soup—the recipe passed to friends with a fresh-picked bagful, recommending a *bruschetta* of fresh tomatoes and basil alongside. And the basil! As soon as it grew tall we'd whip it into freezer packets, each just enough for a single *pesto*, and give away the rest. It was loaves and fishes: even out of that little patch we fed the kids, we fed the neighborhood, we even fed some nicer public officials.
But the yellow cherry tomatoes—that was the crop we gave no one. Fresh off the vine they had at first disappointed us, lacking somehow that last poignant tang. Something told me to cook them, whip them in the blender, put them through the conical food mill—and, *caspita*, that was it! What a stupendous sauce! We had already discovered a factory store in Fair Lawn that made ravioli so good that I'd virtually given up making them myself. We'd cook up a pound with the spinach filling and drizzle them lightly with that brilliant velveteen sauce, untouched by any seasoning and needing none except our own fresh spinach-and-basil pesto on the side.

•

He gave to me and I did cook and eat.

Has any German philosopher ever theorized a *will to lasagna?* Because last year, Sandy, the overreacher, bought the pasta factory. Yes. Went off to make his own. And then I remembered—with a sudden fearful little stab (you know?) like the moment the earth in the garden too suddenly yields to your foot—I remembered that day, like a layer of new memory under my heart. That day in our kitchen, long before we discovered the little factory store, when I was rolling out pasta for fresh ravioli. And he'd stood by, watching, helping, stretching the golden sheets as they oozed from the rollers, thinking, perhaps (as I was), that it was better than minting money.

And he'd said, "I would love to do that." Quite simply. "I would love to make ravioli for a living."

Words are seeds. The little factory is just east of here. This blue-eyed Dutchman, *Italian by marriage,* as he tells his customers, makes the best ravioli in Bergen County, a pasta-eating county if there ever was one. Fresh pasta, too.

It is winter. Sometimes I break from writing and look out the window above the little round table. The yard is a shambles, the raised beds tumbled and splintered and the flagstones torn up—to make a better patio this spring, he says. And I think: the pasta factory is very demanding, as demanding as any novel.

My kids call him their Pasta Man now. They treat him and his bounty as if he were their second mother. He says it is all for me. And sometimes he takes a lasagna pan and sets down the strips of fresh ravioli in layers and spreads sauce and grated fresh mozzarella over them and bakes them for about an hour. It is, honestly, quite the dish.

∽

The Room

Anne Marie Macari

> The weight of the dirt beneath their fingernails,
> the burden of their footsteps approaching my door,
>
> so little time alone I sometimes wanted a sealed room
> like the woman who lived inside the walls

of a church and through the stone squint
heard the world whispering. Days I went

without speaking when the children were away
and made a wall of books around my bed, even kept out

the light, which was nothing compared to her life alone
though someone kneaded her bread,

picked the pocket fruit by her door
or brought honey and tiny nuts

forever patient in their shells . . .
It's something to find the mother everywhere,

to be fed, while rotting pods
fell from wet trees and childlike questions

kept coming multitudinous from their sulfury eggs.
As if we are none of us orphans,

as if my efforts didn't always feel like failure
and my God was not a mother.

In the end the room felt too small though the walls
changed color like clouds

and anyway I found myself averting my eyes
never seeing what she saw: woody thorns,

copious blood. It's not that I had no use for suffering,
but in the end the room itself

was a burden. It was a question of which way to turn
and where the light came from.

I thought of windows and the grasping of summer.
The wind was purple by then and the children and I

ventured toward the water, dragging our things.
It was a question of how to live with anger.

I saw it for a moment when they waded in the shallow bay
and bent over all at once to see some crab or fish,

their backs in white glare. The room
was gone by then, or else so enormous

I couldn't see how we were held.
The sky was pale, quiet, as if calling us with its smallest

voice, as if the sky were a visitor,
approaching, backing off, blue hands waving,

a visitor I stopped and called after,
wherever I was, at least once or twice a day.

∽

Hunger
Donna Masini

Deprived of a kind of salt I grew
to an insatiable craving.
I tried to eat rocks. I snapped
shut on a terrible hunger.
I hid from my mother—her black bras,
her spike heels, her curses and weeping.
I watched her. I dreamed her dead.
Her voice became the noise of my body.
I followed the blue veins on the backs
of her thighs as she leaned out the window
reeling in the clothes. I was taken
by her stories: the yellow pellets
she kneaded into margarine sacks,
a young girl, working it.
How it moved in her hands
deepening, undulant. Hunger I tasted
in the breeze she left behind. I hid from her

in closets that smelled of failure
and wings that ate holes in our clothes.
Where she kept the dead fox she snapped
about her throat. Teeth biting tail.
Coarse fur. Beady eye. I hid
from her teased hair and her lipsticks,
her shadows and powders and tears.
If I am not careful I leak black hands,
my father's desire falls from my mouth
a frail and ashy carbon, a black crease
forms in the folds of my arms. I follow
strange men, a whistle in my hands,
green about my eyes, bending into the night.
There is not enough night for me.
I want to roll through the roots of ancient oaks,
lick salt from the necks of people I love
wake every morning to a human smell,
sex in my clothes, something warm
and salty in my mouth.

Part Six

❧

COMMUNITIES

Dealing with Broccoli Rabe
Rosette Capotorto

three women in one week
told me my broccoli rabe had
changed their lives

if I have perfected one thing this year
it is my ability to prepare
broccoli rabe

to my sister's house I bring
a bunch of broccoli rabe
cook it at midnight
eat the whole bowl myself

to my friend's birthday dinner I bring
wine and bread and three bunches
of broccoli rabe   cook them
in her kitchen
stems first,   the flowery heads
a shorter   softer   time

for Christmas my parents made
twelve pounds of broccoli rabe
it was so beautiful you could
carry it down the aisle my mother said
Andy Boy and gorgeous
only 59 a pound

෨

Sunday
Adria Bernardi

I woke up in a laundry basket well padded with blankets and the first thing I thought was, I'm not supposed to be here yet. All around me it was yellow, fuzzy and soft. The basket was yellow as well, and I could see in between the openings of the plastic weave. I had been sleeping on the backseat of the

Chevrolet and they did not want to wake me. Quiet, quiet, shhh. I was carried in the air, along the stone pathway, one of the handles held up in front, the other one held up in back. I was traveling feet first. The basket was uneven and my legs were higher than my head. I swayed from side to side. My body was tightly bound; they had swaddled me in a receiving blanket in August and I was trying to work myself loose.

If your mother starts in about the dessert. My mother said this, I recognized her voice. *If instead of saying, Thank you, she says, We already have a dessert, you didn't need to waste the eggs and butter.* Quiet, quiet, my father said as they carried me, first through an aluminum storm door that squeaked open, then through a wooden door painted green with a small window and a white ruffled curtain trimmed with red stitching. The entryway smelled like the basement, comforting and damp, with concrete stairs going down to where the cans and jars were stored, to the furnace room and the room with the extra stove where my grandmother cooked when there was company. Here by the door, it smelled like the basement, but it also smelled like onions, garlic, parsley all sautéed together. It smelled like two different kinds of meat roasting. Chicken and pork. Potatoes, both roasted and puréed, spinach cooked with cream cheese. It smelled like olives and peppers. It smelled like stewed tomatoes and broth. It was moist on my face, like vapor.

Then suddenly, it was up, up, the inside back stairs; they were steep and I was now at quite an angle. My mother was in front and I could see the skirt of her dress billowing, it was white stiff cotton with seashells and sea horses. The wide belt was coral. I saw the back of her knees. She had a run in her left stocking. When I came out of her, my balled-up fist brushed against the inside of that knee. It was the first thing that I touched.

We paused in the middle of the kitchen but they did not set me down and I was swaying in the air, faces peering down at me.

Che faccia. A man with a shiny bald head and glasses at the end of his nose looked down at me. This was my grandfather.

L'è un angelo, veh. A woman who wore glasses and an apron with cherries all over it. This was my grandmother calling me an angel.

What a doll. This woman I did not recognize.

A man with a voice like my father's tickled me underneath my chin. Uncle Norm here, he said.

A man with a dry calloused hand that felt like flaking plaster gently cupped the top of my bald head.

The woman beside him brushed her knuckles against my cheek, her wedding band cool against my temple.

When they had all finished looking and cooing, I opened my eyes, and I could see my father lifting up a lid and looking down into a pot.

On four sides around me, draped with a white cloth, was tatted needlework. The cloth hung in undulations, it fell with finality to the edges, it was not flimsy and swayed only slightly. I could see through the netting that the table's feet had knobs that looked like claws. The legs were stained mahogany; they were curved like my mother's legs, and a breeze from the enormous floor fan in the front room wrapped the tablecloth around them.

The men were in the front room smoking. My grandfather Antenore and the man with the rough hand were in armchairs across from one another, a standing ashtray between them. My father and my Uncle Norm were standing in the middle of the room, their voices lowered. The women were all squeezed into the kitchen, and I could hear my grandmother's shoes, they had thick rubber heels, clomp, clomp, clomp, all the way down the staircase down into the basement.

Every so often, someone would lift up the tablecloth, which would brush against the bridge of my nose and my forehead. I would see a face briefly and then it would disappear.

Above, someone would ask

Dorme semper?

Sè.

She's still sleeping?

Yes.

After the cloth dropped back down and fell into place, swaying ever so slightly in the breeze made by the fan, I'd open my eyes again.

Through the tatting, I could see the bottom half of the buffet, its legs straight and ribbed. The door handles were disks, they looked like yellowed tortoiseshell but were made out of hard plastic. The dining room table and buffet did not match and neither did the chairs. Some of the chairs had straight ribbed legs, some had legs that were curved. I liked looking around. The chair right next to me was from the kitchen; it had strange metal legs, no back legs, only front legs that bent backward along the floor into a kind of kneeling position. The seat was red vinyl, stapled into place underneath, and I could see where a few of the staples had fallen out and the material was sagging.

A tavola, my grandmother called from the kitchen.

The men in the front room did not budge. My mother, in high heels and nylon stockings and seashore skirt, began moving around the table.

Clatter, clatter, clatter.

One two three, she counted.

Clank, clank. Four. Five. Six seven. Eight nine ten.

She was picking up the empty soup bowls. The table had been formally set, everyone had seen it. Now the flowers and the soup bowls were coming off. Clank.

Is he coming? My mother asked this, calling out to the front room.

Who knows. My father's voice.

Who the hell knows. My Uncle Norm said this. His voice sounded like my father's.

Is he bringing her? My mother again.

He said he had some business down near Aurora, my father said.

On a Sunday? my mother said.

If we'd a tried half the stunts he does, Ma would of killed us.

It sounded like my father, but it was Uncle Norm.

From the kitchen, my grandmother called out in a sweet, amused voice, *Ma lu lè fa come vôle.* That one there does what he wants.

And whose fault is that? I heard my mother mumble this under her breath in the dining room. I was the only one who heard her.

She held the empty soup bowls in a stack low in front of her. They were heavy, I could see how her wrists were stretched and extended. I could see the circle of the bottom bowl. Heavy white restaurant china with green letters. My mother's charm bracelet slid down on her hand and the charms were dangling in the air.

I saw the back of her turquoise high heels as she walked through the door into the kitchen. I heard a thunk as she set the bowls down on the metal kitchen table, and then a vibrating clatter.

Above, knees pulled in all around me. Dark suit pants and nylon stockings. I smelled someone's shoe polish. There were stripes made of diamonds on my grandfather's socks; the diamonds were black and the rest was maroon. It was hot under all those blankets in summer and finally I kicked myself free of the blanket and could move my legs. I was comfortable in my basket, well cushioned underneath by wall-to-wall carpet overlaid with a cast-off Oriental from a rich lady in Hubbard Woods.

Well, we'll just have to start without him. My grandmother said this in Italian and she sounded disappointed.

Thunk. On the center of the table. The antipasto plate.

Where did you get the olives, Ma? my father said.

Where did you find the peppers? The woman whom I did not recognize.

Find them! *Macché* find them. They're from the garden last year.

The mortadella is from Remo's? My mother asked this.

Macché Remo's. I wouldn't set foot in there if you paid me twenty dollars. They don't sweep enough. It comes from Lenzini's.

The metal chair was nearest the kitchen. My grandmother pushed it back—it slid easily across the carpet—and she stood up and took three steps into the kitchen. Then, the heavy metallic snap of the refrigerator handle being lifted up, the puckering sound of the rubber gasket as the door and the body separated. A plate sliding across a metal rack. One two three heavy steps across the kitchen floor back into the dining room. Thunk again above me, the table shimmying slightly. The other plate of antipasto in place, the one with the coppa and prosciutto. The chair slid back in underneath the table along with my grandmother's knees. Then it slid back out again, another quick trip to the kitchen.

Scordo il Jell-O mold. I forgot the Jell-O mold.

Jell-O mold le nè mica un cibo. Jell-O mold is not food. My grandfather said this.

That shows what you know, my grandmother said from the kitchen. All my ladies in Ravinia and Hubbard Woods and Glencoe serve Jello mold at their dinner parties.

Jell-O is a mineral, like sulphur or bauxite, that they pull out of the ground.

She told him he didn't know as much as he thought he knew and she sat back down again. Then, one more time, the chair slid away from the table. Back into the kitchen for bread.

Up and down, my Uncle Norm said.

Ma stai ferma che te fai 'na burrasca.

Just sit down, you're creating a windstorm, my grandfather said. *A burrasca* is a squall.

In a timid little voice, the woman whose ring had brushed the side of my face asked in the dialect if someone was going to say grace.

My grandfather laughed.

Not here, but they say so many prayers over at Rina's house that they say enough for us, too. He said this in dialect.

Right? He said this to my mother.

She was laughing, but I could hear her voice catching in her throat and I knew her vocal chords were too tight. She tried her best, and said to him in dialect, *Ad ga ragiôn.* You're right, she said, which made everyone at the table laugh, her talking in dialect, she being so modern and so American, especially the man whose rough hand had been cupped around the top of my head.

As they ate the antipasto, I studied the underside of the table top.

I saw where the leaves of the table fit together. I saw the gaps between them. I saw the places where the pegs did not fit so well and where there was a slight warp to the board. Three leaves expanded the table.

The underside of the table was rough unfinished wood, not smooth mahogany like the legs. I looked up and saw writing. I could not read but I tried to puzzle out numbers and letters. 247. G o t t l i n g. The marks were made in a loose black script, written with a black wax pencil like the butcher uses. It could have been directions for shipping or maybe it was the name of the person who had owned the table before.

Every so often, my grandfather's knee would hit a leg of the table hard and the whole table would vibrate. My grandmother would scold, my father and uncle would laugh. My grandmother told my father to make sure everyone had wine. *I bicchieri.* The glasses, she would say. Fill them up.

My grandfather sat at the head of the table. Behind him, the windows were covered with sheers and there was a short radiator underneath the sill.

It's good to have my brother here, my grandfather said, toasting the man whose rough hand had cradled the top of my head. Welcome to America, Ulisse. Welcome Paolina.

When they leave here, they're going to Des Moines and to Phoenix, Arizona, to see Paolina's nieces.

Beneath the hem of the tablecloth, I could see the bottom of the French doors between the dining room gaping open, pushed against the dining room walls. It was impossible to close them because of the thick wool carpet. The doors were stained mahogany, the tiny windows glistened. The floor fan in the front room circulated the air. The fan's head seemed too big for its very skinny neck. I watched the head of the fan pivoting, back and forth, back and forth, even though they all thought I couldn't focus on objects that far away.

All of a sudden, feet were moving all around the table, nylons and high heels. A clearing of plates, a removal of platters. An olive pit fell into my basket.

Oh here, Desolina, let me. The woman whose voice I did not know said this.

Oh, no, here, let me, my mother said.

Paolina, who had wanted to say grace, started to stand up, and my mother told her in very polite Italian that she should just stay seated, that she after all was a guest.

In the kitchen, my mother asked if she should rinse or soak.

Just soak, my grandmother said.

I heard my grandmother's shoes clomping down the back stairs, her voice turning the corner at the bottom of the stairs and into the basement, where she was muttering that you have to tell these young girls everything.

The men pushed away from the table, waiting.

My grandfather and his brother Ulisse spoke in dialect.

Ulisse said that McCarthy was a *mammalucco*.

McCarthy was no idiot, my grandfather said, uncrossing his ankles, revealing more of the black diamond patterns running up his maroon socks.

Better a McCarthy than a Mussolini.

Medesimo, my grandfather said. The same. It's just they stopped McCarthy in time.

At the other end of the table my father and Uncle Norm were talking business, almost whispering.

So you think you're going to take it, Norm?

How can I not?

Dallas?

They say that's where the future is. Opportunity. We'd be moving around a lot but I'd start out in an executive position.

Christ, that's far.

How can I turn it down?

I can just see it now, someday, Norm Gimorri, president. My father said this.

Has a ring doesn't it?

Have you told Ma?

At the head of the table, my grandfather was laying out the beginning of the end of the history that led to the death knell for true trade unionism in the United States. At the top now, he said, you can't tell them apart from the stockbrokers, all speed boats and Cadillacs and vacation houses up in Wisconsin.

My grandmother poked her head back into the dining room and said, Roberto? She thought she heard his voice when she was down in the basement.

Ma, Bobby's not here. My father said this.

Orazio, my grandmother ordered my father, go call him up. Maybe he's still at his apartment.

My grandparents call my father Orazio. Everyone else calls him Ray.

Ma, my father said, either he's coming or he's not coming.

Oh, for Christsake Ray, just go try him. My Uncle Norm said this.

My father pushed his chair away from the table. I could hear him exhaling, exasperated.

All right.

My Orazio's the only one who listens, my grandmother said to Paolina. The other two are just like their father. Stubborn, heads of concrete.

The phone was hanging on the wall in the hallway between the dining room and the sun room at the bottom of the steps that go up to the second floor. Every time my father dialed, it made a scraping sound as the disc rolled around. It sounded like an emery board against a nail, only louder. The two and the three were short little arcs of sound. The nine was long and drawn out, a rubbing all the way around. After he dialed each number, the telephone made a little muffled ding.

He let it ring fifteen times on the other end, you could hear a tiny far off ringing through the receiver. My grandfather was talking to Ulisse about arbitration and a new kind of mortar that was easier to work with in the cold. Uncle Norm wandered into the kitchen. My father hung up the telephone, clunk, and it hung heavy on its cradle. He called out, Nope. No answer.

Coming from the kitchen, there was a sound like a pebble being dropped into water, a liquid plink, a little pucker, then the sound of a full rounded immersing and a swishing all around, a cascading over the rim of the ladle as it was submerged into broth. Then, when the ladle was lifted up, there was a sucking sound, a tapping as it clinked against the side of the pot. A slight click as the ladle hit against the bottom of the soup bowl, the start of a gentle pouring, slowly, slowly, because you don't want to rupture the tortellini as you pour them out into the bowl along with the broth. Another dipping. Another. Inside the bowl, there was a little pond, with its own movements, with lolling and lapping at the sides.

Here, carry it to the table, my grandmother said to my mother. Be careful, it's hot. Be careful you don't burn your fingers. Be careful of the baby.

Should we move her? my father asked.

No, no, my mother said. She's fine under the table, just push her under a little more, in case someone spills.

Above me, it was all a choreographed procession. Slowly, slowly, one by one, my mother and the lady who had called me a doll walked from the kitchen to the dining room. They padded across the carpet in their high heeled shoes, carrying one bowl at a time.

From the kitchen I could hear my grandmother mutter, *Ma con quelle scarpe stupide zoccoline alte alte cum s'portavano le signore di Venezia.* With those stupid shoes like the ladies in Venice used to wear at one time, shoes so tall they needed a walking stick. She was mumbling but my mother could hear her.

I could see that even with their spike heels they managed to stay steady on their feet, that they were not tottering, except every once in a while when an ankle would quiver as a heel sank deep into a carpet divot. They walked slowly as they carried each steaming bowl.

My grandfather wiped the condensation off the lenses of his glasses with the tablecloth. Then he pulled the tablecloth up and bent his head down under the table. He waved his fingers in my face. *Beati quando dormono.* They're blessed—when they sleep.

When he dropped the cloth back down, I opened up my eyes.

Formaio? Formaio? the voices above me said, as the grated cheese was passed around the table and sprinkled into bowls.

Finally, they were all sitting down and no one was talking. Even my grandmother's metal chair was still and all I could hear was a slurping and sipping that was slow and hushed.

Ah, my father said. Holy food.

My mother got on her knees, lifted up the tablecloth and said, Are you all right down here? Oh, you've come loose. Let's just swaddle you back up.

Let me see, let me see. She's such a good baby.

This is your Auntie Florence.

Their heads were under the table. They were pinching the edge of the tablecloth and holding it up, like the flap of a tent. The tablecloth was draped over their heads.

Doesn't this baby ever cry?

She's such a good baby, she sleeps all the time. But when she's awake, my God, she's alert.

They were balanced on their haunches. I could see movement through my eyelids and feel their breath on my face. Aunt Florence smelled like perfume, talcum powder, and honeysuckle. There was a hint of cigarette smoke when they talked, they both smoked on the sly. Aunt Florence kissed me on the forehead, she smelled good, her lips against my skin were a little creamy, greasy, chalky, all at the same time.

Oh look, she said, I've left a lipstick kiss. A Good Housekeeping Seal of Approval.

But really, how *is* she? my Aunt Florence asked.

She's good, she's fine, she's small, she was early, that's the only thing. Everything is very good and she's just as healthy as she can be.

I could hear the slight brushing of their nylons underneath their skirts, thigh brushing thigh, knee against knee. They were both starting to teeter a little on their ankles, slightly losing their balance.

Rina, my Aunt Florence whispered, I wanted to tell you. Norm and I are expecting.

Oh that's marvelous. A cousin, a cousin for the baby.

They moved their heads out from underneath the table and I could see through the tablecloth that they were hugging each other. When the hug was finished, my mother rotated her foot on her ankle and said it was all pins and needles.

I heard snatches of conversation.

Did he say when he was coming? someone whispered.

Did he say if he was bringing her?
He said he had some business.
On Sunday?
The track is open on Sunday.

.

Norm, did you tell them? My Aunt Florence was whispering to my uncle.
    No, for Christsake, I will. Don't have an ulcer.

The meat is delicious, Ma.
    Desolina, how do you make these potatoes?
    John L. Lewis. Now that was a union man. These others are no different from
the capitalists, with their big fancy cars and jewelry and their girlfriends with
mink coats.
    Tomatoes from the garden.
    You put too much salt in the lettuce. She always puts too much salt in the
lettuce.
    Pass me the bread, Ma, I want to sop up the juice.

I must have drifted off and slept awhile because when I woke up they were
clearing the dessert plates.
    The *zupp'inglese* was wonderful, how do you make it Desolina? I'd love to
have the recipe.
    My grandfather and his brother Ulisse were each smoking a pipe, giving off
a sweet tobacco aroma. My father and Uncle Norm lit up cigars.
    My grandfather peered under the table at me and squeezed my big toe.
    A napkin, stained with custard and Chianti and a smudge of cerise Revlon
lipstick, fluttered down past me.
    Someone above said, Oh, to sleep like a baby.

∾

The Oven

Rosette Capotorto

> what are your chances for
> mainstreaming
>
> when you grow up
> in a Bronx pizza parlor
>   and no one

knows your name only that you're
eye-talian and your father makes
the pizza and you
serve the pizza and do
　　your homework after school
　　at the table behind the oven

and no one ever notices your mother
　　but she's back there
　　　　rolling meatballs
　　　　and　tending your little brother and　one in the belly
　　　　that will be your little sister
　　　　　　slows her down a bit

and you will change diapers
　　　　　　in addition to doing your homework
　　　　　　　　in back of the oven
and frying ten pounds of eggplant
for the eggplant parmigiana
and so will your sister
　　　　who is two and a half years younger
　　　　and you both do dishes at the oversized
　　　　　　commercial sink

and after a while you and your sister
will divide the work and it will turn out
that your sister is better at diapers and
baby hairdos and you are better at frying
　　　　eggplant
and then your little brother will be old
enough to make the dough
test his strength against
the stainless arm of the mixer
having been forewarned of its dangers

the little sister
　　the last one born
will make tiny pizzas
　　　　and there will be a photograph
　　　　to remember this by

a little girl rolling pizza dough
which the family
will eat
in six
tiny
slices

∾

Ravioli, Artichokes, and Figs
Nancy Savoca

I read cookbooks like other people read novels. I'll sleep with the Food Channel on, if I'm alone in a hotel, so I can wake up to someone preparing a meal. After twenty years, my strongest memory of my husband courting me is the smell of cold cuts and stuffed peppers that clung to his shirts from his work at the neighborhood deli. Even our first meeting was over the delivery of four pounds of sausage—hot and sweet mixed—a surreptitious order placed by my matchmaking sister.

My eight-year-old has pointed out to me that most of the family stories I tell her and her brothers revolve around food. She's right. I make movies for a living but my other passion is food—I love to cook. (My Sicilian-born father, by the way, was a professional cook. *His* other passion is making home movies.)

How can we talk about our obsession with food and avoid the old standby of "Food equals love," the clichés of "*Mangia, mangia*," Mamma stirring the gravy and the *famiglia* gathered round the table, yelling, laughing, eating—clichés that, let's face it, hold some element of truth but reveal little more than what we already know? But how can we move any deeper into our understanding of food if, like sex or music or meditation, there's a mystical element that escapes definition? In some alchemical way, it changes from a physical act to something emotional, and finally lifts us to the spiritual.

If I could throw a light on the subject of food obsessions, I would. But mysteries reside in the dark and sometimes, if we want to see something in the dark, it's best to turn off the lights. So, instead of analyzing with hard facts, I'd rather tell a story—well, let's make that three stories—about Food and Family and . . . I don't know, other things.

Ravioli

I was three years old when Marta, my then teenaged sister, was going out with her future husband, Vinny. Vinny was a recent immigrant from Potenza, near Naples. My sister, like the rest of my family, was a recent immigrant from Argentina. The reason why she could even communicate with Vinny was because Marta had spent much of her childhood with our Nonna and learned to speak the Sicilian dialect from her—a dialect which, in our Bronx neighborhood, she quickly converted to Neapolitan for survival purposes.

Marta and Vinny were in love. My father, like all Sicilian fathers, couldn't bear to think of his daughter being pursued by anyone of the male species. As a result, my sister became an excellent liar. She'd rip the pages out of her school notebooks so she could say she needed to go to the store to buy a new one. She invented movie plots of films she'd never seen. She gave detailed descriptions of class trips she never took. This would usually work incredibly well except for those times when my parents, maybe suspecting something they couldn't quite know for sure, would yell out to her as she ran out the door, "Take the baby with you!" The baby meaning three-year-old me.

So I vividly remember this particular day when Marta told me—and my parents—that she was taking me to the movies. Some cartoon thing, she said. I was beyond ecstatic, since my sisters, when they actually did go to the movies, would deliberately bypass the children's films and take me to see Hitchcock or *Splendor in the Grass*–type movies which I couldn't make heads or tails of.

So I eagerly went with Marta and was mystified when we walked right past the Loew's theater under the el and headed for one of the residential side streets. She hurried me up a flight of steps leading to a strange brownstone building, much smaller than our tenement. We walked inside and someone opened a door to a tiny apartment. In the living room, a fancy table had been set up. It was covered by a lace tablecloth with plastic over it. I saw a lady (I later learned this was Vinny's sister, Giovanna, whom he lived with) and two noisy toddlers running around. Someone lifted me onto a chair with the Yellow Pages on the seat so I could reach the table. My sister, giddy with nerves, tied a cloth napkin like a bib around my neck.

I didn't know where I was or what exactly was happening and I didn't have much time to think because, all of a sudden, a plate of hot ravioli materialized on the table in front of me. The steam from the plate and the aroma of Giovanna's sauce hit me and made my eyes and mouth water. I was the worst finicky eater, but Giovanna had touched on my only weakness. Pasta was the only food I would eat.

I grabbed my fork and was just about to spear a ravioli when I felt the sting of a *slap*. My sister hissed at me, "Wait for Giovanna to sit down!" How unfair! Suddenly, I was starving. I swooned from lack of food. Giovanna took an eternity to serve everyone. She stopped to chat and joke with each person while I watched my raviolis.

Finally, she sat. I inhaled and the raviolis were gone. I asked for more. Marta laughed and repeated what was already legend in my half-Argentinean, beef-loving family, "Nancy only eats pasta. That's all she eats!" and there were cheers and applause and I felt welcome and accepted into this pasta-loving tribe. They understood.

That evening, when we got home, my mother was in the kitchen beading the costume jewelry she made for work. She looked up from her beading and asked, "So how was the movie?" I blurted out, "I ate the best ravio—"and felt my sister's hand clamp down on my mouth so fast, while she rattled off yet another fictitious movie plot which my mom seemed to enjoy. Marta whisked me off to the bathroom. The water ran—I was thrown in the tub and shampoo put in my hair, running down into my eyes. "I'll give you anything," Marta whispered with no small amount of desperation. "I'll buy you any toy you like. But if you tell her about the ravioli, I'll kill you."

I got a doll the next day. I never told about the ravioli—until now.

Artichokes

Which is better? Stuffed with chopped meat? rice? or just plain breadcrumbs? It was getting to be a pretty heated discussion. No one wanted to seem haughty about it but you could feel the derision from the others as each woman took a turn sharing her recipe for artichokes.

I was hanging out at Marta's stoop, heavy with the pregnancy of my first son. My sister and I and a group of her neighbors were all gathered out front, talking about our favorite foods and enjoying the last of an Indian summer afternoon. Out on the sidewalk, doing his best to ignore us, was Marta's tenant, Jack. Jack was a miserable guy. He never spoke to anyone and mostly grunted if you attempted to say hi. If he looked you in the face, it was mostly to scowl at you. A widowed ex-construction worker, he lived the purgatory life of many retired neighborhood guys—he got to hang with the women. But on this afternoon, he kept his distance—standing out by the curb, snooping but not taking part in what was fast becoming a full-blown argument between the women. As each tried to outdo the other in her litany of ingredients and cooking methods, I cried out, "Please, stop! This is making me so hungry!" Jack caught my eye. His expression darkened and he started yelling at my sister in a guttural Italian—a dialect so thick and hurried, I couldn't pick up anything of what he was saying. He seemed pretty angry, but then again, he *always* seemed angry. I asked my sister what he'd said. "He's mad at us because he says you've got a craving now for artichokes, and if we don't feed you artichokes, it's bad for the baby," said Marta. "He's right," said one of the women. "If you get a desire for something and you can't get it, you gotta touch your ass!" They all laughed, but one of the older women looked worried. "It's true. If you have a craving, whatever part of your body you touch, your face, your hands—that's where the baby will get a birthmark. Better to touch your ass." I laughed. I can be superstitious but this was a bit much. But I found that the entire group of women was staring at me, waiting for me, so I reached back and touched my butt and they all breathed a sigh of relief. All except Jack. He looked more pissed off than usual. He grumbled to himself and stormed off. Now what had I done wrong?

Later that night, I was home alone when the doorbell rang to my apartment. I looked through the peephole and saw my sister standing in the hall with an aluminum-foil-wrapped tray. I opened the door. "What's that you've got there?" I asked. Before I even saw them, I knew by the smell that greeted me that this was a tray of stuffed artichokes. Marta pulled off the foil and I could see that they were made the way I like them best—just seasoned breadcrumbs, grated cheese, and crushed garlic and a little white wine in the cooking water.

"What did you do—" I started to say, but she cut me off. "I didn't. It was Jack." "Jack?" I didn't know the guy was capable of saying hello to me, much less cooking me a meal! "He walked up and down the Avenue. He went to every vegetable stand—he got the best artichokes from each one and he made them for you." Crazy Jack did that for me? I was so hormonal, tears streamed out of my eyes. Who would've thought? Marta put the tray down on my little kitchen table. I got out two forks and some lemons and we sat down and ate the entire tray of artichokes. No leftovers.

I wanted to call Jack and thank him for his act of kindness—even though I'm sure he didn't see it as that. For him, it was more an act of "disaster-avoidance." I called his house but got no answer. He wasn't the kind of guy who answered his phone. So it wasn't till weeks later that I spotted him across the street, heading for a newsstand.

I ran (as much as I could, being seven months pregnant) across the street to catch up to him. "Jack," I said, "thank you for the artichokes. They were delicious! I ate them all!" He looked at me, shocked. Why? Because I had stopped him from buying his Lotto ticket? Because I'd thanked him for doing the obvious? Because I had actually spoken to him? He gave me a furious look and abruptly turned and walked away.

I felt stupid for stopping him. I should've known better. But the artichokes were so good!

Figs

My mother was dying of cancer, although I don't know that any of us had actually accepted this fact. She was spending what would be her final six weeks in a hospital for the terminally ill. It was aptly named Calvary.

Something happened in my family which, at the time I thought was really bizarre. Now I know it's not. Now I know it's common among Italian American families who have a dying relative. We got really obsessed by the fact that my mother wouldn't eat.

Medically, this was no shocker. Liver cancer will do that to you. In fact, the less you eat, maybe the better. Less work for the body to do. But we didn't get that. Love is food and food is love and why oh why was she rejecting our food and love at this crucial moment in our lives? It got to be a little crazy. We would bring her all kinds of foods, trying to tempt her the way my parents tempted me as a child, me the finicky eater who only ate pasta.

And guess what she settled on—the only food my mom would eat as she lay dying? Pasta.

Pasta with a plain white sauce: milk and butter, a little flour and nutmeg. Baked until browned on top. Deceptively simple. Incredibly good.

My mother would eat this and nothing else. My father was so deliriously happy that she would eat, he made it every night. Every evening, he'd take a little Tupperware container of pasta with the white sauce. He'd feed her, a forkful at a time, and she'd eat a bite or two. The weeks went by. Each day she ate less. At night he'd bring home what she didn't eat—each night it was more. She gave up on the pasta in the last two weeks of her life. My father collapsed into himself. I gained seven pounds in those last weeks because I would eat everything my father compulsively cooked. I had to, because she couldn't.

Marta, my niece Maria, and I took turns sleeping with her. At night she'd try to crawl out of bed, or talk about hemming clothes or when was she getting out of that place.

Like the rest of my family, I poured all my worries into obsessing about her diet. How was she going to get better if she didn't eat? The idea that escaped me was that she wouldn't get better. I was walking to the hospital one evening, walking through the Avenue of my old neighborhood. It was sundown and the shops were turning on display lights. I passed by a Korean fruit stand. It was September and the crates displayed the last of summer tomatoes and the first arrival of squash and broccoli rabe and apples. I stopped cold when my eyes caught a green plastic tray with dark purple fruit nestled in it. Figs! When I was little, we'd visited my family in Argentina, and my mother had taught me how to climb up my grandmother's fig tree and find the ones that were so ripe they'd fall into my hands.

My mother also taught me to love figs. Seeing them at the store that day, I felt they were a good omen. I was so filled with optimism, I bought too many figs— maybe a half dozen. I ran to the hospital, which was eight blocks away.

I walked into the lobby of the hospital. As kids, we'd call Calvary the Roach Motel because "you check in but you don't check out." As always when I walked in, I was hit by the energy of all that soul activity. The nuns visiting with ailing patients were midwives in reverse. I wondered how one could ever get used to working with death.

My mother's room was getting quieter every day. Less sound, less movement. I used to try to fight it—I'd brought a radio and played music she liked. I'd bring in films to watch with her. I'd call relatives on the phone and put her on so they could speak with her. But now I began to slow down, too. I'd learned to respect this quiet that was coming down over us in the room. I walked into my mother's room and pulled out the bag of fruit. I broke off a tiny piece from one of the figs and put it near her mouth. "Look, Ma. Taste." She had refused food completely for the last few days so I was surprised when she opened her mouth, childlike. "Figs," I said. "Mmmm," she said. And she ate the little piece I offered her. I was so happy. I ate the rest.

❧

Seventeenth Street: Paterson, New Jersey
Maria Mazziotti Gillan

It was a ceremony, the welcoming of company. The aunts and uncles, the espresso pot, the espresso poured in a dark stream into the doll-sized cups set ever so delicately in their little saucers, a small sliver of lemon rind added to float near the top, then the sugar in its bowl, the spoon, midget-sized, made especially to go with those cups and saucers, and the little clink while they stirred their coffee, the men at one end of the table. Sometimes they passed out little glasses, no bigger around than a quarter and almost one inch high, a tiny handle attached, and my father poured whisky or brandy for them, mostly the men, but sometimes the women, too. The children, sitting between the adults, were given coffee in their cups, a drop or two of coffee and lots of milk and sugar, and they listened to the stories about their parents' friends: the wayward children, the wives who were faithful or not, the men who were fools.

Listening, wide-eyed, believing, I learned more in those moments than I could in years of school about laughter and the way of opening up to others and welcoming them in, and of the magic at the heart of ordinary lives, so that ordinary things transfigured them.

Looking back, I see that ever since, I have been searching for that sweetness, that warm bread-baking aroma, the smoothness of oilcloth, its rubbery smell, the open look of my father's face, sparks flying from him in his pleasure, my mother's hand, delicate, the charm of those moments where I rested in the luminous circle of love.

❧

Passing It On
Maria Mazziotti Gillan

This Easter we don't really need the second table or the extra chairs carried up from the basement: my son, his wife, their two children in Virginia; my daughter, with her husband's family in Cape Cod; my father in a wheelchair and unable to sit at the table; my mother three years dead. I invite my neighbors; still there are empty chairs. My brother sits in the living room all through dinner; he has to have special food that his wife cooks for him before they leave home. He is staring at the white wall, perhaps missing one of his own sons. On an earlier Easter, I remember my Italian mother, looking vibrant and strong, cooking for all of us, seventeen of us gathered around her table, as we had gathered each Sunday and holiday in all the years while our own children grew. My father made a speech, sitting in his black rocker, his metal cane on the chair near him. His hands trembled so much the paper rattled. "Next Easter," he said in his Italian version of English, "I hope we will be together, but if something happened, keep the family strong." I looked over at my mother. Her small, compact body radiated heat, and we gathered around her. By October, she was dead.

After dinner, I call my son. He says they haven't eaten yet. "No company?" I ask. My son, who probably could have been a hermit, tells me we make too much noise. He has been absent for so long, I'm not sure if I miss him or only the idea of him. I wish he sounded happy rather than just tired. My four-year-old granddaughter asks to speak to me on the phone. She tells me riddles. We talk about when they will visit. "I'll bring my pocketbook," she says seriously. "I can't wait to see you, Caroline." I say. "Me, too, Grandma." Then she whispers, "My momma says I'm too loud." "That's OK, I'm loud, too. When you come to my house we'll be loud together."

As my mother said to me thirty years ago, "You don't know yet. Wait." I'd like to say the same thing to my son, but I don't. I want to tell her, "Ma, we're Americans now, and look at all we've lost." She walks toward me and places a loaf of her braided Easter bread in my hands. "*Tesoro*," she says, "give the bread to Caroline," and then she strokes my cheek with her hand.

❧

You Were Always Escaping
Maria Mazziotti Gillan

You were always escaping
We'd hear the sound of the brown door
slamming, the rattling of glass panes,
and you would vanish.

I see us standing in the 17th Street kitchen,
Mamma with her arms around us
and her bruised eyes.
Her voice quivering, she'd say,

"Can't you stay home tonight?"
staring at the empty doorway
then she'd sigh, lift her shoulders,
and begin some project with us.

She'd give us cookie cutters
shaped like stars and bells,
and we'd cut out sugar cookies,
even Alex who was only three.

We'd dye sugar red with food coloring
and sprinkle it on top. The kitchen
would fill with the sweet aroma
of our baking, and we were content.

Other times, we'd make chocolate pudding
or listen to Stella Dallas on the radio.
Sometimes, she'd lift Alessandro into her lap,
and Laura and I would perch on the arms
of the old padded rocker, and she'd tell us stories
about San Mauro, the town where she grew up.
Through the evening hours, she would distract herself
as well as us, but once we were in our beds,
her hunger for your presence
would return and smear the contented landscape.

During the day, you swept the halls
of Central High School, mopped the floors,
picked up the refuse in the Boys and Girls bathrooms.
At lunchtime, you sat in on algebra
and history classes but you were subservient,
your head bent, humble. Though you were louder,
Mamma ruled the house. But at the Società
your friends looked up to you, and you were proud
of your speeches at political dinners,
your awards, and standing ovations.

"You always choose your friends first," Mamma hissed,
her voice rising with anger, and you would struggle
from her grasp, rushing to the next meeting,
the evenings playing *bocce* at the Società

the spaghetti dinners, the women
of the Ladies' Auxiliary
who flirted with you
while Mamma stayed at home.

Mamma peered out of the edge
of the green blackout shades,
waited for your footsteps
on the wooden porch.

Even when you stayed home one evening,
you were restless, pacing the floor
as though the kitchen were a cage
and we the bars that tried to hold you
but that always failed.

∽

Poem
Dorothy Barresi

The enormous courage of the ice cream man
Who has a handcart, bells, no reticence, two soccer games, six

birthday parties, rancheras blaring
from many shouldered estereos,

Who has a park transfused by pink arterial balloons and piñatas
in the shapes of dogs, donkeys, vampires, Bart Simpson, Bart Simpson,

Who has a fixed stare
and both his testicles, PraiseMaryKnockWood,

Who has citron and mango and horchata
but no grape today,

no Ninja Turtle popsicles either, dream pop, cream pop,
Who has eaten the radish of happiness

but not the chicken liver of wisdom,
Whose wife loves him,
Pepita, my chubby, my dove, when he comes and who knows, as he does,
that 29th and Main Street meet in hard opposition, wind,

the eucalyptus and palm trees
shake, there are earthquakes, what's real

knocks at the windows but there is nothing more dangerous
than a young man of a certain smiling

sweating disposition with a gun
and no drugs, or some drugs, or it's got

nothing to do with drugs this time but money: some or none.
Who says I have none.

Who says I have none to the occluded front of the young man's face and
the scary movie hard-on gun in the young man's

pocket in his hand—
Give it up old fucker!—the boy's T-shirt reading

"Chaos ain't what it used to be."
Who says to the boy again I have none, nada, zip,

as the vehement tolling of bells at Our Lady of Ectomorphic
Angels on Dust plays on,

Who says no no no until the gun butt and the ravishing
tones in his head make him spin, pants shitted on the way down

so that later when the cops walk away shaking
their pitiful keys to the kingdom, roger and out, they

hold their noses. Who has mixed credit, four grown children, ten
grandchildren, no license for vending, a baseball game, three

late-breaking parties with their grubby dimes
sweat-fisted; Who has sixteen bridesmaids in red satin dresses

and red satin shoes but no photographer—
what the hell?—who say they are hungry, hot, caliente, give us

something for this muy caliente day in which
we have all failed to be killed, PraiseMaryVirginofGuadalupe,

radiant pincushion of Christ.
Who has the Immigration and Naturalization Service.

Who has a thousand borders to cross
not counting Ghetto Boyz, Primera Flats, and the 29th St. Gang

between one curb and the next bump up.
Who has a clean record because there is no record.

Who has a 1973 Dodge Dart Swinger.
Who has a barbecue. Who has two graduations. Who has ninety-three winos

making out shamelessly with the grass.
Who has a handcart, bells, sky, fame, a wife

alternately weeping and sipping from his left nipple
with the tip of her tongue

in their bedroom later, who raises it, the chill,
the chill nipple of the living ice cream man.

~

Coffee an'
Joanna Clapps Herman

I.

Coffee and sugar were the narcotics that stimulated the days and nights where I
learned about intimacy in that great and terrible school, the Italian American
family. "Coffee an'," we called it. The many cups of coffee drunk all day, invariably
served with something made with sugar to go with it. We pressed up against
one another as if our very breathing depended on our merciless connections.

The adults in my working-class family in Waterbury, Connecticut, drank
pot after pot of coffee throughout the day, from when they woke early in the

morning, until very late at night, when they fell into bed exhausted from their caffeine fueled, furious days.

With the coffee always came the "an." A couple of times a week we baked so that there would always be "an," that little bit of something sweet that inevitably accompanied the many cups of coffee they drank to keep themselves bound to their relentless routines. We used recipes my illiterate grandmother carried in her head from Tolve, her *paese* in Basilicata, in the south of Italy, when she followed her husband to America: *mastachiole, pizza dolce, torta di ricotta, cartadade*. We added to this abundance other recipes our mothers clipped from *Woman's Day* and *Good Housekeeping*, learned on the assembly line at Scovill's Factory, or got from their neighbors: Russian wedding cookies, jam cookies, brownies.

The chemistry of the caffeine, the sugar, the connection with one another (so intense as to make us vibrate), combining as they did with a rage for perfection, made for standards of behavior so exacting that we threw ourselves at every task, work or play, ferociously, with a blind certainty that this *was* reality. Nothing was relative. Everything was absolute. *Must* and *should* was the air we breathed.

Our mothers had been raised in America but with fifteenth-century Southern Italian customs. On the pig farm where they lived as children, they had drawn their own water from the well and baked their weekly bread in the brick oven my grandfather built down by the road. They had risen at dawn to milk the cows and collect the eggs. After school they weeded the garden, cleaned the chicken coops, helped with all the endless chores of farm life. One summer they spent hours in intense heat picking bones out of the pig manure, because my grandfather had heard he could earn money for bags of bones. They grew most of their food. They made their own sausage, prosciutto, many kinds of cheese, of course their own wine. They grew up with screaming and violence as an ordinary response to even minor deviations from these fifteenth-century mores.

This drove them to heights of great accomplishment: whatever they undertook they did flawlessly. They were accomplished seamstresses, amazing cooks, wonderful hostesses, extraordinary gardeners. They were beautiful, immensely strong, extremely hard-working, and had no idea that they were allowed to take note of this. That was the family standard.

For most of my generation the violence had diminished, but fury still raced along our currents. "Get over, here. Who broke this cup? Come here. Right now! I'm going to kill you." The hand hung in the air, swinging, a cupped threat, the twist of skin tight between your mother's fingers. For some of my cousins, real beatings.

In my time, too, the children were expected to work at their parents' side. Our fathers painted and wallpapered the rooms and redid our kitchens after long days of physical work. The kids helped. Our mothers and fathers grew the vegetables and the flowers. The boys were in charge of all yard work, garage work, and basement work. The mothers and daughters did the house-cleaning, the laundry, the ironing, the sewing, and the shopping. We canned the tomatoes, the peaches, the pears, pickled the eggplant, made the jam.

For fun we made our own liqueurs, fresh pasta, baked panettone, pizza, bread, focaccia (*fucazz'* we called it), made ricotta, scamozza, and provolone.

It wasn't as if we didn't play. When we gathered for our annual Memorial Day picnic there was first an homage to America, bowls of chips, trays of nuts, dips. Bowls of macaroni salad, potato salad, trays of cold cuts. Our food followed: trays of manicotti, lasagna, meatballs, sausage, roast chicken with potatoes, sausage, onions and peppers. Coffee carried in jars wrapped in *mappine* to keep it warm. Gallons of lemonade, orangeade, iced tea, the bottom of each jar coated with a thick syrupy layer of sugar. Platters of desserts.

If ferocity was our code, oblivion to the code was our commandment. Making any comment on how the family operated was a sin. Calling attention to yourself was another. "Can you imagine she had to go and brag about her sauce? We all make sauce. Who does she think she is?"

You weren't allowed to get credit for what you naturally worked so hard to accomplish. Instead, there was only blame for trivial failures. Perhaps we thought that if we were silent maybe someday we would be declared *good*.

Often, deep in our night's sleep, my sister and I were shaken loose from our dreams by my mother's screams, "Peter, Peter, Peter," she'd cry out for my father to protect her. "There's a man, a man, he's coming in the window." That murderous man came to get her so many nights. He was there to tell her she hadn't done enough. She should rise from her sleep and wash the kitchen floor again. Her father had repeatedly condemned all his daughters, in his Tolovese dialect, *"Quest' non mai ess' femin' della cas'"*—"You'll never make good housewives."

II.

Weekday afternoons after school the girls helped their mothers start dinner. Then the kids all went outside to play while the mothers had their coffee an'. The only time these women sat still was when they served each other coffee.

"Papa had no business leaving everything to Rocky." They are sitting at one of the formica tables that dominated our kitchens. It's four o'clock, four thirty. A *chambotte'* or *pizzaiola* simmers on the stove while we're waiting for our fathers to come home, dirty, sweaty, and hungry from their jobs on construction sites or at the factories.

"We worked on the farm just as hard as Rocky did when we were kids. Didn't we get up at six o'clock in the morning to milk the cows and feed the chickens before we went to school? Those freezing cold mornings. The fire in the stove out." My Aunt Vicky, the youngest daughter, starts the conversation. After my mother calls to say the coffee is on, she combs her hair and puts on bright red lipstick.

"After Mamma got her arthritis I had to get up before everyone and light the stove to make Papa's coffee. Some mornings I had to break the ice on the top of the water jug to make the coffee. Oh, it was bad. Papa forgot all that." My mother interjects.

"We all worked hard. I was always the one who had to carry up all the wood for the stove the night before. And carry in all the water. God, how I used to worry about how I was going to smell going to school after I milked the cows. I'd scrub my hands until they were raw." This is Aunt Tony.

"What are you going to do? That's the way it is in Italian families." Auntie Ag, the oldest, the one who accepts her fate. She raised these sisters and their only brother, Rocky.

"I know, Ag," Aunt Vicky says. "The boys are everything. The girls are nothing. But that's not right."

The girls, my mother and her sisters, nursed that conversation, nudged it along the same road for twenty years after my grandfather died. Leaving everything to Rocky, he had declared their work null and void. "Do you know in Italy—I read this somewhere—it's illegal to do that? You can't do that in Italy. How's that?" One would remind the others again.

"And Mamma, too. She could change it now if she wanted to. It's not right."

"You know Rocky's her favorite. I told her, Mamma, that's not right to leave it like that. You have five children. Not one."

"Here, try these cookies. Marie gave me the recipe. Her mother, Donna Paola, used to make them. I don't remember Mamma making these. They must be Sicilian."

"I shouldn't. We have to have dinner soon. Just a little piece."

"Wait, I'll heat you up." The half-empty cup gets filled.

The coffee, the sweet, and the talk got them through. But it never changed anything.

Sometimes the fathers arrived home at the end of these "gab sessions." They'd sit and have a cup before they went to take a nap or went out to their gardens. "You girls have nothing to do but sit and have coffee." In their greasy and ripped work clothes they'd stand in the doorways, teasing their wives and sisters-in-law.

"*You* should have our 'nothing to do,'" the women would turn their heads away in mock and real fury. "At least your day is finished. We're not even halfway through. I don't go to bed sometimes until two, three in the morning."

More often, though, before the men started pulling their trucks into the driveways, one or another aunt would say, "I have to get home. I haven't even started dinner. Joe hates it if I'm not there when he walks in the door. Men are such babies."

"I know," my mother would chime in. "You know what Peter asked me the other day? Where did I keep the toilet paper."

"Men! Such a bunch of babies." All the aunts agree on that.

III.

On a Saturday morning as the light was just cracking the horizon, I'd hear from the kitchen the gurgle of the percolator start in the coffee pot my mother had prepared for my father the night before. This was a moment for a different kind of intimacy. My first romance, just him and me. An ironworker, my father often worked on Saturdays to get in a little extra time on the jobs that were crowding in on him. I'd get up and go sit at the kitchen table and watch him, first as he sat there barefoot, in his sleeveless undershirt, as he drank his first cup of coffee of the day, then as he pulled on his socks and shoes. There would be no coffee for me. I only wanted to be with him, hoping he'd relent, invite me to go with him. I'd follow him around the house while he grabbed a gray work shirt filled with holes from welding sparks, looked for his red and black plaid wool work hat, until he finally gave in. "Can you get dressed fast?"

I'd run back to my bedroom, throw on some dungarees and a blouse. He'd throw back a last slug of his coffee before we climbed up onto the high seats of his truck, the welder clanging along behind us like a clunky metal tail. Off we'd go through the dawn light on the back roads of Connecticut to some obscure spot in one or another corner of the state where a fire escape had to be put up on some old wooden clapboard building at a private school.

He'd sing, in his high, nasal tenor, as he drove to the job site, and as he worked, the old songs, songs full of yearning and longing: "Ramona," "Somewhere Over the Rainbow," "They Tried to Tell Us We're Too Young." The timbre of his voice was from the Old World, as he sang about losses in this one. The singing held at bay the early brutality of his life: his mother institutionalized when he was three, his father's drinking and philandering, his brother Mike's suicide, his brother Frank's early death from leukemia.

On the job I'd stand on one foot amidst stacks of lumber, piles of concrete blocks, iron beams that waited to be lifted into place, listening to him sing, or I'd follow him around the muddy construction sites so I could hand him tools while he worked. He'd explain why one job was filled with problems. Another with pleasure. Why he loved his work.

He'd tip the brim of his hat back. "Take a look at this. This son-of-a-gun railing had been cut a half-inch short. You can't know how that makes all the difference. I had to decide. Am I going to take the whole thing back to the shop and make them redo it or am I going to make it work? I stayed with it, cutting a little off an old piece of pipe I found on the back of the truck, welding it on, then smoothing the edges. What a terrible day that was." His voice was dry with disgust at the memory, "But we got it done, somehow." He'd shake his head. "Somehow we got it done."

One of those Saturday mornings on the way home we stopped at a diner for breakfast. It must have been about ten-thirty in the morning by then. By that hour, my mother would have the sausage sizzling for the start of the sauce. She cooked a pound of sausage and one of meatballs for Saturday lunch, a pound each for the sauce for Sunday. There would be a quart of cold coffee fixed from the morning's remaining brew waiting in the refrigerator to go with my father's lunch, a loaf of Spinelli's crusty bread delivered that morning. But that day my father decided we would stop for something before we drove home. I peered at the menu, not something with which working-class kids in Waterbury had much familiarity.

"Bring me a cup of coffee," my father said when the waitress appeared. "Would you like a piece of apple pie?" He put his cracked hand over mine. I nodded. "Put some vanilla ice-cream on it," he told the waitress. "How about a glass of chocolate milk to go with it?" turning back to me.

A wide smile on his face, he leaned across the table as he made these extraordinary suggestions. Apple pie with ice cream and chocolate milk for breakfast!

"I'll have some of that pie, too." I've never eaten that particular combination of sugars again. The thrill of that moment. Breaking the rules. Apple pie, ice cream, and chocolate milk for breakfast, behind my mother's back.

And my father. My father all to myself.

IV.

Having my father to myself was a singular moment, but it was usually the family, the rich confines of each other's lives, that enveloped and imprisoned us. We barely knocked on the door as we ran in and out of each other's kitchens. We knew the damp smell of each other's cellars, where tables of dusty tools rested near shelves full of jarred tomatoes, pickled eggplant, canned peaches. When one of our aunts' or uncles' hands began swinging like a small scythe, threatening one of their kids, we knew enough to make ourselves scarce, slipping off into the yard, whispering to the victim's sibling, "What'd she do? Why's your mom so mad?" Someone was going to get a *palliade*.

We formed the populace of our own claustrophobic nation, gulping each other's air. Sometimes only our depleted exhalations were left in the room.

But on weekends and summer nights, when there was usually another round of "coffee an'," another kind of air filled our lungs. After the dinner dishes were washed, the stove was cleaned, the floor swept, the ironing done, when the relentless appetites of the beasty gods of duty had been appeased and they dozed briefly, most nights someone would suggest, as if it were a brand new idea, "Let's have company."

Phone calls would be made, "Come over," even though only an hour before my mother might well have said, "You can't believe what your Aunt Tony told me on the phone today." Her full complaint would follow. "She said that she and that other one, your other prized aunt, went to the movies last Thursday. They didn't even call me. After all the rides to New York your father has given those girls." This slight would have been cultivated through the day, nurtured into full insult, given room and time to bloom into noxious anger.

But it was evening now. What were we going to do with this brief respite if not bind ourselves to one another more tightly?

"You can't call Auntie Ag and not call the others. They'll be hurt. I don't want to be like them. Call them too. Tell them the pot's already on." This time period straddled the pre-TV and the early TV years, so evenings were still open-ended, waiting to be filled with talk and coffee an'.

Sometimes the men joined us. The old stories came out and were repeated. All the sweet things the little kids had said were passed around the table again and reminded us of other family stories. But the men got tired earlier than we did. My father went down the street to play cards at the Italian Social Club. By the end of the evening it was always the women and the kids. That was when the deepest intimacies curled up around our ears: in the world of women, kids, coffee an', and talk.

Whatever bitterness rocked and roared among these women, when they gathered, they naturally fell to alliances with each other again, murmuring assents and assurances, righting each other's worlds with simple certainties: "Cripes, she had no right to say that to you." Nursing each other's miseries: "Peter and I will drive up with you and Gilda to the hospital in Boston. Don't worry. I'll stay with you through the operation." Swelling each other's pride: "He looked so beautiful in his First Communion suit. His hair slicked back like that." Or gossiping. My great grandmother would be quoted: "*A che murmurade?*"

At the end of these attenuated nights, long after the men had left to go home or had gone to bed, with cup after cup poured out for each woman, with plates of cookies and cakes emptied, refilled, reluctantly one of the aunts would say, "It's late. I have to get home." That aunt would rise from the table and begin to carry the cups and saucers to the sink to be washed. That was the signal for everyone to get up and help. Although siblings might fight after dinner—"It's your turn to do the dishes"—when there was "company," even our aunts, each of us wanted to show, almost ostentatiously, that she had been "brought up right." We'd push the grownups away from the sink. "I'll do them. Don't worry about that, Auntie Ag."

Although coffee an' was officially over for that night, the real "and" wasn't. The mothers might pick up the conversation while their girls did the dishes. Then we'd walk each other to the door and pause just inside, not quite ready to let go. There the talk might well continue for another half hour. Whatever the main topic for the evening had been, the talk would go deeper now. "You know what I think it *is* about her?" A piece of information that had been hidden through the whole extended discussion would be revealed now. "You know what she did one time to me?" And the murmured one's horrendous act, having lain dormant under the normal rules of discretion, would now be fully exposed. Everyone would add new cluckings and comments. "I always thought it was just me she did those things to. So, you too?"

"Well you know maybe it's because she never was that pretty. Even when we were girls. She was kind of chunky. Remember?" Then another addendum, "Well, her father was so mean to her. I hear he beat her terrible. She always had, like, this scared look. Once I saw some marks on her back when she was changing her blouse, all bruised, red and blue. It was terrible. Like she had been hit with, I don't know what, who knows—"

"Well we all were scared of Papa, too. Don't you remember the beatings he gave us?"

"Yeah, Tony, but her father was even worse than Papa. At least Papa laughed and sang, too."

"Yeah. When he wasn't whacking us."

"Yeah, but not like that. That was terrible."

"I gotta get home. Joe must be wondering where I've gotten to."

Then we'd leave our posts around the door frame and walk our company down the driveway to the sidewalk, really a dirt path at the side of the road, and kiss each other goodnight again. We were at the edge of the visit now, under the clear stars, the cool of darkness. A couple of the younger boys would be playing tag on the lawn, the rest of the kids were hanging onto their mothers, but not saying a word. We didn't want to break the spell. The grownups were *saying* things. One of my aunts would quickly dart a look around at the kids' upturned faces, asking herself, Should I say it in front of them? before she turned her gaze back to her sisters. But the night would beckon, restraint was loosened a bit more. "I feel sorry for her. You know what I heard about her husband? He's stepping out on her."

Maybe my mother's hand would be stroking my hair—a brief recess from our daily fights. "I gotta go. It's late. I don't know what we're doing standing here." We'd all laugh.

Then, "We'll walk you home. It's dark." We'd walk them home just up the street. Another excuse to extend the visit, the talk. Then my aunts and cousins would have to walk us back down the street. Two of my aunts lived side by side. We lived two houses away. "It's dark. We'd better walk you back."

Finally, at maybe one, one-thirty in the morning, just between Mrs. Goodenough's and Miss Simpkin's houses, we'd tear ourselves away and say goodnight. "Come on girls, we *really* have to get home," my mother's arms around each of us, shepherding us home.

Each of those almost-goodbye moments allowed discretion and defenses to loosen and fall. Each time we declared the night at an end the conversation was free to go in a little deeper, allowed to rise up more. Out there in the safety of the late dark night, the rules slipped. This intimacy had about it love born of the animal grouping, life lived in clusters, the connection of house to house, body to body, breath to breath, whispered secrets in the dark.

Coffee was the elixir, the fuel. Sugar sweetened the bitter, the talk, and being together was the "and." We had each other in a way that has spoiled me for the thin and ordinary connections in currency now. I escaped my family in a rage, needing to loosen their claustrophobic bonds, but I miss the "and."

～

Jeanie
Phyllis Capello

Jeanie walks to work on snowy days
when the bus doesn't come;
the stretch from home—past bodegas, factories,
the broad graveyard—is three miles of trudging,
hands in pockets and two cigarettes
(the strong kind, drawn deep) smoke
twirls up; her belly growls;
but at the store they let her eat.

Halfway there and it's snowing harder;
cars struggle up the hilly streets;
wide flakes cobweb her hair; the city turns
from ghetto to fairyland.
She wishes she'd taken the old boots
her mother offered and the ugly red hat.

Deliveries will be late, she thinks,
unlocking the riot gates, schools

will probably close; she eats two cupcakes,
lights up, watches the store cat purr over his bowl.
Ma's partying again and Little Julie's got a cold,
but she lets that go; thinks for a moment
about winning the Citywide: sweet arc of the ball
dropping clean through the rim,
the beautiful cheering.

All day, over the register, bent low,
she will tally and pack; the same old lady
will wander down the bread aisle like a lost child,
the cat will twirl himself between her long legs,
and today, like yesterday, she'll let
the gypsy-kids steal another box
of high-priced cookies.

⤫

Working Men
Phyllis Capello

They are the kind that whistle.
Crisp in gray-blue uniforms, they warble
unnamable melodies; streams of notes,
incomprehensible as birdsong, trail them.

Dollies piled high they shuttle
        between double-parked trucks and shopdoors,
delivering everything:
teeth, yarn, vitamins.
They know everyone's name: "How's it goin'
Al," they say: "What's
shakin', Lou?"

Amidst rattling plates,
and mumbled news, they'll have
the meatloaf, at the diner, in December; eat
        a sandwich on a shady bench in June.
Their days divide

into traffic lights, routine
runs, coffee breaks, available bathrooms.

Nothing hurts them yet.
Their legs are strong; their arms well-muscled,
        eyes, still keen, unspectacled.
They could go to war, play baseball at picnics,
make their pretty wives moan in thankful rapture.

When they get home the youngest ones
clamor at the door, lifting up
their red, red lips for kisses.

༄

Moving In and Moving Up
Donna Masini

1.

At first they stood outside, five men and a dog.
Occasionally someone peed in the hallway.
When the cold hit they moved in, broke
the light, the lock, seven mailboxes,
spread an old yellow blanket over the grease-
tracked floor, half a doorknob, flannel shirt,
pile of shit, two empty bottles of Nighttrain,
and a plate of dried *frijoles.*
And now I see it's my old yellow blanket.
There's a cup of wine in my mailbox slot,
three white rocks, several pennies,
and a pink plastic Happy Dolly Dream
House tipped against the wall.
By Chrismas two make it to the first landing.
The dog looks dead. The man deader.
They've yelled *Ivanhoe* through my dreams.
I hear them starving my nights.

2.

The world is structured on its own displacement,
I read in the *Times.* I think of this as I step

across the yellow blanket. Something moves,
grabs my leg. I kick it, feel for my keys.
"If I lost my keys I'd kill myself," a voice
behind me says. "Why don't you," I say.
His tongue dangles, drips on his shirt.
"I love you," he says. "God bless you, mommy."
"Fuck off," I say, holding the keys around my finger.
"How come you so pretty? How wide you spread
those pretty legs, mama, white girl, tight pussy?"
"Merry Christmas, mommy," the blanket shouts.
"Drop dead," I say, taking the stairs two at a time.

3.

I flip open the *New York Times Cookbook*
like it's the *Modern Witches' I Ching.* P. 175:
Wash tongue and place in large kettle.
Cover tightly and bring to boil.
Simmer until tongue is fork tender.
Let cool in broth. When cool
remove. Cut off bones
and gristle at the end. Slit the skin
from the thick end to the top.
Return tongue to broth to reheat—
or serve cold.

4.

The coldest night of the year.
The one called Angelo falls down
Delancey Street, a plate of *habichuelas* in his hand,
pants around his knees, penis like an old balloon.
In the hall a man stumbles, tucks
another inside his blanket,
covers him with a cardboard box top,
wedges a clump of foam under his head,
pats it three times before he falls.

5.

Night life. He rises above me, rooting
in the caves of me. The Williamsburg Bridge

a halo behind him. I watch my legs flying in the shadows
the bridge lights strike against the wall.
That's when I feel them
climbing through the halls
moving slowly up the stairs
hand over hand, to the
second landing. *I love you,*
baby, love you, mama.
I hear them wheezing in my room,
crawling in my air,
slowly, slowly
nesting in my bed.

∼

Fatso
Mary Cappello

> *"You son-of-a-bitch! . . . Don't die, will ya?!"*
> —ANNE BANCROFT TO DOM DELUISE IN FATSO

Some things were past now: a dinner party in which a man prepares chicken cutlet with a wedge of lemon, pasta with pancetta, cheese and bread; where he lays out milk glass water pitchers, multiple utensils for soups and well-oiled salads, greens and potatoes, anchovies and olives, seagreen glasses overflowing with red. He has always made too much for the crowd of people he invites but sits, not eating himself, afraid everyone won't be fed. Once the party is over, he imbibes the leftovers, which, now, *must* be eaten, then tells, not confesses, tales of sinful excess.

Jean and I are sitting at Larry's dining room table. The table's surface is empty except for a lace covering that suddenly feels terribly reminiscent of Miss Havisham's abode, the politics of a lifetime evaporating like the last drop of water in a tin lapped up by his companion cat. He's twisting a handkerchief into a tourniquet around the space of air in front of him and unrolling in hurried succession one piece of Toblerone after another. He's eaten a dozen.

This afternoon, wracked with flu-like symptoms that wouldn't subside, he's been told that a strain of hepatitis has been busy in his liver for years. His liver is decimated; he has "one to three years to live." Another doctor tells him, "Additionally, you tested positive for AIDS."

In the middle of winter the radiators in Larry's apartment make clanking noises, as though a specter is banging on them with a wrench. Jean and I have fallen into a constant state of worry, but when I'm with Larry, I launch into avuncular coach mode. "OK," I turn to Jean, slapping the front of my thighs with my palms, "Let's go get some soy milk and fresh fish."

Human beings may not have agency, but the liver certainly does. It detoxifies, breaks down, synthesizes, converts, stores, inactivates, accumulates, produces. Disease can cause it to degenerate. And the effects of liver degeneration are ugly and grave, ranging from the inability to urinate to the inability to think, if one should become so unlucky as to fall prey to the condition whereby the body produces ammonias it cannot expel.

"According to what I read," I tell Larry, "you need foods rich in vitamin B, protein and carbs. We're going to have to shop at your least favorite store," by which I mean Bread and Circus—a posh health food nook.

Later, Jean prepares trout in Larry's kitchen. I've set the rice and string beans to steam. The cat is swatting, jumping at the smell of fish cooking. We offer to stay with Larry, but he insists we go home. He's going to make some phone calls, then try to sleep.

In the most difficult first month of his illness, Larry stays with a friend he has known since their years as altar boys. Gradually, the swelling in his abdomen—ascites—begins to diminish, but his condition is still grave.

During this period, all we seem to do together is watch movies, curling up under a blanket on the couch, swept into the self-contained, moving image drama of other lives. Each flicker of passing images imbibed together assuring us of the lasting story of our friendship.

This evening, after breaking sticks of spaghetti into boiling water, which, once drained, will yield a bland spur-of-the-moment meal for Larry, who still can't really eat, we watch a film with the remarkably crude title of *Fatso*. Anne Bancroft, a.k.a Anna Maria Louisa Italiano, wrote, directed, and starred in the film, the only film she ever directed, Larry explains. Larry owns this film—maybe the only feature title in a small collection, mostly of gay male porn; he counts it among his favorite films. "So it's a comedy?" I ask, dreading a vulgar farce along the lines of Fat Albert. "Meah, Meah, trust me! You'll see," he says, "there's a lot going on. I think you're gonna love it."

A roly-poly Italian/American baby gurgles and pouts center stage; an adult hand breaks the frame to feed the baby a pacifying *connolo*. Cut to an over-wrought gathering of Italian American mourners attending the viewing of Sal, a one-time tuba player, who is now "playing his tuba for the angels," having died young of a heart attack from overeating. Sal's cousin (played by Dom DeLuise) weeps at the edge of the coffin until a priest instructs him to get his distraught aunt a glass of water. In an adjacent kitchen, where he goes to get the water, a pot of tomato sauce is bubbling on the stove. Sal was like a mother to him, he explains to his sister, Antoinette (played by Bancroft). Sal always had "something on him to eat," he remembers, and together brother and sister chant, "Always, always, always, always."

Alone in the kitchen, Dom eats a piece of Italian bread dribbled with a teaspoon of the sauce he has skimmed from the edge of the pot, covering it with an even layer of parmesan. He has forgotten to fetch the water for his aunt. He eats until his breathing becomes regular and he ceases to cry.

Meanwhile, Antoinette addresses the dead body of Sal: "You son-of-a-bitch . . . How many times did I tell you to lose weight?. . . You could've been sitting here next to your mother rather than laying in this box." "You're good people," she tells Dom, "the good people are the fat people and the fat people die young."

Italian/American, fat, queer—to Larry and me the terms are interchangeable in this funny, sad film about tenderness between men, and a brother/sister relationship between this delicate, funny man and this earthy, commanding Italian/American woman, and what Larry calls "feeding disorders"—the condition of she who bloats her children.

The raucousness of the filmspace is momentarily stilled: Dom DeLuise, back home in the kitchen of the apartment he shares with his brother, Frankie (played by Ron Carey), raises the frying pan in which he is about to prepare eggs, as though to smash it against the wall between the stove and refrigerator. "What do you say to a mother that buries a child?" he weeps, the first of many tears that just might make this film set a record for the number of times it shows a man weeping.

I think about the beauty of the word *spooning,* and its correlative in bodies bent like matching utensils. I wonder if there is anything more intimate than literally feeding, spooning food into the mouth of another human being. I remember brightening, one day, to the thought of surprising my mother with a soft pretzel from the Catholic grade school I attended, soft pretzels imported from the nearby city of Philadelphia. But each time I advanced to another streetcorner, I took a bite from the pretzel until all I had to offer my mother when I arrived was a crumb.

It was obvious to me now, the fact of Larry's body. He "felt fat" so much of his life, but only now do I feel his belly when we hug, his bloated, ailing belly.

"You don't know how to run your plate. You're thirty-two years old and you don't know how to run your plate," Dom DeLuise addresses his brother, Frankie. "The omelet is supposed to come out even with the bread." Almost in despair, he goes on: "You don't even dip your bread . . . you don't even butter your bread." Frankie yells back that he's told him for one hundred years that he doesn't like bread! And it was too much bread, bread and jelly, that killed their cousin, Sal, "Thirty-nine years old and he's dead, dead, dead!"

To each family member his own running of the plate. My father approaches food with trepidation, the possibility of poison, toxicity, harm, or he eats ferociously, like one starved. My mother eats freely with gusto, drugs herself with coffee, recites "The Raven" while we eat. My grandmother, my father's mother, puts her hand down her throat after eating a large meal. My brother invents towering desserts, special moundlike concoctions, and takes deep breaths between shovels. My other brother hides a piece of toast with jam between the slipcovers or behind the refrigerator where my mother finds it. I like to melt an entire sugarcube on my tongue. I appreciate that my father grows the food we eat, but then, why does he expect to be poisoned? I detest the thin broth made out of water and brown cubes that my father feeds me—he swears by them—when I'm sick. Is there anything worse than swallowing chlorinated water or ocean? Yes, having your stomach pumped at age four because the bubble bath you drank did not have ingredients on the bottle and it might have been worse if they hadn't pumped your stomach, or so they said.

Making pasta with butter for my friend who may be dying is not a sacred ritual. It doesn't *really* mean anything. It's just a basic fact of survival, one of any number of simple acts that, if we're lucky, accumulate without interruption, certainly without the corruption of meaning, to make a life.

Is it enough that Dom runs a card shop for a living, Di Napoli's Card Shop, where he daintily arranges pastries on a doily-covered plate on a small wooden table with two chairs in the middle of the store? Isn't it rich? "Stop," Larry would say; "Go on," I'd echo, incredulous before what we identify with (as in, want for ourselves, know, know to be possible, know to be true) and love: the idea of a man who runs a card shop, who offers you a Danish while you shop, then helps you choose the right card for the particular occasion—he listens to you describe it in detail—then moves with you through his own feelings as he opens each card to read its kitschy verse.

More than once I'd arrive at Larry's to find him ironing a damask tablecloth. He likes to keep his tablecloths warm, not crisp, as though at first to press into the fabric the impression of the last meal, almond scents and sugary *torrone*, the indentation of the soup tureen, the words, the untold temptations and inaudible sighs, the breaking of bread, crumbs ground beneath an elbow, the leaning forward to listen. In ironing, the meal was momentarily stowed in the cloth, and then, shaken out, transmuted into sky.

I thought of the creamy surface, damask mint, of the tablecloth he gave us but that, for some reason or other, we retired to a drawer; of taking it out into a garden party one evening, not wanting to consign it to the tomb; of the carafe of red wine that toppled, crushed grapes, wasted, and the red stain that would never wash out.

The one thing left to be thankful for was his aunt's habit of smoothing the tablecloth beneath her hand between sentences, on either side of the brink of words.

It was obvious that *Fatso* was a gay film, and yet no one we knew had ever heard of it. It came and went, it didn't do well in the theaters, and Italiano never directed another film.

Made in 1980 with nary an image of male-male love on Hollywood's horizon, *Fatso* catches the tightknit nature of Dom's New York City neighborhood. When Dom leaves his house, everyone he sees greets him with sympathy for Sal's death, and, as he walks to work, two men holding hands skirt past Dom unselfconsciously, part of the life of Bleecker Street, where he lives. There are campy references in an antique store to "two American cocks," a Chinese delicacy called "narcissus balls," an episode in the card shop where Dom's wooing a woman with wrapping paper is "too gay," a man at the counter clutching his shoulder bag. Then there is the group orgasm where three fat (read queer) men confess their illicit pleasures to one another—jelly donuts and chocolate covered grahams—that sets off an all-night group binge. At its end, one of the revelers strokes Dom's face, saying they must now be considered dropouts of Overeaters Anonymous, a.k.a. Chubby Checkers (whose sponsors come to rescue him from breaking open the locks he's put on his cabinets). After the binge, Dom cries as he pleads, "Why do they want me to be skinny? I'm not so bad as I am. My mother liked me this way."

Imagine if all were denied. From what would you make a meal? If the only thing left to be thankful for was snow.

Snow was dirty, it was said, on the outskirts of acceptable pleasures. At a sweaty pause between plunges down the local inclines on my sled, I'd feel thirsty. More transgressive than sipping the head off an uncle's just-poured beer was the act of sucking snow. It was sky food, manna, like eating of a piece of cloud, and thus the enormity of the pain when I learned that snow could not possibly be good for you.

I thought of the story that my mother felt compelled to repeat, of the day she came home from school to find her mother gone—her mother's father, a grocer, had suddenly died and she was called on the instant to go by train to the house in North Philly. Of arriving home to find her own father clueless in a bare kitchen. Of how he found a pomegranate and cut it in half for the two of them to eat for dinner. Of how they sat silently eating pomegranate, not understanding where her mother had gone to. Of drops of red soaked onto her white school blouse like a light suddenly illuminating her place at the table.

Dom had placed a sign in the window of his card shop during Sal's funeral: "Closed On Account of Death." I felt Larry's belly press into my belly and it gave me such a sense of well-being to know he was alive.

I wept at every scene where Anne Bancroft exploded like moonlight across an empty prairie, begging Dom to love himself. (Bancroft's character represents a particular kind of love—affectionate brusqueness: she never knows whether she wants to be hugged or left alone, whether she wants to strike her brothers or embrace them. She'll love like no other, but she has a limit for taking any shit. We both knew someone like her.)

Larry was most moved by Dom DeLuise's brief soliloquies on compulsive eating as self-consolation. The family knows that Dom is trying to diet, but they send him to the pastry shop to pick up their nephew Anthony's birthday cake. Waiting in line, Dom breaks out into a sweat when he sees the sumptuous layered sweets that other people are ordering. Dom restrains himself and purchases only the cake, but when sister Antoinette opens the box, she discovers a piece missing, the piece with the last three letters of her son's name. She lunges at Dom with the pair of scissors that she's used to cut the box's thread. "You ate the 'ONY!'" She commands Dom to get another cake. When he asks what she's going to do with this one, she grinds and mashes what's left of it with her hands.

Who knows which end of her rope led my mother to shower my brother and me with Cheerios one morning, or to pound a sandwich until the dish broke beneath it, or my father to turn the dinner table upside down?

Am I laughing at Anne Bancroft because I recognize that brand of unabashed rage, or because I love her guts and her gravelly voice, her chutzpah—or both? It is an anger that goes right to the source, no soft-shoe, no subterfuge, no nonsense. What's more dangerous—Antoinette's throaty screams or Dom's appetite?

Dom is sent to pick up a huge takeout order of Chinese food for Antoinette and a group of cardplayers who gather at her home. He hasn't heard from a new girlfriend and is convinced she doesn't want him. Dom eats all the food on his way back home, skids his car onto a curb, and deposits numerous boxes and bags into a garbage can. Back home, he tries to secrete himself in shame, but Antoinette realizes he's returned and what he's done. She whips the dresser beside Dom, but it looks like she's whipping him, too. "I ate it all," he says, "I'm sorry." But for Antoinette, a confession won't do: "Ya got crazy blood in your brain," she says. "Maybe I am crazy," he replies. "I don't know. Do crazy people hate themselves? Always trying to find an excuse for eating . . . but I don't need an excuse to eat. I have to eat. When I eat, I'm me. Like when I was a kid, it felt more natural when I was eating and eating and eating and eating."

Occasionally I'd have nightmares of eating paper. What made the dreams ugly was that the paper was hard to swallow, but I was compelled to eat it as though I knew it was the only real form of nourishment available. Always the paper had words on it.

I'm convinced that food tastes differently the moment you know what it's called. I'm convinced that I can neither write about nor make a decent tomato sauce if I don't take the pains to know that the etymology of tomato is "ball of gold," and one of the many uses to which the word has been put include "whore."

And *these* words, the words with which I fill *this* page? Can we partake of them? Can we reap this banquet of words in honor of my friend? Can I be a host at the table of these sentences?

The film kept taking us to the mirror. We knew why we laughed and we knew why we cried. We quoted in code: "You ate the 'ONY!'" when no other words would do. We munched on fragments:

Don *smells* the gift-wrapped present Lydia brings him when he's sick: "It smells like buttered beets."

Dom tells Lydia to "watch for the cars" when she leaves his card shop to return to her giftshop a few blocks away.

A character dabs her index finger into some stray sesame seeds, once, twice, three times, and licks.

The word *dead* recurs with deadpan regularity.

A piece of spaghetti drops from the ceiling onto Frankie's shoulder the morning following his brother's binge.

Larry's illness, I notice recently, warily, has made him look more delicate, less "stocky," less "fat." Lying across my couch, he seems to grace it like one of his lacey throws, except for his belly, which is still swollen.

I have the sudden desire for us to massage each other with eggshells in the light of an eggnog-colored sun. I was thankful, now, for the memory of my father drawing a face onto the shell of a soft-boiled egg, and knowing that I did the same for another little girl some windowed breakfast long ago in which her laughter broke through the morning to ask for another; that I learned to crush eggshell as loam to feed my roses, and that there is nothing more quiet or sane than turning those chalky petals into earth on a summer day.

We are speaking on the couch where Larry will sleep tonight in our house.

When I lost my sight, I thought, "my mouth will do what my eyes can't"

You were embarrassed

I was always too embarrassed

Do you still see the face of the Italian gentleman

Like a welcome film blocking the nauseating light through the train window

I can feel my voice fading

No, you are illuminated at the table and it only takes a drop of color to admit you're still alive

I'm falling

Hey, remember that line from Fatso, *"Christ fell three times and he was Christ!"*

I've been thinking a lot about whether there is life after death

Yes, after Marjorie died . . .

There's the idea of giving a sign
Probably something funny
The only man I loved
I feel like I know him
When he died, he wasn't speaking to me
My mother held the hand of her father on his deathbed, but he didn't want her,
he wanted his work or his God
Just breathe, somebody said
I can help you with that
Too much to think about, but I'm less and less afraid
That's amazing, I'm not
To be given the opportunity to return to the table. To touching under the table, hands knees feet. To have hidden under the table, a stowaway on a different boat to a world elsewhere. To catch your finger in the table; to extend a table with leaves. To sit at your assigned seat at the table, triangulated. To lie under the table, as though it were yesterday, pretending not to breathe, making my poor mother find me there, pretending to be dead, dead, dead.

Needing no invitation, in the afternoon, to arrange the table, especially the glasses and the flowers, many hours ahead of time. To sit in the next room, waiting in a length of sunlight and quiet for the guests to arrive.

Part Seven

❧

PASSINGS

The Lives of the Saints

Susanne Antonetta

When I first learned about atoms in high school
nothing seemed more ridiculous than life
if that's all it was: tiny, disintegrating, empty, all-the-same.
Dustdots streaming
toward an even larger collapse.
Everywhere. My mother in her pinkchecked party apron
spun in bits to the dining room, a duck nucleused
by *Joy of Cooking* sauce l'orange in her arms.

& my lubehaired dad sighing his paper down
to come to her.
He was something else totally,
really just a bundle of nervous hoops.

He knew my mother as small
already, the TV
blaring *I love ya little cutie but the office is my duty*
as legions of husbands left their wives onscreen.

What I saw kept showing me
its rounding Ferris wheels of movement, its poor parts.

.

At Mary Star of the Sea High School, 5th period science class
it got hard to believe in anything, seeing it all
as the same at the root—
one or two dot's difference, carbon's diamond,
or bound with other, almost identical
atoms, it's me.

Then 7th period Religion we read about
the lives of the saints, so it was like
hearing them try to yank the absurdity to something else.

Or maybe the saints knew it
too, Catherine
with her puslicking, her meals of celery & vomiting.

I loved those people & their comic gestures.
Rose of Lima rubbing pepper on her skin, Jerome
turning restlessly on his nails
showed their indifference to the state of matter.

They were the first atomic scientists.
Francis' parents'
cast him off, Catherine shamed her mother, they blew up
the world around them.
Like they had to start that way, freed electrons,
so the way in front of them could be clear.

                              .

Later I saw them all the time
when my mother grew their look.
I say *grew*. It emerged, a new life, from her face.
The one where you smile & it's real
but the rest of your face does something else completely.

Looks beyond the room, your eyes heavy with the weight
of two existences, the pupils carved almost.

It seemed my mother's cancer hungered for her eyes.
Ovarian: massive, larger than the organs
it consumed.

They took out everything, the first plushed bed
of my babyhood. "All gone," says my mother
then tells me how she bled, "like
saffron threads" (Indian cooking
with Craig Claiborne, a phase of hers).

She took to eating bacon & eggs & liver.
She'd had her thyroid & appendix removed
& tells me she feels like a bladder or balloon, a skin
clung to a wind that's scraping her clean.

After chemo I set her hair the way she likes it, the strands
cytoxin didn't gobble up.
I trapped them in pink rollers the size of fingers—she used them
on me a few times—they had little spikes all around,

& she'd emerge redone, scrollheaded,
a fountain of those Jewish scripture-curls
over the shell she'd become, a child's Visible Woman, pieces lost.

·

For a while I couldn't justify my love of sweets
with all I knew of the world, it was evil
or emptiness, Catherine
lived years on the Host, & I
took a cake decorating class and squeezed the icing bag
straight into my mouth.
It saved me: the frosting
mostly powdered sugar, only heaps of sugar
can make a good form & keep it.
Flavors like chocolate just a whisper of elseness

& my secret love became that sugarshock
of icing, that knock to the jaw,
your tongue & teeth can actually vibrate from it.
Your mind screams *pleasure*
your teeth hit with that corruption nervescream *hurt.*

I made strange cakes & brought them to my mother
first her favorite flowers like roses & bleeding hearts
then drip bags, syringes, & whatever
they took out of her, I made.
I even made a sheetcake using fondant to mold
the smug, sporebearded face of an oncologist she couldn't stand.

She couldn't eat them & I didn't want her to.
It was a way of seeing her life as holdable, slapstick, nothing
but the sweet inside.

After We Bury Her
Dorian Cirrone

How many times without complaint
did her hands mix cold, raw meat, cheese,
eggs, parsley, bread crumbs.
Fingers freezing, yolk oozing
through knuckles, hours spent
molding, mixing, browning,
hands still slippery with fat,
washing bowls, scrubbing pans.

I watch my own hands
while following my mother's recipe
and think of the note my five-year-old son
placed in her coffin: a picture of
spaghetti and meatballs, to remind her
to make some for God.

Only weeks after we bury her,
I loathe this chore,
the standing, the stirring, the serving,
the sameness of each Sunday.

ᐁ

Ma, Who Told Me You Forgot How To Cry
Maria Mazziotti Gillan

Soothsayer,
healer,
tale-teller
there was nothing you could not do.

In your basement kitchen,
with the cracked brown and yellow tiles,
the sink on metal legs,
the big iron stove with its pots simmering,
the old Kelvinator from 1950,

the metal kitchen table and plastic chairs,
I'd watch you roll out dough for *pastichelle.*
"Be quiet," you'd say,
and work at super speed.

Today, when we walk into your hospital room,
you do not speak of your illness,
do not mention the doctor
who tells you bluntly,
"You have three months, at most, to live."

Your shrewd, sharp eyes watch us,
but you do not cry.

Soothsayer,
healer,
tale-teller,
always ready with a laugh and a story,
ready to offer coffee, cakes,
advice at your oval kitchen table,
your chair pulled close and your hands
always full.

We are like little children gathered
around your bed. Al, with his doctor's bag
full of tricks and medicine,
Laura, in her nurse's uniform,
her hands twisting, and me,
my head full of words
that here, in this antiseptic room,
are no use, no use at all.

We wait for you
to get up out of that bed,
to start bossing us around,
the way you always did.
Tell us a story
with a happy ending,
one in which the oil
of Santo Rocco that you put on

your swollen belly each night
works its elusive miracle.

Soothsayer,
healer,
tale-teller,
there was nothing you could not do.
Tell us again how the bluebirds
came to sing at your window
that January, when Al was so sick
all the doctors said he'd die.

⌒∾

The Day Anna Stopped Making A-Beetz
Suzanne Branciforte

Visits to my father's family in Connecticut always began with a stop at Mamma's house. Mamma, my father's mother, was Mamma to seven children and fifteen grandchildren. She lived in an apartment in the house that had once been home to her children, her husband, and herself. Now there were four apartments, and Mamma lived in one of them. We never really had a meal there. At most we ate lunch with Mamma, and looked forward to a more complete meal at one of my aunts' and uncles' homes later in the day.

Mamma was a bad cook. She left us no recipes. Really, the only thing she made well was pizza, which she called "a-beetz." Mamma made two versions of a-beetz, one with sauce, and another with chunks of tomato, fresh basil, slivers of garlic, sprinkled with oregano and Parmesan cheese. This was Sicilian pizza, the thick-crusted kind made in an oblong pan, its soft white dough rising up an inch.

Pizza was Mamma's offering. When she knew we were coming, she made sure it was fresh and waiting for us on top of the washing machine. That's where she placed the cookie sheets to cool.

Pizza was the one food Mamma continued to make now that she lived alone. I don't know what she ate the rest of the time; I never saw a piece of meat or a salad or a plate of pasta in her house. She'd offer us a-beetz, and we had to have some, even if it was ten o'clock in the morning.

There are photos of Mamma when she was still robust, squeezed into her flowered apron, her black dress underneath. She was solid, sturdy in her black widow's shoes, her white hair pulled severely into a bun. I remember her flabby underarms, their doughy white flesh gently moving with each stroke of the rolling pin as the pizza was rolled out. Somehow, all that work did not make her upper arm muscular.

As she aged, we would find long, thin, gray hairs on the pizza—and then Dad would tell her, "That's enough, no more a-beetz, you're getting too old. I won't tell you when we're coming, this way you won't know and you can't make a-beetz."

"Oh, Johnny," she'd say, laughing, as if to say, *Naughty a-boy, playing a-trick on your Mamma, a-Mamma.* She was coquettish with my father. "Oh, John, oh. I know, I a-know, yes a-Mamma, Mamma too old, a-Mamma." And she laughed because she knew she had a good thirty years still in her and that she would continue to make a-beetz.

Those squabbles delighted her: they gave her a chance to remind my father that he was still her little boy and she was the parent. More than the chubby, sweet, nurturing granny who makes special treats for her grandchildren's visits, Mamma was a kind of field marshal, making battle plans and strategies for the continuation of her matriarchal rule. A-beetz was the food that accompanied discussions with my father, her youngest, about family politics and strife. My father's protests about a-beetz were his way to assert his authority. In the complex passage of command from a parent to a child as a parent ages, the struggle for decision-making power is played out in strange ways. As long as Mamma was making a-beetz, she was in control.

"Anna" was how my Sicilian grandmother was known to her friends. Her real name was Sebastiana, a name that she hated. Anna was the name she had given herself in a remarkable assertion of independence.

And it wasn't enough that Sebastiana had become Anna. She wanted all her granddaughters to be Anna, too, and she imposed this rule on her seven children in a demonstration of the force of her will, which marked the next generation of her progeny. Which is how my cousins and I came to be called Ann Karen, Ann Marie, Joann, Betty Ann, Mary Ann, Diane, and Suzanne.

Later in life, this led to enormous confusion, with Mamma reciting a litany of names before finding the one she was looking for and smiling with relief. "Suzanne, ah, Diane, ah, Joann, ah Mary Ann, *si*, Mary Ann, you bring a-sweater a-mamma."

For a long time I didn't understand why my grandmother abhorred her real name, Sebastiana. It was unusual to me—exotic, even. It didn't have an English equivalent, and couldn't be reduced to a silly sounding nickname. Saint Sebastian, I later learned, was the name of the parish of her small Sicilian hometown, Melilli.

Sebastian, the martyr, pierced through by many arrows in popular iconography, turns his pitiful gaze to heaven, his eyes rolling to the back of his head. Could this image of suffering have upset my grandmother? Sebastiana was no martyr, that's for sure. That look of pious resignation was not among her countenances.

Determination, anger, indignation, revenge of the I'm-not-saying-anything-now-but-you'll-get-yours-later variety—those were the faces of Anna. The tightened lips, the piercing stare from the slightly narrowed eyes meant to stop you in your tracks, the stony face that meant trouble—these were Mamma's looks. Looks accompanied by silence.

Mamma's hands were gnarled, her bony fingers curved, her joints enlarged. Somehow, though, she held a needle to cross-stitch the tablecloths we brought her once a month from New York. The tablecloths my grandmother Anna stitched with irregular crosses were bright, haphazard, colorful. There was no pattern to the colors, but there was something *allegro,* buoyant, fun, in how the colors swirled together.

My mother used to complain to my father, "Why doesn't your mother follow the pattern? We buy her these things to keep her busy, to give her something to do. Then she plows through them so fast, paying no attention to the color scheme, that they come out looking like she's on drugs." Sometimes my father would talk to his mother, explaining that my mother wanted the tablecloths in a particular color scheme, all shades of blue, or red. What would come back was a many-hued mosaic of color, a phantasmagoria of red orange purple blue yellow green brown.

Years later, on a trip to Sicily, my grandmother's homeland, I realized: those were the patterns of her origins. They were Anna's reminders of the bright sun of Sicily and the sharp and vivid colors of that land. Anna recreated the landscape of her youth. I learned this near Siracusa, looking at a Sicilian cart, the yellows, reds and greens of its brightly colored wheels, the dizzying designs on the body of the cart, the multichromed plumage of the horse leading it. Now, when I take out my grandmother's multicolored tablecloths for formal dinners, my friends admire her handiwork.

The hands that stitched those tablecloths were hands worth studying, hands that told a story. The babies' diapers they had changed, the socks they had darned, the food they had prepared. They say Mamma turned the blackened roasting peppers on the stovetop without the protection of pot holders or gloves. The history of that family was seared into Mamma's hands.

Anna had her own language, which wasn't English, wasn't Italian, and wasn't even the Sicilian dialect. It was something *resembling* Sicilian without *being* Sicilian. During the eighty-six years she lived in the United States, Anna stubbornly refused to give up her own language. She never really mastered English and added the vowel *a* before words. "Dat's a nice a-boy." "You go-y a-store a-buy a-ice cream."

But perhaps the linguistic tic that most defined her was the habit of adding "a-Mamma" to every sentence she pronounced. "I sorry, a-Mamma." "How you, a-Mamma?" "I no like a-dis, a-Mamma." Everything was "to Mamma." As a child, I thought this was simply an Italian way of reminding everyone that Mamma was the center of the universe, that all things revolved around her.

Mamma was only a teenager when she made the transatlantic crossing with a few of her older siblings. She had the courage to leave her parents behind, not knowing if she would ever see them again, to go to a country where she didn't know the language or the landscape.

Mamma had crossed an ocean, borne nine children, watched four sons march off to World War II and come back again. She had buried two infants, a husband, and a daughter, and had raised two grandchildren as her own. She had directed family politics and strategy, marshalling six sons and their wives for over five decades, and through the years, the only person able to stand up to her was her only daughter, Mae.

The day Anna stopped making a-beetz is the day our family started to come undone. It had gotten to be too much, my father determined. We had found one too many gray hairs on the pizza; her eyesight, he said, was going. She had to stop, she had to stop making a-beetz, she was too old.

And so we would arrive unannounced, ambushing Anna so she could not prepare for our visits. We started taking her out to lunch in New England–style restaurants that served crab-stuffed scrod to distract her from the fact that she was no longer making a-beetz. And she was a little less Mamma as a result. Sitting in those restaurants, she suddenly seemed older, smaller, almost meek. I liked her better the old way, when she was making a-beetz.

It was the beginning of the end. My father had taken the reins. He was now "taking care of Mamma" by bringing her to the fancy restaurants he could afford. But what he didn't anticipate was how this broke her spirit. And what he couldn't know was that he wouldn't always be there to take care of her.

After my father died, "the boys" decided Mamma would be "better off" in a nursing home. It is hard for me to imagine how Anna must have felt when her sons took her from her home to an assisted care facility. She reminded us often, those first few years when we visited her there, that this never would have happened if my father had lived. She was right.

There had been a time when Mamma's prayers that the Lord take her seemed to be an insurance policy that He wouldn't, a Sicilian warding off of the evil eye: If I ask God for this, I'm sure not to get it. But now, when she said, "I pray a-God a-take a-me, a-Mamma. I no a-wanna live a-no more. I pray a-God," she meant it.

She spent over ten years there, in the little room that contained only the barest trace of the life she had lived—a few photos, her rosary beads, and some of her housecoats and cardigans. I don't know where the things from Mamma's apartment went, all those small tokens of her past, reminders of her life, of her passage through this world—photos, furniture, ceramics, and jewelry. They were things without value, except for the fact that they were *hers*, that those gnarled hands that had once made a-beetz had touched them, those same hands that had touched and cradled my father when he was a baby.

I have her tablecloths, the pieces of her handiwork that no one wanted when she was alive. These are the truly precious heirlooms I inherited. The bright colors arranged in that artfully haphazard way, like a mosaic path that I can trace back to my Sicilian roots.

And I have the pathless memory of a-beetz, sitting on the washing machine on the white macramé doily, its sweet aroma mixing with the fresh scent of newly washed laundry.

∽

My Mother's Career at Skip's Luncheonette
Janet Zandy

She had the morning shift,
breakfast and lunch, home by two.
Squeezed between grill and counter
one hand on a plate, the other on a pot
she concocted banquets of heavy food
for the working poor.

Sausage, peppers and onions on hoagies
pasta shells stuffed with ricotta
and covered with gravy.
She knew her customers,
who liked their sandwiches trimmed a certain way
heavy on the butter or the cheese.

The aroma of her cooking settled on the
four-year-old Hallmark cards,
kids' comics, daily scratch sheets.

When she left, pressure sky high,
ankles swollen, grease stains on

all her aprons, Skip closed the grill, figuring
Who would do that kind of work?

A few customers still remember Millie's cooking
how important a full belly was to her sense of the world.

And Ma, all the time you worked there
I never came in
once
to say
hello.

∾

Secret Gardens
Janet Zandy

When my mother died
the only thing I wanted,
really wanted, was her black silk scarf.

A black field
covered by purple iris
bordered in bruised blue.

I've seen her wear it
hundreds of times
hurrying to novenas,
hasty protection against the cold,
always tied, peasant style,
around her head.

Last fall for the first time
I planted twenty iris bulbs.

My mother was not a gardener.
She was the oldest daughter
and the best cleaner.
Nine brothers and sisters felt
her hands brisk in hot baths

heads checked for lice
underwear boiled in cauldrons
on scoured stoves.

When you spend so much time inside
battling for clean white space
dirt is, well, dirt
and digging in the yard
a leisure for another world.

My mother had a mangled nail,
an injured thumb that never mended,
too small for a doctor
too large for time.
She called it her witch's thumb,
a joke for children.
At the end of the story,
hidden beneath the folds of her apron,
she would jerk it out
like a happy ending.

She wanted me
in the kitchen
with her
but I would not come.
Or, if I came,
I would not stay.

But the scarf is soft.
Its petals fold and unfold
to the place
she could not name
where our love
our rift
our beauty
would visit.

I want to crush it
in anger, in regret,
for the life she did not have.

In dreams, smiling,
she reminds me:
"I had a life."

I touch the scarf
put my face into its soft folds
smell the memories.

"Keep it," she says, "it's yours."

❧

The Exegesis of Eating

Alane Salierno Mason

And thou shalt treat the food that touchest thy lips with reverence, in recognition of the labors and traditions of thine ancestors, and in communion and fellowship with those to whom thou art tied with ties of blood and love. Thou shalt not neglect to share the fruits of the earth with thy neighbor. Thou shalt not neglect to feed the old and the sick . Thou shalt serve first the pasta, then the meat, fish, or fowl, then the salad, and thou shalt sprinkle no grated cheese on the fish. Thou shalt give thanks before the meal and kiss the hand that feeds thee. Except in condition of necessity, thou shalt not eat in haste, in distraction, or alone.

These are some of the commandments I took in at my grandparents' table, along with string bean salad, chicken cutlets, potatoes and eggs, stuffed and roasted mushrooms, thinly sliced beef rolled and tied with string. But in my adult life, I've broken them all, except for the commandment not to use grated cheese on linguini with clam sauce.

I spent much of my childhood in my grandmother's kitchen. As I watched her cook, she would give me something from her preparations to assuage my hunger—a carrot, a piece of celery. Most of the foods she prepared took time. They needed first to be "cleaned," trimmed of fat or organs or bones in the case of chicken or meat or fish, or of stems and seeds in the case of vegetables. Then basted in egg and bread crumbs, for cutlets or zucchini flowers, or stuffed, for mushrooms. String beans had to be snapped at both ends, and after they were cooked, each one had to be carefully sliced along its length; for artichokes, every leaf had to be trimmed, then stuffed with chopped garlic and bread crumbs.

"Such a big bag of string beans your grandfather brought me, a whole hour it took me to clean so many, he doesn't know the time it takes!" Or, "He brought home calamar', still with all the bone in, it took me all morning just to clean them and cut them up, doesn't he know you can ask the fish market to do it for you?" She often cleaned the foods under running water, and her hands were rough. Once I tried to squeeze the peeled tomatoes through a strainer the way she did when making sauce; I couldn't do it, it made my knuckles raw.

"All the time it took to make it, and we ate it in no time!" she'd exclaim as soon as our plates were empty. These were often the first words to break the silence my grandparents preferred while eating. When I chattered, merrily rushing through my food to get my words out faster, they'd both chasten me: "Eat slow, you can talk after. It's no good to eat fast."

My grandmother was always rotund; she took pleasure from eating if not from cooking. Her flowing bosom made for an especially comforting embrace. She snacked through the day, from nervousness, perhaps, but when her depression became overwhelming, that was when she lost her appetite for sweets as well as for life, and when she went on strike from the kitchen. The depression then could feed on itself, as she punished herself with the idea that by not cooking, she was a terrible disappointment to us all.

The thought of preparing the Christmas Eve meal always undid her, disabling her with "nervous tension," as she called it, a blend of fatigue, anxiety, and tears. At ninety-one, as pain in her feet and legs made it increasingly difficult for her to stand long enough to cook, her depression returned and was more difficult than ever to treat. That year she was hospitalized twice for trying to die. Left alone for several weeks each time, my grandfather (younger than she, but only by a month) struggled to learn to cook.

My grandmother was born in New York of Italian parents; her maternal grandparents, the Carbones, had a restaurant on 116th Street in Italian East Harlem. My grandfather was born in Naples, where his mother and father had a trattoria on the Via Orefice. They served pasta marinara, veal scaloppine, chicken cacciatore, zuppa di pesce—"everything," my grandfather says. His father's family was in the wine export business, and his mother's, in the grocery business. The maternal family nickname was "Cocchiamichele," which probably meant that someone in the family named Michele had made *cocchia*, round loaves of bread with a split across the top.

His father and mother fought over the trattoria. Gennaro thought he should greet the customers out front, a public relations job, while Giuseppina stayed back in the kitchen, doing all the work. She didn't agree.

So Gennaro left for America, and my grandfather's mother took the children back to her hometown, where she ran a tiny grocery from the corner of her house and sold bread that she baked in a large wood-fired oven across the street. The children fired the oven, and they baked both white bread and *scagnozzi*, a corn bread. During World War I, she sold the bread to soldiers. Almost all my grandfather's stories of Italy have to do with the preparation of food—the few cents a day he made picking grapes, and how they made wine by crushing the grapes with their feet; how his mother would wring the neck of a chicken, and how she would slit the throat of a pig while he stood with a bowl to catch the blood she would use to make blood pudding, *sanguinaccio*.

His mother's relatives, who had set up a grocery in Brooklyn, made it possible for him to come to America. Later, their grocery business grew into a chain of supermarkets. My grandfather, who had gone into contracting, built the first of the Danza supermarkets on Avenue X in Brooklyn at the end of World War II. At the groundbreaking, he said to his cousin Albert, "*Compare*, what are you going to do with this big store?"

"*Compare, la gente*," Albert said and made a gesture towards his mouth with the bunched fingers of one hand—a gesture to say, "People always need to eat."

My grandfather always hated the idea that Americans think of pizza as "Italian food," even though his birthplace is famous for it. He always claimed it wasn't Italian, wasn't real food. "I never heard of pizza before I came to this country. Pizza, pizza, that's junk. Why do you go out for that kind of junk when you can come over here and have a good dinner with us?" he'd say. Pizza is everything he doesn't like about America: quick, sloppy, cheap, eaten on the run, away from home. (He makes a gesture like a turkey gobbling to show how people eat on the run.) "Eat and run, eat and run, that's what they do in this country," he says.

Real food takes time, preparation, care, he might say. A good Italian restaurant can be trusted to provide it, especially when you've gotten to know the owner—when he comes out front to chat with the customers. But best of all is when it is made at home, for the family. Home preparation is what makes it good, what slakes hunger and thirst.

While my grandmother was in the hospital, I went to visit my grandfather, bringing a box of linguini and a jar of marinara sauce. My mother, from her own sickbed, made sure I also brought a baked chicken. "Bring whatever we have," she said.

My grandfather had tomato sauce on the stove, and he had some jars and packages of alfredo sauce and egg noodles; I think he was going to mix it all together, whatever was in the cupboard. For my grandfather cooking is like a second crossing to the New World, bringing his life experience with him: his idea of cooking is mixing everything together, the way he used to mix plaster or cement.

A home care assistant might come a few days a week after my grandmother was released from the hospital, my grandfather told me. "But do they cook?" he asked. "Those people, they know nothing about cooking. At most, they open the can of soup. Do they know how to prepare the spaghetti marinara, the veal scaloppine?" He laughed.

We had some linguini in the tomato sauce, and we had some of the chicken. But his stomach was bothering him; nothing seemed to sit well. "I have to push it down with a shovel, with a stick," he says, making a gesture like pushing a balled-up rag through a length of pipe. "Not to enjoy it, just to live." He'd lost his appetite for eating since my grandmother had lost hers for life.

After our lunch, he took an ice cream roll out of the freezer. "I have some Friendly ice cream for you to take home to your mommy and dad." This was part of the meal, too—the necessity of sharing it with those who are absent.

"Oh, that's all right, Grandpa, they don't need it, really," I said, but he was taking a baked hen out of the freezer. "Take this home, also," he said.

"Grandpa, she just gave *you* a chicken, and now you want me to bring one back to her? You keep it, you'll need it."

"Why not? Here, take whatever you want, I have so much stuff here," he said, gesturing to refrigerator shelves that were almost empty.

"Like father, like daughter," I tried to tease him. "If you and my mother had your way, I'd spend all my time carrying food back and forth from one house to the other."

But I did as I was told, and took the ice cream and the frozen hen back to my mother. Who am I to argue with the currency of their concern for one another?

"I want to show you something special," my grandfather said. "I want you to meet some wonderful people, some friends of mine. They do things the old-fashioned way, the real, old-fashioned way," he continued, as he drove slowly in his brown Cadillac with SALIERNO on the license plate. "They even have chickens. And you want to see how many peaches he had from his peach tree, my god, how many peaches! Three hundred peaches he had on one tree, you want to see how many he gave Grandma and me the last time, and eggs from his chickens, tomatoes from the garden—what a big garden! So much stuff he gave us, that's why Grandma baked him the cookies. But I don't want to tell you, I want to surprise you."

As I later learned, a few months before, my grandmother had been feeling so well, she made vanilla cookies to bring to them. She carried them in a paper plate covered with tinfoil on the tray of her four-wheeled walker.

We crossed over the railroad tracks into the East Village, an Italian and Slav hamlet of neat one-family houses built close together, with tiny gardens sprinkled with lawn ornaments and whirligigs, and stopped in front of a white cottage with a clothesline along the side.

A trim middle-aged man in slacks and t-shirt and my grandfather greeted each other with *buongiornos* and handshakes that went halfway up the arm, and my grandfather said we weren't stopping, we didn't want to interrupt them, we were just dropping off something Grandma made to thank them for everything they did, and so on, and naturally the man insisted that we get out of the car just for a minute, and my grandfather said he told me all about the peaches and the man took us to see his garden.

The garden was perfectly enclosed in a chain-link fence to keep out the deer, and though it was September, the tomato plants still had that sweet-bitter smell as strong as pine. His basil plants were small bushes and he still had some zucchini, overgrown now, very fat and yellow on the underside—maybe he was keeping them for seeds for next year.

Before we left, the man insisted my grandfather take a dozen fresh eggs, and he leaned into the car with two jars of homemade marinara sauce (one with eggplant), and one of preserved peaches.

"You see?" my grandfather said as we drove away. "What did I tell you, dear? You don't find people like that anymore these days. They do things the old-fashioned way, like I remember, the real Italian way."

My grandmother was in the hospital for a long month. After those weeks without good food cooked at home, without balanced meals—food eaten just to survive, not to savor or celebrate, food eaten alone—something went out of my grandfather. He was confused, off balance; he no longer felt like driving or grocery shopping or planting his garden. Even with my grandmother home again, he wasn't the same.

I called before going over to visit to see what I could get from the store, but "No, we don't need anything, we have everything here, don't worry about us, you just come over and have a nice lunch," my grandmother insisted. But there wasn't, for lunch, the usual bounty. My grandmother had made a soup from pastina and egg. In the toaster oven, she was reheating a half-piece of leftover chicken parmigiana one of my uncles had brought from a deli.

"All he wants is soup, soup, soup," my grandmother declared. "He says he's not hungry for anything else. "

"I have no appetite whatsoever," my grandfather said. "I have to force myself to eat to live."

I scanned the refrigerator shelves—no fruit, no vegetables, no cold cuts— and later in the afternoon, claimed to have to go out on a personal errand.

In the supermarket, I found sliced Italian bread from Arthur Avenue, ground turkey my grandmother likes for her low-fat meatballs, cold cuts and lettuce and tomatoes, grapes and pears, the waffles they like for breakfast, bananas easy for my grandfather to digest, zucchini easy for my grandmother to prepare, the beets they mentioned they like—not the artichokes, since the moment she looked at them she would see "a lot of work" to trim and stuff them. Some fresh corn-on-the-cob, some frozen peas, some thinly sliced beef, some Progresso soups, some extra olive oil. And chicken, carrots, celery, spinach—the fixings for a homemade soup.

I was raised in my grandmother's kitchen, and I am the only daughter of her only daughter. My mother's own illness now keeps her from fulfilling her traditional role of caring for her parents, and I often think I should be living with them, shopping and cooking for my grandparents and my mother, too. That's how things went in the old country, and who's to say there isn't a poetry and justice in it? To prepare, for one's elders, the kind of food they prepared for you, in the way they taught you to prepare it, is something that goes beyond eating food for survival. It can't be replicated by Meals on Wheels (which doesn't go to their neighborhood, anyway) or home care nurses or store-bought preparations, ready-to-heat. It is the richer nourishment of memory, love, and gratitude.

So I think, but I live over an hour away, working in one of those jobs that devours time. A professional job, a privilege. And yet a dozen times a week I eat alone, in a way that is against my cultural religion. Should I tell the priest, next time I go to confession, the number of times I took my food in vain? I make quick 'n' easy versions of Italian comfort food—frozen tortellini or gnocchi, boiled then sautéed in the same pan with some garlic and oil and frozen peas, unlike anything I knew in childhood. And each time I cook, I make enough for three. The leftovers harden in the fridge. In the kitchen (where so many Italian American women once ladled out the years in one meal after another) I spend only a little time at the beginning and the end of the day, eating while reading the mail, paying my bills, listening to radio news. It takes me longer to do the dishes than to cook; and what I cook, I eat alone, heedlessly. I don't bemoan my freedom from the ancestral bond to the pot waiting to boil, and yet and yet— and yet, in my gut, I know there's something wrong with the way I feed myself and the fact that I so rarely feed others.

My friends remind me that the needs of my family could devour me. But my friends don't say this about my job. They are New Yorkers; they assume the job is identical with the self—the independent self that women have struggled so hard to realize.

As I drove to do my grandparents' grocery shopping that day, a strange, potent fear washed over me—of having an accident, of never returning with the groceries that might sustain my grandparents. Was it a fear of losing myself in their love and need, fear that if I set off down that road of caretaking, I might never come back? Or was it the fear that no matter what, despite my best efforts and intentions, I would end up failing them, that I wouldn't be there each time they needed me?

I wasn't quick enough in getting back to make them dinner. Since my grandfather began feeling unwell, he'd become ever more insistent on eating at particular hours: noon and 5:00 P.M. At 5:30, he was already eating some glutinous egg and pastina soup leftover from lunch. Still, I made the beets and corn-on-the-cob and some salad with some ricotta salata sprinkled on top, and the salad seemed to go into him like water into the leaves of a drooping plant.

"A balanced meal is very important," he declared. "I think that's part of why I got so weak. You can't just eat pasta and pasta and pasta."

"I'm sorry I wasn't around more these last few weeks," I said, feeling the unimportance of the travels and obligations that had occupied me while he had gone into decline. "I'm sorry I wasn't around to cook something once in a while."

"Oh, no, my dear," my grandfather said. "When opportunity knocks, you have to take it. That's the way it goes. One leads to another. You have opportunities, you take them."

I took most of the skin off the chicken and baked it first so the soup wouldn't be oily, as my grandmother taught me, and I got the garlic, onions, celery, and carrots simmering. Then I added the cooked chicken and the spinach, and boiled it a while. The broth turned a rich auburn; it smelled delicious.

"So much cooking you did," my grandfather said to me, "now you can stay away for a month!" Then to my grandmother, "She fooled you, dear. She said she was going shopping for herself, but she was going shopping for us." Then to me: "Take some home to your mother." Before I could stop him, he had begun packing up a bag for me to bring back to my mother.

"You pulled a fast one," he said as he walked me to the door.

"I do as I was taught by my elders," I said. "If you taught me the wrong way, you're just going to have to live with it."

"Oh, no, sweet-aht," he replied—he never pronounces an initial English *h*—"you learned the right way."

Whenever we hear of a friend concerned with family illness or need, we Americans have learned to say, "Don't forget to take care of yourself, make sure you take care of yourself"—but it rings to me a little unconvincing, a little hollow. Is another's need such a threat to the self? The American self is the doing, achieving, self-realizing, independent self. A self rattling freely in the large jar of the world. Zooming along in a car, stopping off to refuel with gas and pizza before getting on the road again, the forever youthful, autonomous

American self, needing for true nourishment only the air of liberty. A self that I can never really believe is something other than a well-intentioned lie, a deceptive seduction.

The ideal farm, for Jefferson, was one that produced everything it needed. America was meant to be a nation of such self-sufficient farmers. Yet the world is continually telling us that its truth is one of universal need, of mutual dependency.

What if the self does not stop at the borders of the body, but is a small constellation of elements including those who need us? Then, in taking care of others, we'd be taking care of ourselves, too. Women have always known this, have always attended to the larger self, and yet we also know that, too often, they've lost themselves completely, burying their own talents and desires, and then when they're no longer needed, what are they? Frustrated, angry, depressed—I sometimes think there is an unspoken epidemic of depression among older Italian American women, those who've ladled the pot of nourishment dry. A lifetime spent feeding their families, and somehow they're left without sustenance.

When my grandfather started to feel better, my grandmother's sister died, and my grandmother slowly took a turn for the worse. It became an effort to get her out of bed to eat, though my grandfather tried his best to nurse her. Sometimes he ordered pizza, or Chinese food, or heated restaurant leftovers or trays of lasagna or manicotti his sons brought by. "Cooking is a problem," he admitted. "Three times a day, someone has to cook!" he said in amazement. Even accounting for illnesses and occasional meals out, my grandmother had prepared almost seventy thousand meals during nearly seventy years of marriage. No wonder she had gotten tired.

But with practice my grandfather was getting better at it, coming up with his own recipes. On Sundays, he didn't give me a chance to cook but already had pots bubbling on the stove when I arrived. He put store-bought baked chicken in a pot of marinara sauce from the jar, and added a lot of a lemon-pepper-garlic spice. It was surprisingly good. He said he was going to open a trattoria like his parents had in Naples. As my grandmother, on new medication, began to feel better, she criticized his cooking. "He can't cook, he doesn't know the first thing about cooking, those meatballs were terrible," my grandmother said. That she took enough interest to complain was a good sign.

"I just don't feel like cooking," she lamented the following week. "But he's a man, what does he know about cooking?" We told her men cook, too, even become famous chefs, but she wasn't convinced. She didn't want to be convinced, she wanted to be needed, she was on the mend.

I, too, want to be needed, but not too much. When my grandfather tells me women in the workplace have put an end to family love, the family meal around the table, I ask him if he thinks it would be a good thing for me to spend my life in the kitchen. He doesn't have an answer. Nor do I have one for him, for his sense of a world wobbling free of its axis of the family dinner table. I only try to convince myself that it is necessary, also, for me to do the other things that I do. If they are a part of me, it must also follow that I am a part of them—the part of them writing this essay; the part of them out in the world, with opportunities still before me. Words, I am sure, can be another currency of love. But what are words without flesh?

To feed each other as we have been fed, to eat and be eaten, a good priest says, is an embodiment of our greatest commandment. Nourishment is spiritual, metaphorical, yet palpable and real. Still the literal hungers of those near to us seem infinite, recurring daily. The vat of soup is soon empty again, and washed. Love refills it. How many times? Seven times seventy times, or a thousand times seventy?

Eat slow, my grandmother would say, and tell me afterwards.

In memoriam, Joseph R. Salierno, June 12, 1908–January 15, 2002

The Vinegarroon
Dorothy Barresi

Once, out walking the low pass between two hills
of no particular beauty
save they were there, like the couple,
half green,
blind to the other faces they wore
in the other resonant valleys below,

and the crows' unhinged articulations
ringing out, the first stars
invisible, for this was a summer evening and light,
bearing invisible witness to—what,
pure seeing?—

they saw a vinegarroon,
plated in its bright coppery

sectioned shell
with whip-tail joints all business, pincers
vised on a baby tarantuala
it was dragging across the road.

Taken together,
spider and scorpion,
the scene was fantastic, a brooch one's grandmother
might have worn in the thirties
with rhinestones for eyes.
Imagine a keepsake tarantula,
a prize catch for dinner
and may the best venom win!

The man and woman shuddered. Ahead
lay chaparral and sky
nicked here and there by clouds.
Behind them, the sounds of the party they'd left to be alone
and unobserved
rose on the wind like uncertain mantras;
separate voices were indistinguishable
even as the air disclosed them,

though someone might have said *pesto*,
another *sabbatical,* or *ruin.*
The music was vintage Sinatra.

"Once," the man said slowly, enunciating, circumspect, not mean
but not yielding, either,
rubbing wild sage
between his palms for effect,

"once I put the bones of some leftover childhood dinner—
chicken paprikash, I think—
into a jar of cider vinegar and waited two weeks.
When they were done steeping,

I brought them out and amazed my chums—
they were rubber bones then. Bendable
as the joke chickens they used to use in vaudeville
to whack a gullible

fellow over the head,
but more stripped down, of course,
and to the point.
Post-post-modern, I guess you'd want to call them.
Though this was before your time."

Now this is how the young woman came to feel like crying.
Understand she had trusted him
as any good grad student would trust her best professor,
and he a married anthropologist with tenure!
She watched his fingers grow
lightly stained with green; the knuckles
ground a little.
Fingers that had raised

her clit in pleasure:
the smell of sage was everywhere, clean heaven.
The vinegarroon, when she remembered to look for him, was gone.

The walk back was uneventful. No one had missed them.
In fact, during the dissolution of this love affair,
the party had grown gayer.
Smart women wearing expensive, idiosyncratic jewelry,
sat on antique milking stools,
smiling as their men recounted
oral exams
which might have been taken yesterday,

so fresh was their terror.
Tipsy, the host with great magnanimous gestures
fed the giant koi he kept
in a stone pond where the newly risen moon
had just begun to writhe
and settle
and calcify.
The fish jumped for every magic bite. These pellets

that kept them spangly and false
made their orange tails
work the water to a boil.
And dinner? That was a late matter of some artichokes,

a sauce for dipping,
and some well-built steaks.
Sour cream for potatoes, baked, and chives, alfresco;
you get the point,

until each in turn had scraped the green petals down
with his or her sharp teeth, sipped
some Pinot Noir
to stiffen the backbone, the long
drive home with one's long-suffering spouse . . .

I knew a guy once, who,
a young professor started, then looked out
beyond her plate and laughed
and shook her head.
Last March she'd tried to kill herself
with a Swiss army knife.
Victorinox.

Nobody dared move or chew. No one said a word.
Then, as sometimes happens
here on earth, the moonlight
grew amazingly, idiotically bright,

like a loutish man with a metal plate in his head,
who after the accident keeps asserting
it's stainless steel,
and go ahead,
go ahead and hit him.
These things happen. It never was your fault.

Then a phone rang twice inside and stopped.
A pair of brown bats,
stirred by whatever instincts drive
so fluttering an engine,
dove one after the other for the speck
of a crumb of an insect

smaller than a mote in the eye.
Then Sinatra came and went again, feelingly.
Then the embarrassed laughter that swims, feckless,

up to the surface, and relief,
signaling the end of the meal.

∾

Triple Bypass
Annie Lanzillotto

For Amelia King, Joseph Lanzillotto,
Rosa Petruzzelli, Al Paoletta

Mai più ci vedremo faccia a faccia.

You have to understand the basics to survive a whole life.
"L'arancia, di mattina—oro puro; nel pomeriggio—argento; di sera—piombo."
Mamma never had an ice cold drink till she was nineteen and in America.
Water, wine, and a squeeze of the goat whenever she had a cold.
Hank didn't listen. "If you call the Bronx America," was all he said to me,
licking the last malt off his lip.

If she sang to herself while her fingers pulled my shoelaces tight
I knew I had a good chance of getting an ice cream cone
outside the slaughterhouse.
I held my mouth full of cream
till it dissolved as her arm dove into cages
where feathers became her hand.
Her face reddened and her mouth gathered spit to knock
the price down. Feathers everywhere
as she pointed at the chicken whose breast
passed her inspection. Feathers in my mouth as its blood fell
into a pail. "A spezzia!" she sang triumphantly.
And onward we marched, up and down the market aisles, hunting and
    gathering, feeling
the heads of lettuces like the skulls of babies, feeling
for the soft spot, smelling each peach at a microphone's distance,
remembering something there, then moving on,
pocketing garlic, pocketing parsley. Some things in life
you shouldn't pay for. "*L'aglio è essenziale. L'aglio è l'essenza della vita.*"
I tried to tell Hank.
Garlic will straighten you out, if you know how to eat it.

Garlic will push an ocean through your aorta.
Sammy he ate fried foods. Vinny was a soppressata man.
And Hank loved milkshakes.
We all had the same operation, the American
senior citizen barmitzfah. They were all dead in six months. Me?
I'm not really here. I'm on borrowed time. I boil everything.

Last Supper

Jennifer Lagier

While other women
tore lettuce and arranged china,
I was in our hosts' bedroom,
undressing with your older brother.

Outside the closed door,
you speared smoked oysters,
jangled ice cubes, smoked,
drank your third V.O. and water.

The lasagna I brought
got too hot, burnt cheese
and singed tomato sauce
pouring smoke from the oven.

After, I paced
alone in the garden,
knew in a year I'd be gone,
this catastrophe over.

For the last time, we sat
together at the family table.
Your father lifted his wineglass;
you nervously touched me.

I looked into your Lazarus eyes
and delivered the final defiant kiss,

resurrected myself
with an act of betrayal.

❧

New Year's Eve
Dorian Cirrone

I spin the silver bundt pan with one hand,
swirl in the batter with the other.
Yellow flecks of lemon skin speckle the mixture.
Theoni removes a coin from her pocket, drops
it in. Hand on stomach, I watch
the thick, creamy substance slowly swallow
the edge of the shiny disk. Too soon
to feel anything, my baby, no bigger
than the coin, waiting, weightless, inside.
It's an old Greek custom, Theoni explains,
At midnight, we'll cut the cake: whoever
gets the coin enjoys good luck all year.
I hope to hang the coin on a silver chain,
above my swelling belly. I watch expectantly as
the cake rises, yellow bursting open at the top.
By moonlight on the porch, we play
cards, drink champagne, only a sip for me.
We begin the backward count. At midnight
we cut the cake. I am giddy
when the silver coin sparkles in my plate.

•

When I think of that night,
I remember the sweetness of the cake,
the anticipation of a lucky year,
those moments suspended
just before midnight in Times Square.
The thing I always forget,
that doesn't fit, is the fetus,
already dead, floating inside me.

༄

Baked Ziti

Kym Ragusa

The video footage is degraded now, pixels dropping here and there. The camerawork is shaky, the images are blown out so that all the white objects in the frame take over, bleeding into everything else. My father, his girlfriend Susan, and his mother, my grandmother, are standing in the kitchen of our house in New Jersey, making baked ziti.

Baked ziti is a specialty in my family, and my father is the master of the dish. He makes it for Christmas and Easter, for birthdays and other celebrations. Sometimes, if we're lucky, he makes it just because he's in the mood. On days like this he'll cook alone, making enough to feed an army, which he once did. He'll give me a huge tin of fresh macaroni, plus a few containers frozen and extra gravy, I mean sauce, just in case.

I have always wanted to record this recipe in some special way, as it's one of the only traditions my family has left. Most of the old people passed on long ago, relatives have moved away, scattered across the West, or, like us, around New Jersey. Or stopped speaking to each other out of sometimes real, sometimes imagined, slights and offenses. Those of us who are left live in the absence of history, our days rushing ahead of us, the anchor of memory long unmoored from our lives.

I am two people in this narrative: the student filmmaker beginning a documentary about my father that I will never finish, and the me of five years after, who has been through the war that was to come. The me that watches the images on the screen, receiving them from my younger, hopeful self.

I'm in the kitchen, recording the making of the baked ziti. This is no holiday— my father is cooking just for the shoot. I follow him with the camera as he goes through the preparation step-by-step, and I follow Susan and my grandmother moving through the periphery, sometimes trying to help, but mostly just commenting on my father's technique, acting as his captive audience.

I see now how clumsy I was with the video camera, how I forgot to check the iris of the camera so that everything looks blown out: the light coming in from the kitchen windows, the reflection of the knife as my father chops onions and garlic, the mozzarella resting soft and exposed as flesh on the wooden cutting board. Everything glows with some otherworldly light—the kitchen looks like heaven, a room filled with ghosts and those who are becoming ghosts right before my eyes.

Ghosts: my grandfather Luigi at the head of the table by the wall, drinking espresso and cracking almonds with his old nutcracker, dead almost twenty years ago of heart disease. My aunt Evelyn on the inside of the table by the door, drinking her Pepsi and smoking a Parliament cigarette, gone ten years later of cervical cancer. The ghosts of myself and my cousin Donna as kids, impatient then to leave the table. To leave the table, to leave this life behind and have no idea how much we will miss it one day.

I am hiding behind the camera. Through the lens I watch what's left of this family, which is my own family, go through the motions of an ancient ritual, preparing the feast day meal. This meal that would have been prepared for at least thirty people before we moved to the suburbs and dissipated. Back in the Bronx. Or East Harlem. Or in the hills of Calabria and Sicily where our old ones were born. I don't know which is more absurd—the absence of the context for this food or the desperation with which I record its preparation.

I pan around the space of the kitchen and dining area with my camera-eye, my camera-heart. Across the wood-paneled walls, the linoleum floor. The black-and-white TV on the counter, beneath it the cabinets that hold pots and pans and lentils and cookies. The old brand names: Progresso, Ronzoni, Contadina, Polly-O. The formica dining table that welcomes and waits. The windows behind the table. Flood of light. I see myself as a child sitting at that table, dunking biscotti into milky tea with four teaspoons of sugar, watching Grandma fry meatballs at the old stove, a huge pot of sauce simmering on the back burner and all the smells filling this warm space flooded with light.

Out the window to the wild backyard that was once my grandfather's garden. Past the dry, tangled grapevines whose meager fruit was eaten by birds year after year. Past the memories of eggplant, tomato, zucchini.

Ghosts: my grandmother, who will soon die of cancer, and Susan, who will go two weeks after her, lost to AIDS. And my father, who is a ghost of himself, of what he might have been. He too hovering between life and death, or perhaps between two deaths, AIDS and heroin. Three people becoming ghosts, my family.

I watch through the lens now as my father fries the tomato paste. Susan is behind him, saying how good it smells. "That's just the beginning," my father beams. He is so proud of his ability to make magic from food, his special gift. My grandmother wanders in and out of the frame, tidying up in the kitchen. Always cleaning. When the rest of the tomatoes are in the pot and the sauce is starting to bubble, to become,

she will pass by every few minutes with her dishcloth and wipe the tiny red splashes
from the stovetop.

My father's pride in himself. The kitchen is the only place where he has this confidence, the only place in his life where he is in control. Cooking has been the constant, unbroken thread that has run through his years, from the time that he was a child in his own Calabrese grandmother's kitchen. He always tells me how he learned everything from her, and I imagine him a soft, quiet little boy, standing on a chair at the stove with an ancient wooden spoon, stirring her sauce while she holds him steady.

They cook together, my father and his grandmother, in this Harlem kitchen, while other boys his age are out protecting their turf from the Puerto Rican boys who have begun moving into the neighborhood with their families. Out learning how to fight, to be men. Is there any language for the man my father is becoming in his grandmother's kitchen? For the first time, I think about how he must have been named as much after his grandmother, Luisa, as after his own father, Luigi. Now he is JR or Junior, or June, as my grandmother calls him.

"June, when you gonna put the meat in?" "Now, Ma." He ruffles a little at her
attempted intervention and slides browned pork ribs, then fried meatballs, from
the battered cast iron pan into the sauce. His girlfriend Susan gestures toward me.
"JR, tell Kym about your toys when you were little." "Wow, I almost forgot about
that—that's right, honey, I had a little cooking set, my own pots and pans, even
then. Remember Ma?" "I remember. He didn't want to play with nothing else, only
the little pots. And he's still the same!"

Still the same. As a young man, he would cook for his platoon in Vietnam. He knew he was going to get drafted, and figured that if he volunteered to go as a cook, he would be spared spending any time on the front lines. But he was sent immediately into the center of the "conflict," and though what he did was cook and though he didn't have to shoot anyone himself, he saw all the killing close-up, the murder of Vietnamese women and children, the torching of villages, his friends blown to bits. It was 1968. He was twenty-three years old.

My father in the jungle in a war that made no sense, reproducing the domestic space of the kitchen in the mess hall tent. Feeding dying young men chili, spaghetti, and yes, on special occasions, baked ziti. Trying to do whatever he could to help, with whatever supplies were available, trying to make the meals special and memorable to the other soldiers, who were his family now. A boy-mother in the jungle, surrounded by exploding bombs and flames and blood and poisonous snakes. And no comfort but one.

I was just turning two, and the man my father would become in this war would be the only father I have ever known. I have a photograph of him during this time—actually, I stole it from him. To remember the father I never knew. He is wearing his fatigues, surrounded by lush trees, and he is terribly handsome, with his dark skin and hair, his blue eyes shining through the black-and-white of the image. The mustache that makes him look like any young man in any village of his ancestral land, except for the small monkey on a leash that is perched on his back. The unbelievable irony of him literally carrying a monkey on his back.

He returned from Vietnam, like many others, addicted to heroin, an addiction that continues. Almost the entire span of my own lifetime. This is the other thread that runs through my father's days and years, what he turns to when even the cooking can't hold back the nightmares. I have hated my father for this addiction, pitied him, excused him, and hated him once more.

I zoom in on my father's hands stirring the béchamel. He has always been slight—thin and wiry—even in times of relative good health. His hands seem to belong to someone else, large and broad, with thick fingers. A worker's hands, like his father's, who was a bricklayer before he became a bartender. Unmistakable markers of masculinity that betray how soft and delicate he is. He stirs the dense mixture of ricotta and egg that will bind the macaroni together. "Can I lick the spoon?" I ask, knowing he'll caution me on the dangers of ingesting raw egg, my response to him: "For me, it's safe." This small ritual we once shared, the tasting of that mixture, that now could kill him.

Did I recognize the change in him when he came back from the war? At three years old, what could I have known except "Daddy's home!" My mother says, looking back, she can't remember having noticed anything different about him, although soon after, they broke up. When I asked her why, she says she can't remember even that, only that they were young and that it just didn't work out. I do know that my father started having nightmares that wouldn't go away, about helicopters, the horrible whirring of their blades, and the screams of his friends as they died.

His life soon revolved around the heroin that would temporarily calm his nerves, and soon he had a new family, a new culture, that he shared with the other junkies he met when he came home to the Bronx. From one war-torn landscape to another, to a new family. He disappeared for weeks at a time, he lied and stole and raged. Once he took me and a friend to the movies, and left us on line, two little girls alone at night, while he searched for a fix. It seemed like hours until he came back. By that time everyone had already gone into the theater. And my friend crying, "I want to go home." Another time he pulled a knife on my grandfather as I stood by and watched, as my grandfather, himself no stranger to rage, shouted in dialect, "Go on, kill me, I dare you."

What is it about our fathers and their fathers, the violence whether there has been a war or not? What is it about Southern Italian culture that feeds and nourishes male rage? Even my father, who grew up in his grandmother's kitchen, the sacrificial lamb with his pots and pans. That wellspring of fury. Yes, there was a war. And there were/are the drugs. I have always made excuses for him and disguised them as compassion, have never asked myself when the seed of violence was really planted.

It seemed as though my father might turn himself around when he got the news that he was HIV positive. This did not have to be a death sentence, but a second chance, particularly with the advances in medicine in the early 1990s. This was when he met Susan, who had already developed AIDS. She was all goodness and kindness, despite the violence she had seen all her life. My father loved her, and I thought this love might save him. Thought he might wake up, join the living. He took care of her, kept her alive, and for a moment this was his redemption.

My father cuts two slices of Italian bread, puts them on a small, flowered plate, and spoons sauce on top. "Here," he passes it to Susan, "try to eat." I zoom out so that I get my father handing the plate to Susan. "I don't know, I'm still not that hungry," she says as she takes his offering. "You need your strength, come on, just try." Susan picks up the bread and nibbles on it. She is unbearably thin, but her eyes shine softly through the gauntness of her face. Her red hair in fine wisps on her head, fine as my eighty-five-year-old grandmother's. My father's illness doesn't show like this, not yet.

To this day he does not know that I know. It isn't long before my father's addiction pulls them both under. On a rare day alone together, Susan tells me she wants to leave my father. How he keeps doing drugs around her even though she's trying to stay clean, fighting for her life. How their food money is always gone before the end of the month. How they have nothing to eat. There are no words for the shock I feel at this revelation. Everything that I believe about who my father "really" is falls away. Sick and frail as she is, Susan is trying to escape, to save herself from him. When she dies, her friends will blame him for cleaving fragile years from her life. To this day he does not know that I know.

I follow my father to the sink as he drains the macaroni. Again the blinding light of enamel, pasta, and rising steam. My grandmother in a chair on the edge of the frame: "June, did you sign the papers yet?" The business of the house, from which I've always been removed. The baby of the family, the outsider looking in. "Not now, Ma, let's talk about it after dinner." I follow behind, adjust the lens. Always chasing partial meanings.

My father still relates to me as if I were a little girl. He even speaks to me in a slight singsong voice that one might use with a child. "Don't forget, always use flat-leaf Italian parsley—that American parsley has no flavor," he tells me again and again, each time as if for the first time, as if it were a revelation, a gift for being a good girl. A good girl is quiet and doesn't tell secrets. Maybe it's more comfortable for me to play that role with him. To pretend that I don't know what I know. To simply watch him cook, with innocence and awe, ignoring the rage that has settled inside me like a too-heavy meal that I can't digest.

As I am writing I realize how much I have needed to see my father as strong and healthy, as any daughter might. And that this is connected to how I focus on what I believe to be my incompetence as a filmmaker, as I watch this footage of my father cooking that I shot as a beginning filmmaker. I write about my shaky hand as I hold the camera, my awkward questions. How I don't compose my shots so much as follow the action, follow, like a toddler. This, against my father's control and expertise with his materials: bay leaf, butcher knife, peppermill. He makes cooking look so easy. I stumble. The kitchen is where *his* power is, the only place where he has any power. The camera should be the site of my power, but I couldn't claim it then.

This past Thanksgiving my father wasn't feeling well, so I decided I would make the meal myself, with the help of my husband. My first Thanksgiving dinner, after years of watching my father cook. He was weak and pale, and had lost a lot of weight. I forbade him to even come into the kitchen. We had a small group of family and friends over, and there were candles and appetizers and music, and it felt right, that I had finally made a home for myself. But my father barely spoke to anyone all night. He sat in a chair by the kitchen door and watched as my husband and I prepared the meal. "Are you sure you want to use that pot," he would call out, or, "You need more salt." He wrung his hands and grew more and more panicky as we cooked.

Of course, the turkey was underdone and the dressing burned. But the rest of the meal was fine, and my father grudgingly acknowledged this. And I understood for the first time how my relationship with my father exists only in relation to food. Cooking, feeding people, is the only way he knows how to communicate, to show love. But it is also where he hides, and how he cooks, a kind of bravado that disguises his fragile sense of self. For me, food has been both his gift and a deprivation, what has been given with one hand but taken away with the other. I have my own kitchen now, and it is time for me to stop being the little girl nourished and silenced by my father's cooking.

•

Grandma and Susan set the table. Grandma's good dishes, white with tiny gold diamonds and gold around the rim. My father is mixing the macaroni with the béchamel and the sauce. Then the mozzarella and the grated pecorino. Mix again. More cheese on top. He puts the huge baking pan into the oven. Enough to feed an army. He leans against the counter, wiping the perspiration from his face. This is hard work. Suddenly it seems very quiet. The kitchen air is thick with the aroma emanating from the oven, thick with exhaustion and anticipation. I think of questions I should ask, what more I might need to record. But the shoot feels done. We are finished here.

Soon my father will take out the baked ziti and present it at the table. We will marvel at its beauty, and then I will sit down with my ghosts and eat.

Part Eight

LEGACIES

What They'll Say in a Thousand Years

Maria Terrone

Glassy as mirrors, the huge eyes of the Easter lamb took me in, a child of seven. Had they seen the glory or unspeakable horror? Not knowing filled my mouth with a new taste, sharp and dry like metal—my first taste, I suppose, of ambiguity.

My cousins, offspring of my mother's two older, Sicilian-born sisters, were seemingly unfazed, but I kept seeing another, disturbing image: the head of John the Baptist on a platter. Years later, I imagine his eyes all-knowing, projecting a steady, intense light. He's seen something Salome hasn't; even the seers with their second sight haven't a clue. Unable to avoid that powerful gaze, Salome shrivels as if burned inside-out, and for the rest of her life, tastes only bitter crumbs from her gilded plate.

As a child that Easter Sunday, I wanted refuge from what I couldn't understand. So I darted into my aunt's kitchen with its veils of steam and otherworldly heat; jumble of knives; potatoes musty as earth, laid on a board for scrubbing; espresso pot poised to erupt a black, Vesuvian brew. How reassuring, but different this was from the kitchen at home, where my mother, the American-born "baby" of the family, preferred her vegetables in frozen, scentless slabs, her bread presliced, fruit vacuum-packed, and all living creatures beheaded somewhere else.

That lamb's brilliant eyes followed me for years, persistent in their dumb death. When I was a teenager, I dreamed that sinister men bundled in drab, bulky overcoats stood with me in my mother's kitchen. There was no food in sight. A ping pong ball contained the secret of the universe; a hidden spring, if touched just so, would unlock it.

We grappled for the ball, scuffling on the black-and-white checkerboard floor like breakaway knights. The face on the wall frowned 8:20 A.M., but night might arrive the next moment. Could the world, here in this kitchen, be won or lost to the sound of panting, the smell of old wool? The clock ticked impatience: Seize the moment. So when I wrested the ball back, I crushed it like an egg. Instantly the men gathered around me, coats heaving with their ragged breath. An eye filled my palm and I heard my voice say, *The eye sees all things.* Or maybe the voice said, *The I sees all things.* It doesn't matter; by now, I've come to accept uncertainty as a permanent state.

Yesterday, walking home from the subway after work, I noticed a truck double-parked outside the Halal butcher. Its doors were flung open wide like a charnel house that welcomes all visitors. Inside, skinned goats were piled high, stiff as factory-made objects. The driver, wearing a blood-splattered white jacket, emerged and hoisted a single goat over his shoulder. As he hunched towards the shop, the animal stared straight back at me with eyes that were awe-struck, absorbing the whole world I still inhabit. Something powerful circled there, then moved outward to encompass me on the pavement where I'd paused briefly after a long day that fall evening, tired, cold, hungry, but not far from home, my hands clutching the thin plastic bag that bulged with vegetables I'd just bought for dinner.

Two Women Waiting

In a kitchen, hungry
for news of his accident, the women
pass the time with a carving knife
and a bursting squash.
Better to save than watch it rot,
each thinks but does not say.

They sit face to face across the table
and pass the knife to and fro.
Wordlessly, they slice,
pushing till the rind
yields perfect curves.

Silently, they make their preparations,
sprinkling oil, applying spices,
striking a match for the oven.

Will he ever taste this?
each thinks but does not say.
The room swells with heat.
Under a frozen-starburst clock,
these hands move as one.

Strawberries

Close your eyes, you order, hands behind
your back: propped up late in bed reading,
I obey: my mouth opens
to ice cream, Chambord, domination

of strawberry. Then my eyes open
to you, the overflowing spoon held above
a bowl where slices float like pods
in a cool, fermenting pond. So heady,

at the end of a day that began with burnt
toast and jam, an old jar of pulp clouding
the kitchen table, the taste
of our words lingering in charred

silence. And then we went
our separate ways into the muddle
outside: stacked on my desk, half-truths
disguised as the morning news, plain

talk smeared by winks and irony—
you know, love, that read-between-the-lines
mishmash. But I'm back home,
where there's no mistaking your gaze

and my own drowsy contentment.
I could end this now with similes:
dissect the fruit to discover hearts,
cross-sections of trees, and poppies. Instead,

I'll close my eyes on today
with the sweet, simple truth
of these berries, ripe
just with the meaning of themselves.

☙

Ceres Explains the Soul of Pasta

In the center of a perfectly cooked pasta strand there should be a white ghost,
a tiny spot of not-quite rawness. This is its anima.
—ITALIAN CHEF QUOTED IN THE *NEW YORK TIMES*

Shivering in my sheer goddess-gown
and my thorned crown of vigilance, I checked
wheat stalks from sunup to sundown.
Durum is the toughest kind,

the longest-haired, restless each time
a new wind blows, eager to strike out
beyond the fencing and mingle
with every bad seed. That wine

you're sipping gave me no heartache;
grapevines soon give up their dusty,
nomadic life and cling to my stakes.
But imagine trying to rein in a field

of rash youths who dip their heads
to whisper, hang together, wave
you away. Fearful thoughts spread
in my mind like hell's rank weeds.

I pictured my tawny beauties lost, fallen
among the uncultivated, and in the end,
cut down to line a horse's stall.
Yet I never despaired, pouring

my very soul into theirs. Now when I see
steam rise from that *al dente* pasta
you eat with such gusto, I'm at peace:
my offspring have met their destiny.

Uncorking the Aged Wine

I imagine the grape-tinctured air
      escaping like a genie
who's bidden time for years,

his power growing deeper, more complex
      in its knowledge
of the human heart: We all want more

than three wishes. But I'll gladly surrender
      my first to taste
the sun's honeyed flight and the sobering

down-pull of must jousting
      on my tongue,
that willing vessel of poetry and mayhem.

∾

Rosemary

> *Grow it for two ends, it matters not at all*
> *Be if for my bridall, or my burial.*
> —ROBERT HERRICK

Wreathed in the herb's scent of sea and pine,
my two aunts leaned over the uncooked lamb,
dabbing blood from the stainless pan
gently, as if to nurse a wound. Words twined,
sometimes tangled across the tabletop like vines
in Italian hills where they played, girls not yet stunned
by the climb into new lives. They were orphans
disguised as grown women, tending the shrine
of the past until their memories became my own
Paradise Lost (and Gained, to know that once, in spring,
sky inclined to earth as rosemary's blue flowers).
Aunts Sarah and Anna signed X over and over
the lamb's flesh: I see a flash of knives and wedding rings,
nettles pressed deep, to keep the taste of those hours.

❧

Salt for Uncle Charlie

Like Apicius, who preferred death
to ingesting a bad meal, my uncle,
forbidden salt, declared, *It's just not worth it.*
A month later, he was dead—betrayed

not by his bounteous heart, but his cells,
suddenly massed against the prospect of a bland
life. My uncle, happiest in the kitchen
patting his dough, felt condemned, denied

even the condemned man's banquet.
But the last time I saw him alive,
a sheet lay tucked under his chin
like an oversized napkin. Reclining

in that hospital bed—eyes half-closed,
lips curled—he seemed to me suspended
in that ecstatic moment between the scent
and taste of his own homemade feast as,

drop by drop, his veins sipped
saline clear as eau-de-vie.

❧

White

After dinner, my cousin Ron offers
white peaches and white cherries, the sweetest,
most costly kind. The sun is dropping
like a fat yolk into the bowl
of woods that surround his new house
while we plan the summer days ahead,
pressing our luck as we might test
a fruit's ripeness, hoping we'll taste
perfection.

So hard to believe he'll soon turn sixty.
Twenty-five years ago, seeking
Maine's simple life, he came to hate
that state where nothing grows
for long. Even berries were puny,
he said, covering the land like buckshot,
staining skin with the devil's blue ink.
But mostly he came to hate the gluttony
of white that long, jobless winter—how
it gulped at windows but wanted more,
devouring space, time, his faith
in his own senses; white that billowed
like priest's robes, then felled trees,
killing power and a man at his stove
who wasn't found for a week.

The room darkens.
In two years, I retire, Ron says,
lots of time to catch a record-breaking striper,
to cook more meals like this one.
He'll put behind the years of teaching,
the restaurant that almost ate him alive,
the Christmas eve spent selling trees
in a frozen city lot. I watch
the pits accumulate on his plate,
only the barest shreds still clinging
to the spots he could not
scrape clean.

∾

At the Knife-Skills Workshop

"First you must choose the proper tool,"
the chef proclaims, lording

over his empire of carbon steel.
He raises the twelve-inch knife,

then tours the room checking thumbs
for proper placement. "Be sharp!" I command

my faltering mind to become like the blade
I hold, but I'm thinking of tools

besides these knives—the files and pens,
picks and awls that people take up,

along with their daily bread. I'm thinking
of my cousin, who lies now in a hospital bed,

fixing a customer's car. He's crawled
out from his head and underneath

the chassis; all day long, hands no longer
veined with grease gladly twist the air.

～

Beets

I think they must be very old,
holding fast for years in a tight cold place,
escaping the scythe through sheer
homeliness.

They wobble on my cutting board,
big awkward knobs smelling
of rain-soaked soil, sparse hairs
trailing from greyed, misshapen domes.

When I boil and slice them open
I find a tree's concentric rings
closing into one tiny secret core.
Peeled, their skin is smooth as a youth's
and radiant.

I love the way they yield their essence
with such ease,
surprising me the way my gashed knee
surprised me as a child.

We are lively, they say, vibrant,
not at all what you thought.

Let us mark you with our brilliance,
spiral scarlet over your fingers,
stain your hands with our sweet ageless blood.

I want to carry their stain for days.

∽

Blood Oranges

Provenance: Sicily

Two nails deftly applied to skin expose
an interior life not red—
though that would shock enough—but red
blackened by the color of blood spilled
and dried in history's shadow.

You would expect a thousand years
of conquest to produce a bitter
taste. Then how can this sweetness
be? *Beware of strangers,*
my mother warned, joined

by her parents' blood to a sun-blinded isle
of secrets. *Never trust appearances.*
The Sirens were enchanting,
bird legs and claws hidden
behind long hair that blew glorious

as their song over the Strait of Messina.
Sometimes, when fierce currents
force up the deepest dwellers,
their phosphorescence makes the sea
a silver lure to ensnare unwary

travelers—one more fata morgana
in a place that loves mirage. So what to make
of these gifts concealed in twisted
tissue? As someone before me has said,
Beware the fruit of your darkest wishes.

∾

What They'll Say in a Thousand Years

Ice spikes the rungs of our fire escape
  like the teeth of a prehistoric creature
that would swallow us whole, if it could

reach through this fiercely shining glass
  into the kitchen, where we sit, together
at breakfast again. After this winter passes,

the next and the next, hors d'oeuvre for a monster
  fattened on time, what will survive
of us here? I think they'll find the plainest tools—

a grainless spoon, enamel stock pot stripped
  to iron core, oxidized black skillet.
Mistaking petrified dill for pine, they'll speculate

that a grove rose at the site of the granite counter.
  A primitive people who ate outdoors,
a plaque above glass might say, skipping

the words passed across this wooden slab
  hundreds, no thousands of days.
But then they'll get it right: as if arranging

a hominid's scattered bones,
  they'll reconstruct the frame that held
life together: each morning, a flame,

then egg and bread, water,
  at night, oil and wine—each burned
to heat, propelling us daily from caves

of sleep, outside, into the beast's
  maw and back to the fire
again and again, to eat.

∾

Polenta

Denise Calvetti Michaels

When I go back far enough, I hear Nonna say *senti*, hear this, *senti*, smell this, *senti*, taste this, *senti*, *senti*, *senti*, to the sound of the ravioli wheel spinning through dough. The language of my hands came first. Always, another language behind the first. Our table was not a piece of furniture, but a hearth. If I could, I'd go back, find who made this possible, thank them.

I write the first page.

It begins in mud that is black or rust red, with a puddle my brother and I are stirring with sticks as we drop in handfuls of dirt. It is summer on my grandparents' farm.

A cowboy who works at the rodeo down the road knocks on the kitchen door, asking for Dago Red. He's a tall man with spurred boots who can see into every niche of our world. Yet he wants only the homemade Muscatel. My grandfather refuses his money. *Vieni*, he says. *Mangia con me*. Agostina maka ravioli. Come in, please.

In the autumn of 1958, I turn ten and can play Santa Lucia and a few tarantellas on the piano. My father tells me it is my turn to cut the polenta for Thanksgiving, a ritual that he hopes will tie me to my Italian roots. He asks, too, that I write the stories my family shares while the polenta is cooking.

Guests are invited at the last moment, in the midst of our polenta-making, to celebrate our Italian American version of this holiday. Family and friends gather at our home in Redwood City from all over Northern California—the prune ranch in Morgan Hill, truck farms in Gilroy, Salinas, and Monterey, neighborhoods in San Leandro, Lafayette, San Francisco, and Oakland.

Grandfathers and uncles arrive first to rinse out the spider webs from Nonna Agostina's voluminous old pot stored in the attic and kept just for this purpose.

Cooking gallons of cornmeal to feed forty or more guests requires vigilant stirring to prevent lumps and scorching. No ordinary kitchen spoon will do, so my father improvises a sturdy stirring stick by cutting off the wooden handle of a new broom. The cooks, wearing long white butcher aprons, laughing and telling stories, are at the stove, shirt sleeves rolled, collars unbuttoned. They wait to add salt and handfuls of coarse ground corn to the pot when the water boils.

Because I keep a diary, ask questions about the old country, and have published a short story in the children's page of the *Tribune*, my father looks to me as the family historian. My job is to translate dialect and broken English. My job is to record important stories before they are lost.

Nonno Bianco tells why he left Montaldo Scarumpi. *Mio papà arriva alla sua casa senza niente per mangiare.* . . . *My father came home with nothing to eat, a table of eight children waiting for supper, a scant cup of ground corn swirling in a pot of lukewarm water. He picked up a spoon to taste it, then hurled the thin gruel at the fireplace where it dripped down bitter yellow, too thin to stick. Soon after, we left for America.*

Scrive what your Nonno tells you, my father commands.

There is the story of great grandfather Giacomo, who left Balangero for America. Jenny, my mother's mother, was born under a scoop of Oklahoma stars. But the family does not stay long on the prairie. Lonely for Balengero, they leave howling coyotes and a Big Dipper just beyond a blue moon.

Thirty years later, my younger cousin Lorella, who lives near Balengero, tells me the story. She asks me how to pronounce *coyote*, the animal our great-grandfather remembered.

Did you write it down? my father asks, believing that to write is to mark territory, that to write is to declare.

He is not a writer. But, he understands how the senses make and liberate memory.

He tells us, *You will remember this place, you will remember this meal,* as he carries a loaf of thick crusted bread, a bottle of wine, and grape juice for my brother and me, to a large boulder on the Merced River in Yosemite.

We have lunch in the sun while the ice cold river splashes and swirls on the bare feet we dangle off the warm sandpaper-rough granite rocks. Tearing the bread with his river-washed hands, he gives us each a piece, and, for a moment, we find sanctuary on this tiny island, then wriggle away to find an elegant rainbow trout holding firm against the current.

It was not easy for my father. He was a veteran of World War II, stationed in the South Pacific. He saw his buddies killed on Guadalcanal.

One night, searching for hope, he walked a white sandy beach, gathering delicate pastel cowry shells in the moonlight. He saved them in a poker chip box and gave them to me years later.

Stirring the polenta conjures Piedmontese villages—Balangero, north of Torino, home of my mother's family; Montaldo Scarumpi, near Asti, home of my father's. Whoever holds the stick speaks the names of those left behind. *Caterina Calvetti, Domenico Airaudi, Giacomo Bonino, Orsula, Maria Teresa, Agostina Gonella, Ercole Bianco.*

One summer when I'm a teen, I visit Montaldo Scarumpi, where two-year-old boys mock shadows, stand naked to the wall, and pee the dust to life. I imagine Nonno in a field, holding a hoe like a staff, rough-hewn hands, the texture of gunny sack, durable. I sketch scenes of vineyards, fields, *cortili*.

I write *Nonno is like a bird, an Italian village bird, migrating so the rest can stay.*

When I return to America, I cannot explain to my friends that Italy, for me, is more than the cathedrals, fountains, and paintings on the postcards I've sent from Rome, Venice, and Florence. It is a string of peasant villages where my women cousins are living sculpture as they kneel over boulders washing clothes, hanging them out to the bleach of sky. It is cisterns filling with roof rain in the courtyards, wooden-lipped dippers on hooks. It is hillsides covered in strawberries, wild blood-red fruit eaten ripe on hot afternoons, shop shutters pulled closed, flies asleep on glass, a pail for Maria Teresa, who is pregnant and doesn't know it.

But there are some stories that no one will ever ask me to write down.

Blame is an ugly animal, Nonna Agostina once told me. *No one wants him.* We were mincing basil and garlic with the *mezzaluna*.

Does he have claws, Nonna? Teeth? I asked.

Only desire, Bella, she replied. *In the eyes.*

There is the sister I never meet. She is missing at the table. Her hair is the color of wheat. I learn this when I am pregnant with my first daughter and tell my mother I am considering *Catherine* for a girl's name. We are in my grandmother's kitchen.

Don't you remember? she asks, taking me to Nonna Agostina's linen closet, where a picture of Catherine is hidden under the towels. She insists that she has told me about my sister, born with cerebral palsy eight years before me to my father's former wife.

Years later, I have a dream that my grandmother includes Catherine in the same world I blossomed in. I call my mother to ask *Did Nonna spend time with Catherine? Did she introduce her to baby chicks and rabbits, to seeds and planting, to egg gathering on a foggy morning in the barn?*

Yes, my mother says. And I am glad.

Toward the end of polenta-making, the kitchen fills with adults holding up children at a safe distance from the roiling cornmeal to see down into the cavernous pot, into the throat of the volcano.

Va piano! Va piano! The polenta is ready. *Go slow,* my grandmothers warn, as the cooks carry the cumbersome pot into the garage.

This is the largest space in the house, so we convert it into a dining room with three cloth-covered tables made into one. It bears trays of paper-thin salami, prosciutto, and mortadella; baskets of long crunchy bread sticks and golden crusted rolls; a bowl of pitted black olives that the children wear on their fingertips before eating them; Salinas's *insalata;* wild mushrooms from Monterey; Morgan Hill plums; sliced meats from the delicatessen in San Francisco's Little Italy; Gilroy garlic; tiny bud artichokes soaking in olive oil from Castroville; bread from Pisano's Bakery; the wine our grandfathers made from a Lafayette vineyard's grapes.

The lava-thick polenta is poured onto a large wooden board in the center of the table. It slowly flows to the edge. Windows, eyeglasses, and the watches the *paesani* wear on chains fog from the steam.

Vieni qui! Vieni qui! mothers call. Little ones are lifted to high chairs and benches with telephone books to boost them to the table. My mother and Aunt Winnie carry plates of Gorgonzola to melt on the polenta. They reappear with bowls filled with rabbit stewed in tomato sauce, chunks of red pepper, mushrooms, onions, and garlic.

Nonno Bianco stands at the head of the table, holding a glass of wine. *Salute,* he says. Welcome, cheers, give thanks.

Nonna hands me one end of a long piece of string in a ritual that winds back to Montaldo Scarumpi.

I walk to the other side of the table, holding it high. We hold the string taut and slice the topaz mound into its rich golden core.

Nonna Jenny and my mother scoop up thick slabs as plates are passed.

After another round of toasts, the first bite of earth-textured corn permeated with tomato sauce, and creamy, melting Gorgonzola.

Molto buono, everyone chimes. *How delicious the polenta,* this simple peasant food so woven into imagination, transformed into story.

I will never let go, never let go of the string, never let go of my family's history.

❧

Lament in Good Weather
Lucia Perillo

So would this be how I'd remember my hands
(given the future's collapsing trellis):
pulling a weed (of all possible gestures),
trespassing the shade between toppled stalks?
A whole afternoon I spent chopping them back, no fruit
but a glut of yellow buds, the crop choked
this year by its own abundance, the cages
overrun. And me not fond of tomatoes, really,
something about how when you cut to their hearts
what you find is only a wetness and seeds,
wetness and seeds, wetness and seeds.
Still, my hands came gloved with their odor
into this room, where for days I've searched
but found no words to fit.
Bitter musky acrid stale—the scent
of hands once buried past the wrist in vines.

∽

Mafioso
Sandra M. Gilbert

Frank Costello eating spaghetti in a cell at San Quentin,
Lucky Luciano mixing up a mess of bullets and
calling for parmesan cheese,
Al Capone baking a sawed-off shotgun into a
huge lasagna–
            are you my uncles, my
only uncles?

      O Mafiosi,
bad uncles of the barren
cliffs of Sicily—was it only you
that they transported in barrels
like pure olive oil
across the Atlantic?

   Was it only you
who got out at Ellis Island with
black scarves on your heads and cheap cigars
and no English and a dozen children?

No carts were waiting, gallant with paint,
no little donkeys plumed like the dreams of peacocks.
Only the evil eyes of a thousand buildings
stared across at the echoing debarkation center,
making it seem so much smaller than a piazza,

only a half dozen Puritan millionaires stood on the wharf,
in the wind colder than the impossible snows of the Abruzzi,
ready with country clubs and dynamos

to grind the organs out of you.

࿆

Picking Apricots with Zia Antonia
Maria Famà

Late afternoon in June
when the sun was less intense
my aunt and I picked apricots
   in a terraced field
    on a mountainside

We picked buckets
I on a ladder
she below
her everyday life
special for me
fresh from a city
an ocean away

From the ladder
I saw the dusty roads
snaking through the town

the laundry waving on balconies
I heard goat bells and bleats
         a motorcycle buzz, a fiat horn
I breathed sweet apricots and sun

I slowed and swayed
my aunt called up to me
she said I was not used
         to the power of Sicilian apricots

at sunset   we carried the buckets home
some to sell, some to trade, some to eat ourselves

at twilight I sat in the kitchen
a little dizzy

my aunt was right
her everyday life
my ancestors' lives

~

Mortadella

Rosanna Colasurdo

It is another March morning. I am on spring break and do not want to be up so early. But the birds are chirping annoyingly outside my bedroom window, disturbing my sleep. In the kitchen, the coffee pot is making those coffee pot noises. I turn over, not wanting to open my eyes. My sister is complaining about one of her coworkers. My mother tries to console her. My eyes refuse to open as I struggle to get more rest.

The sound of the telephone is the final straw. I open my eyes.

Everything is spinning. Chandelier, television, night table, ceiling, glass of water on dresser. The room spins and spins. I feel like I have just gotten off the Tilt-a-Whirl at the boardwalk in Point Pleasant.

My heart is pounding. I am sweating. My mind is racing, imagining I have an inoperable brain tumor. I call out my mother's name, but she doesn't hear me. The vomit rises in my throat.

I need some air. I stumble out of bed and to my front porch, holding onto furniture and wall. Brisk air touches my face. My nausea dissipates. I look up into the bright, sun-drenched day and instead of seeing the familiar tree facing my house, I see two fuzzy, lopsided shapes. The dread rises in my throat, a volcano about to erupt.

I stumble to my bathroom, sit down hard on the toilet seat. I call out my mother's name again. I need to splash water on my face. The water will help me. It will make the dizziness go away. Up off the toilet, slowly. Concentrate on a single green button on my green-and-white pajamas. Turn the faucet on, glance in the mirror. Face is fuzzy. Thoughts are scattered. I have not eaten a meal for twenty-four hours. After yesterday's breakfast, I had decided that more meals were out of the question for the rest of the day. I think that this is the cause of my sickness.

My mother finally hears me. She must have been down in the basement. Her face is fuzzy. She is trying to help me out of the bathroom, but I will not let her pull me out. My clammy hands grasp onto the bathroom sink. She is speaking to me, but I can barely hear her. I fall to the ground. I lose consciousness. Everything is gray. My mother is next to me, but her voice is very far away. I concentrate on the gray. I believe I am going to die.

The brown hallway tile slowly comes into focus. I concentrate on it. If I take my eyes off it, the gray will capture me again and not let go of me this time. My mother is on the ground next to me, crying. I am crying too. She is saying, "You're okay, you're okay."

"I'm fine," I keep saying. But I am not fine. I haven't eaten in a day. I do not think that I have an eating problem, but one is knocking on my door. I am making myself sick, yet I refuse to go to the doctor.

My father comes home, sees me lying on the floor, yells at me. He tells me that I need to eat right. That I am not fat. That to think I am fat is crazy.

Why do I need to be so perfect at school, at work, in my social life? Why is my body image so warped? Why do I still let hateful words that old classmates said years and years before haunt me?

"Rosanna, *mangia!*"

I hear this yelled to me often throughout my childhood. By my mother, father, grandparents, aunts, uncles, even my sisters.

My family owns Roma Italian Imports, a delicatessen. Making food, selling it, is how my family has survived and thrived. Without the lunch meats, sausage and peppers, hot roast beef sandwiches, chicken parmesan, pizza, stuffed shells, and other dishes the neighborhood craves, my sisters and I would never have had toys and clothes, a college education.

The family has always loved to cook. But as a child, I refuse to eat most of what my mother cooks. I sit at the kitchen table, scrunch up my face, and reject whatever my mother has specially prepared for me. Spaghetti, ravioli, lasagna, pizza—all would be pushed aside. Spitting out veal cutlet covered with mozzarella was a common occurrence during Sunday dinners. My favorite food was pasta with butter. I would eat it three times a day if I could; if I could, I would eat nothing else.

Though I had been a chubby baby, I was a very thin child. Skin and bones. In photographs, my ribs are clearly visible. I look fragile, like a porcelain doll, easily breakable. I was often ill.

Playing with my older sister was not allowed unless I finished my scrambled eggs and orange juice. I would force everything down and then run into my room to play Barbies. I ate not because I wanted to, but because I had to. Food was no pleasure. I had to eat to play with my dolls and toys, watch my favorite cartoon, spend time outside after dinner.

Then I discovered brick oven pizza. Pizza with thick, bright red tomato sauce and a paper-thin crust. I ate as much of it as I could during my sixth summer, the one I spent in Italy. The sweet smell of the sauce, the taste of salt, oregano, onions, and garlic in my mouth was heavenly. Brick oven pizza was the first food that I ever enjoyed, that I looked forward to eating. Every time we entered a restaurant on our summer-long trip through Italy, I would always ask, "Do they have pizza?" My mother was thrilled to watch me consume quantities of it with reckless abandon.

On the trip, we had many meals with relatives I barely knew. I would put on a happy face and choke down whatever they served. There would be no spitting out of veal cutlet. My father made sure of that.

My sisters and I were not allowed to be disrespectful about food. Our culture taught us to respect family members, including those we had never met before. To respect them meant being kind to them, and eating all the food they offered us, for doing so is the ultimate sign of respect in an Italian family. My Nonna Lilla would smile proudly as she served her ziti and fresh sauce. If any was left on the plate, her smile would be replaced by her famous scowl, and a spattering of unpleasant words muttered under her breath. Nonna created masterpieces in the kitchen, and she felt that everyone should appreciate her works of art.

In one of the first portraits taken of me, at age two, I am sitting down. My poker-straight, jet black hair is held back by two red barrettes, thick bangs falling across my forehead. My thick eyebrows are knit together. My eyes are big and wide. My skirt and blouse were brought back by my Nonna Lilla from Sicily. The skirt has little horses pulling carriages around the bottom and along the pockets. The white blouse is decorated with donkeys pulling carriages, and tiny men and women dancing. My crocheted socks with red trim are pulled all the way up my chubby legs. I am the perfect little Italian doll, posed on a brown stool.

When I am young, I think that everyone in America speaks two languages in their households, has grandparents who live with them, and dozens of aunts, uncles, and cousins who are "not really" aunts, uncles, and cousins. That everyone kisses family on both cheeks in greeting. That everyone calls their grandma and grandpa "Nonno" and "Nonna."

When I start school, I learn that children around me are different. They look different, smell different, speak different, dress different. I learn, in kindergarten, that we should appreciate our differences. We are all friends in kindergarten.

My best childhood friend is Catherine Mary. She lives two houses away from me. Catherine Mary is Irish Italian with light brown hair and freckles. Her parents were born in the United States. They speak only English in her house, and dinner on Sunday is at six, not at two. As we get older, I love that Catherine Mary's mother serves TV dinner on trays in the living room. I am jealous that Catherine Mary can eat Chef Boy-ar-dee ravioli. I am taught to hate it, told that it is disgusting, artificial Italian food.

Once, when Catherine Mary is eating, she dips her finger in the beet red sauce and dangles it in front of my face. She asks if I'm positive I don't want any. I scrunch up my face, make gagging noises. I tell Catherine Mary she doesn't know how lucky I am. Nobody can cook like my mother and father. She shrugs, continues to eat. My mouth is watering. But I do not give in to my desire. I have learned to reject foods that come from aluminum cans found in brightly lit supermarket aisles. I must eat what my mother prepares with a smile on my face. It is food that I do not enjoy eating, though I pretend to.

But when I am seven, I discover mortadella. My uncle slices it thinly for me at the store, and I do not even take the "dots" out or pull off the plastic casing before I devour it. I eat it with bread, without bread, with crackers, with cheese, with just about anything. For a long time, it is all I want to eat. Catherine Mary thinks this is strange.

My passion for mortadella dies when my sister announces to me that the little white dots are not just dots but tiny pieces of fat. If I keep on eating so much mortadella, she says, I am going to turn into one. I stop eating, drop the sandwich, nauseous. I run to my mother and ask if this is true. She tells me, no, the little white dots are pieces of salt. I know she is lying. I try to eat again, but I do not touch another piece of mortadella for about ten years.

When I lose my enthusiasm for mortadella, my obsession with Nutella begins. I spread the chocolate hazelnut cream all over my toast in the morning. I eat it for lunch, for snacks. I sneak into the kitchen in the middle of the night, pull out a spoon, dip it into the jar, and lift the Nutella to my awaiting lips.

Nutella becomes the center of my food universe. I sneak into my family's store to grab a jar and shove it into my book bag. But my mother doesn't mind when I slather it on bread at dinner and lick the knife. She is happy to see me eat, to put on weight. She was born in Sicily and thinks being plump is being healthy.

Plump is what I become. Pleasantly plump. I discover salty snacks. Then Hostess cupcakes and Twinkies. Homemade lasagna. My father's homemade pizza with pepperoni and chunks of garlic. A ham, salami, provolone hero from the deli. I eat and eat. I drink and drink. I gain more and more weight.

My mother is happy. She loves to cook. Preparing meals for her family is her passion. And we all show how much we appreciate her cooking by gaining weight. This is my mother's great accomplishment. It means that she is a good cook. That she feeds us well and takes care of us.

I am at the park one day, on a swing. Catherine Mary is swinging next to me. We are shouting, giggling. It is a school day, we have finished our homework, and our mothers have let us go to the park. Life cannot get any better for two nine year olds.

Shawn and Geraldine, two kids from our class are playing directly across from us. Catherine Mary suggests going to say hello. I cringe. We walk across the small grassy playground. It is early autumn, the air is crisp, and leaves are scattered on the ground. My legs feel leaden. On most occasions, I can tolerate Geraldine. I cannot stand Shawn. He is a bully. He tortures me with words. I do not want to see Shawn. But I also want to prove that I am not afraid of him, that I am not a coward.

Shawn is a mediocre student, not very popular in school, though he likes to believe he is. He likes to do whatever he can to impress people. He puts people down to make himself feel good.

Shawn and Geraldine are sitting on the playground horses that bob up and down. Catherine Mary and Geraldine want to talk. So I sit, silent, on a horse, right next to Shawn. Shawn tells me that he does not like my mother because she "talks funny." He asks me why she sounds so weird. Is she abnormal? His parents, he says, don't talk like that.

I do not speak. Catherine Mary explains my mother was born in another country and that I learned to speak Italian before English.

Shawn laughs and laughs. He throws his head back, his beady eyes tear. He mimics my mother's accent. His voice is high-pitched, shrill. It shames my mother's beautiful, liquid speech. Geraldine and Catherine Mary tell him to stop. Tears fall down my cheeks. He insults my family. My family who had nothing when they came to America, my family who started a business and made a wonderful life for us. I get off the horse and run all the way home. Catherine Mary runs after me. I hide in her basement until I calm down. I do not want my mother to see me upset, do not want her to know what happened.

When I go home, I see my mother in her usual spot, at the stove, in the kitchen.

My mother grew up in Sicily, where Nonna Lilla and Great-nonna Giovanna taught her how to cook. She graduated from college, and moved to Canada when she was nineteen. There she met my father, also Italian, also born in Italy, also a great lover of Italian cuisine. They saw each other only twice before getting engaged. After they married, my father, my mother, and her family moved to Jersey City, where he and his parents had been living. He knew how to speak English, he had a job in a factory, he would take care of everything. He worked and worked. Saved every penny so that he could accomplish his dream. The American Dream. To open his own business.

I eat if I'm at the store. Food surrounds me. My mother encourages me to snack even if I have already eaten lunch. That I am gaining weight is no problem. When I am thirteen, I do not know how much I weigh because I never use the scale. My doctor does not weigh me, but he looks me up and down when I go for checkups.

I want to lose weight, but I can't. I only care because there are those around me who torture me about it.

I am thirteen, and in the eighth grade. In the school year book there will be a section called "Can you imagine . . . ?" Each student chooses the name of a classmate out of a hat and writes something about that person that no one could ever imagine that person saying or doing. I have chosen my new best friend, Lori. I think I will write, "Can you imagine Lori ever giving a speech in front of the entire school?" because Lori is such a quiet girl. I think she will get a kick out of that.

As I write my submission, laughter surrounds me. Richie, the class clown—and the class idiot in my opinion—has picked my name. "What should I write about Rosanna?" he asks, purposely raising his voice. "I know! I'll write, 'Can you imagine Rosanna not being fat?'"

Richie laughs but no one around him laughs. The girl standing next to him punches him. I remain seated. I feel sick, ready to retch. My eyes water, hot tears roll down my cheeks. I have never cried in school before. I hate myself for showing Richie how much he hurt me, but the tears fall. Soon I can no longer feel anything. My teacher asks what is wrong, but I cannot answer. I shake my head and look ahead.

It is January 1995. I am a student at Jersey City State College. And I still have a weight problem. I live in sweatpants, leggings, and big sweatshirts. I never enter a fitting room at the mall, but simply grab the loosest thing I can find in large or extra large and run to the cash register, not even looking at the clerk as I hand over my money.

My best friend, Amy, and I have many things in common. We like the same music, sports teams, television programs. Amy is overweight, too. She likes to eat as much as I do. Amy is Egyptian. We compare our cultures all the time. She complains about how her strict parents will not give her freedom. She consoles herself by eating.

I console myself by eating, too, but not for the same reasons. I am angry. Angry that I spent our years of high school without a boyfriend. Angry that I commute to school because my parents want to keep a short leash on me. Angry that I cannot parade around in a bikini at the beach. Still angry, after these many years, for harsh words spoken by little boys. Angry at my mother for cooking the good foods I love to eat. Angry at my father for owning the store, filled with treats I cannot resist. I am angry, yet I do nothing to lose weight, and when my mother puts a plate of pasta in front of me at night, I eat it all, and then have seconds.

Amy is losing weight. I can see it, but I ignore it. I never comment because I am jealous. Amy has always been pretty. Now she looks even more attractive. One night we are at Pizzeria Uno. I order an individual pizza with pepperoni. Amy orders the special pizza. I eat all my pizza. Amy eats only half of hers. An old friend from high school, Cassandra, comes by. She comments on how much weight Amy has lost, on how wonderful she looks. Inside I am screaming and crying. Amy is leaving me behind in a scary world where my only comfort is food. She likes to go shopping now; she goes every weekend with her mother to buy new clothes. I still walk around in sweats. I am eighteen years old and should be having the time of my life, attending parties, going out on dates, having an active, full life. But food is my true best friend. I look forward to meals more than I look forward to anything else. My mother yelling *"mangia"* to me plays over and over in my mind. But how can I blame her now?

It is the summer of 1997. It has been two years since I started to lose weight, and to take food and make it my worst enemy instead of my best friend.

I began that night at the pizzeria with Amy and Cassandra. I was 190 pounds, the heaviest I had ever been. I lost weight quickly at first, and then slower and slower. I went from eating heroes at lunch to eating turkey on rye bread with lettuce and low-fat mayo. Everyone was happy about the way I looked except my mother. She was worried. Worried about my not eating enough, about my passing out. Although I refused to admit it, she was right to be concerned.

I was obsessed with my weight, and still obsessed with food. But instead of finding food to shove in my mouth, I thought of ways to psyche myself out of eating. I never starved myself, but I deprived myself. No more chips and cakes and ice cream. The only pleasure I allowed myself was pizza, on Friday nights. The first food I loved was still the one I could not deny myself.

March 1997. I am browsing at the Gap, one of my favorite stores. I need a new pair of jeans. I head into the fitting room with two pairs, one a size twelve, the other a ten. I try on the twelve first. I pull them on, button them up, then glance in the mirror. They are baggy. I smile as I pull them off and reach for the size ten. I pull the ten on, slowly, feeling exhilaration. They button comfortably. I examine myself in the mirror. They fit my hips and thighs nicely. I savor the feeling of accomplishment, the same one I had when I dropped from a size sixteen to a fourteen, from a fourteen to a twelve. It is like passing a difficult exam, receiving an award, getting a bonus at work.

The next morning I pass out in my bathroom.

I watch commercials on television and think about a culture that is obsessed with looking good. There is nothing wrong with looking good. I want to feel good about myself, too. For too long I have hated myself, could not look in the mirror because I felt disgusted by my reflection. I hate myself when I am young for being a person who lets others make me feel bad because my parents are from a different culture, because we have different customs, a different language, and different eating habits. I hate myself when I am a teenager because I'm fat, and being fat makes me feel ugly and undesirable. And I hate myself for blaming my parents. I hate myself at nineteen, twenty, and twenty-one for becoming so obsessed with my weight that I would forgo meals and deprive myself of the foods I love and curse Italian food and Italian culture. And I hate myself for being so critical of everything I do. I hate myself for not being able to love myself.

I look in the mirror now and see a woman who looks somewhat foreign. She believes in herself, thinks that she is pretty, smart, funny, creative. She writes. She has friends and a family who love her. She comes from a rich culture. She is the correct weight for her height.

Still, I have my "fat days," days during which I feel huge, unattractive, and forlorn. But I also have days when I have what my mother taught me to always keep inside, *speranza*, hope. On the bad days, the spoon comes out of the drawer, the Nutella comes out of the cupboard, I dip the spoon, fill it, lift it to my lips, savor, swallow. On the good days, I am happy, and I wonder, "Can this really be me?"

∾

Keep the Wheat and Let the Chaff Lie
Mary Ann Mannino

There's an old pair of shoes
resting on the extension ladder

in my garage. A pair of black Florsheim
wing tips, now scuffed, worn down in the heel
white paint splattered across the tops
the lining of one torn and curled, the other missing.
They've been nesting on that ladder since 1980.
Twenty years I've cleaned that garage, spring and fall.
Forty times, I've returned them to their perch.
My papa's shoes. Once proudly polished
preserved with metal shoe trees inside.

Papa never bought sneakers or casual clothes.
When his good clothes wore, he used them to
work around the house or yard. Once, he'd been
depression poor. Lost his house and sun-kissed fig tree.
Later, he spent money on beef roasts, schooling
for his children, books and bikes for my babies.
Throwing out old clothes, buying new ones for work
a frivolous waste.

These shoes he kept in my garage
along with frayed dress pants
a faded oxford shirt, a torn sweater.
He'd walk five blocks from his home to mine
impeccably dressed, not to embarrass me
before my neighbors. This gentle man
immigrant with broken tongue
former farmer, friend of grape vines
olive trees, and sweet, black soil
displaced in a city.

He'd change clothes in my garage
sweep the leaves from my winding drive
nourish my azaleas with cow manure
weed my favorite flower beds
plant forsythia and hydrangeas he'd rooted
make my house and yard look loved
richer than the houses of my neighbors
whose hired gardeners manicured their lawns.

No one's perfect.
My mother had stories.

My older brother too.
Mother used to say
"You don't know your father.
Once, he ripped his custom-made
silk shirt in two because he lost a
button, and us with no money."
My older brother'd say about my parents
"When I was a boy, they'd go at it."
He'd shake his head.

But I know none of that.
I remember him legally blind at eighty
gently lifting tomato seedlings he'd grown
as if they were eggshells or Waterford
placing them in rows in my garden
staking them with tree branches
he's stripped for the purpose
tying them with rags he'd uniformly cut
to save us money.

∾

The Northside at Seven
Lucia Perillo

Gray sulfurous light, having risen early this morning
in the west, over the stacks of Solvay, has by now
wafted across the lake and landed here on Lodi Street,
where it anoints each particular with the general grace
of decay: the staggering row houses, the magazines flapping
from the gutters like broken skin, the red Dodge sedan
parked across the street from where I'm hunched in the pickup.
The Dodge's driver was ahead of me at the counter
in Ragusa's Bakery, making confession before an old woman
who was filling pastry shells with sweetened ricotta:

I put a new roof on her house, he was telling the woman,
but the lady don't pay me. I do a good job; she got no complaint.
But see, a man must hold his head high so I took her car.

The old woman trilled as she stuffed another log of cannoli.
Turning to me he said, *She can call the cops if she wants—*
I'll tell them I got kids to take care of, I got a contract.
I shrugged: all the absolution I could bring myself to deliver
before grabbing the white paper sacks the woman slapped down
and walking out the door, leaving the man in the midst
of what he needed to say. I don't know—

there was something about his Sicilian features, his accent,
his whole goddamned hard-luck story that just gnawed on me so,
like those guys who came to unload on my own old man, muttering
Bobby, Bobby, we got a little problem here Bobby . . .
the cue for women, kids to leave the room. But since then
my father had tried to draw me back into that room,
driving me along the tattered Bronx streets of his boyhood,
sometimes lifting his hands from the steering wheel and
spreading them, saying: *Look, these people are* paesan,
you're paesan, *nothing you're ever gonna do can change that . . .*

We'd spend the rest of the day on food, eating spiedini,
the anchovy sauce quenching my chronic thirst
for salt, and shopping for the dense bread made from black
tailings of prosciutto, I forget the name of it now.
I forget so much. I even forget why tears come on the freeway,
mornings I drive by these old buildings when bread is cooking—
why? for what? Sometimes I feel history slipping from my body
like a guilty bone, & the only way to call it back
is to slump here behind the wheel, licking sugar from my chin,
right hand warmed by the semolina loaves riding shotgun,

the way my father might have spent his early mornings years ago,
before he claimed the responsibilities of manhood—of marrying
and making himself a daughter who would not be trapped, as he
felt he was, by streets washed over on the slow decay of light.
Making her different from what he was. And making her the same.

☙

Words

Maria Laurino

Each time I traveled to Italy, I longed to use the correct Italian grammar and speak with just a trace of an accent. I learned Italian in my late twenties, by which point my brain was too rusty and my tongue too lazy to form new sounds. I also carried with me an assortment of dialect words from my childhood, and I tried them out on my Italian friends. My friends, however, were befuddled, unable to decipher what I was saying. Their confused stares confirmed that I had once again committed some gross violation of their language, and the look on their faces brought back my sense of childhood shame about dialect. When I was a child, we tried to mask our susceptibility to shame by keeping "ethnic" details, the keys to our identity, under lock and key. Secrets and shame converged daily in our use of southern Italian dialect.

We spoke only English at home, but my parents kept alive an assortment of southern Italian dialect words that signaled a quiet intimacy or set off the alarms of subterfuge. These homegrown foreign words captured the musings and jags of daily life but had to be uttered solely among ourselves.

"Do you understand me? Are you *stunod*?" my mother would say.

Stunod. Someone who is out-of-it, spacey, not a practical person who knows that life is labor and that only the sturdy can get the job done. You lock the keys in the car. You pause, ponder, lose the moment instead of seizing it. You're *stunod*. You can be momentarily *stunod*, or the word can describe a general state of mind that applies both to the ethereal dreamer and to someone who's a little slow. Or a person, like a nonstop talker, can make you *stunod*, the type who consumes so much of the room's oxygen that you're left gasping for air. To me, the emotional clarity of each meaning is so perfect that I have kept this word in my adult vocabulary, and share it with my Russian Sephardic Jewish American husband, who immediately understands my linguistic shorthand when I declare a person *stunod*.

My American-born parents grew up communicating with their parents, whose knowledge of English was extremely limited, in southern Italian dialect. (Actually, my father listened to his parents' dialect and responded in English). After my grandparents died, my mother and father had little reason to speak what they knew was not the "real" Italian, Tuscan Italian, but the language of an illiterate people from the south of Italy.

It was impossible, however, for my mother to keep her beloved dialect in storage, and a steady stream of words emerged throughout the day. When I refused to change my mind about something, she called me *gabbadotz*. When tired and unresponsive, I was *mooshamoosh*. If I grabbed too many free samples in the food store, I was acting like a *mortitavahm*. Dropping a plate, stubbing her toe, or encountering any stumbling block to getting the housework done, my mother let out a cry of *footitah*. I was left to fill in the blanks, to figure out the general category of emotion to which each word belonged.

Despite the harsh assessments, when my mother used dialect the gesture was affectionate, not a reprimand. I was comforted to hear words spoken only between us, words that no one else knew. The tone was often humorous, sometimes ironic, an interpretation of the world that my parents were passing along to their children.

But I also understood that I would face undue embarrassment if our code of silence was broken, if I repeated dialect to outsiders. Suburbanites say hello to passersby and comment on the lovely day; they entertain with barbecues and bring out steaks and corn on the cob; but they don't speak or eat like peasants, and we had to imitate their behavior. I could get myself into trouble if I used odd-sounding words or told neighbors about the strange foods that I devoured.

My love of my mother's cooking (many of the dishes felt doubly foreign because they had dialect names) and her expressive use of southern Italian provided the simmering flavors of a life that I never knew but felt intimately connected to. But at the same time, southern Italian food and dialect words, my closest cultural links to our past, collided with everyday life in our suburban cul-de-sac. And as a child, I realized that I couldn't afford to repeat the kind of mistake that I had made with Joey Unger.

Joey Unger was our neighbor and my brother Bob's junior high school pal. During one of Joey's regular visits to our house, I joined him and my brother on the front steps. I was always a bit of an annoyance, being eight years younger than they were, but that afternoon I managed to nudge my way into the conversation.

"What's your favorite food?" Joey asked me.

As I was about to answer, my lips pronouncing the first syllable, I felt a large hand firmly cover my mouth, preventing me from even turning my head. I could barely breathe, let alone respond to Joey. Momentarily confused and afraid, I soon realized that the arm connected to the smothering hand on my mouth was Bob's. How could my kind and affectionate brother be trying to suffocate me? Was I going to die right there on our front stoop while attempting, desperately, earnestly attempting, to tell Joey Unger that my favorite food in the entire world was chicken feet? With my brother's hand rudely clamped on my face, it was impossible to explain how I loved to suck on the wrinkly claws shriveled as a witch's finger steeped in tomato sauce, and describe my favorite part, the large chewy piece of cartilage at the base of the foot, which slid around my teeth with each satisfying bite. It never occurred to me that others might not have tasted this food, a dish common among southern Italian farmers like my grandparents, who raised their own game before settling in New Jersey.

My muffled screams became louder and louder: "Chicken feet. Chick-ken feeet. CHICKEN FEEEET."

"Chicken?" Joey asked.

"Yes, that's right," my brother said. "She loves chicken."

"No, no," I said, shaking my head forcefully. Chicken couldn't be my favorite food; it was dry and tasteless compared to the lower reaches of the bird.

"Chicken FEEEEEET."

"Chicken something," said Joey, a bit confused.

"Chicken FEEEEEEEEEEEEET."

"Did she say chicken feet?"

"No, she didn't," my brother responded, his hand still wrapped around my telltale mouth.

I began to violently nod yes.

"She eats chicken feet?" Joey said, scrunching up his boyish white face as if he had never heard anything quite so disgusting.

"I don't know what she's talking about," my beet-red brother replied as he opened the screen, deposited me inside the house, and slammed the door. I ran up the steps, furious about my mistreatment, and watched them walk down the street, my teary face plastered against the windowpane.

Our ancestors were people who worked the land, and even if my father had been born in Millburn, New Jersey, even if he had never touched the hilly terrain of Picerno in southern Italy that yielded barely enough crops for them to eat, somewhere deep in his blood was the instinct to pick edible food wherever it was available. As a boy, my father worked weekends as a caddy at a fancy golf club that restricted Italian-Americans and other swarthy types. An enterprising twelve-year-old, one day he discovered a fertile patch of green off the silky eighteen-hole course. He quietly sat on this less traveled path and began to pull up *chicoy*, our dialect word for dandelions that are eaten as a salad.

"What are you doing?" asked one of the golfers who happened to walk by.

"I'm picking these for tonight's dinner," he said.

"You eat grass?" the incredulous golfer replied.

Yes, my father nodded, too embarrassed to explain the satisfying bitter taste of *chicoy* or lie when caught green-handed.

The shame that my father must have felt on that golf course as a child was, in a diluted form, passed along to me, contained in the nervous grip of my brother's hand on my mouth. My father munched on weeds, I ate the feet of chickens; neither was appropriate in our town, either in the roaring twenties or the rebellious sixties. My brother recalls that my mother never cooked chicken feet again after the Joey Unger incident. My parents were mortified to have been caught serving such a low-rent meal. Their shame turned everyday acts into small secrets, as we lived out the stereotype of trusting only the family: don't mention our foods; don't use our dialect words.

This decision caused some emotional trepidation, because I would find myself refraining from mentioning subjects as innocuous as a dinner meal. How could I tell friends that my dinner had been a dish made with *kookazeel?* The word sounded more like baby talk than baby zucchini (*cucuzzielli* in dialect, I discovered years later), which my mother sautéed with peppers, onions, and eggs, calling the mixture *jombought.* I had to devise my own rules of nomenclature: if asked about last night's supper, I would describe in general terms what I had eaten, but I'd never assign a name to the dish.

Lettuces seemed bound to get my family in trouble in America. In high school I became friends with an Italian-American girl whose parents lived on the right side of the tracks but still indulged in, I discovered, the foods of the wrong side.

"Do you eat beans and greens?" she asked me one day.

"What's beans and greens?" I replied.

"Oh, it's a soup my mother makes with escarole and beans."

Meneste, I thought to myself. I've finally met someone else who eats *meneste.*

I loved *meneste.* My mother made it every Monday night, this thick soup of escarole, cannellini beans soaked in olive oil, and sliced pepperoni, which we sopped up with chunks of soft Italian bread. It was considered a poor person's soup because the ingredients were so cheap (although a less tasty version of this dish sells for $4.50 a pint in Balducci's today). *Meneste,* from the dialect word *menesta,* which means vegetables boiled for soup, looked quite unattractive, with lumps of mushy white beans separating from their filmy skin and seaweed-colored escarole floating in the plate. To me, *meneste* was a delicious mess. I loved the dish, but would never mention it to anyone else.

Beans and greens, however, sounded American, fine to say.

"Yes, my mom makes that, too!" I replied with childlike enthusiasm, delighted by a connection that made my household seem less foreign.

"What do you call it?" she asked curiously.

I'm not sure if my friend was testing me, trying to find out if my family, like hers, had an arsenal of embarrassing, hushed-up words. Was "beans and greens" a code phrase, a rhyming sobriquet that could unite us in a shared ancestry and common dialect? Or was her family more "modern" than mine, knowing the dish only by this name?

"Oh, we don't call it anything," I replied, playing it safe.

I'd soon rename the dish "beans and greens," which, unlike *meneste,* was much less of a mess to explain.

•

Deeply uncertain about my place in the world, I couldn't make the self-confident leap in early adulthood that would have allowed me to have fun with dialect, to give others a taste of my culture through its language. In my job as a newspaper reporter, the only woman among a group of scruffy men, I once offered a colleague one of my mother's homemade *tatalles*. *Tatalles* is an Italian-American word for the southern Italian food known as *taralli*, which are made with flour, eggs, olive oil, fennel seed, and pepper. Pieces of this thinly rolled dough are shaped into circles, boiled, and then baked until a crispy golden brown.

I handed a *tatalle* to a newspaperman who spent his day editing words, and he asked the obvious question: "What is this called?"

"It's an Italian pretzel," I responded.

"I've never seen this. What's its name?"

"I don't know," I fumbled, never a good liar.

"It must have a name."

"It's an Italian version of a bagel."

"How can you not know what it's called?" he repeated, exasperated by my food comparisons.

"I don't know its name," I replied, and walked away.

I was afraid of being laughed at if I said *tatalle*, an odd-sounding word spoken only at the kitchen table. By keeping dialect separate from my daily discourse, I both increased its importance, allowing me to hold secrets that no one else possessed, and devalued its relevance, believing that I would be taken less seriously if I repeated illegitimate words.

Because so few Italian-Americans openly use dialect, I could only confirm its existence by listening to my family or by randomly encountering a person who retains these words in everyday discourse. It wasn't until I traveled to the south of Italy and met a scholar in Naples whose father, like my maternal grandparents, grew up in a village near Avellino that I discovered the etymology of many of my dialect words.

The drab gray facade of Università Federico II looks like many old Neapolitan buildings, its color indistinguishable from the endless stream of smoke that spills each day from car exhausts. Inscribed on the entrance archway are the words "Faculty of Letters and Philosophy." Through the arch was a lush green courtyard, and students breathed in this small offering of peace, their heads bowed over books. I made my way past them, turning into a corridor of staircases and walking up three stories of old cement to the philology department. In one of the small cramped offices shared by several faculty members, Professor Nicola De Blasi was waiting for me.

A philologist trained in the love of learning, De Blasi was naturally frustrated that he couldn't speak English well enough to converse with me about the history of Italian dialects. This left us to my Italian.

Italy was divided for many centuries by the accents and speech patterns of regional Latin dialects. In the late nineteenth and early twentieth centuries, when my grandparents left Italy, they would have spoken, like the vast majority of immigrants, the southern dialects of their regions; and my grandparents knew that their language was thought of in America and in their homeland as substandard Italian.

The words that I learned growing up were not pure southern Italian dialect. Their roots are in my grandparents' language, but the pronunciations changed over time, as an American tongue prevailed, abandoning Old World sounds for the strange hybrid of Italo-American speech. Like a hothouse lily, this Italian-American lingua franca was bred from the regional dialects of southern Italy, gradually mixing with the vowel off-glides and staccato rhythms of English speech. The information shouldn't have surprised me; but when you grow up hearing dialect, you assume, or at least I did, that the language was Italian, spoken somewhere in Italy. All the pieces of my life considered to be "Italian"—the food, the dialect, the dark hair—I kept distinct from the American side, forgetting about the hyphen, about that in-between place where a new culture takes form.

I had typed a list of dialect words for the professor, and I cautiously began with my favorite.

Stunade, I wrote, a bad transcription because the sound is closer to *stunod*.

He stared at the word, looking quizzical.

"*Stew-nod*," I pronounced carefully, allowing him to examine what my American tongue had done to his dialect.

"*Sì, sì, sì*," he responded. "*Stonato. Fuori da testa.*"

"Yes!" I restrained myself from pounding the desk in my enthusiasm. I had found a wizard who made my words real.

Out of one's mind. In dialect, *stunod* means a person who can't understand anything because he is senile or doddering, and is used to describe anyone who acts a little out of it. In Tuscan or standard Italian, the professor explained, the word *stonato* exists, but its meaning changes. *Stonato* is a person who sings off-key, the opposite of *intonato*.

As the intimacies of language bridged the gap between native and foreigner, professor and student, De Blasi became my linguistic confidant. He began to decipher my connections to the south of Italy.

I learned that one reason why my northern friends didn't understand my southern dialect is that many of these words, which all have Latin roots, exist in standard Italian but without the pejorative connotations found in the south. *Citrulo* (pronounced "chee-trool-oh"), for example, is southern dialect for the standard Italian *cetriolo*, cucumber. In the north, the word has no metaphorical meaning, but in the south, where it's impossible to separate the people from the land they cultivate, *citrulo* describes a person whose brain is as fleshy and watery as a cucumber.

The Italian-American version of this southern word, in which the *ci* sound changes to a soft *g*, is *gedrool*. Anyone who has ever listened to that 1950s Anglo-Saxon paean to Italian-American culture, "Mambo Italiano," which continually creeps into contemporary movie sound tracks, has encountered the *gedrool*. As Rosemary Clooney swooned in her fake Italian-American accent: "Hey *gedrool*, you donnuh have to go to school. / Just make it with a big bambino. It's like a vino. / Kid you're good-ah lookin. But you donnuh know what's cookin."

Other vegetable words have second meanings in dialect: deep purple egg-plant, in dialect *mulignan*, describes black people; and fennel, *finucch* in dialect, is used for gay men. I often heard *gedrool* growing up, but I was unaware of the figurative meaning of these other two words. My brother Bob, who is an assistant prosecutor in Newark, New Jersey, tells a favorite office story about the importance of understanding the metaphoric meaning of dialect: An old Italian-American man who spoke broken English went to the police station to file a complaint that he had been attacked by a big *mulignan*. The officer took down the story verbatim and later asked a colleague, "What is *mulignan*?" The final report read that the man had been assaulted by a large eggplant.

With the professor's help, I was discovering a set of rules that enabled me to link my hand-me-down words to a real language. For example, the standard Italian word *cafone* (cah-fone-ay), meaning an ignorant person, is pronounced "cah-fone" in the south, where the final vowel, always used in standard Italian, trails off. In the Italian-American pronunciation, the hard *c* changes to a hard *g*, and becomes one of my favorite dialect words, *gavone*.

Understanding this pattern, I discovered why we called the pie my mother made the night before Easter *pizza gain*. I remember how my mother would chide herself all day if she had mistakenly tasted its prosciutto filling on the meatless Good Friday, and how we voraciously ate thick slices of *pizza gain* after returning from Saturday night confession. My dislike of confession compared with my love of this pie could not be measured with worldly cups and table-spoons, but it was worth any penance to commune with this mixture of moz-zarella, parmigiano, and ricotta cheese, egg, peppery salami, and prosciutto baked in a crunchy bread shell. The words *pizza gain* made no sense to the American ear, so the dish remained nameless to outsiders, added to the list of family culinary secrets. Fortunately, when I was in high school, quiche Lorraine came into fashion, allowing me to serve *pizza gain* to my friends as "a kind of Italian quiche."

In southern dialect, the *pi* ("pee") sound in standard Italian often changes to *chi* ("key"). So the word *piena*, meaning full, becomes *chiena*. *Pizza chiena*, stuffed full of good things, sounds like *pizza gain* to the Italian-American ear. Northern Italians would describe a similar type of pie as *pizza imbottita*.

De Blasi went on translating with blooming vigor, as if he were rediscovering the ties between southern Italians like himself and his transplanted compatriots. My inclination to act like a *mortitavahm* when gobbling down free food comes from *morto di fame*, literally, "dying of hunger," and used to describe someone disgraced by poverty.

Dialect must have been a relief, a kind of escape for my mother. After many exhausting years of trying to fit into American culture, she could return to the comfortable language of childhood, when life is as plain as your parents' voice. To be raised by the sturdy hands and ancient customs of people from a traditional culture creates an adulthood of confused aspirations and conflicting values. What a simple luxury, especially in moments of frustration, to slip into one's peasant tongue, allowing language to transport you to the cozy safety of the past.

When I use a dialect word, I am repeating the sounds of my grandparents—perhaps the closest contact I could have with them. I am now their young grandchild, uttering playful words, oblivious to the meaning of what I am saying. How could I have understood all those years ago, innocently mixing my own batch of sounds, that dialect brought their faraway culture to our little white house, making us, in some tiny way, carriers of their abandoned way of life?

When my father left for work early each morning, my mother said he had to "go *zappà*," to put the food on the table. I always sensed that the word had more power than plain work. Decades later, finding a dictionary of the dialect of Picerno, I saw that *zappà* was a dialect form of the standard Italian verb *zappare*, meaning to hoe.

To hoe? My father, like the rest of the commuter dads, took the train to downtown New York to work in an office. He was manager of international shipping for the Allied Chemical Corporation. I don't think he knew how to use a hoe. But he had to go *zappà*, literally, "to labor in the fields," the exacting ritual of rural mountain people. If my mother had said he had to "go work in the fields," we would have questioned her grasp of reality. But *zappà* made sense, good sense. My mother's word choice, her interpretation of the meaning of work, unconsciously restored the lost culture of her parents.

As I decipher the meanings of my childhood language, I'm bombarded with relentless negativity, notes of jealousy, belittling quips; these are no Hallmark card messages for a warm and fuzzy day. The culture of southern Italy, in which hope was as elusive as fertile land, may have created a special place in language for expressions that let judgment and envy free. De Blasi joked that dialect descriptions are often derogatory because if you thought highly of someone there was no need to say anything at all.

Not a bad code for exploited, exhausted peasants to live by. Which suggests another interpretation. The words are sharp, funny, distinctly Italian, absent the self-righteous quest for moral perfection found in nineteenth-century American life, and yet filled with a belief in the ultimate worth of human beings. The opposite of the *citrulo* is the self-examining mind. The *morto di fame* maximizes self-pity. Like a diptych, the well-lived life hangs on the opposite hinge, a knowledge so implicit that no words are necessary; honor lives in silence.

∾

How To Sing to a Dago
Rachel Guido deVries

> Wop wop wop, wop wop a guinea guinea,
> Wop wop wop, wop wop a guinea guinea
> all day, all day, as the dagos on
>
> I mean I can laugh at myself, greaseball
> that I am with a bumpy nose and a mouth
> full of garlic. Hardy har har you all know
> how the ginzo can laugh up a storm and how she
> loves to get laid. Put your tongue inside me,
> I'm a putana, give me spaghetti with bacon,
> one big wooden spoon and I'll be happy
> with my shoes off and no babe in the room.
>
> > Wop wop wop, wop wop a guinea guinea,
> > wop wop wop, wop wop a guinea guinea
> > all day, all day, as the dagos on
>
> When I'm quiet I'm thinking, a surprise to you
> all, but my voice is like thunder inside of
> a storm. I listen to voices that tell me to hush
> but I'm hungry for music, in love with all touch.
> What I want is more feeling, what I want is too much
> for the white girls who tell me Italians are loud

and the others who say they will not take me out.
I might yell in a fury or scream in my joy.
That makes them feel funny, ashamed of their choice.

> Wop wop wop, wop wop a guinea guinea.
> Wop wop wop, wop wop a guinea guinea
> all day, all day as the dagoes on

When you sing to this dago my ears come to life
and it don't matter if the words aren't perfect
or nice. What matters is singing at the top
of your voice and then being ready to listen
to mine. When I lay my mouth to your ear,
my tongue in its shell, I'm singing a love
song and singing it well:

> Wop wop wop, wop wop a guinea guinea,
> Wop wop wop, wop wop a guinea guinea
> all day, all day, as the dagos on.

ᕔ

The Post-Rapture Diner
Dorothy Barresi

A thought you cannot call back,
and empty shoes like
exclamation points
on every road from here to Tucson.

Who will knock their boots against the doorjamb now
and enter shyly?
Who will peel the vegetables?
Pie domes cloud over. Old sugar

makes a kind of weather in there—
webbed, waiting.
Tiers of doughnuts go woozy with collapse.

We deed and we will.
We bow to what providence we understand
and cede the rest: our lies and doubts, our human,
almost necessary
limitations. *Probably I should have,*

we whispered more than once, shaking our heads.
Probably. Now what's left of the past
hangs in a walk-in freezer,
fat-shrouded, bluing,

and all we know of the present
is a spatula in a coffee can
on a cold grill, pointing to heaven.

༄

Cutting the Bread

Louise DeSalvo

The Bread

My grandmother is in the kitchen cutting the Italian bread she has made. The bread my grandmother has made is a big bread, a substantial bread, one you can use for dunking, or for scraping the last bit of sauce from a bowl of pasta, or for breaking into soups or stews, or for eating with a little olive oil and a shake of salt, or with the juices of a very ripe tomato and some very green olive oil *(pane e pomarole)*.

My grandmother's bread is a good bread, not a fine bread. One that will stay fresh, cut-side-down, on the breadboard for a few days. A thick-crusted bread. A bread that my grandmother makes by hand in our kitchen, much to my mother's disgust, twice a week. A bread that my mother disdains because it is everything that my grandmother is, and everything that my mother, in 1950s suburban New Jersey, is trying very hard not to be. Coarse. A peasant. Italian.

My grandmother's bread and the pizza she makes from her bread dough are the foods that sustain me throughout my childhood. Without them, I know I would starve because I hate absolutely everything my mother cooks, have hated it for years. Hate it because it tastes awful because my mother burns the food she cooks or puts too much salt in it or forgets to time the chicken and brings it to the table running with blood. Hate it because it's terrible food—gristly meat, bloated bratwurst, slightly off hamburger gotten for a bargain that she tries to disguise with catsup and Worcestershire sauce. Hate it because I can taste the rage in her food, can hear it in the banging of the pots and pans in her kitchen, in the clash of metal against metal in her stirring, can feel it against my skin.

The kitchen, when my mother is cooking, is not a place I want to be.

And my mother's rage—at me for not being a "good" daughter, at my grandmother for living with us, at herself for her never-ending sorrow despite her loving my father—scares me, makes me want to hide in a closet or rush from the house. It is a thick, scorching rage that I cannot predict, cannot understand. But it is something I do not want to catch from her (though of course I do).

And so. I do not eat her food if I can help it. Do not enter the kitchen when she cooks. Do not help her cook, for she prefers when I am not near her, when no one is near her. Do not help her clean up after we eat. And I leave the table as soon as I can.

My eating my grandmother's bread and my not eating my mother's food is another reason my mother screams at me, another reason my mother hates my grandmother, her stepmother, not her "real" mother who died when she was a baby. A mother, she laments, who would have taken care of her, not resented her, as this woman does.

And so. My mother doesn't know how to be a mother to me. No cookie baking in the kitchen. No lessons in how to make sauce. No cuddles. No intimate chats at bedtime. No very much of anything.

The Other Bread

My mother does not eat the bread my grandmother bakes. My mother eats the bread she buys from the Dugan's man, who comes round in his truck to our neighborhood a few times a week. This bread, unlike my grandmother's, has preservatives, a long shelf life, my mother boasts.

This bread my mother buys is white bread, sliced bread, American bread. A bread that my grandmother would never eat even if she were starving. Maybe my mother thinks that eating this bread will change her, will erase this embarrassment of a stepmother, all black dresses and headscarves and guttural Italian and superstitions and flurries of flour that ruin her spotless kitchen and tentacled things cooking in pots, this woman from the South of Italy who, my mother swears, never bathes, who treats water as something to pray to not something to wash in. Maybe my mother thinks that if she eats enough of this bread she will stop being Italian American. And that she will become American American.

My mother's bread is whiter than my grandmother's, as white, as soft and spongy as the cotton balls I use to take off my nail polish and the Kotex pads I shove into my underpants.

My sister and I like having this bread in our house, not because we like its taste, but because you can do many things with it. You can take a piece, pull off the crust, smash it down, roll it into a little ball. You can play marbles with this bread. You can pull the middle out of a slice and hang it over your nose or twirl it around your finger.

You can also eat this bread. But it sticks to the roof of your mouth and you have to pry it off with your fingers. Then you get yelled at for your horrible table manners.

My grandmother's bread doesn't stick to the roof of your mouth. Which is why my father likes it. Which is why I like it. That my father likes my grandmother's bread makes my mother angry.

From the Dugan's man, my mother also buys apple pies, blueberry pies, chocolate-covered donuts, crullers, to satisfy my father's sweet tooth when she is too depressed to make a dessert, and she usually is.

"*Merda*," my grandmother calls everything that my mother buys from the Dugan's man. Sometimes, unsure that my grandmother is correct, I take a tentative bite of something and conclude that, yes, it is *merda*, it tastes like cardboard, and the canned stew my mother feeds us because she is too depressed to cook is also *merda*, and the canned spaghetti and raviolis, too.

Kneading the Bread

My grandmother makes her bread by hand in my mother's kitchen, much to my mother's disgust, at least twice a week, sometimes more. Making it takes a lot of time. To make it, my grandmother dumps flour on my mother's kitchen table, makes a well in the middle, and into it pours warm water in which she has dissolved some yeast. She flicks the flour into the yeasty water with her fingertips a little at a time, until the shaggy mess comes together into a ball. Then my grandmother starts kneading.

When my grandmother kneads the bread, she takes off her dress, because kneading the dough is such hard work. She stands in the kitchen in her underwear. Coarse unbleached white undershirt. Coarse unbleached white pantaloons (these she makes herself because you can't buy them here). Black stockings. When she strips down, my mother huffs and leaves the room. When my grandmother kneads the dough, she gives me a little batch to knead. Then she shows me how to shape the dough into a little crown, which she bakes for me after it has risen.

While our bread bakes, my grandmother takes some scraps and shapes them into little figures which she fries for my sister and me. This is my lunch on baking days. My mother violently disapproves but lets us eat them anyway because, as usual, she hasn't made lunch.

My mother is always angry when my grandmother bakes her bread. "There's flour all over the place, even on the floor. Jesus Christ Almighty," she says, "how much more of this can I take?"

My grandmother cleans up but not the way my mother wants her to: clean enough so you can eat off the floor, although we don't eat off the floor.

My mother's face is red with rage. She rescrubs everything with Ajax. She curses. She spills water on the floor, makes a bigger mess. It's impossible to ignore her while we eat our *zeppoli*, yet we try.

The Knife

The knife that my grandmother uses to cut the bread is not a bread knife, not a serrated knife, like every well-equipped American kitchen now has. No. The knife that my grandmother uses to cut the bread is a butcher knife, the kind that figures in nightmares, in movies like *Psycho*. The same knife, incidentally, that my father used when I was a teenager when he threatened to kill me. (Years later, I bring up the subject, of how he came at me, how I got away because my grandmother put her body between us. "I never meant to hurt you," he said. "I was just trying to make myself clear.")

My grandmother would take a gigantic loaf of the bread she had made, and pull the knife towards the center of her chest where her heart was located, as if she were trying to commit an Italian form of hara-kiri.

"Stop that," my mother would shout, half-fearing, half-hoping, I think, that this stepmother who didn't love her would pull the knife towards her breast just a fraction of an inch too far, so that we would finally have bloodshed in our own kitchen, finally have a real mess on our hands that would take my mother a very long time to clean.

"Stop that, for Christ's sake," my mother would shout. And she would pull the bread away from my grandmother and often she would cut herself in the process, not much, but just enough to bleed onto the bread. And she would throw the bread down onto the counter and say, "Why can't you cut that goddamned bread like a normal human being?" And my grandmother would make the sign of the cross over the bread and kiss her fingertips and bend over the bread that she had made, weeping. My grandmother would weep because to her the bread was sacred and to her the only way to cut the bread was to pull the knife through the bread toward your heart.

My mother was afraid of knives. Before she went to bed at night, she would gather up all the knives in our kitchen and put them in a drawer. "This way," she said, "if a burglar comes into the house in the night, they'll have to look for them. This way," my mother said, "we'll have a fighting chance."

Peeling Onions

When I was a girl, my mother cried every time she peeled an onion. Not cry the way everyone cries when they peel onions—you, me, the stinging unbidden tears annoying the corners of the eyes. No. When my mother peeled an onion, she really cried, her chest heaved, her eyes bled huge tears that dropped onto the scarred Formica counter where she did all her cutting.

She wouldn't use cutting boards, my mother. She thought they were unnecessary, an extravagance, like raincoats and rainboots. And besides, she didn't need one often. When she moved to the suburbs, she abandoned the preparation of Italian food that required chopping, mincing, in favor of American food, convenience foods or things that were easy to prepare—hamburgers, meatloaf, hot dogs, toasted cheese sandwiches (though for Christmas or New Year's she might still make a lasagna or some meatballs and spaghetti).

My mother would rub her eyes with the backs of her hands to try to staunch the flow of tears, which only made it worse. And although my mother had a lot to cry about—that her mother died when she was a baby, that she was abused by the people who took care of her, that my stepgrandmother never loved her, that her beloved father died so young, that her husband came home from the war an angry man—the only time that I ever saw her cry ("having a good cry," she called it) was when she was peeling onions when she cooked, and I often thought that she specialized in dishes containing sautéed onions (liver, meatloaf) because making them gave her an opportunity to cry.

Oh yes, my mother had a lot to cry about, but I didn't know that then. I knew if I ate her dinner, I would eat those tears, and I was afraid that I would be as unhappy as she was. And I didn't want that. I wanted a quiet, ordinary, peaceful life. Not the commotion, the bitterness, the unhappiness of her life.

Sometimes when she cried, I ventured into the kitchen to see if I could cheer her because I worried that the crying would turn into something worse than crying, and that she would enter the world of her deep depression again, as she so often did, a place where she was inaccessible to us, inaccessible even to herself. Then my sister and I would be hauled off to relatives where we were cooked for, but not cared for.

"Your mother had a hard life," my father would say. But why her life was hard, he never told us. What he said was "All your mother wants from you is a little love." And that was something I couldn't give.

Scars

When I was growing up, my mother was always cutting herself, always burning herself, because when she cooked, my mother was depressed or distracted or shouting at my grandmother. Whenever they were in the kitchen together, they shouted at each other. Screaming: the condiment that sauced our food.

My mother yelled about how my grandmother had used up all the flour. About what a pig she was. About how she stunk up the kitchen. About how she ruined the pots and pans. My grandmother yelled about how my mother showed her no respect. About how she forced her to live with her. About how she stole her money. About how my mother would have died if it weren't for her. About how my mother wasn't even her blood.

And because they were always yelling, my mother wouldn't pay attention.

And so. She'd slice a piece off her finger. Or peel her hand instead of peeling the vegetables. Or she'd pour the boiling water off the potatoes too fast and scald herself. Or she'd bang into the side of a cupboard and get a black and blue. Or she'd stick her head too far into the oven and get a blast of steam on her face and it would be red for days. "Battle scars," my mother called them. And they were.

While my mother and my grandmother were in the kitchen together, I kept my distance. And so I never learned to cook from them.

When I got married, I needed a cookbook even to boil water. I learned to cook Italian from Italian cookbooks, not from my grandmother, and certainly not from my mother. So that the kind of Italian cooking that I cook is nothing like the Italian cooking that was cooked in my house. I learned nothing in my mother's kitchen about what sustains your soul. In my mother's kitchen, I learned about violence, about rage. I learned about using food and the implements used to cook food as weapons. Against others. And against yourself.

And after my mother died, and I found her recipe box, and went through it, the only recipe I wanted was one for pumpkin pie. She made a good pumpkin pie, my mother.

Wiping the Bowl

Just after my grandmother fell out of bed one morning, tore her nightdress off, and crawled around the floor naked, my mother decided it was time for her to go to a nursing home, that final stop on the railroad of life's journey.

So they took her there and she went unwillingly, strapped onto a stretcher and raving in an Italian no one could understand.

The nursing home was not a fancy one with private rooms and a solarium, but a bare bones piss-smelling nursing home run by the county where the very poor and the very unwanted came to die in giant wards cared for as well as the overworked underpaid nurses could care for them, which is to say they were not cared for at all.

My mother went to see her stepmother almost every day and came home crying because my grandmother wouldn't eat. My mother believed she wouldn't eat to spite her.

"Go see her," my mother said, exhausted, terrified. "Maybe she'll eat for you."

And so I went to see my grandmother on a day when the maple outside the window of her ward blazed red. And on that day, I fed my grandmother applesauce. She didn't eat much, a teaspoon or two, from the small quantity I dished into a little bowl.

I could tell she was near dying because she could not pick up her head from the pillow, could barely lift her arm, and couldn't speak. Still, she looked at me and her eyes teared and I told myself that coming here to feed her was a good thing, and necessary; told myself that these few spoonfuls of nourishment would, perhaps, prolong her life; told myself, who hadn't yet been to see her, who wouldn't see her alive again, that it was the least I could do for her after all she had done for me.

When she was finished, weak as she was, she reached for the bowl. It took much effort, this reaching, and I could not understand what she wanted, what she needed to do. And she took the napkin I had tucked under her chin to keep her clean. And she wiped the inside of the bowl. She cleaned the bowl as best she could.

In dying, as in living, she tidied up after herself, this Southern Italian woman who wanted no other woman to make clean what she had messed. This is what I think about when I remember my grandmother. How she baked her bread. And how she wiped the bowl.

No More Cooking, No More Food

In the final autumn of her life, my mother could not move. Could not move her arms, her hands, or her fingers. Could not move her legs, her feet, her toes, her head. Could not speak, could not say anything. Could not move, could not chew, could not swallow. Hence, could not cook, could not eat.

A tube inserted in her body, now her only means of sustenance. I looked at my mother, through those dying days, wanting conversation, which I would never again have, for she had long since ceased to speak. Wanting what I had never had, really: normal talks, ordinary talks, ones like other people have, about what we did during the day, what we cooked for dinner, what we felt about our lives.

Come closer, I said to her, once, as she lay dying, though she couldn't hear me, couldn't come closer. *Come closer*, I wanted to say, *and I'll tell you something wonderful, something you've been waiting for me to tell you for a long time.*

I wanted to speak to her, for she was moving into the land of death, a place I didn't know about, didn't want to know about, though a place I will one day follow her into, but not, I hope, too soon.

Would she remember me after she died? I wondered. Would she remember light? Music? The taste of grapefruit?

What I wanted to say was *I love you*, although I wasn't sure I did. I thought that if I said the words, words I'd never said to her before, words she'd never said to me, then the feeling might follow. I wanted to love my mother before she died.

Tearing the Bread

My mother died in autumn, like my grandmother. Though these two could agree on nothing in living, they agreed that autumn, with its leaves all dry and sere and red and bronze and gold and falling to the ground, was a fitting time to die.

As my mother lay dying, I wanted to tell her this story.

Imagine we are together. And imagine that, just once, we aren't fighting, we don't hate each other, you aren't disappointed in me, and I am not disappointed in you. Imagine we know it will come to this; imagine that because we know that it will come to this, we have learned to love each other.

Imagine us having a picnic. There is a cloth laid upon the ground and on it are simple things: some cheese—the smoked mozzarella from Dante's you liked so much—and roasted peppers (I might have made them myself); some mortadella, because neither of us likes prosciutto. And bread, yes, bread. Not my homemade bread, for today, I was too busy for baking bread. But good bread, sturdy Italian bread.

About the bread there would have been some disagreement. You would have wanted a fat crusty loaf without sesame seeds. (You had, by now, given up your taste for American bread.) I would have wanted them—the seeds, that is—for the added flavor they gave the loaf. But we decided that at this time in our lives, we could buy two breads and enjoy them both: the one you wanted (without the seeds), and the one I wanted (with).

Today, we sit together on the cloth in a grove of almond trees in full blossom, this place that we return to where we have never been before, and we eat. How beautiful the trees are, you say, their flowers, so silver-pink, the searing eyes of the individual blossoms seeing that we are together. They are, I say, a transfiguration, a predilection, and a blessing, and I tell you that I am so happy that you have chosen this place for us to be together.

And, finally, we eat, and drink the milk of almonds. And we talk. We have an ordinary, normal talk, about our day. Mine was filled with writing, reading (books about the South of Italy and the life your parents left there and, yes, they are helping me at last understand you, understand how you were between two worlds, how both despised who you were, so that you had to become "American," had to bury the Italian in you, had to hate your stepmother for what she was so you would not hate yourself for what you were). Your day, you told me, was full.

You had changed the lining in all the cupboards in the kitchen, made a soup for
dinner, a nice minestra, *and had sat down in the afternoon to embroider: prim-*
ulas, roses, poppies on a beige ground for pillows that now decorate my bed.

Today we do not cut the bread, for we have forgotten to bring our knives. Today,
we tear the bread with our hands. It is hard, this tearing of the bread, this partak-
ing of it. It is hard because the loaves have been well baked and because they have
a thick, nearly impenetrable crust. Yes, it is hard, we both agree, to break the bread,
to tear into it, to get at the tenderness inside. Yes, it is hard to break the bread. But
it is not impossible.

Playing the Bowl

One Friday, I take my granddaughter, Julia, to her toddler music class. She calls
the class "Oh my" because these are the first words of her favorite song, "Oh my,
no more pie." When Julia sings, I hear a young voice, but there is something old
about the voice, just as there is something old about the child. She is one of
those children who look as if they are older people locked in childish bodies.

On this day, the teacher shows how to improvise musical instruments at
home. "See," she says, picking up a cheese grater and playing it with a spoon,
"you don't need to buy musical instruments to make music." She's smiling; she's
making music seem like so much fun.

On this day, preoccupied with a piece of writing that has not been fun in
the making, I am cranky. I think that this is the wrong message. Writing, art,
music, I think, aren't fun. They're essential. They're bone, flesh, blood, sinew,
soul, spirit. And music can be hard. To hear it; to make it; to play it. But these
are kids, after all.

The teacher dumps little plastic bowls and wooden spoons onto the floor.
"Just watch the children; see what they do," she says. She turns on a recording of
African drums, the rhythms insistent, intricate, energizing. The children start
moving. Even I start moving.

One little boy picks up a bowl, a spoon, turns the bowl over, starts beating it
with the spoon. Soon, all the children are beating on their improvised instru-
ments. All but Julia.

Julia sits in the center of the circle, flips her bowl, takes her spoon, starts stir-
ring. She's stirring as quickly as the other children are drumming. She's shaking
her head and stirring. She's stirring and tasting. She's closing her eyes, lost in the
stirring. She's pretending to cook as if cooking were all that mattered, as if her
life depended upon it, as if the gods cared.

And she's making waffles, sauce, biscotti, scones, she's making pudding, she's
making pie, and she's calling out the names of what she's making, and she's tast-
ing what she's making.

So here is this little child with the wise face, who seems to have seen all things, this child with her mother's face, and my face, and my mother's face and my grandmother's face, and her other grandmother's face and her mother's grandmother's face, and the face of every woman in the world, and this child is stirring and cooking and singing through the celebrations, through the pogroms, invasions, bombings, evacuations, emigrations. She's stirring in Russia and in Austria-Hungary, in Puglia and in Sicily, and she's singing, this child who sees the future, who sees sorrow, sees joy, this wise, wise child.

She stirs and tastes and cooks and tastes and sings, and she sings, "Oh my, no more pie; oh my, no more pie; oh my, no more pie. No more pie. No more pie."

About the Contributors

Kim Addonizio is the author of three books of poetry, *The Philosopher's Club* (1994*), Jimmy & Rita* (1997), and *Tell Me* (2000), and a book of stories, *In the Box Called Pleasures* (1999). With Dorianne Laux, she coauthored *The Poet's Companion: A Guide to the Pleasures of Writing Poetry* (1997). Her awards include two National Endowment for the Arts fellowships, a Commonwealth Club Poetry Medal, and a Pushcart Prize. She lives in San Francisco, where she freelances as a teacher of private workshops.

Flavia Alaya, whose distinguished eating career began in her father's market when the sawdust still clung to the soles of her baby shoes, is professor emerita of literature and cultural history at Ramapo College. Recipient of Fulbright, National Endowment for the Humanities, and Guggenheim awards, she has made notable contributions to nineteenth-century Anglo-Italian and women's studies. She is currently writing a historical novel featuring the food and Italian anarchism of her home city of Paterson, New Jersey. She has published a memoir, *Under the Rose: A Confession* (1999).

Susanne Antonetta grew up in New Jersey and now lives in the Pacific Northwest, where she teaches and writes. She is the author of *Body Toxic: An Environmental Memoir* (2001) and *Bardo* (1998), a book of poems, which won the Brittingham Prize. She is currently finishing a book of poems titled *The Lives of the Saints*. Her father's family emigrated from the town of Gesualdo in Campania.

Pamela E. Barnett is assistant professor of English and African American studies at the University of South Carolina. Her essays have appeared in *PMLA, Signs, Women's Studies,* and the *Southern Quarterly*. She is currently working on a book about representations of rape written in the wake of the sixties-era liberation movements.

Regina Barreca, professor of English at the University of Connecticut, is the author of *They Used to Call Me Snow White . . . But I Drifted* (1991), *Perfect Husbands—and Other Fairy Tales* (1993), *Sweet Revenge* (1995), and *Too Much of a Good Thing is Wonderful* (2000). She is the editor of *The Penguin Book of Women's Humor* (1999) as well as *The Signet Book of American Humor* (1999). She is working on the forthcoming *Penguin Book of Italian American Writing*.

Dorothy Barresi is the author of *All of the Above* (1991), which won the Barnard College New Women Poets Prize, and *The Post-Rapture Diner* (1996), which won the American Book Award. Her third book of poetry will be published in 2002 by the University of Pittsburgh Press. She has received fellowships from the National Endowment for the Arts and the Fine Arts Work Center in Provincetown. She is professor of English and chair of the creative writing option at California State University, Northridge. She lives in Los Angeles with her husband and son.

Adria Bernardi is the author of a novel, *The Day Laid on the Altar*, which received the 1999 Bakeless Literary Publication Prize from the Bread Loaf Writers' Conference; a collection of short stories, *In the Gathering Woods* (2000); and an oral history, *Houses with Names: The Italian Immigrants of Highwood, Illinois* (1990). She is the translator of Gianni Celati's *Adventures in Africa* (2000) and of Tonino Guerra's *Abandoned Places* (1999). She lives in Worcester, Massachusetts.

Mary Jo Bona is an associate professor of Italian American studies at SUNY-Stony Brook. Her poems have appeared in *la bella figura*, *Voices in Italian Americana*, *Footwork*, the *Paterson Literary Review*, *Unsettling America: An Anthology of Contemporary Multicultural Poetry* (1994), and *From the Margin: Writings in Italian Americana* (1999). She is the author of *Claiming a Tradition: Italian American Women Writers* (1999) and the editor of *The Voices We Carry: Recent Italian-American Women's Fiction* (1994).

Suzanne Branciforte teaches at the University for Foreigners in Siena and the University of Genoa. She is the author of *Parliamo italiano!* (1998), a multimedial program for learning Italian, and the translator of Renata Viganò's collection of short stories, *Partisan Wedding* (1999). Her research and writing focus on linguistic and cultural mediation between Italy and the United States. Born and raised in New York, she currently lives in Bogliasco (Genoa).

Dorothy Bryant is a native San Franciscan, daughter of immigrants from northern Italy. She has written ten novels, including an American Book Award winner, *Confessions of Madame Psyche* (1987). *Dear Master,* the first of her five bio-historical plays, won the Bay Area Critics Circle Award for Best New Script of 1991. "Dizzy Spells" is an excerpt from her novel *The Test*, reprinted by the Feminist Press in 2001.

Cheryl Burke (a.k.a. Cheryl B.) is a writer who has performed her work throughout the United States, Canada, Great Britain, and Australia, and in Paris,

France. Her publications include five chapbooks of prose, as well as selections in many publications, including *The World in Us* and *Poetry Nation*. She is also the editrix of the literary website www.motoroilqueen.com. She received a master's degree in creative writing from the New School in May 2002.

Mary Bucci Bush is professor of English and creative writing at California State University, Los Angeles. Her book of short stories, *A Place of Light* (1990), won a PEN/Nelson Algren Award. She is working on a nearly completed novel about Italians illegally imported to the Mississippi Delta at the turn of the century to work on cotton plantations. She is a 1995 recipient of a National Endowment for the Arts Creative Writers' Fellowship.

Anne Calcagno received the San Francisco Foundation Phelan Literary Award and National Endowment for the Arts and Illinois Arts Council fellowships for stories in *Pray for Yourself* (1993). A dual citizen, Calcagno grew up in Rome and Milan, and has written about parts of the world rich in Italian history for the *New York Times*, the *Chicago Tribune*, and the Italian American Historical Society. She is the editor of *Italy: True Stories of Life on the Road* (1998). An associate professor of English at DePaul University, she can be found on the web at www.annecalcagno.com.

Phyllis Capello, a.k.a. Ukulele Lady, is a writer/musician. Her poetry and prose have appeared in many anthologies and literary magazines and she is a New York Foundation for the Arts Fellow in fiction. As "Dr." Ukulele Lady, she gives family concerts and performs year-round in the Big Apple Circus Clown Care Unit, bringing music and the delight of classical circus to hospitalized children. She teaches writing in New York City schools.

Rosette Capotorto is a writer whose work has been published in *Long Shot, I Am from the Lower East Side* (Italian/English), the *Paterson Literary Review*, *VIA: Voices in Italian Americana*, and *Curaggia: Writing by Women of Italian Descent* (1998). She runs poetry workshops for children and adults in classrooms, museums, arts festivals, and senior centers. She teaches in the After-School Literacy Outreach programs at the Brooklyn Children's Museum.

Mary Cappello is the author of *Night Bloom: A Memoir* (1998) and numerous pieces of literary nonfiction, poetry, and cultural criticism. She has recently completed an experiment in prose titled *My Commie Sweetheart: Scenes from a Queer Friendship*. She is currently working with Italian photographer Paola Ferrario on "Pane Amaro/Bitter Bread: The Struggle of New Immigrants to Italy," a collaborative project for which they have received the Dorothea Lange–Paul Taylor Prize from the Center for Documentary Studies, Duke University.

Nancy Caronia is a contributing editor for *Government Video* and a feature writer for *Videography* and *Pro Sound News*. Her work has been published in *Curaggia: Writing by Women of Italian Descent* (1998), *Women on Campus, Footwork: The Paterson Literary Review*, the *girlSpeak* journals, and *phati'tude Literary Magazine*. She is working on a novel, *Paper Napkins*, and a collection of essays and memoir pieces entitled, *Mario Is Dead, But I Ain't Done with Him Yet*.

Mary Beth Caschetta is a medical copywriter and an adjunct instructor of writing at Fordham University, Vassar College, and New York University. She is the author of a collection of short stories, *Lucy on the West Coast* (1996).

Rita Ciresi is the author of *Mother Rocket* (1993), winner of the Flannery O'Connor Award for Short Fiction; *Blue Italian* (1996), which was chosen for the Barnes and Noble Discover New Writers Series; and *Pink Slip* (1999), winner of the Pirate's Alley Faulkner Prize for the Novel. *Sometimes I Dream in Italian* (2000), a volume of linked short stories, was a Book Sense 76 pick and a finalist for the Paterson Fiction Prize. She teaches at the University of South Florida.

Dorian Cirrone has published poetry, memoir, and literary criticism in *Parting Gifts*, the *Paterson Literary Review, FEMSPEC*, and several anthologies. She is currently at work on a collection of linked short stories about growing up in the sixties in South Florida. She dedicates her poem "After We Bury Her" to the memory of her mother, Eleanor Zona Cirrone.

Rosanna Colasurdo was born and raised in Jersey City. She graduated from New Jersey City University with a degree in English literature in 1999. She currently works as a kindergarten teacher in a Jersey City public school. Her parents, Robert and Antonina, were both born in Italy. They continue to run a business together in Jersey City.

Mary Russo Demetrick is a Sicilian, Neapolitan, Slovak American poet and fiction writer. She has published two collections of poems, *First Pressing* (1994) and *Italian Notebook* (1995), the latter cowritten with Maria Famà. In 1994 she established Hale Mary Press, "founded to commemorate all women who lost their ethnic, given names at Ellis Island and who were renamed 'Mary' in legal immigration documents."

Louise DeSalvo is professor of English at Hunter College. She has published thirteen books, among them *Virginia Woolf: The Impact of Childhood Sexual*

Abuse on Her Life and Work (1989), *Breathless* (1997), *Adultery* (1999), *Writing as a Way of Healing* (1999), and the award-winning memoir *Vertigo* (1996). She is currently writing a memoir, *Crazy in the Kitchen*, and a book about Charles Darwin.

Rachel Guido deVries is the author of two books of poems, *How to Sing to a Dago* (1996) and *Gambler's Daughter* (2001), and a novel, *Tender Warriors* (1986). Her recent work has appeared in *Voices in Italian Americana* and the *Paterson Literary Review*. She teaches creative writing in the Humanistic Studies Center of Syracuse University.

Diane di Prima is the author of thirty-four books of poetry and prose, which have been translated into twenty languages. Born in New York in the 1930s, she currently lives in San Francisco, where she works as a writer and a teacher. Her most recent books include *Pieces of a Song: Selected Poems* (1990), *Loba* (1998), and the memoir *Recollections of My Life as a Woman: The New York Years* (2001).

Maria Famà is the author of three books of poetry and the cofounder of a video production company. Her work has appeared in numerous publications. She has read her work in many cities across the United States and on National Public Radio. She received the Honorable Mention in the 1994 and 1995 Allen Ginsberg Poetry Awards. Her poem "6:35 a.m." was a finalist in the 1998 Allen Ginsberg Poetry Awards.

Rina Ferrarelli is a poet and translator of modern Italian poetry who came from Italy at the age of fifteen. She has published a book and a chapbook of poetry, *Home Is a Foreign Country* (1996) and *Dreamsearch* (1992), and two books of translation, Giorgio Chiesura's *Light Without Motion* (1989), and Leonardo Sinisgalli's *I Saw the Muses* (1997). She received a National Endowment for the Arts fellowship and the Italo Calvino Prize from the Columbia University Translation Center.

Sandra M. Gilbert, professor of English at the University of California, Davis, is the author of *Kissing the Bread: New and Selected Poems,* 1969–1999 (2000), which won an American Book Award from the Before Columbus Foundation. She has also edited *Inventions of Farewell: A Book of Elegies* (2001) and received the John Ciardi Prize for Lifetime Achievement in Poetry from the Italian-American Foundation. She has published five collections of poetry and a memoir, along with a number of critical volumes coauthored or coedited with Susan Gubar.

Maria Mazziotti Gillan is executive director of the Poetry Center at Passaic

County Community College. In 2001–2002 she was the head of the creative writing program at SUNY-Binghamton. She has published seven books of poetry, including *Where I Come From* (1995) and *Things My Mother Told Me* (1999). She is coeditor with her daughter, Jennifer Gillan, of three anthologies, *Unsettling America* (1994), *Identity Lessons* (1999), *and Growing Up Ethnic in America* (1999). She is the editor of the *Paterson Literary Review*.

Daniela Gioseffi is the author of four books of poetry, *Eggs in the Lake* (1979), *Word Wounds and Water Flowers* (1995), *Going On Poems 2000* (2000), and *Symbiosis: Poems* (2001), and a novel, *The Great American Belly Dance* (1977). She has edited two award-winning anthologies, *On Prejudice: A Global Perspective* (1993) and *Women on War: International Voices*, to be reissued in 2003, and she currently edits www.PoetsUSA.com. She founded the Bordighera Poetry Prize to promote Italian American poetry.

Edvige Giunta was born in Sicily and came to the United States in 1984. She is associate professor of English at New Jersey City University, where she teaches memoir. Her most recent publications include *Writing with an Accent: Contemporary Italian American Women Authors* (2002) and a special issue of *TutteStorie* devoted to Italian American women writers that she coedited in 2001. She lives in New Jersey with her husband and two children.

Joanna Clapps Herman teaches in the Graduate Creative Writing Program at Manhattanville College and at the Center for Worker Education, City College, CUNY. She has published in many magazines and anthologies, including the *Massachusetts Review,* the *Paterson Literary Review, Italian Americana, Voices in Italian Americana, Kalliope, Critic, Fan,* and *Woman's Day.* She has an essay forthcoming in *The Penguin Anthology of Italian American Writers.* She is the winner of the Bruno Arcudi Prize in fiction for 2001.

Adele Regina La Barre is a New Yorker whose mother was born and raised near Sulmona in the Abruzzo, where Adele has lived briefly herself. She is an independent scholar with a doctoral degree from Columbia University in art history (Byzantine studies) whose current research concerns textiles, especially *biancheria,* the needlework arts of Italian and Italian American women, and *lavatoi,* laundry houses. Adele's recent work has appeared in the *Northwest Review, Differentia, Chelsea, New Digressions, Turnstile, Art Mag, Chasm,* and *Voices in Italian Americana.*

Jennifer Lagier is a member of the Italian American Writers Association and the National Writers Union. She earned a master's degree at California State

University, Stanislaus, an M.L.I.S. from the University of California, Berkeley, and is working on her doctorate at Nova Southeastern University. Her two books are *Where We Grew Up* (1999) and *Second-Class Citizen* (2000). She teaches at Hartnell College and California State University, Monterey Bay.

Annie Lanzillotto writes, directs, performs, and produces works in theaters and communities. Her performances include *Confessions of a Bronx Tomboy Part I* (1991), *Pocketing Garlic* (1993), *Opera Vindaloo!* (1994–1996), and *How To Wake Up a Marine in a Foxhole* (1998). She has taught writing and drama workshops with at-risk and ex-offender youth, inmates at correctional facilities, and the formerly homeless living with HIV and AIDS. Lanzillotto's "A Stickball Memoir," a performance and installation, was part of the Smithsonian Folklife Festival in Washington, D.C., celebrating New York City culture.

Maria Laurino is the author of *Were You Always an Italian? Ancestors and Other Icons of Italian America* (2000). She is a former staff writer for the *Village Voice* and chief speechwriter for former New York City mayor David N. Dinkins. Her articles and essays have appeared in numerous newspapers, magazines, and anthologies.

Loryn Lipari studies English literature and creative writing at New Jersey City University. She has presented her memoir and poetry in many venues and published in *Paths* and *Women on Campus.* She received the New Jersey City University Poetry Prize (2001) and Honorable Mention for Prose (2000). She is a freelance writer for *Hi-Rise Expressions.*

Anne Marie Macari won the 2000 APR/Honickman First Book Prize for *Ivory Cradle* (2000). She has published in many magazines, such as *Field, TriQuarterly,* the *Ohio Review*, and others. She is on the faculty of the New England College low-residency master of fine arts program and has taught and read her work at the Prague Summer Seminar and other places.

Mary Ann Mannino is visiting assistant professor of English at Temple University. She is the author of *Revisionary Identities: Strategies of Empowerment in the Writing of Italian/American Women* (2000). She is coediting, with Justin Vitiello, an anthology of Italian American women writers discussing the influences on their works. Mannino is also a fiction writer and poet. Her poem "Jimmy Fahey" took first place in the 2001 Allen Ginsberg Poetry Awards.

Donna Masini is the author of a collection of poems, *That Kind of Danger* (1994), which won the Barnard Women Poets Prize in 1994, and a novel, *About*

Yvonne (1998). Her second collection of poems, *Turning to Fiction*, is forthcoming. A recipient of a National Endowment for the Arts fellowship and a New York Foundation for the Arts grant, she has published poems in *TriQuarterly*, the *Paris Review, Georgia Review*, and other magazines. She is a full-time professor in the creative writing program at Hunter College and teaches poetry at Columbia University. She lives in New York City

Carole Maso is the author of six novels: *Ghost Dance* (1986), *The Art Lover* (1990), *Ava* (1993), *The American Woman in the Chinese Hat* (1994), *Aureole* (1996), and *Defiance* (1998); a collection of essays, *Break Every Rule* (2000); and *The Room Lit by Roses: A Journal of Pregnancy and Birth* (2000). *Beauty Is Convulsive: The Passion of Frida Kahlo* is forthcoming. A recipient of the Lannan Literary Fellowship for Fiction, Maso is a professor of English at Brown University, where she has also been director of the creative writing program.

Alane Salierno Mason is an editor of literary fiction and nonfiction at W. W. Norton & Company. She has published reviews and essays in *Vanity Fair*, the *Boston Review*, the *Baltimore Sun*, *Context*, and *Commonweal*, and her essays have been reprinted in a number of anthologies. Her new translation of Elio Vittorini's *Conversations in Sicily* (2000) was recently excerpted in *American Letters* and *Commentary* and was published in a New Directions Classic edition.

Cris Mazza is the author of nine books of fiction. Her most recent novel, *Girl Beside Him*, was released in 2001. Some of her other notable titles include *Is It Sexual Harassment Yet?* (1991), *How to Leave a Country* (1992), and *Dog People* (1997). She is coeditor of *Chick-Lit* (1995) and *Chick-Lit 2* (1996), anthologies of women's fiction. Her nonfiction feature essays, which have appeared in the *San Diego Reader*, have been collected into *Indigenous / Growing Up Californian*. Mazza was a National Endowment for the Arts fellow in 2000–2001.

Denise Calvetti Michaels writes poetry and memoir. Her poems have been published in the *Paterson Literary Review, Crosscurrents*, and *King County Poetry on Buses*. Her grandparents immigrated to the United States from Piedmontese villages in Italy around 1910. Born in Salinas, she grew up in Redwood City, California. Mother to three daughters and grandmother to Holden, she works to develop quality, culturally relevant child care.

Lucia Perillo has published three books of poetry, most recently *The Oldest Map With the Name America* (1999). Her work has appeared in many magazines, including the *New Yorker* and *Atlantic Monthly*, and has been reprinted in the *Pushcart* and *Best American Poetry* anthologies. In 2000 she received a

MacArthur Foundation fellowship for her writing. Currently on leave from teaching, she lives in Olympia, Washington.

Kym Ragusa is a filmmaker, curator, teacher, and writer of Italian American and African American descent. Her work, including the documentary films *Passing* (1996) and *fuori/outside* (1997), draws upon her family histories to explore the politics of race and community. Her work has been shown in festivals in the United States and Europe. *Passing* was broadcast on the PBS-WNET series REEL NY in 1997. She is working on *Neighborhood Goddess,* a documentary film about women immigrants of East Harlem and the Madonna of Mount Carmel, and a film about African and Asian immigrants in Sicily.

Vittoria repetto is a native downtown lesbian New Yorker and a second-generation Italian American. She has published in *Mudfish,* the *Paterson Literary Review, Voices in Italian Americana, Harrington Lesbian Fiction Quarterly, Lips, Unsettling America: An Anthology of Contemporary Multicultural Poetry* (1994), and *Curaggia: Writing by Women of Italian Descent* (1998), among others. repetto is the vice president of the Italian American Writers Association and hosts the Women's Poetry Jam at Bluestockings Bookstore.

Agnes Rossi is the author of *The Quick: A Novella and Stories* (1992), which was named a New York Times Notable Book, and the novels *Split Skirt* (1994) and *The Houseguest* (2000). She was the finalist for the Granta Best of Young Novelists Award. She lives in Brooklyn with her husband and four children.

Mary Saracino is the author of *No Matter What* (1993), *Finding Grace* (1999), and *Voices of the Soft-Bellied Warrior: A Memoir* (2001). *No Matter What* was a 1994 Minnesota Book Award Fiction Finalist. *Finding Grace* was awarded the Colorado Authors' League 1999 "Top Hand" Adult Fiction Mainstream/Literary Award. Her work has also appeared in *TutteStorie, Hey Paesan! Writers Who Cook, Sinister Wisdom, Voices in Italian Americana,* and *Italian Americana.*

Nancy Savoca is the daughter of Sicilian and Argentine immigrants. She graduated from film school at New York University. Her first film, *True Love,* won the Grand Jury Prize at the 1989 Sundance Film Festival. Savoca has directed *Dogfight* and *Household Saints,* an adaptation of Francine Prose's saga of three generations of Italian American women. She was cowriter and director of the HBO production *If These Walls Could Talk,* produced by Demi Moore. Savoca also directed *The 24-Hour Woman,* starring Rosie Perez. Her work has been the subject of retrospectives by the American Museum of the Moving Image and the New York Women's Film Festival.

Maria Terrone is the author of a collection of poems, *The Bodies We Were Loaned* (2002). Recipient of the 2000 Elinor Benedict Poetry Prize from *Passages North* and the 1998 Allen Tate Memorial Award from *Wind*, she has published work in anthologies and magazines, including *Poetry,* the *Hudson Review,* and *Poet Lore.* The former executive editor of *Attenzione* magazine, she is now director of public relations for Hunter College in New York.

Gioia Timpanelli is one of the founders of the current worldwide revival of storytelling. A winner of two Emmy awards, she has received the Women's National Book Award for her work in the oral tradition and the Brooklyn President's Award for "lifelong dedication" to Italian culture. Her *Tales from the Roof of the World: Folk Tales from Tibet* (1984) was a New York Times Notable Book, and *Sometimes the Soul, Two Novellas of Sicily* (1998) won the American Book Award.

Camilla Trinchieri has published seven mystery novels under the name Camilla T. Crespi. Under her own name, she has completed *Looking in My Shoes,* a fictionalized account of her American mother's harrowing years in Prague and Rome during World War II. A native Italian, she came to the United States as a teenager with her diplomat father and returned to Italy after she graduated from Barnard College. In Rome she worked in the film industry as a dubbing producer/director with Federico Fellini, Lina Wertmüller, and Luchino Visconti. She lives in New York.

Janet Zandy is professor of language and literature at Rochester Institute of Technology. Her books include *Calling Home: Working-Class Women's Writings* (1990), *Liberating Memory: Our Work and Our Working-Class Consciousness* (1995), and *What We Hold in Common: An Introduction to Working-Class Studies* (2001).

Credits